A CIP catalogue record for this book is available from the British
Library.

ISBN 978-0-9552466-1-6

Published by
Hot Air Publishers,

10 Marigold Court,
Red Lake, Telford,
Shropshire TF1 5ZN

Reproduced, printed and bound in Great Britain by Cox and
Wyman, Reading, Berkshire

PAST AND PRESENTS

Dave Armitage

ABOUT THE AUTHOR

Dave Armitage was born in 1958 and is a journalist with the Daily Star newspaper. Past and Presents is his second novel following his successful debut Born to be Mild. He lives in Shropshire with his partner Jo.

ACKNOWLEDGEMENTS

Special thanks to Jo, Phil Shaw and Janine Self for being prepared to be guinea pigs and give the first draft the once over. Many thanks for their advice and encouragement. Special thanks also to Steve Fulford whose fantastic Toys of Yesteryear Museum in The Peak District provided the images for the cover. Also a big thanks to John Wheeler at Cadbury Schweppes plc, Nick Chandler at Hornby and Gillian Acomb at Corgi for their co-operation with the cover images.

1

SPERM WAIL

I've always been more M&S than Eminem. As billionaires go, you could say I'm fairly run-of-the mill.

I object to paying more than ten pounds for a haircut, I keep old clothes for the garden even though I've got a gardener and I still haven't quite got my head around cassette tapes being phased out. I'm 50 and I still jump off the bottom part of escalators for fear of being chewed up by the jagged bit. For God's sake!

I've mellowed. I'm not mean, I'm just set in my ways. I buy the same colour socks to prevent the aggravation of losing one, I sigh audibly if I'm in the chip shop queue and the person in front orders a kebab with all the trimmings. I'm Antiques Roadshow and Radio Two - it's just the way it is. It kind of happens.

But it hasn't always been that way - when I was a teenager I did something so daring, it could so easily have been the death of me. I had fathered a kid in Australia for a start off - no mean feat when you are just turned sixteen and live ten thousand miles away.

It really doesn't get much more adventurous than managing to get one of your sperms all that way. I should point out that's not quite the mystery it may appear. It was incredible to think that one of my inconsequential microscopic tadpoles managed to get himself all the way to the other side of the globe. Without devaluing the feat, by the time Qantas had offered their assistance, the damage had been done. It was the first few inches that had done the fucking damage. The little sod hadn't actually donned a frogman's outfit and swum the whole way. If it seems vaguely amusing, believe me, there had been nothing remotely funny about this. I recall her raging father coming to our house that Christmas Eve all those years ago with the kind of festive surprise nightmares are made of. Pregnant? He was fucking joking wasn't he? To be fair, he didn't even remotely look like he was joking. News of my impending fatherhood was just about the worst surprise Santa could have bundled down the chimney of No 2 Orchard Grove. I might be a wealthy man now, but even during the times when I was staring down both barrels of financial ruin, bad news really never came any worse than this. My mum's face. Jeeezus.

She was screaming about taking precautions but apart from putting my hands over my head I was hopelessly exposed. I'd been careful - or so I thought. This was 1974. The Wombles were the top selling group of the year for God's sake. The humble jonny was still years off being elevated to anything which sounded even as vaguely exotic as a condom.

There were only three flavours back then - Michelin, Goodyear and Pirelli. Take your pick. The days of pina colada, strawberry milk shake and passion fruit were a long way distant. You had Nu-Form, Gossamer and Fetherlite. They weren't ribbed, nobbled or anything elaborate and, roughly speaking, they came in two colours - a shade resembling magnolia and pink. They did come in machines, but not in places I frequented. These were the barbers-shop days of 'something for the weekend, sir?'

Rubber jonnies certainly weren't given out free at school to teenagers lucky enough to even know someone who would even consider having it away with them. God forbid. If they had been, then this story would be struggling for a beginning, middle or end.

Getting a girl in the family way was not part of the

equation. These were days when being pregnant at 12 didn't automatically book you a place on The Richard and Judy Show or mean social services would send around a team of helpers to look after your every need. I couldn't have envisaged my parents on Jerry Springer or Trisha saying anything remotely like how proud they were about such a sorry state of affairs.

Mine were far less-enlightened times. Bastard was still a really bad word and unmarried mums got a broom cupboard not a new flat. There was no such thing as a love-child. Mixed race? Only if you ran the 400m and 800m - that was about the size of it. Had condoms or abortion been as readily available and socially acceptable when I was a lad, then everything might have been sorted. Morning-after pills being given out at school? I think not! No, these were days when getting in the family way, in the club, up the duff, up the stick or whatever term you care to choose was a serious, serious business.

Her dad came to the house and went absolutely mental. He said I'd never make anything of my life. He was right to go mad but he certainly called the next bit wrong.

Now over thirty years later I find myself just staring at the photograph. There we all are smiling away as the golden penny sun seemed to sizzle down into the huge, shimmering African lake behind us. Just a photograph, yet behind that picture lay the story of the greatest Christmas present I'd ever had. Who could ever have imagined it all turning out this way?

It's a time of year that should be special to everyone, but for me there was no escaping it. Not with a name like John Christmas and a story like mine to tell.

2

PHOGEY PHONES

The last time I'd seen her dad he was clambering into a Ford Granada looking every bit like he was on the verge of a nervous breakdown. Virtually his final words before pulling away was how I was next-to-useless with no hope of ever making anything of my life. Whoops. Eight years ago I sold my business for £898m and I haven't had to touch a single penny since. That's mainly because the interest just keeps accumulating and also because I get a 'pension' of around £4m a year from retaining the rights to my revolutionary Phogey Phone.

The Phogey has a Mars Bar size handset, big numbers, no camera, no games, no e-mail, she-male, Wi-Fi, Hi-fi or sci fi. It's a phone that works on the old-fashioned concept of just making and receiving calls - how bizarre! I threw in a text messaging facility because most of us find that useful and a money-making monster was born.

Never mind Bluetooth, this is more slightly yellow teeth - and proud of it. I made it cheap to buy, cheap to use and made sure it came in a range of colours that would bring any 14-year-old out in rash if they even went near the fucking thing. If I could have knocked them out in woodchip, Anaglypta or Vymura, I would have done.

People slap me on the back and ask how I managed to dream up such an idea. Well, to be honest, it was hardly a flash of brilliance. I just wanted a phone that technological half-wits, like me, might find to their liking.

When your eyesight is not quite as sharp as it was and your co-ordination just one degree up from arthritic, why does anyone think a phone the size of a fucking credit card will suit your needs? It's preposterous.

What's more, let's have the darned thing devoid of anything that would make it worth pinching. I wanted to invent a phone that worked perfectly well, but if a mugger turned you over, he'd throw it back in disgust. That's the one for me!

Now I have so much money that, frankly, it's bloody obscene. If I'm truthful, it's probably the ridiculous success of the Phogey that has put everything in perspective. It was a runaway hit from the minute it went on the market and backed my judgement that sometimes technology can run away from a lot of us at far too rapid a rate.

Considering I've made such a colossal amount of cash from the boom in mobile phones, you could have imagined me not even entertaining something that prides itself in flying in the face of the latest cutting edge technology. But necessity is the mother of invention and I was just getting totally fucked off with the phones companies like mine were making available. Where was one that suited me?

At first you had kids saying 'God it's a brick.'

And defiant, delighted, 40-somethings the world over roared 'Exactly!'

And guess what? People went absolutely crackers for the Phogey. It was one of last year's must-have accessories for the Betamax brigade. They were so seriously untrendy that they became fashionable. Now people carry their Phogey's with pride. Six million units later and there's no sign of a let-up in demand. It's a badge of honour. The Saga louts love them and the money continues to pour in.

It's just a question of hitting a market - luring the sort of people who never quite managed to master the video before it became obsolete. It's for all of us who suddenly turn to jelly when they are given a TV remote. For that army of people who wander around HMV and Virgin Megastores asking some bemused 16-year-old sales assistant if they are *absolutely* sure they no longer stock video cassettes. For any of the legion of good souls who still don't own a DVD - fogies of the world unite.

There's nothing wrong with being a middle-aged tosser. Once you've learned to live with it, there's no problem. Just because you are on your feet financially doesn't mean you have to chuck your cash away. I couldn't do it all those years ago and I'm certainly not about to now. Don't interpret that as being mean. I'd like to think I'm just not stupid.

Don't get me wrong, I like nice shirts or shoes, whatever, but I won't pay £500 for a pullover or be persuaded to part with £200 for a designer t-shirt. I just can't do it and I'm seriously fucking loaded! If anyone managed to sell me a ripped t-shirt for a couple of hundred quid then they might as well embroider *'prick'* right on the front, because it's the least I would deserve.

I now come into contact with people who happily boast they have paid £5,000 for a suit. Am I supposed to be impressed? I feel like saying 'knob,' but you just have to let them get on with it. Tell the truth, I'm at that stage in my life where I don't really like any kind of writing on my t-shirts, but I accept that makes me sound a right twat. Why would I want meaningless babble on the front of me? All it's going to say is something like 'Blue Oyster Club' or 'Beach Bar.' What the fuck's that about? I can't be arsed. Perhaps that goes back to the 'Frankie Says' shirts that were everywhere in the early 80s. Who gives a toss what Frankie says?

I'm the kind of guy who can be heard saying 'well, the toilets are immaculate' if I'm weighing up whether to eat somewhere. It's the sort of thing that just creeps up on you and then you find yourself a resident of Sensible Land.

Anyone of around the 50-mark was brought up in a world

totally unrecognisable from the one youngsters frequent today. Days when colour TV was a revolutionary thing and having the phone put in at home was quite an event. The times when if pubs did food, it was in a tiny cellophane packet with a couple of silverskin onions, a cheese triangle and a cracker. The revolution was barely under way.

3

THE SANTA CLAUSE

Once you no longer believe that some sherry-sodden fat man with a beard drives a fucking sleigh onto your roof, the magic of Christmas takes one massive dip. It's an unlikely tale really, but we all buy into it and as long as we do then the true magic of Christmas remains with you. Your dad tells you that you must go to sleep and wait for this odd-looking bloke to somehow get down the chimney, creep all around the house, come into your bedroom and leave you loads of pressies. Then he scoffs a mince pie, has yet another alcoholic drink and kisses your mum before fucking off to some unknown address in Lapland. Call the police! You couldn't make it up! Or, more to the point, someone did. It's the great Santa deception and our lives are all the richer for it. But uncover that one and suddenly you stumble on all sorts of things that adults palm off on you.

Surely one of the biggest cons of all has to be pomegranates. The minute you realise a pomegranate is not so much an exotic fruit as a tool to keep a kid quiet for at least an hour; you've made a significant leap towards adulthood. For some strange reason, these weird bloody things only ever seem to appear at this time of year. No longer could my mum slice one in half, hand it to me with a pin and expect me to think she'd given me the elixir of life. Pomegranates? Just what the fuck use are they to anyone? I swear to God I've spent more hours than I care to think about, meticulously plucking seeds from them and thinking I was enjoying a

8

special treat. There's certain Christmas things which will forever be fantastic and then there's others . . . well, you just get wise to them. It's like dates. We always had a couple of boxes of dates in our house come mid-December. Nice looking boxes, sort or rounded off at each end; picture of a camel on them and they had that stupid plastic stalk type thing which you were supposed to pluck them out with. When I got to the stage where I was confident enough to ask just what was the point of dates, my mum had a stock answer.

'Well, they're good for you. They keep you regular, for a start off.'

Brilliant. Perhaps that's why they are called dates. I can give you a stack of dates that are regular - Easter Monday, Shrove Tuesday, how about October 13 - maybe that's why they are called dates.

I'll tell you what dates and pomegranates are - they are fruits which no one really knew what to do with, so they convince gullible nations that they are missing out on something special and create a whopping great demand.

It's PR bollocks and I'm all for sticking to the traditional Christmas things that have been standard fare seemingly for ever.

Chocolate brazils? Wow. Can you ever tire of those? Well, yes, the minute you start throwing up, but you get the idea. Orange and lemon sweet slices in a round box. That sort of stuff crosses the boundaries, but once you start questioning the whys and wherefores of pomegranates and dates, then you really are on the slippery slope zooming away from childhood.

Before you can say 'Jack Robinson' you'll be yearning for a Fry's Chocolate Cream or a Barley Sugar. When you dip into a box of chocolates, you won't scrutinise the lid and you'll feel genuinely delighted to get a coconut ice or a coffee cream. You are entering dangerous territory. Your ice cream of choice will be a tub or a Cornish wafer. You won't think gooseberries are just sour, lime-flavoured phlegm. It's the end. It's adult stuff.

9

You've had your last strawberry bon bon and the days of grown-up sweets are upon you. Actually I did always have a soft spot for Newberry Fruits and the way that little ball of sugar-coated juice could be nibbled away at. But it doesn't alter the fact that it's sensible stuff. It's like pickled eggs - fantastic things, but I don't think you should be allowed to have them until you are 18. I am a child of the days when a Heinz Sponge pudding took three-and-a-half days to boil and then you ended up tossing it around the kitchen like a grenade because it was too hot to hold even with a tea towel. Now you can cook them in a microwave in next to no time - it just takes the edge off it somehow. I still like them - but I'll never be convinced they are exactly the same.

Nothing's the same. It's the nature of life. Everything now is so much quicker and yet the one thing you can guarantee, is that despite these great labour-saving devices, no one has any more spare time.

And so I glanced at the photograph once more and somehow the magic of Christmas glowed brightly again. I began to reflect and tried to see how far back I could remember. When was the first Christmas I could genuinely recall? I'd be four by my reckoning. Yeah, definitely, I'd have been four . . .

4

1962 - WHITE CHRISTMAS

My dad said the icicles were so big that if one fell off it would kill a horse. We hadn't got a horse, so I wasn't really sure what all that was about. He had told me to stand well clear while he used a broom to smash them all off the guttering at the side of the house. That is my first vivid recollection of Christmas. Deep, drifting snow. Mittens, wellies and snowballs. It's not my childhood memories being given a dusting of romance - winter 1962 was very cold and very white.

The first thing that really springs to mind is unbelievably deep snow and my dad showing me some iced lollies he'd made outside. He'd made them out of squash in eggcups with a lolly stick skewiff in the middle. I vaguely recall him pulling me on a tiny homemade sledge; red wellygogs; scarves and gloves. It was really cold and when you got inside by the roaring fire it gave you pins and needles. That is still fixed in my mind and so it would have been December 1962. Now it's referred to as the Winter of '63 but it actually set in late in the previous year and so my mish-mash of memories - of snow and slush and dad clattering colossal icicles must have been around then. What I actually would have had for Christmas is too specific but there's a little montage there in the deepest corners of my mind. A Pinky and Perky record, those little square letter and number games I found so fascinating. A flattish grid of eight plastic tiles which you had to shift around to get them in the right order; a plastic assortment of noses, lips and ears you attached to potatoes to make funny faces. Just stocking fillers like that really, which come flooding back at random.

There were astonishingly beautiful, yet simple things. Like mum's silver-coloured metal jelly mould in the shape of a rabbit. I couldn't wait for it to be ready just to see it. And when it wobbled free of it's casing, I just must have looked dumbstruck at the vivid, translucent red of the strawberry jelly. The shape of it, the smell, just everything, filled me with wonder. And being allowed to touch it even though mum said you mustn't was such a wondrous thing. The gentle quiver of the perfectly shaped rabbit, lingers with me to this day. It's hard to explain. It's just there and will be forever.

I'm sure most of the things I remember up to being five are courtesy of my parents passing stories on. Mum never tires of telling the story that as a youngster I once tried to poison my auntie by serving her up a special brew of mine in a plastic tea service. I guess a tea set isn't really a textbook boy's thing, but apparently I had hours of fun with it, right up to the point where my auntie almost passed out. We often went to my gran and grandad's on Christmas Day, so that would explain how Auntie Irene was around to be given the shock of her life. On account of my tender years and it being over forty years ago, I'll have to give my own special interpretation of the scene.

'Tea, tea . . . tea Auntie Ibreem, tea,' I apparently insisted.

'Okay sweetheart. You pour me a cup of your best tea and I'll have a biscuit with it.'

I carefully pour it out into a red plastic cup and wait for Auntie Irene's approval.

'Mmm it's lovely,' she says politely.

'You know what, he's had more pleasure out of that little tea service than half the other things he's had. It's funny isn't it,' mum interjected fondly.

'Mind you, I don't know what he's made this tea out of but it's a bit funny.'

Mum comes over and starts quizzing me on where I've got the warm liquid Auntie Irene has sipped politely.

And so why has mum slapped me across the legs? I mean, improvisation that's the thing. I'm four years old - a little bit of creativity should be applauded. So, I've pissed in the teapot. What's the big deal? Aunties eh? They're so fussy!

Mum squeals: 'Don't you ever let me catch you doing that again!'

Crikey mum, it's not the sort of thing you do twice to be fair. It's not the sort of thing most people do once in all honesty. I'm guessing her protestations were mainly for the benefit of my aunt who is trying not to make too big a deal of the fact that she's just taken a swig of my piss. I thought dad was going to wet himself when she told him, supposedly out of my earshot. He thought it was one of the funniest things he'd ever heard. I'm sure he said he'd wished he'd been there to see it before coming in and giving me a right ticking off.

'Don't you ever do that again,' he scolded me.

What is it with parents eh? Both of them seem to think that after having my legs slapped and being thoroughly chastised, the first thought on my mind is going to be trying to stage a repeat performance. Nah, it would be a pretty tough act to follow that. Definitely the sort of thing you only do once.

But I remember those magical mornings, rushing in to mum and dad's room and pleading with them to get up and take me downstairs.

'Merry Christmas John,' they'd both say giving me a huge hug.

'Do you think he's been?'

'I hope so dad.'

'What d'ya reckon love?' dad asked mum.

'I didn't hear him,' she'd say.

'Daaad. Muuuum. Come on.'

The rustle of the presents and the flickering lights of the tree were just marvellous. And there was one present there that all these years haven't managed to dim. To this day I get a shiver down my spine just recalling my dad explaining how it worked.

'There you go. Now just turn it carefully. No, point it to the light. That's it. Can you see?'

'Wow.'

'Good isn't it.'

Good? It was fantastic. Like having your own stained-glass windows in your head. A kaleidoscope. Wow. I can't remember ever being so enthralled, to be honest. It was just a whole new magical world. There were a couple of selection boxes and toy farm animals and the like, but that kaleidoscope just edged it. Does it ever get better than your first glimpse through a kaleidoscope? I'm not sure it does. It wasn't until later that you realise it's a pretty flimsy, unspectacular piece of equipment. They don't stand up to close scrutiny. Very little does. The lessons in life had already started. But through the eyes of a child, who had never seen anything like it before, that kaleidoscope still ranks as one of the most marvellous things I'd ever seen.

I wondered what sort of Christmases my kid would have had in Australia. Now I had family there, I couldn't help thinking the whole thing with the Aussies had been a bit of a one-way affair. I mean to say, we'd got them started in terms of their modern population even if it was a few hundred boatloads of murderers, thieves and rapists. We'd given them The Queen, scurvy and syphilis - what more could they ask for? And what did we get in return? Skippy, Olivia Newton John and Rolf Bloody Harris. It hardly seems like anything resembling a fair swap, though having said that, could we ever have imagined that Rolf would prove to be something of a constant in our lives?

Forty years on and he's even painting Her Majesty. That's longevity for you. I just get this picture of Rolf whistling and making all those strange noises of his as our monarch sits there patiently with the bearded one saying 'Can you guess what it is yet?'

I guess all men of around 50 have one rock-solid dependable character from those early days - Rolf. Yeah sport, he's been there like some favourite uncle for my entire life. And I wouldn't have it any other way. I don't know when I would have first come across Rolf, but when he was singing 'Sun Arise', 'Jake the Peg', or Tie Me Kangaroo Down Sport' I'd only be a nipper. God, my dad used to laugh at him doing that Jake the Peg routine with the mackintosh and wellies.

'Look close, see if you can see which is the false one,' dad would chortle.

'See, you can't tell can you? Brilliant. Absolutely brilliant.'

And who would have thought that the silly geezer with the beard who made all those wonderful noises with didgeridoos and suchlike would still be with us today? He's a stayer is Rolf. Singer, painter, comedian, king of the Stylophone, master of the wobble board, star of Rolf on Saturday and Pet Rescue overlord. Christ he even did Stairway to Heaven. Hats off to you mate - a nation stands in tribute. You were always there for us. You kind of came and . . . well, never went and we're grateful. If you were a young kid in the early part of the 60s, Rolf would have been there somewhere.

5

1963 - HOT MAIL

How does Santa get any of those notes that fly up chimneys all over the world? How the fuck does he piece them back together and read them if their charred remains ever manage to reach him? It's a source of some bemusement to me, but is all part of the marvellous fantasy that is Father Christmas. Reindeers with red noses and even Santas with red noses. Fantastic, magical times in your life, you can only hold on to but never fully get back.

I kind of resented the fact I'd missed out on that with my son. I doubted they even had chimneys in Australia. Maybe they just put notes on the barbecue or something. No one should miss out on writing to Santa and sending it via chimney-mail.

I'd never had the chance to do that with my lad. My lad. How odd did that sound? It hurt a bit to be honest. It was like I'd not been there for him which, given the circumstances, was spot on. But just thinking about it, brought memories flooding back.

'Let me do it . . .'

'Here give it me,' said Dad.

'Daaaaaad!'

'Now be told . . . you don't want to get your hand burned do you?'

Dad took the carefully compiled note and held it into the fire towards the top and I shrieked with a mixture of both delight and concern as my Christmas list flew skywards and disappeared.

'Dad, how will Santa read it, if it's burned?'

'Don't worry son. Santa can read everything. He gets lists from all the little children all over the world and still sorts them out.'

That's another thing you see. Old houses had proper chimneys. Proper places for Santa to get in. We'd leave him a mince pie and some sherry. I can't remember him coming because, no matter how hard I tried, I just never managed to stay awake long enough.

The roaring fire at my gran and grandad's was the central point of the house and yet I was always quite scared of it. There was a guard - a brass mesh affair to catch things when it started to spit. The fire was warm and lovely, but I was always told to keep my distance.

There was another thing I was never quite sure of about gran's house - the bath. The taps were ancient and by the plughole there was a sort of rusty stain. I wondered if I was in it too long, whether I might catch old age. Mum used to plonk me in there with some grey plastic battleships. I'd stay in there until my fingers were textured like the roof of a cat's mouth. I recall having a kind of frogman figure thing as well. I think you put a little pellet in his back and he'd rise up and then dive with bubbles coming out of him. I had a pretty good time in the bath at gran's; it just worried me a bit getting into it. Once I was in there, I was okay. It seemed a very safe place. Maybe it was the big ingots of green carbolic soap, or just the smell of the place, but it felt secure. Strange really, because I'm usually not totally at home in water. Those fishmen used to frighten me in Stingray. Them and the Daleks - they were the most behind-the-couch scary things I can remember.

It was around this time that my love affair with telly programmes like Fireball XL5, Stingray and Thunderbirds began.

Steve Zodiac, Troy Tempest, Scott Tracy . . . how cool

were names like that? Now, you have kids called Troy and Scott, but not back then you didn't. These were tough names. Hard names. Names from . . . oh, America I suppose. Well, everyone has their own opinion and the right to interpret things their way, but I don't think names come much better than that. I think it's probably that 'Z' in Zodiac that swings it. When you're a kid it's like names, numbers, colours and things acquire a certain status. Having a tough name is something rather special when you are younger. It's all right people saying they were bound to have good names because Gerry Anderson, or whoever, gave it careful thought, but it doesn't have to be that way. What about Illya Kuryakin or Joe 90 - they weren't such great names were they?

Back to our man from Fireball XL5 - ten out of ten for that. Troy's in there with a mark of at least 9 out of 10 along with Scott Tracey. Virgil? One. Gordon? One. Alan? Five, I guess.

It's like with colours, when you're a child, there's a definite pecking order of colours and the boundaries are fairly rigid. Ask a kid for a favourite colour and they will be definite. 'Blue' or 'red' the answer comes back. It's only when we're adults that people start fannying around with them. You can't have blue - it has to be described in one of a million shades like aquamarine or topaz. When did a child ever reply 'barley' or 'oatmeal' when asked their favourite fucking colour? It just doesn't happen. It's only when tossers like Laurence Llewelyn-Bowen start distorting everything that the problems start.

Numbers are the same. For young boys, I think the ranking of a number depends largely on your favourite footballer, which one he wore and the general perception of the position that particular number reflected. These were the days before everyone fucked around with football shirts. It used to be simple. Favourite number? Nine. Easy. Centre forward - cool position. Loads of good players had the number 9 on their backs. Take your pick. Ace number. Seven was in the same elite bracket. Lucky seven. It looked good as a number. Nice when you wrote it down. Meet a kid who said 'three' and I'll guarantee one thing - wanker. Full back. Three? Ray Wilson? Keith Newton? Terry Cooper? Exactly. And again, it's all gone haywire. None of the professional footballers keep the same position anymore and so the entire equilibrium of the thing is shot to bits. Ask a kid now what his favourite number is and he's likely to say '36.' I rest my case. What sort of an answer is that? If you said your favourite number was '36' or maybe '42' when I was a boy, you'd have been put in the spaz class as it was innocently known. You might even have been locked away in a broom cupboard for a week - and quite rightly so. Special needs? Na, just a bit thick. Simple, if that's the right word, as that. It just didn't happen and the world was a richer place for it.

Steve Zodiac didn't have to fly around the universe to be rated a really top guy, but there's no getting away from it - it helps. Astronaut just gives you so much more of a chance than, say, postman. No disrespect to that respectable occupation, but I've yet to meet anyone who doesn't think astronaut just edges it.

Anyway, being a postman might just be a slightly better bet right now as my Steve Zodiac toy dangles precariously from a power line, held aloft only by his entangled parachute.

If Steve Zodiac were to meet an untimely end, it would have been more fitting if he'd been incinerated on re-entry to the earth's atmosphere rather than having been wrapped up on a power line after being hurtled through the air on the end of a thick elastic band. Having a tough name was all well and good but being stuck 18ft up a pole was bit of a leveller in all honesty.

Fireball XL5's pilot hadn't had to go whizzing around the universe to come to a sticky end, but the back garden of No 2 Orchard Grove did seem a slightly incongruous and unglamorous place to be hanging around for what eventually turned out to be months.

But while I was fiercely upset at the time, I didn't have any trouble making my own amusement. There was a new revolution starting and though pop music puritans would quite rightly say I missed it, I hung on to its coat tails. The Beatles had started sending the nation crazy with their outrageous haircuts and they were tailor-made for a little lad like me who had already discovered that my impression of The Shadows went down a storm with the family. When I put on my battered pair of sunglasses with no lenses in, I WAS Hank Marvin. I'd appear from behind the settee with anything resembling a guitar in my hand - usually my dad's old tennis racket - and play to my admiring audience.

Now The Beatles were here - they were everywhere - and I'd happily shake my head uncontrollably and belt out the few words I knew of 'She Loves You' and 'I Want to Hold Your Hand.'

This was family entertainment at its best and I was centre stage. This was my Sunday Night at the London Palladium.

The Beatles songs were clearly so different to anything I'd ever heard before. Up to now I'd been fed a diet of those comic offerings like I am a Mole and I live in a Hole. Cliff Richard and The Shadows had bridged the gap until now. Suddenly Terry Scott singing My Brother or Peter Sellers grumbling Goodness Gracious Me didn't have the same appeal.

My gran and grandad were outraged at the Fab Four.

'They want to get their bloody hair cut for a start off,' grandad would groan.

'What do they think they look like?' gran asked.

'Bloody big cissies, that's what they look like,' he answered.

But they'd already started a tidal wave of admiration in people a lot older than me and it was obvious even to a five-year-old that something quite special was happening.

And as it turned out, it wasn't the only revolution going on

- this would be our last Christmas in the house just across the road from my gran's.

In the summer we would be moving to Orchard Grove - a new estate of around 50 semi-detached houses built in a large loop just a few miles away in Linshaw.

It seemed a big upheaval for me because gran and grandad living so close meant I got to spend an awful lot of time there. It was warm and safe and there was a comforting air of familiarity about their house.

Grandad would show me things - great things. He would carefully peel an orange into quarters with his penknife and make the segments into fake teeth. Scary teeth. He'd methodically cut into it, first a line across the width and then small cuts in the opposite direction to accentuate the teeth. Then he'd turn it inside out, pop it into his mouth and bare that hideous grin at me with a snarl. It would make me jump even though I knew what he was about to do.

And another thing he'd often do was give me one of his Callard and Bowser butterscotch sweets and then take a three-penny bit or a sixpence from his pocket and take a big white hankie from his pocket.

He'd place the silver foil sweet wrapper on top of the coin on the table. Then he'd rub away, methodically and slowly until the imprint started to show through. It was perfect. Sometimes he'd give me the coin and tell me it was mine to keep if I could make a good copy. And so I'd spend ages carefully making my imprint. They never seemed quite as good as the ones he did, but I must have done something right because I never had to give the coin back.

It was nice my gran's house but another thing I remember about it was that I seemed to spend a lot of time on the floor. I don't think it's a case for a psychologist or social services to investigate. Maybe it was just because I was always playing with my toy cars back then. I'd cut holes in the side of shoeboxes or cereal packs and use them as garages. I had such

21

fun with those cars. Not a care in the world. Days when the only thing you had to worry about slightly were the fishmen off Stingray and catching old age from your gran's bath.

Those were my only concerns, though I guessed the fishmen would never get me where we lived. I just didn't want to have my teeth in a glass or not be able to eat toffees or have grey hair or wear glasses. Not unless they were those Hank Marvin ones - they were okay.

6

1964 - TOY GARAGE

It might just be the greatest Christmas present I've ever had. It's hard to put them in any order. But if time spent enjoying playing with something was the determining factor then the Shell garage I had when I was six, would have strong claims to be number one. I'd never seen one before. My eyes must have almost popped out of my head the minute I clapped eyes on it.

There was no indication of what it was because it had been put in a square cardboard box before wrapping. It wasn't that heavy for its size. I remember dad picking it up from under the tree and placing it in the middle of the floor before getting alongside me and helping me tear the paper off it. There seemed to be loads and then, once you were inside the box, there was lots of scrunched up newspaper and stuff to make sure it didn't get broken.

I couldn't quite tell what it was looking down on it from above and it wasn't until my dad lifted it clear of the brown box that I could fully take it all in.

Up to now, I'd kept my toy cars in a small battered suitcase, but this was just like nothing I'd seen before. Now I had my very own garage. It had three petrol pumps on the front that you could move about and a ramp that came down the left side. You could put cars in the bottom of the tower that had a red 'Shell' sign on the top and wind them up to the top floor on a lift. From the roof you could put cars into the ramp entrance and watch them go down past the middle floor and all the way down the side. They got stuck sometimes but it didn't matter. It was, quite simply, magnificent. It was definitely a present to rank among the all-time greats. The same can't be said of everything . . .

It's just two words and the first one is *blow*. How promising a start is that? Bearing in mind it's designed to give lads endless pleasure, I can barely disguise my disappointment to this day. Blow Football . . . now just what is that all about? What a shite game. I mean really, really mind-numbingly crap. The thing is it's dressed up as something wonderful and exciting and its only salvation is that it enriched my life forever by introducing me to the little guy who would become my blood brother and best mate for life - enter Mouse.

Mouse's real name is Ian Ratcliffe but there are significant numbers of people who have known him for years, who simply wouldn't have a clue what his first name was. Mouse was plain Mouse from the first time I met him and he remains that to this day. Some assume it was because he was quiet; others that he had a squeaky voice when he was younger. Some wonder whether it was because he had slightly protruding ears, yet the actual source of his distinctive nickname was nothing quite so dramatic. Mouse was the youngest of six - four brothers and a sister. The eldest brother - Nev - was eight years older and was universally known as Rats. Then came Gary - 18 months younger - who seemed to be answer to any permutation of Ratter or Little Rats. Then there was Kevin - a year younger than Gary - who simply answered to Kev. Brian, the next boy up from Mouse also managed to hang on to either his proper name or merely 'Bri.' Then there was the only girl Sandra followed by the youngest - Ian. And because he was the Junior Rat, one of their uncles labelled him Mouse and it stuck. And not long after we struck up a friendship, it was Mouse who gave me the nickname that would stick with me to this day - Santa. I did have misgivings in the early days when it quite clearly showed signs of sticking, but it was something I quickly grew comfortable with.

Our friendship has managed to survive everything - even the unpromising start of him introducing me to the dubious pleasures of blow fucking football. Didn't we just love it? Well, no, not really. But that's a confession I still have to make well out of Mouse's earshot to this day. He always loved it and I had to go along with it. I did that for all the right reasons and like a little white lie that never gets uncovered, it's taken on a life of its own.

I still look back on those days in the back room of Mouse's house with such affection. The Ratcliffes lived in a council house that directly backed onto our new home.

It was a chaotic house with the brothers diving in and out and Mrs Ratcliffe always seeming to have some domestic implement or other in her hand. If she wasn't cooking, she was ironing a shirt for one or a number of them. Our house in comparison seemed almost sedentary, but I loved going to Mouse's. He was fun. He had a cheeky laugh - a wheezy affair, similar to Mutley. He was stick-thin but as tough as old boots - undoubtedly virtue of being playfully slapped around by his big brothers. Mouse did have slightly protruding ears, which stuck out beneath his basin cut mop of jet-black hair. Mouse's house was very rarely anything other than disorderly. Music invariably thumped from one of the bedrooms and downstairs seemed to stay in a state of perpetual untidiness. Mrs Ratcliffe tried her best but she was always swimming against the tide. It was an open house but sometimes just getting inside could be like tackling an army assault course. There were inevitably a couple of bikes propped against each other in the tiny outhouse by the back door. No one ever seemed to use the front, which was just as well because there was always ironing piled up against it waiting to be taken upstairs.

She would always have a pinny on and could often be heard screaming 'you little bleeder' to whichever one of her kids had either deliberately or inadvertedly played her up. Mouse's mum could say 'bleeder' without it sounding offensive. It was just part of her make-up and the whole family were fiercely protective of her.

The two cats, Blackie and Graham, seemed to have a continual look of panic on their faces. When they weren't being sat on, they were carefully being hurled outside, just so someone could have the space they had occupied. Graham was actually a she cat, but the story goes that when they were picking her from the litter, one of the brothers said to little Sandra 'Have the grey 'un'.

And so when she finally decided which one she wanted she told Mr Ratcliffe she wanted 'Graham.' And so the poor cat was lumbered with that name for life. Graham and Blackie knew their place at No 1 Castle Street - they just couldn't always find it. Orchard Grove was a newly developed spur off Castle Street, which was affectionately known as Vinegar Hill by locals. No one seemed to quite know why it had been given that name, but the best offering was that in days gone by it was the smell of beer from the two pubs that sat at either end. At the top of Vinegar Hill on the junction with Vicarage Road was the Farmers Arms, a black and white pub with a large car park and a bowling green at the back. At the bottom of the hill, but on the same side, was the Green Man, a spit and sawdust type place favoured by an older clientele. The hill was quite steep and had recently been made a dead end to vehicles. Pedestrians had access to Main Road, but it had been cut off to cars as part of the development plans for Orchard Grove. Walking up the hill from the Green Man, the entrance to the new houses was about 200 yards away. Beyond the pub was a row of eight semi-detached 1950s council houses. Mouse and his family lived in No 1 and they rose in odd numbers up as far as a hawthorn-hedged field that bordered the Farmers Arms' car park and spanned back as far as the path that cut its way from an alley at the top end of the grove. Behind there was the best area to play in the world. There was a cornfield where we made dens leading up to what was known as the first banks. There were two small ponds to the back of the first banks, bordering the high gorse-covered bank that dropped steeply down to the railway line.

A straight path, about 150 yards in length, took you to the second banks, a small clay mound with a hollow middle where we would spend hours biking, diving in and out of the dip. There was a small wooded area on the back slope of the second banks comprising mainly hazel, birch and elder, which funnelled down to a large grass field the size of two football pitches, which was the mid point between the second and third banks. It was known as Bluebell Wood because of the fragrant carpet of blooms that arrived without fail every April or May. The third banks were real adventure territory, a gently undulating larger mound where skylarks hovered feverishly over sporadic clumps of gorse. This was Cowboys and Indians Land. War Land. This was Bike Land. It was Boy Land and in our teenage years it was to be very much Boy and Girl Land. There was a thousand and one little hidden away spots on the Third Banks and though it was to become familiar territory to us, to others it must have seemed miles away.

Opposite The Farmers Arms on the other side of the junction was a small grassed area with a bench, which had been put there by the Linshaw British Legion. We'd mess around there sometimes until we were told to scarper. Going back down the hill, there were five detached houses with big bay windows, the last of which was just past the mouth of Orchard Grove. Next to that was Maggie's Shop, a small newsagent-cum-general store where we'd get our sweets. And down from that, at the bottom and directly opposite the Green Man, was Roly's Chippy where we'd go for bags of chips and some batter bits. Sometimes we'd get a can of Coke or Shandy Bass and Roly would open it for us. You can keep your smoked salmon. If there's anything beats the taste of chips and batter bits smothered in sharp vinegar and washed down with Shandy Bass, I've yet to come across it. It was food of the gods. Our very own ambrosia and we'd have eaten them every night of the week if we'd had our way.

The living room of No 1 Castle Street was like a stinging grey cube of Park Drive smoke. Mr Ratcliffe virtually chain-smoked and the tiny coffee table in the middle of the room almost creaked under the pressure of tea mugs and ashtrays. I was always fascinated by one of the ashtrays. It was metallic green in colour, a kind of globe shape at the bottom, with a push down handle rising up through the middle. When you pushed down on it, three or four metal panels all opened up on each other to let the contents drop through. I liked to push it - trouble was it was nearly always so crammed full that it would barely move at all.

Mr Ratcliffe seemed to be quite a quiet man most of the time, unless instructed by his wife to lay the law down to one of the boys. When he bellowed, dust literally flew as someone was brought to task. You didn't mess with Geordie Ratcliffe. Not in his house and not outside if his reputation was anything to go by. He wasn't a particularly big man - about 5ft 8in at a push - but he had sinewy strong arms, courtesy of years straining at the pit face. He had a tattoo of an eagle on his left bicep and a lion's head on the other. He threatened to murder any of the lads who ever thought of having a tattoo. He was nice to me, Mr Ratcliffe. He'd rub his yellowed fingers through my hair and usher me in whenever I went there.

'Come on Santa, get yourself in son,' he'd say.

Mum would often remark that I stank of smoke when I got home - a touch disconcerting when you are six or seven, but bloody useful when you reach your mid-teens and need a failsafe way to cover your tracks. And it's all down to my mum that I got wrapped up in the whole Blow Football deception, even though I think I'd worked it all out long before she delivered her thoughtful mini-lecture.

'John, just a word. I know you're pretty good, but you must be careful love when you go around to Ian's house.'

'What do you mean mum?'

'No I didn't mean that to sound the wrong way. It's just that well, you know Ian's mum and dad have got a lot of mouths to feed and money is probably a bit tight you know.'

I must have looked puzzled, so she continued her address.

'What I'm saying is, be very careful what you say because Ian won't be able to have the games and things that you have.'

'I know mum.'

'Good, I know you know, but it's just it's very easy to hurt people's feelings without knowing it. It's too late if you say something wrong, even if you don't mean it that way.'

'I know mum.'

'Good. He's a lovely lad is Ian and he's always welcome here but I don't want you to say something which could come out sounding wrong.'

'I wouldn't mum.'

'Well maybe not, but me and yer dad only have you to buy for so sometimes you'll be able to have things that Ian can't - there's nothing worse than a show-off.'

'I'm not a . . .'

'I'm not saying you are. Just bear it in mind. No one likes big heads. Run along with you, I'm busy.'

Sound advice and - as I said - the reason to this day, I've never been able to tell Mouse that Blow Football is a fucking nightmare.

We were in the backroom when Mouse got his game out. Two thin steel goalposts with a tin goalie hanging from the crossbar and two straws - one luminous green and the other bright yellow. We mocked up a pitch using the big table and we each agreed to have four similar obstacles to double up as players - a salt cellar, pepper pot, two match boxes, a small ornament, two egg cups and a dog-eared pack of Waddington's playing cards.

And so it was that the big game got under way - bear in mind this was long before the PC health and safety brigade had been dreamed up, let alone let loose to outlaw such an innocent pursuit as Blow Football. Imagine it now - various mouths being allowed within the vicinity of just a couple of battered old straws. And as Mouse's big brother Kev was soon to discover, goalkeepers made out of such wafer-thin tin plate that they were absolutely lethal.

Kev intervened and thought it would be a great laugh to send his young brother's goalkeeper rattling around the crossbar with one carefully aimed flick. But he was immediately sent wailing from the bloodied playing surface as he inspected the damage he'd inflicted on himself. The keeper had sliced into his forefinger with such ease that Mrs Ratcliffe dared offer the observation that he might need a stitch in it. Blood was gushing everywhere and, much to Mouse's amusement, Kev was left holding his sliced finger under the cold water tap for what seemed an age as his mother attempted to stem the flow of blood.

'Jeezus Christ,' he bellowed as if it were the work of some divine force.

'Well it's your own stupid fault,' Mrs Ratcliffe intervened.

'I'll kill you,' Kev mouthed at Mouse.

'Why me? I didn't do anything.'

'It's your stupid bloody game,' he groaned.

'Language Kevin,' Mrs Ratcliffe roared.

'Well, what a stupid thing. It's dangerous that is.'

'Not if you don't try and wreck it,' Mouse complained.

Everyone seemed to agree that it might be time to pack the game up for the time being. And what with me winning 7-5 as well. Ah well . . . maybe another day.

7

1965 - JOHNNY SEVEN

There just had to be more than seven reasons to hate Guy Digby. First, he sowed the seed with me that Santa Claus didn't exist. Secondly, he was a fat kid with freckles and a gormless expression. The rest all came rolled into one - Johnny Seven. That's nine for starters.

The first time we met Guy was late morning that Christmas Day. It was cold and we had wrapped up. As Mouse and me made our way to the brow of Vinegar Hill, we spotted him, though he didn't have too much problem catching our attention with the impressive green gun he had slung cockily across his chest. Johnny Seven - O.M.A. One Man Army indeed. One man arsehole more like, but Guy Digby was worth getting to know even if it was just to have a go on one of the most fuck-off superb toys known to 1965 man (or boy, if we're splitting hairs). Wow, there were guns and there were *guns* and this beauty had the lot. It must have been a yard long with a list of functions the like of which had never been seen before. I swear to god, Bush and Blair could have sent the troops into Iraq armed with nothing more than Johnny Sevens and still frightened the shit out of anyone who dared cross them.

Guy Digby and the Johnny Seven were somewhat unlikely partners. He was one of those dumpy kids with a kind of self-satisfied expression that could instantly rub you up the wrong way. Facially he had a more-than passing resemblance to Skippy's pal Sonny Hammond. It wouldn't be that long before

31

the Double Deckers arrived on the scene and he would forever be branded with the nickname Doughnut.

But for now anyway, he was certainly worthy of our attention if only for the wondrous weapon he was playing with on the front drive of his house. It was Mouse who decided to go over and introduce us to the new lad making peculiar noises with his impressive new toy. Up to now the only guns we'd seen were cap guns, the silver cowboy rifles and the pistols that came with a 'gem' encrusted holster. Peashooters were about as menacing as we got. This monster was immediately recognisable as something completely different. The chubby figure smiled at us as Mouse acknowledged him and was clearly desperate to show off the gun's stunning array of tricks.

'You new here?' said Mouse.

'Yeah, you?'

'Nah, not really . . . bin here a bit.'

'Oh right.'

'Great gun,' said Mouse excitedly.

'Yeah, it's a Johnny Seven. It does everything.'

'Well, not *everything*,' Mouse begged to differ.

'It does the lot this one, fires grenades, bullets, it's got a rocket launcher and a separate gun if you need it.'

It was a gorgeous green American army kind of colour. I'd never seen anything like it before.

'Can I have a go?' I asked.

'Yeah. But be careful, mind. I don't want to lose anything.'

Guy detached the pistol from the handle and handed it to Mouse, laughing uncontrollably when he accidentally fired one of the caps.

'Wow,' Mouse said, regaining his composure. 'I wasn't expecting that.'

'Like I said, it's got everything this one,' gushed Guy proudly.

'That's the grenade launcher,' he continued.

'That one there - that's the anti-tank rocket. Armour piercing shell there. That bit is the err, I can't remember what that is now,' Guy said.

'Oh yeah, that's a bunker missile thing. There's 10 bullets there and that bit is the Tommy gun.'

It was my turn to reel back as the gun made a rat-a-tat-tat sound the like of which I'd never heard before.

It seemed to weigh a ton. What a weapon. While we had both looked upon the new kid with some suspicion there was no doubting this was a magnificent machine. Mouse and me had cap guns, sure. And we'd made rifles out of pieces of wood, which did the job. But this, well, it was just the kind of thing dreams are made of.

'Must have cost a fortune,' I said.

'I'm not sure, I think it was quite a lot,' Guy said, adding that his dad had bought it for him. His dad was in the army in Malaysia he said. He reckoned his dad had the real live version, which could kill over a hundred men in one go. We weren't sure whether to believe him.

As Guy went on to tell his very eventful life story up to this point, it all became a bit of a mystery. He lived with his Nan and grandad in one of the posher houses - the second one down on the opposite side of Vinegar Hill. His parents were abroad on army duty, he said. His dad flew helicopters and his mum was in some kind of secret service, he assured us. It all sounded rather far-fetched to two kids from Linshaw. A shade too elaborate, we couldn't help wondering.

Guy had one older sister - a whole lot older - like at least 20-odd and a fat brother called Cameron who was a couple of years older than us.

According to Guy, he'd spent lots of time in the jungle when his dad was on leave; been bitten by a snake and nearly died and survived a crash landing when his dad's helicopter had to come down in a forest. He said he'd eaten spiders as big as your hand, if not bigger, and all sorts of bugs too. It was just the sort of thing you had to do if you didn't want to die, he said matter-of-factly.

It all seemed a bit made-up to us, but with no way of disproving it and with this fuck-off beautiful gun in his hands, we were prepared to go along with it.

Eventually we left him because we knew our big dinner would be ready soon. Mouse and me agreed he wasn't going to be one of our close mates, Johnny Seven or not.

'Did you think it was that good?' Mouse asked me, looking straight at me for a true answer.

'It wasn't bad was it?' I said trying to take the middle ground.

'Yeah but what happens when he loses all the stuff. All them bullets and stuff? What then?'

'He'll have to call it a Johnny Six or summat like that,' I said.

Mouse laughed. 'Yeah, Johnny Four-and-a-half eh?'

'Johnny Two,' I took it even further.

'What about Johnny Nowt? Johnny Nothing. Guy Digby One Man Arsehole!' Mouse collapsed with laughter.

He was crying as tears poured down my face too. 'One Man Arsehole' I liked the sound of it. It was naughty. We laughed and laughed, as we made our way home. Better not let our mums or dads hear us saying words like that or there'd be trouble.

'One Man Cakehole,' Mouse roared. We didn't like to admit it - we were impressed. That was one hell of a gun

'Yeah, but . . .' said Mouse clearly intent on putting everything into perspective.

'Yeah, but . . . listen. If you could have that gun and had to have him as your bestest friend and not me, what would you do?'

'The gun! The gun! Gimmee the gun!' I yelled.

'Get lost. You wouldn't would ya?'

'Course not stupid.'

'Nah nor me.'

I told mum about meeting Guy but she seemed less than impressed with some of his claims.

'It sounds an awful lot for a little boy to me. Are you sure he wasn't having you on?'

'I dunno mum, but he meant it. When he was eating snakes in the jungle . . . he said . . .err.'

'I should take it with a pinch of salt son if I were you,' dad interjected.

'He sounds a bit of a dreamer to me. Anyway, think about putting those cars away now.'

It was then that I asked mum whether Santa really did exist, which I could tell, took her aback a bit. She assured me he did and asked who had suggested otherwise.

'Guy said there was no such thing,' I told her.

'Did he now? It strikes me that boy knows a little bit too much - or so he thinks,' mum said sniffily and pointed me in the direction of my cars which were scattered all over the floor.

'Clear those up for me, love,' she said.

I loved playing with my cars. My favourite was the James Bond car - an Aston Martin DB5 - I'd had as a present. The things I liked best were all the great gadgets on it.

Best of the lot was the ejector seat. You just had to press the lever and the little blue man shot out of the roof. It was brilliant. I think on the real car, the button was on the gear stick. Yes, it was. It was on the gear knob. But they couldn't do that on a little car like this. It had a bulletproof shield, which popped up at the back, tyre shredders, which came out of the wheels and machine guns, which came out of the front. What a car. I'd love to be able to drive the real thing. I wouldn't be able to drive for a long time yet and even if I could I wouldn't ever have enough money for a DB5.

I'd got a driving school car. It was light blue and it was great because if you turned the red thingy on the top the front wheels moved. So you could steer it sort of like a proper car. I loved my cars. I still put them in the battered suitcase and kept the garage separate. You couldn't really pick them up if they were in the garage because they rolled around all over the place and ended up falling off.

The James Bond car was my favourite by a mile, though I quite liked the Chipperfields Circus wagon with a trailer too. You could put animals in the back behind the bars. One day I put the milkmaid in there so as the lions could eat her. Dad said it wasn't a nice thing to do.

My next best car was The Saint car. I liked The Saint because he was a really good guy and always beat the baddy. I didn't understand all of it though. Mum said Roger Moore was really good looking. What I didn't get was that when he was just about to do something or whatever, this ring appeared above his head and he had a silly smile on his face. I don't know - I just didn't quite get it. Dad said it would have taken too much explaining and to just enjoy it.

My toy Saint car was white with red seats and a transfer of the stick man thing on the front. I was never really sure about that. The real Saint didn't have the transfer on his car. That's why I thought it looked a bit stupid, but I knew if I tried to scratch it off, my dad would shout, so it stayed there.

It was like they were saying 'this is The Saint car' and we'll put a matchstick man on the front just so there's no confusion. I knew what the fucking hell it was. Why do adults treat you like kids?

8

1966 - TRIFLE

Mum always made a huge trifle at Christmas. They looked great - fantastic layered colours, a fresh cream topping, coloured hundreds and thousands with bits of crumbled Flake. But more importantly, they didn't just look good, they sounded great. I can immediately tell if a trifle shapes up by the sound it makes when you cut into it. If it doesn't make a really funny noise like pulling your wellygog out of thick mud, then it's strictly second division. My mum's trifles hit the button every single time. The minute she cut into it with a large spoon, you just knew as it started to squelch that it was another award winner.

God knows how we managed to eat it sometimes after ploughing through the main course, but we did. Firm trifle - it's the only way. My grandad used to say you could tell a lot about a man by the state of his shoes. Well, trifles are the same.

My mum was meticulous about the way she made them and I'd often just hang around the kitchen knowing that she'd hand me a couple of sponge fingers before she set about soaking them in the raspberry juice. I swear I could have eaten a whole packet of sponge fingers, but she would warn me that she needed them to make the trifle properly. It never disappointed. I used to love playing in the kitchen, giving my mum a hand - a grubby one at that - which she could have well done without. If only I'd have known the money to be made from being a celebrity chef, I might have paid more attention.

But just messing around with pastry, rather than making it into an art form, was more than enough to occupy me.

If I wanted proper entertainment there was no shortage. The Woodentops, Pinky and Perky and Andy Pandy had only been the start of it. By the time 1966 had arrived we were all model citizens. Supercar was just before my time; Troy Tempest and Steve Zodiac kicked it off, but in their slipstream came, Thunderbirds, Captain Scarlet, Joe 90, the fucking lot. Pretty soon all the serious entertainers on telly would be puppets - Basil Brush, Lambchop and Lord Charles. I'd had two Thunderbirds toys as presents - Thunderbird 3 and Thunderbird 2 with the all the pods as accessories.

The list of puppet masters was endless and that's not even counting the Tufty adverts, which regularly cropped up on the telly. For the uninitiated, Tufty was a squirrel whose key role in life was to teach kids road safety. I'd been a member of the Tufty club a few years back, but had grown out of that - if you can ever grow out of the principle of not getting squashed by a lorry. Tufty was the good guy while Bobby Brown Rabbit was the little shit who continually flouted the rules and was forever getting knocked down. If you've ever wondered why you see so many dead rabbits on the road, it's because their very first real hero was a fucking half-wit. Watership Down was light years away. And so rabbits the length and breadth of Britain gave short shrift to the squirrel and followed the one with the shorter fluffy tail - big fucking mistake. Thus, rabbits end up mashed on the road covered in fleas and having their eyes pecked out by magpies.

There were a lot of public information films around at that time. I liked the one where there was a man with a knotted hankie on his head sitting on some cliffs by the sea with his wife. There's a man flapping around in the water and the guy on the cliff says: 'Oh look, now he's waving at us Petunia!' It was for the coastguard or something like that. I lived in Shropshire, so it didn't seem to apply to where we came from.

Then there was 'Dip don't Dazzle' and stuff like that, urging you to be considerate with your headlights. But then again, we hadn't a car, so that wasn't much use to us either.

The summer success of the England World Cup team meant that anyone would have been hard-pressed to top that in terms of drama - enter Gilbert the barber.

Mum didn't need to scratch her head to come up with a culprit when I came home one day scratching mine.

Her anguish at the very thought of even the most audacious head louse daring to set foot anywhere near her beloved and well-groomed son was too much for her to bear.

'They say they only go for clean hair,' I heard her impassioned address to Mrs Ash who lived in the first detached house up the road, next to Guy Digby's. Mr and Mrs Ash were both teachers and had three daughters. They were the epitome of clean and respectable and mum was clearly working on the theory that three immaculate girls with parents who were in contact with countless children at school was a recipe for disaster. If I was going to have to share lice with anyone, mum would rather it have been someone respectable like the Ash sisters.

'Have any of your girls had them yet?' asked mum, assuming it would be a formality. If I were by some peculiar twist of fate the first, I certainly wouldn't be the last. My mum would have seen to that. I swear to God she would have captured every last one off my head and let them loose at junior school.

'No,' Mrs Ash said somewhat indignantly. 'But I shouldn't worry. All kids get them at some point,' she tried to reassure the demented woman who doubled up as my mum. This was not all kids - this was me.

'Well, they've got my lad,' mum grimaced as if I was the innocent victim of a terrorist attack.

'Touch wood, the girls have stayed clear of them so far,' Mrs Ash said with a mixture of relief and pride.

'Well, be warned - they're everywhere apparently,' mum continued, readily inviting every neighbours' child to become a fully paid up member of the summer of '66 Nit Club. Behind closed doors she was blaming the Rogers kids who lived in the ramshackle terraced house halfway along Vicarage Road.

'They're bloody filthy,' she groaned indignantly.

'There's not one of them had a good bath in months by the look of them,' she continued.

'Haven't seen a bar of soap in God-knows how long. I doubt whether there's any in the house, truth be known.'

Dad intervened. 'That's a bit unfair love.'

'Oh I knew you'd take their side. Unfair? Unfair? That house is filthy. It's a health risk. I bet they're all crawling with nits - the lot of them.'

'Well, if they are, then that buggers up your theory love.'

'What theory?'

'Well you can't go around on one hand blaming those poor little mites for spreading nits and then, on the other hand you're telling everyone they only go for clean hair. It doesn't make sense.'

'Mites? Mites be damned. Well they do only go for the kids with clean hair - that's a fact.'

'That's as maybe,' dad said softly, holding his hands up in conciliatory fashion. 'But if that's right then you can't pin it on the Rogers tribe.'

'Oh my God,' said mum with an exasperated gasp. I got the feeling she would like to have said 'good point' but it was all getting too much for her.

Losing an argument was one thing - losing her only son to terminal ticks was another.

'Well, it's that barbers then. That one you take him to.'

'What Gilbert's?'

'Yesss. It has to be.'

'Why does Gilbert suddenly become the chief suspect?' dad asked.

40

'Well because the Ash girls don't go there for a start off. I'll bet good money it's his place.'

'Well possibly, but don't say it like it's my fault for taking him there. The lad's got nits not leprosy. There's no use getting in a state about it.'

'State! State! Who's in a state?' mum chuntered.

The Ash girls were the unlikeliest recipients of nits you could imagine. My mum might as well have asked The Queen if Charles or Anne were crawling with lice. Melissa was my age and the youngest; Mandy was about 12 months older and then there was Barbara who was another couple of years on. Melissa had a sticky plaster patch over her glasses on her left eye and she seemed upset when Mouse and me were asking her about it the other day. We referred to her as Nelson behind her back. She was a bit of a goody-two-shoes to our way of thinking. The three of them were for that matter. They all wore pretty patterned dresses and Clark's shoes over white ankle socks. They went to Sunday school and the only time you would see them in the street was when they were either going to or returning from school. They didn't seem to come out to play too often, certainly not any further than their own driveway.

Mouse and me thought they were a bit snobby. Their parents wouldn't let them watch telly - they didn't even have one in the house. We could hardly believe it when Nelson had told us they never had chips and the only chocolate they had was on a Sunday when their dad would give them the money to buy a couple of bars to share between them as a special treat.

It must have been last Sunday when we had seen her. She was walking up from Maggie's shop with a Bar Six and a Whole Nut. She said the whole family shared them which seemed like you wouldn't get much. She'd looked at us as if we were from a different planet when we looked shocked at the seemingly severe regime they lived under.

41

Mr and Mrs Ash didn't permit them to have fizzy drinks or comics or any of the rubbish we liked.

They had books and the radio and that was it. Mrs Ash was an art teacher so they did lots of drawing and stuff and Melissa was learning to play the cello. Mouse and me looked blankly at her. We didn't even know what a cello was. It all seemed very harsh and I thought it was a good opportunity to tell mum that the fact that Nelson hadn't got nits wasn't that surprising at all. Huge mistake.

'Don't you *ever* let me hear you call that girl *that* again John,' mum said sharply.

'What?'

'What you just called her - THAT'S what.'

'Oh it's only a joke.'

'Well, it's not funny. How would you like it?'

'Well . . .'

'She's got a lazy eye and that's why she has to have that patch on, not because she thinks it looks great. Poor girl's probably beside herself about it, I shouldn't wonder. Never, ever let me hear you say that again.'

'What's a lazy eye then?' I said faking ignorance in a bid to get myself off the hook.

'Well, it's when you have one good eye and one that doesn't work properly. It's like it's a bit lazy, so they put a patch over the good eye.'

'Over the good eye?' I said incredulously.

'Yes . . . that way it makes the other one work, sort of catch up with it, if you like.'

'I don't get it.'

Mum looked exasperated. 'Look, if you had a leg that didn't work as good as the other one, they could put a splint on it, so as the other one would get stronger and then you'd see what would happen.'

'I'd fall over.'

'Stop being so silly. It's not funny and I never want to hear

42

you say that again. Got it?'

I think I'd got it. Nelson, sorry Melissa, had got a bad eye and a good one. So they completely cover the good one so you can't see out of it and leave you with the bad one. Perhaps they worked on the theory that if you bumped into something and hurt yourself, you'd completely forget about your bad eye.

Cor blimey, complicated things girls, aren't they?

And there was my mum worrying about just a few lice . .

9

1967 - FATMAN

Batman must have munched his way through some selection boxes and mice pies in his time - well OUR Batman certainly had. How the fuck did Adam West become The Caped Crusader? Let's face it he was a bit of a podgy git. He didn't look like he could punch his way out of a wet paper bag to be honest. Let's get this straight. I adored Batman as much as the next kid. It was just fantastic and when the end came, you were just kept hanging on for a week to see if Robin and him really could get out of a dire fix this time. Common sense should have told you they always did, but that wasn't in abundance when I was nine. I had Batman cards and Batman stickers and my mum even made me a cape out of some material she'd found somewhere. And so maybe the same quality which allowed me to be in suspense for a week, actually worrying about Batman and his mate, allowed me to forget that Adam West was more paunch than punch. He must have known the producer or something. How else would he have got such a plum role and become a cult hero? There must have been thousands chasing that part.

I would have auditioned for sure even if my cape wasn't quite black. In fact, it was mainly royal blue with some kind of swirl, on account of the fact that in its former life it had been a pair of curtains. Holy smoke!

It had been a funny Christmas for mix-ups. Mum thought she'd give me a nice surprise because she'd heard Mouse and me going on about Batamarangs. She didn't quite get it

44

somehow. She must have heard us going on about how great Batman's secret weapon was. If someone tried to escape his clutches then one quick throw of his bat-boomerang and he'd have them tied up and at his mercy in no time.

Don't you just love mums? Mine decides to make me a cake. A cake? Yeah, a cake . . . It was delicious mind, but she's got it into her head that it was a bat-a-meringue and made a scrumptious lemon meringue pie with a marzipan bat symbol on the top. How good is that? No wonder Batman was so fat - he was secretly wolfing down desserts rather than catching his arch enemies. Adam would have needed to let out another couple of notches on his bat belt by the time my mum had finished with him. Fatmaaan . . .dinner . . . dinner . . . dinner . . . dinner. Fatmaaaan.

When we weren't hero-worshipping our very first supermodels we were making them. If there's anything more satisfying than building an Airfix Flying Fortress, Spitfire or whatever then I'm damned if I know what it is. Even those German Fokkes had something about them. Personally, if I had to pick a German one, then it would be the Stuka with that funny seagull type wing, but Fokke just sounded great as a lad.

That is until your dad overheard it from a distance and delivered that 'What did you just say?' piercing glance. I'd kind of look back at him vacantly as if to stress any alleged profanities were as a direct result of the plastic cement I'd been sniffing throughout the model making exercise. It'd be by-passed with a knowing smile and one of those typical dad nods, eyebrows raised, which just kind of told you to be careful. What a fokking relief.

Dads were duty bound to clamp down on that kind of stuff I suppose. The other day, Kenneth Wolstenholme had said 'And that was a real let-off in the Everton defence,' and I'd started giggling. Dad told me that if I couldn't watch the football without being stupid I'd have to go to bed.

But mainly, I recall nine being the sort of age where your

parents latched on to buying you stuff that required you having a real input and so Airfix and Frog models were the mentally-stimulating diet we were gleefully fed on. And it wasn't just the building of them - more the colours and smells of all the peripherals which made up the package.

Take the glue, or rather plastic cement, for example- now how good is that stuff? The smell of the stuff we used to stick model planes together was just out of this world. It's only retrospectively that I realise we were all high as fucking kites for days on end. There was the glue, the fantastic tiny tins of paint and the transfers you had to soak in water. It all made up for the kind of appealing package that could keep a young boy occupied for hours on end.

But the one present I can recall magically appearing on Christmas morning, 1967, wasn't even mine. I'd gone around to Mouse's house as early as was permissible to go and play and just happened to be there when his big surprise present was unveiled. It was almost eleven and mum warned me on pain of death to be back for no later than one o'clock in time for dinner. I remember it being a bit wet underfoot and I almost slipped over in my urgency to get around the corner.

Geordie Ratcliffe was a dab hand at making great things - which must have come in handy with a family as big as his. Since I'd known Mouse he'd often get things his dad had made especially for him. He'd had a homemade catapult and a bagatelle kind of game in the past. Oh yeah, and a sort of Shut The Box game, his dad had made where you rolled two dice to close the numbered panels. Oh and there was the brilliant bow and arrows he'd made both of us this summer.

But this one was the one to beat all-comers. This baby was the one to leave the rest standing hands-down.

I'd said Merry Christmas to Mr and Mrs Ratcliffe, had a

playful clip round the ear from his big brother Neville and gratefully accepted a sweet from the big tin of Quality Street. I tried to make out I wasn't looking, but I was a master at that, and managed to get one of the purple ones, just by chance.

'You've got something else lad. Show him where it is Neville,' said old man Ratcliffe, motioning his eldest towards the kitchen.

'Come on wetneck,' Nev said playfully.

'Come on, Sant,' he said urging me to follow.

We made our way through the narrow kitchen and out to the back door and turned left out of the outhouse towards the dilapidated shed. Nev turned the key and scrambled around for what seemed like an age before telling us to give him some room. We were right on his heels, trying to peer in, Mouse asking excitedly what it was.

'Hang on a mo. Just hang on,' said Nev.

'Come on,' urged Mouse.

'There's that much crap in here. Move back. I need some room. Cover his eyes Sant,' his brother urged me.

'I covered Mouse's eyes with my hands and moved him out towards the tiny bit of lawn at the back where Nev had pointed me to go.

'Wow.' It was fantastic. I managed to see it just before Mouse, who squealed with excitement as he wrestled free of my hands.

'Oh man alive,' Mouse squealed as his proud dad looked on from the outhouse entrance. It was a trolley - a fantastic go-cart and I've got to admit I was quite envious when I first saw it. Mr Ratcliffe had made it out of a number of pieces of wood and on the front part, which had the piece of rope to steer it, he'd made a number plate - MOUSE 1. It was tremendous.

'Cor, thanks dad. Can we go out on it now?'

'Well, yeah, but . . . Nev just take the pair of them out there for ten minutes and show them how it works.'

Mrs Ratcliffe didn't seem quite so enamoured with the

idea of her nine-year-old son hurtling around the street on a few pieces of wood, no matter how lovingly assembled.

'You just take it easy you pair. It'll end in tears if you don't. And don't expect me to come and visit you in the hospital if anything happens,' she warned.

That's what mums did - worry. What could possibly go wrong once we had got the hang of it? It wasn't long before Neville went indoors and left us to it with a curt 'Just watch it - and if any cars come up the road, get off the bloody thing. Dad! What time's he gotta be back for?'

'He can have an hour - no more.'

'Okay,' Mouse shouted. 'Thanks dad.'

'It's all right son, but just go steady,' Mr Ratcliffe shouted back.

Mouse agreed that we would share rides, but that he would have the first one down from the top of Vinegar Hill as far as our cul-de-sac towards the bottom of the road. This was fantastic.

I gave him a push just to get him started and then followed him as he rapidly picked up momentum. I managed to keep up for quite a way, then as the speed increased, he flew away from me as fast as you could imagine. The water was spraying up off the road and soaking me, but I didn't seem to mind. This was too much fun. I could hear Mouse's chortles of delight as the distance between us got greater and he urged me to try and keep up. He knew I couldn't - this thing was just so darned fast and as the slope on the hill plunged, I breathlessly gave up trying to keep near.

'Jeronim-oooooooooo' Mouse exclaimed as he disappeared into the distance. It was only my desire to have a go that kept me going down the hill to meet him. There weren't any brakes, so he had to make a sharp turn at the bottom and try to slow himself down by putting his feet down.

Eventually I caught up with him, just past Guy Digby's house and you could tell he was pleased I was so keen to have a go.

'You've got to pull it all the way back to the top - that's the deal,' he said.

'I don't mind.'

'God it's so fast. I could feel the air gushing past my cheeks,' he said excitedly.

'You just went away from me - in a flash.'

'Couldn't you stay with me?'

'Nah. You were just gone. Like lightning. Just gone. Man alive. I don't know how fast you were going. Forty I reckon.'

'Forty? That fast?' Mouse asked.

'Easy. Maybe fifty. I dunno. Fast though. Real fast.'

I dragged the trolley to the top of the hill, desperate to clamber on board. Mouse made sure my feet were in the right place and barked out final instructions.

'Before you get to the bottom, start thinking about stopping. If you don't you'll go straight onto the main road and get smashed up.'

'Okay,' I assured him. 'I will.'

Mouse made one last check and nudged me off the brow and I was on my way. I'd never experienced anything like it. It was like being The Saint, Batman and the fastest man alive, all rolled into one.

As I got towards the bottom, I stuck my right leg out and dug the heel into the tarmac. I thought I was losing control for a minute. So I stuck my left leg out too and managed to stop the darned thing just inches before I would have smacked into the kerb.

I turned to see Mouse hurtling down Vinegar Hill. He was a pretty fast runner but he couldn't keep up either. It wasn't just me. I doubted any of his big brothers could have kept up. This thing was fast - very fast. We both had one last go and then Nev shouted that it was high time we were back in to get ready for our dinners.

We were playing on the trolley a few weeks later when Guy Digby saw us and came out to see what all the fuss was about. Mouse was a bit reluctant to let him have a go, but on account of the Johnny Seven episode, felt he didn't have a lot of choice.

'Okay then, but be careful right. Damage that trolley and I'll damage you,' he warned.

Guy was steering like a girl. As he got halfway down the hill it became clear he was in trouble. He was all over the place and well before the accepted stopping point he veered across the road and onto the pavement. For one horrible moment it looked like he'd smack into the lamppost half way down Vinegar Hill, but even though he missed it, things got worse.

He ploughed straight past the entrance to the grove towards the front garden of No 10 - the fifth and last detached house at the bottom completely dismantling the small picket fence, before cutting two grooves through the lawn and stopping just inches short of the bay window.

'Christ,' Mouse exclaimed.

'He could have killed himself,' I agreed.

'I'll kill him,' Mouse snarled.

But there was worse to come. Guy jumped off crying his eyes out and ran off towards his house, leaving the trolley perched on the edge of a flowerbed right in front of the house.

'Come back,' Mouse screamed. It was too late. Guy had hurtled around the back of his house, never to be seen again.

The two of us had a summit meeting and decided we'd better come clean. Even if there was no one in, which was our number one preference, someone was bound to have seen us. Mouse agreed he would knock the door, while I was to stand at the top of the drive to verify his story if required.

Mouse was snivelling a bit as he knocked the door and

when the shape of a figure drew nearer through the glass, he turned to me and looked skywards.

Barely able to get his words out, he pointed to the trolley and the fence . . . and the lawn . . . and the fence . . . getting more breathless by the second.

'Hey don't worry lad. Are you okay? That's the main thing.'

'Yeah, it wasn't me . . . but err.'

'So long as you're okay. I was going to take that fence down anyway. Saved me a job. Get on with you.'

We couldn't believe it. What a result. THE result of all results.

'And, hey,' the man interjected as Mouse hauled his pride and joy off the lawn.

'Just be a bit more careful eh?'

'Yeah . . .thanks,' Mouse gasped.

It was more than either of us could have asked for. What to do with Guy fucking Digby was another matter.

This was to be the first time I saw Mouse in action and it was a ferocious sight. Two days had passed and Guy had resisted all attempts to lure him out onto the drive, when there was an unexpected development.

His older brother Cameron strode down the drive in a deliberately forceful manner and begged to be let in on what was going on. Cameron was a large boy, well overweight, but quite strong looking and virtually two years older than us. He had a scramble of unruly wiry blond hair that accentuated his round face.

'What's yer problem?' he asked looking at me.

'Well, we just want a word with your brother that's all,' Mouse took over.

'What about?'

'Between him and us,' said Mouse.

'Well what if he doesn't want to talk to you?'

'He should really.' I said rather meekly.

'Why's that then?'

'Cos he nearly wrecked my trolley and then he ran off like a right scaredy cat,' said Mouse.

'You saying he's scared?'

'Yeah,' Mouse said sternly.

'What of? You?' the big boy said dismissively.

'Well yeah if you put it like that,' Mouse countered.

'Why should he be scared of you?'

'You just tell him, I'll get him that's all,' Mouse warned.

'Oh yeah, you and whose army?' Cameron said boldly.

'I won't need an army,' Mouse assured him.

I felt like telling him to ease back on the bravado. Guy's brother was a lot bigger than us and looked capable of snapping my little mate in half.

But he wasn't prepared to give ground and seemed to be almost relishing the prospect of conflict with a much larger foe.

'Do it yourself would you short stuff?'

'Yeah.'

'Go on then,' Cameron goaded him.

'Go on what?'

'Hit me if you fancy throwing your weight around.'

'You'll regret it,' Mouse said, his teeth gritted.

'Talk's cheap. Don't say you're gonna do it. Just do . . .'

SMACK! Mouse pulled a punch from god knows where and damn-near poleaxed Cameron Digby before he'd even managed to finish his goading.

I wondered what response he'd come up with, but Mouse had his head in the bigger lad's midriff and was flailing away with punches.

'Whoa, whoa, hang on. There's no need for that. Stop. Stop,' Digby senior urged his attacker.

'You had enough?'

'Enough.'

'No tricks.'

'No tricks. Enough.'

Cameron wiped the back of his hand across his face and looked horrified to see his suspicion confirmed. He was bleeding. A trickle of blood was coming from his nose and he looked like he was having to hold back tears.

'You fucking maniac. You still after my brother?' he asked trying to rescue some pride from his intervention.

'Nah,' said Mouse generously. 'You can sort him out.'

'I will. It's his fault this happened,' he wheezed.

'No. You've got a big gob. And that's why that happened. You should learn to shut your cakehole,' Mouse sneered.

Cameron turned and sloped off back up towards his front door his humiliation complete.

Mouse rubbed the back of his right hand and smiled at me.

'Wow. Where did you learn to do that?'

'What? Punch?'

'Yeah,' I cooed, unable to hide my admiration.

'When you've got brothers like mine, you learn,' he said with a grin.

'That was some punch, Mouse. Some punch,' I said.

'Ah, that was nothing. He's just a big blubby pudding Cameron Digby.'

'I know but he's older than us . . . and a lot bigger.'

'Yeah, but he's a big soft pudding who shoots his mouth off when he shouldn't.'

'I wish Scotty could have seen that,' I said somewhat proudly. Winston Scott was the tough nut of our class, who had been throwing his weight around in every direction just recently.

'If he carries on he might see it closer than he likes,' Mouse said nonchalantly. And he obviously meant it, too. Wow!

10

1968 - WINNING FORMULA

If Formula One bosses want to know how to put some excitement back into the sport they could do a lot worse than ring the manufacturers of Scalextric. When it comes to great toys, Scalextric takes some beating. And who thought up the idea of the chicane? Whoever it was, it was a master stroke. There was only one drawback with Scalextric and that was it seemed to take an age to set up. Whether that was accentuated because of my eagerness to get started, I'm not sure, but it seemed to take a lifetime. It was always worth it though.

We'd see just how daring those overpaid Formula One guys were if they suddenly had chicanes installed at every track. Murray Walker tossing on endlessly about how all the brave drivers put their lives on the line each time they got behind the wheel of their cars. Fuck off Murray - they get paid absolute fortunes and, these days, you barely ever see a crash. Call me sick, but until one or two drivers start getting barbecued again, the sport's appeal will be lost to millions of us. I can't be alone. In recent years it's just become a procession and the only way the front car generally doesn't go on to win is if it breaks down. Danger? They can barely overtake now and it's all become one massive yawn. Crikey, they'll be having speed cameras and zebra crossings next. Liven it up for fucks sake!

I don't give a toss about how good Michael Schumacher is, what brake horsepower his Ferrari generates or any of the technical crap they like to throw at you. If all he's going to do is get into pole position and then lead for 72 laps, I just can't see the point in it. I want him surrounded by high-octane fuel and in grave danger of being engulfed in a savage inferno. It's nothing to do with him being German. I just want him to really earn his dosh and put his life on the line now and again.

The Grand National lost a certain something when the health and safety people got their grubby mitts on it. I KNOW it was sometimes a bit much for the horses, but hey, this is entertainment. It was a lot more of a spectacle when horses were crash landing all over the place causing total chaos.

Show jumping is exactly the same. Back in the late 60s and 70s it was massive. Show jumping was on TV all the time and the likes of David Broome and Harvey Smith were household names. But I'll tell you where it all went tits up for show jumping - the cruelty police stopped them having to jump that huge wall and that was it - curtains. The wall was ace. The horses would go around and if they had a clear round, they would put another row of 'bricks' on the wall and see if they could jump that. It got to the stage where you could almost see the horse saying 'Are you serious?' before sending them scattering everywhere. It was great.

And so because it's basically a sport for moneyed twits with half-a-brain cell, the powers that be decided that we didn't want to see horses and riders seriously injured attempting the wall and that, perhaps as a replacement, they would throw in a bit of dressage. And the great British public told them exactly where to stick that and show jumping is hardly ever on the telly now. Give the people what they want just like Scalextric did and you won't go far wrong.

Formula One is no different. These guys get paid squillions of pounds for a dream job so I don't think it's too much to ask to see some carnage now and again. Call me extreme, but I expect a whole lot more than that. I want an instant explosion, stewards desperately trying to get the flames out while the driver can feel his eyeballs melting.

Seriously, if they are going to get mind-blowing amounts of money to spend their lives on yachts shagging the world's elite crumpet then I want them to at least be badly scarred. The occasional missing limb is passable, but I definitely want some evidence that they put their bollocks on the line.

Things have just got far too safe. The fuel doesn't instantly ignite anymore, which was definitely a backward step to my mind. The construction of the fuselage is now all geared to ensuring maximum protection against impact. It's that nanny state thing. For me, they could even consider scattering some tin tacks on the track as well just to ensure some serious destruction.

Now see, if they had taken a leaf out of the Scalextric book, we would still be having some serious fun. The chicane must have been something they just kind of made up. Brilliant! Absolutely fucking brilliant. Let me tell you, I was swinging from the rafters with delight when I realised I was actually unwrapping a Scalextric. When I found it had the chicane as well, I must have darned near pissed my pants. How cool is that?

All these years later, a present would struggle to make the long-lasting impression of a Scalextric. It was quite an expensive toy, so not everyone could have one, which I suppose made it all the more special. These things weren't ten a penny. But boy, oh boy, were they fun. My dad and me were up playing Scalextric at around seven that morning and raw anticipation and impatience threatened to burst me apart. There was transformers to get sorted out, the wire-brushes on the front of the cars which made contact with the track and that was before you were ready to start.

Dad got it up and running and just as we thought it was ready, one of the cars would suddenly stop. Several books, magazines, fag packets in strategic places later and we'd have a race on. So, if anyone tells you it was flawless, it wasn't. But overall, I'd have to say that Scalextric would probably come in tops with a lot of lads on what was their all-time, best ever, most exciting gift.

But faster than any Scalextric car was the pace of technological change. These were heady times indeed. Guy Digby's family are THE talk of the immediate vicinity because they have boldly gone where no resident within a square mile has gone. Yep, they've got a colour telly and that is a really big deal. The fact that most of the programmes are still in black and white doesn't seem to matter. This is big news. Mouse says his dad isn't bothered about getting one and my dad says we will when they are not so expensive. Imagine being able to watch Star Soccer or Match of the Day in colour? How good would that be? Ah well, I'm sure we will get one some day.

Guy is really into Captain Scarlet which, when you've got a colour telly is understandable. Mouse and me like it, but it isn't quite the same in black and white really. Not when all the characters names are like Captain Green, Captain Blue and the man himself. Thank god for Captain Black that's all I've got to say.

It is an ace programme though. Mouse sometimes hides behind the back fence or the shed and goes 'This is the voice of the Mysterons - we know you can hear us Earthmen!'

He's nutty is Mouse. If we're playing out and we are okay about something - whatever - we'll often say 'S.I.G' like they do in the programme. 'Spectrum is Green' it stands for and it's become our sort of codeword, even though every kid knows what it means which defeats the object a bit.

Our latest step into the technological age is to have the phone put in at home. It's quite a big job really. A couple of men came around and were stapling wires all over the house for most of the day. Two-tone green we've got which mom thinks is a bit posher than some of the others. Brown is common she said. We're on a party line, so mum's told me to be very careful and that if I pick the phone up and I can hear someone else talking then I should put it down. Wouldn't it be great if you heard someone say something they shouldn't be saying? Just say you heard something that was really supposed to be a secret.

So, our phone was green and Spectrum was green - just not on our telly they weren't. They were one shade lighter than black.

11

1969 - TWO LITTLE BOYS

Big school. Big changes. Big satchel. I've had a brand new brown leather satchel for Christmas. I had to make do with one my Auntie Eileen had given me for the first few months. Now I've got my very own. Despite what my mum and dad say, I can't wait to get it broken in a bit and get some stickers on it. My satchel sticks out like a sore thumb. I stick out like a sore thumb. My satchel is like me - it's got first year written all over it. I can't wait until it takes on that battered, soft look like some of the older boys' satchels.

Four months in and I'm getting used to the massive switch in my daily life. I miss Mouse and find increasingly that I'm leading a sort of split existence. Although Wellington Grammar is only three miles away, not too many of the kids from our village go there. It's not a snobby place at all but by now I was getting used to being tagged a 'grammar grub' even by lads and girls I'd knocked around with for years. It's a strange one when you come from an area that outsiders consider to be a bit of a dump.

The main source of their humour was that Linshaw had an extremely large immigrant population. Thousands of West Indians, Pakistanis and Indians had sought work there at some of the major engineering shop floors. And so while my new school mates playfully looked down on the place they referred to as 'Little India,' the friends I headed back to after the 4pm bell all took the micky out of my recently elevated status. And so, to my Linshaw mates I'd gone all Sandhurst while my new grammar school pals viewed me more Parkhurst.

Big school brought with it new attitudes, new views on things. Now, more than ever, you would be judged by a fresh and less forgiving audience. Big lads . . . some very big lads, walking around with LPs under their arms beyond my first year status. Black Sabbath, Led Zeppelin, Deep Purple, Hawkwind, Pink Floyd and the like were a diet far too rich for my young ears. The only way you could get away with any such deception was if you had an older brother and could argue that you'd been virtually weaned on the stuff. Mouse would have got away with it, but he wasn't here. There was always an almighty racket coming from one of his brother's bedrooms at his house, so the names of the big heavy metal bands were something I was familiar with. But I didn't like them very much so there was never a chance of me being seen carrying anything that would have appealed to the older lads at school.

It seemed like every corner you turned there were new things. Some were great, but a lot were a bit intimidating at first. Bunsen burners, gas taps, science as a lesson, form teachers, detention, a music room, and all stuff like that. Just stuff that I'd never seen before and though it would quickly become familiar, I just remember it being a lot to take in. I swear to God, the first few months at school from September to now have just flown by. There's just so much to take in that they even give you a small diary to put all your things in. Fucking hell, what is happening? Everything was new. New classrooms, new subjects, new kids, new masters, new expectations. Suddenly your world is turned upside down because almost everything that you could count on being constant had changed. Well almost - Rolf spends six weeks at number one and Two Little Boys becomes the biggest selling single of the year. Good old Rolf . . . there's one thing you can rely on.

One of the small things I've had for school this Christmas

is absolutely fascinating - a plastic rubber. How good are they? They must rank as one of the really seriously stupendous innovations of the 20th century. Up to this point every school kid had to put up with rubbers that only really managed to erase anything because they completely wore away the paper. That slightly defeats the point you'd think. You might as well have just used the edge of a fucking matchbox. All over Britain, kids' exercise books - their best ones - are ruined by little telltale scuff marks where the old-fashioned rubber has been put to work.

They were next to useless, especially those hard ones you'd get on the end of cheap pencils - the sort that got stuck in your ear or you could swallow so easily. But now someone has invented the plastic eraser and it has to be said, they are mind-numbingly superb. Call me sad, but they are *that* different. You can keep your pack of 64 different coloured felt pens or the biro which has 50 colours but is so fucking thick you can't grip the bastard thing - it's plastic rubbers for me. They just take the mistake away and leave the paper as it was. God's teeth! Give the man a knighthood.

I missed having Mouse around in the daytime. Not least because he was such a little tough nut that being his best mate afforded me a luxury and status in Linshaw that counted for nothing here. Luckily, the fact I'd passed for grammar school was no big issue with him. The fact that he wasn't considered bright was a puzzle to me. Mouse had a certain street awareness and an eye for an opportunity that was way beyond many of the kids I now brushed shoulders with. Some may well have been academically astute, but they were as dozy as fuck in so many other respects.

Mouse was cool. We'd always team up together over the fields when we were playing war with all the lads. There were usually at least a dozen of us ready to fight it out with bits of sticks doubling up as guns. The hazel sticks were the best if you could find them - really straight, like walking sticks.

Mouse and me would always make sure we were on the same side and we'd make a point of covering each other. He was mad on John Wayne. We'd hide together most of the time. I doubt anyone knew those banks as well as us two.

'Be my eyes,' he barked at me.

'What?'

'Be my eyes! Cover me, you idiot.'

I'd never heard such a thing and must have looked bemused.

'It's what that guy said in that film the other night on telly. 'Be my eyes.' It sort of means, watch my back while I run over there and see if they're hiding in those bushes.'

'Oh, right.'

'Ready.'

'Yeah!'

Mouse hauled himself over the grass bank and stormed towards the gorse bushes on the far side making rat-a-tat-tat noises.

He knew all the lingo did Mouse. They weren't in the bushes, so he swung his arm over his shoulder, urging me to follow him.

'Thanks pal.'

'No problem. Where now?'

'I reckon Jonno and Mark are down by the pool. C'mon.'

Mark and Jonno were hiding behind some corrugated metal sheeting just where he'd said. We took them completely by surprise and got them to surrender. They said they'd shot us first, but they didn't. I didn't mind getting shot sometimes because you could dive all over the place and roll around groaning. Not this time though - we'd got them both good and proper. Those summer nights playing out until it was dark seemed an age away now.

Mouse was always one step ahead of the game and, not that I needed the point ramming home to me, that became perfectly clear with his announcement just a few weeks before

Christmas.

'Hey, Sant, I've got a great idea to make some cash. You in?'

'Depends.'

'Trust me. You in or what?'

'Well what do we have to do?'

'Just you and me, right?'

'Okay.'

'I don't want Guy Digby or any of those other fuckers getting in on it right?'

'Okay.' I wasn't really sure what I might be getting myself into, but I agreed.

'I've seen this on Blue Peter . . .' Mouse cooed enthusiastically.

'I reckon it's a great way to make some cash.'

'I'm all ears.'

'Well, what it is, is this. You make some Christmas logs and flog them. I reckon we could do them for next to nowt and make some real money.'

'Christmas logs?'

'Yeah. What you do is get some nice logs and decorate them with holly and stuff, a candle and a bit of glitter and Bob's your uncle. Easy. Thing is we need somewhere to make them. Reckon your dad would let us use your garage? Ours is full of shit.'

'Where we going to get the stuff from? And who's gonna buy them anyway?'

'Neighbours. Take them round the streets. Knock some doors.'

I needed to be convinced but agreed to give it a go. There was a catch. Mouse needed me to stump up the cash for the things we needed with the proviso that I'd get it all back straight away once we went into profit.

Mouse had it all worked out. We needed a bag of logs that we could get and bring back on his trolley. We would need a box of candles, a tube of glitter, some plaster of Paris and we'd have to go and cut some holly down from over the second banks. It sounded okay.

That Saturday morning we got the logs, with decent bark on them; Mouse brought some big staples from his dad's shed and in the afternoon we went to get the other bits. We came back from over the banks with a supermarket box full of holly and set about our money-making venture. Mouse split the logs lengthways and tacked on sprigs of holly with nice berries on and left a gap in the middle for the candle. I mixed the plaster of Paris and the minute it had stiffened sufficiently, poured a dollop in the middle so it looked like snow and gently placed the candle in. A few little dollops of the beautiful white mix to cover any visible staples and we were almost done. Once we had a dozen made, Mouse set about putting dabs of modelling glue on the holly and sprinkling them with glitter. We made about a dozen and agreed to meet later and set about seeing if we could sell them. I was a little worried that the five bob we'd spent on materials might take some getting back.

There was no need to worry - within an hour we'd got rid of the lot and received orders for at least six more and we hadn't even ventured off the estate. People seemed more than happy to pay five bob each and we sold the first twelve in no time at all. That was three quid. Three fucking quid. I took the cash out to cover the initial investment and we split the rest.

'Told you . . .' Mouse yelled enthusiastically.

'If we can knock these out a bit sharpish we can make a fortune,' I agreed.

'Yeah . . . easy peasy.'

We went to the chippie and had pie and chips EACH and toasted our new enterprise with a can of coke between us. We still had well over a pound each and we hadn't even started.

In the region of 50 logs later, the days ran out more quickly than our enthusiasm. We'd made over a tenner each and realised the only real mistake we had made was not starting making the darned things in October!

'Who says money doesn't grow on trees?' Mouse said triumphantly.

'You're a fucking genius mate. Ten quid! We're millionaires,' I said giving Mouse a bigger pat on the back than was necessary, prompting him to spray a mouthful of coke all over the place.

12

1970 - BANDY LEGS

It was Christmas morning, 1970, when I suddenly began to walk like a cowboy. Seemingly instantly the urge to chew gum took on addictive proportions and I was able to spit further than ever before. Had my balls dropped? How else could anyone explain why my legs had gone bandy overnight and I could seemingly rake phlegm from the pit of my stomach? Why else would I be on two packs of Beech Nut a day? There was a simple explanation. I was now the proud owner of a pair of Gola football boots with screw-in studs.

Screw-in-studs - plastic moulded puberty. I swear to God I could feel hairs sprouting out of my legs the very second I tried those lovely new boots on. If the distinctive click-clacking of those studs on the concrete path didn't do it then nothing would. It would have been easier to just go straight over the grass, but what the fuck point was there in doing that? You wouldn't hear anything that way. No, when you owned a pair of screw-ins - the boots the pros wore - you find the nearest available strip of concrete or slabs and do a proper footballer's walk right over it.

You don't have to perfect a proper footballer's walk - it just comes with the boots. It's a peculiar thing. Suddenly, without any real explanation, your legs bow a little in the middle and you get the desire to slap liniment on them just like you had seen the top footballers do. Embrocation it was called. Elliman's rub, I think - white stuff with a smell that could knock out a horse. I wanted to look like a footballer, walk like a footballer, spit like a footballer and smell like a footballer. It doesn't get much better than the sound of those studs.

Who knows? In no time at all I might even be heading a proper case-ball without being rendered unconscious. School team here I come! I told myself that Pele must have worn something similar in this summer's World Cup. Well, no actually, he wore Puma. There was a Pele white boot that had just come out. I'd never seen the great man wearing them either to be honest. Alan Ball wore them, but I thought they looked a bit odd.

My previous pair had been mouldeds. They were Adidas with bright blue soles and Bobby Charlton's signature on the side. They weren't grown up boots. It's not that Bobby Charlton isn't grown up, but he just didn't wear the moulded ones himself. He just put his signature on them - but he probably wouldn't be seen dead in them. That's no slight on Bobby - even though he played for Manchester United and had a ridiculous comb-over hairstyle everyone took the piss out of.

He had his name on boots because he had a thunderbolt of a shot. Dad said that when he hit that goal from 30 yards to beat Mexico it had stopped the traffic in Mexico City. That was how hard Bobby Charlton could hit a fucking football. He didn't really look like he had it in him, but the minute he pulled back that right foot, boy you just knew what was coming. THWACK! It was like a rocket when he thumped one. He was a bit like Henry Cooper, was Bobby Charlton. Henry didn't really look like that tough a bloke at all - he looked more like your dad, really. But, fuck me, had he got a wallop on him. Enery's Hammer they called it and it had put Cassius Clay on his backside.

Mouldeds, you see, just weren't the same. With screw-ins, you had a special aluminium spanner to take the studs out. You could put metal ones in. They made you a better player - it's just one of those facts you either know or you don't. My mum said it didn't make any difference. What did she know about football boots? She should stick to mum things like pastry and washing up.

I felt just like one of the England players you saw in Shoot magazine or on the telly. I'd been collecting the Esso World Cup coins from the garage. They were just fantastic. I only needed Paul Reaney and Francis Lee to complete my set.

Why don't petrol stations do all that kind of thing these days? Collecting that stuff was just the best. One little silver coin in a sealed packet - free with every four gallons of petrol. My dad hadn't even got a car! Fortunately a couple of his mates at work had cars and no kids - not unconnected, dad often pointed out. So they'd pass them on to my old man.

Any garage that could do that now would make a fucking fortune. But I suppose things have changed. Players have image rights and would want a zillion pounds to appear on a coin. I'll bet Bobby Charlton and Francis Lee and all that lot probably only got a free car or something. Only!!! That's enough isn't it, to be sought after and treasured by a nation's children?

We were a generation of collectors. Football stickers, American Civil War cards (what the fuck were they about?) and - to my shame - birds' eggs. I've still got The Observer's Book of Bird's Eggs - how marvellously politically incorrect is that? Time was I could tell you what colour a particular bird's egg was, how many they laid and, in some instances the fucking thing's Latin name. How have I remembered that a magpie's Latin name is pica pica? I can't remember what I had for lunch, yet I can recall so much out of that fantastic little book.

Collectors? We took some beating. And those coins were the bollocks. Somehow the mounting card wasn't quite right - the coins just never seemed to quite fit. But they were magnificent to a young boy. It's like the show jumping - petrol stations have never been quite the same since really. They were always giving away things. Drinking glasses? Fucking hell, there was every permutation of glass up for grabs - ones that wobbled but wouldn't fall over, plastic ones which sat in a separate coloured holder type-of-thing, big ones, slim ones, tall ones. You name a type of drinking vessel; you could get it free from a garage.

We were a fanatical nation of collectors. I badgered the arse off my gran and mum to only drink PG Tips because they gave away a free card in every carton of their tea. And over a period of years I collected stacks of their cards and put them into my special album, that (I think) you bought for sixpence, or whatever. How brilliant a concept is that? Buy our tea above all others because we'll give you a card that we can make thousands of for a few pence and then we'll charge you for the album to stick them in. Superb. And a grateful nation followed . . . they brought in series after series and we stuck with it. I can remember Wildlife in Danger, Flags and Emblems of the World, Wild Flowers, Freshwater Fishes, British Trees and Butterflies for starters. But they were great to collect. There was a kind of excitement waiting for your gran or mum to open the new box. It was like the lottery to us! It was that serious. Then you suffered the searing disappointment, if it was one you already had, and you'd have to put it in with your swaps.

You'd get all sorts of things in your breakfast cereals back then too. Glow in the dark figures, cartoon things, anything. I'm just guessing the safety police came in and stopped all that because some stupid fuckwit child from Stockton-on-Tees swallowed one and died. Choke you little bastard! You've ruined it for everyone.

Shoot magazine launched on the back of giving away free League Ladders - cardboard press-out things of the different teams which slotted in to a league table. They were brilliant. Absolutely brilliant. You could make your own tables, if you weren't happy with the way the actual ones were working out.

You could put Leeds and Chelsea down at the bottom if you wanted. But it wasn't just the kids either. Adults were enticed to buy things on the promise of triple Green Shield Stamps or Co-op stamps and there were Embassy and No 6 cigarette coupons that you could cash in for prizes. My mum had the Embassy one and you know there was actually a Rolls Royce you could collect for but it was God-knows how many coupons. A long time after you'd died of lung cancer or coronary heart disease, that's for sure.

13

1971 - TALE OF THE TAPE

Jonathan King, under various guises, had spent 37 weeks in the charts this year. How did he ever get time to even think about young boys?

I wanted to be Jonathan King this Christmas - I mean in the sense that I wanted to be a record producer. I'd had a Binatone tape recorder for Christmas and pretty soon, I reckoned, I'd be making albums of my own, compiled courtesy of the Sunday Top 40 chart show. These were pre-compilation album days. You made your own, which was great because you could have just what the hell you wanted on it, for the first time ever. Dad warned me to be careful about taping things and to mind who I told. He said you needed a licence to do it officially and that if you got caught you could be in trouble. I liked that - it made it sound like I was doing something illegal, which was about as close as I got to being troublesome - or so I thought.

One of the first things I was going to do was tape my new LP - Electric Warrior by T Rex. I fucking loved T Rex. Jeepster, Get It On . . . fantastic. My dad struggled to see the appeal of a five foot midget who wore make-up and women's shoes, but I wasn't alone in thinking T Rex were just the best.

I-pods? Christ, I'd only just about got eyebrows in 1971. The main problem was going to be finding somewhere totally quiet to ensure recording any given track wasn't suddenly interrupted by the sound of mum Hoovering around the place. You see, the big stumbling block with this revolutionary, but still fledgling technological breakthrough, was that there were still one or two teething problems. The main one being that you had to place the microphone in front of the radio or record player speaker to tape it. The only direct input was actually pleading with your mum and dad to keep well clear of the bedroom that had now become your own personal recording studio. Parents just don't get it though, do they? My dad seemed to think it was okay as long as he knocked first. I lost count of the songs I recorded which were peppered with my dad knocking quietly, followed by a louder one because he thinks I can't hear him over the 'racket' his son is so pre-occupied with. Then there's me going 'Shhh . . .'

'Never mind shush.'

'Ahh daaad, you've ruined it.

'Ruined it? I'll give you ruined it. It wouldn't take much to ruin that rubbish.'

The fact that he'd just stumbled in on Dave Edmunds' I Hear You Knocking, just kind of made it suitably fitting.

'Anyway, tea's ready so go and get your hands washed.'

'Ah daad, I was just goin' to . . .'

'Never mind, *just going* to do this and *just going* to do that . . . your tea's ready. Get yourself down stairs and step on it. What's a matter with kids today . . . '

Kids today? Can you believe your parents saying that? My generation might not have been deprived but this was pre-Now That's What I Call Music 86. The only compilation albums were ones not sung by the proper artists called Top of the Pops and Hot Hits. They had fuck all going for them except a cracking looking bird in a bikini or hot pants on the front cover.

And you know the ironic thing about those Winfield specials 99p Top of the Pops LPs? Some of them are worth an absolute fortune now. It's true - rare ones have artists singing on them who went on to become big time like Elton John. So you see, who knows what we chucked away?

But if you went for the home-made compilation route then invariably you had the sound of the bog flushing, your dad saying 'sorry' or the distinctive wailing of an ice-cream van passing by. And they seem to think we had it easy!

It's Christmas 1971, and that Binatone cassette recorder would go down as one of the top five best things I ever had. At last, I was entering the realms of album production. I could have what I wanted and where I wanted it. Today my bedroom - tomorrow Abbey Road. Sundays were best when the chart show was on. The whole Top 40. Fucking marvellous. In those days, it really didn't get a lot better than that. The modern generation just wouldn't get it would they? It sounds ancient to them. They'd be wondering if this was the part where the show is interrupted by the sound of Noah trying to coax another couple of animals on board.

Well, that's the way it was. And the odd thing about it was that when you had made a particularly fine compilation and played the arse out of it, it became really weird when you heard one of the songs in a different environment. You would automatically assume what would follow it, and when it didn't, it completely flummoxed you.

So the I-pod can just fuck off really. What if you can get 10,000 songs on a machine the size of a credit card? Someone had to be the pioneers and we were the chosen few. Scratching records? Our generation invented scratching records.

All this rap bollocks and bands making albums in their bedrooms - well, just get lost. We were doing it years ago. I can't begin to think how many records I scratched long before Fatboy Fucking Slim came on the scene.

We had to master cutting off recording the very second the nuisance DJ started chipping in again - then click play and record as soon as you thought he's shut the fuck up and was going to let the following record play. Not as easy as it sounds.

'And it's new in this week . . . yes . . . it's that man from somewhere other than Mother Earth . . . you've got it . . . it's

David Bowie . . . it's Space Oddity . . .'

CLICK! Got it, play and record down together (how fucking annoying was it when one sprang back up?) Yeah!!

'Lotta soul . . .' says Bowie.

Suddenly. No. Don't do this. Please. She isn't? She fucking well is.

'Johhhhhn! John! Come on love, gran's got to go now. Come and say goodbye.'

'Oh fuck gran. Silly old sod. Fuck, fuck, fuck, fuck, fuck.' I said to myself.

I was kind of hoping the machine hadn't picked up mum's interruption, but that would have been a ridiculous wish really if you think about it. Why would you want to be the proud owner of a tape deck that didn't pick up things?

So I made my way downstairs to see gran off, give her a kiss and thank her for the ten-shilling postal order she'd brought me. She'd also got me a Dymo label printer, which I was planning to use for labelling my tapes - come the glorious day when I actually completed one.

I'd bought gran a decimal currency calculator on a key ring. The country had gone metric back in February and she had struggled to get her head around it. You couldn't have escaped the fuss about it all. Dad said to wipe the slate clean and just forget the old stuff, which considering I'd just spent five or six of my most formative years (half my life to be precise) learning, was a touch disconcerting.

'Just completely forget it - that's the only way,' dad would say.

'There's no use saying something is 10p so that's two shillings. It's pointless. Just forget you ever heard that stuff and start afresh.

Dad blamed Ted Heath; mum blamed the French while gran blamed the Japanese for some odd reason. Gran blamed the Japanese for myximatosis, smallpox and decimalisation. She'd got it in for them ever since Uncle Eric was tortured during the war.

Anyway, the Dymo came in handy. I made a label saying 'John's - Strictly Private' and stuck it on my tape recorder. Pity dad didn't think it applied to him and the whole episode ends with me getting one of the biggest triple-pronged bollockings of my life.

When I came in, I was 15 minutes later than arranged and the fact that dad was prepared to virtually dismiss that, led me to the conclusion that there was real bother coming my way. Apparently the continuous clack-clacking of the lolly stick in the spokes of the back wheel of my bike had been driving the entire neighbourhood up the wall. Quite how he knew that I wasn't sure, but it wasn't a point worth pursuing. What he meant was, it had driven him to distraction all afternoon.

'Yeah, but it wasn't just me, dad.'

'Oh I know. You've all bloody well got them. Well that's got to stop. For one thing, it'll ruin your wheel and I don't suppose you're planning on buying a new one when all the spokes fall out are you? And two, the noise is unbearable.'

'Well, the thing is . . .'

Dad intervened. 'The thing is, nothing. Take the stick out of your wheels or I'll take it out. But anyway, there's something else that concerns me far more right now.'

'Something else?'

'Yes, far worse.'

Worse?

'Yes. Much worse. I can't believe a son of mine would come out with such stuff. I'm actually quite shocked if the truth be known.'

'What?'

'I'll give you what. Have you heard what's on here?' Dad pulls the tape recorder from the side of his chair. I didn't expect him to like Jeepster, Coz I Luv You or Tokoloshe Man, but this was a bit rich.

'If I EVER hear anything of this sort again, you will be for the high jump. You'll jump so high, your feet won't touch the ground.'

It wasn't a good time to say that your feet generally didn't touch the ground when you were jumping. It kind of defeated the object, but I'd leave that for now.

'I don't get it, what's the problem.'

Dad presses play and the nightmare unfolded.

'Lotta soul . . .' says Bowie.

'Johhhhn! John! Come on love, gran's got to go now. Come and say goodbye.'

'Oh fuck gran. Silly old sod. Fuck, fuck, fuck, fuck, fuck.'

Dad was furious, so I sloped out of the door and made my way towards the end of the road and turned left - any direction would have done. Things were going to take a turn for the worse - there was Guy Fucking Digby hurtling down the road on his new bike - a bright yellow Raleigh Chopper. They were like no other bike you had ever seen and I admit to going a slight shade of green. I'd got a bike, there was no problem there - and I couldn't complain about my lot. I knew Chopper bikes were expensive - over thirty quid. It wasn't just that Guy Fucking Digby seemed to get everything he wanted. He was a total spaz - that was the problem. I pretended I hadn't seen him and made my way towards the alley.

Just between the end of our road and the Farmer's Arms pub was a small field that had been empty for as long as we had lived there. It had a hawthorn hedge on three sides, with gated entrance on the far side, furthest away from the road. Mouse and me would often hang around there doing nothing much, or climbing the oak tree which, if we got past the tricky bit, would give us a panoramic view over Orchard Grove.

I made my way under the canopy of the large oak with a view to maybe walking over to the first banks for a while. Dad would have cooled down in a bit. It was quite mild for the time of year, though there was a crisp wind blowing across the path as I made my way towards the gentle slope, which took you to the top of the first mound. As I came to the end of the path, a figure with a small brown and white mongrel-type dog on a lead, approached me. It was a girl of about my age, but one I hadn't seen in these parts before. She was slim, with long, dark hair that fell in slight waves onto the shoulders of her Afghan coat. She had black loon pants on and those Jesus-creeper type boots, which gave her a kind of hippyish look. She had a slightly turned-up nose but was very pretty and when she smiled at me as I made my way to pass, I couldn't resist trying to make conversation.

'Hi.' I sensed I'd have to move quickly or she'd be gone before I'd worked out how to find out more about her.

'Hi,' she smiled. She had Jagger-esque lips and striking teeth with a slight gap in the middle. She was lovely but in an almost unconventional way.

'Nice dog! He looks a bit wet.'

'Yeah, the grass is soaking.' she replied. God, now she thinks I'm stupid.

'Not from round here are you?'

'No. I'm just visiting my grandpa. He lives over there,' she said pointing to a small cottage a couple of hundred yards away up towards the stile which crossed the railway line at the side of Vicarage Road.

'Just here for Christmas eh?'

'Well kind of. Couple of days I think.'

'Oh right.'

'Just thought I'd get out from under everyone's feet and take the dog for a walk. You?'

'Same, I just got in a bit of bother with my dad. It's a long story. Decided to get out of the way.'

'It's quite neat around here isn't it?' the girl continued.

'Neat? Not heard it called that before but yeah, it's okay. Nothing special but . . .'

'It's great having all this stuff. You know trees and things like that and being able to walk the dog without getting knocked over. I like it!'

'Where are you from?'

'London. Well just outside really. But down that way and it's just a lot busier than around here. Just don't really know where I'm going round these parts - that's all. Who cares eh?'

It was too good an opportunity to miss. Whether she had intended it that way, I wasn't sure, but I'd been presented with the perfect opportunity to ask her if she wanted me to show her a bit further afield without making myself look stupid.

'Hey that would be great. By the way, my name's Suzie.'

'Sant. Well, John . . oh everyone calls me Sant. It's a long story.'

'Another one? You seem to specialise in long stories. Come on then Sant, tell me all about them.'

Suzie had the loveliest smile I'd ever seen. She laughed out loud when I told her the tape recorder mishap and then I explained how I'd got my nickname. She was quite tall - almost level with me and so I was surprised to find that there were only a couple of months between us. I'd assumed she was a bit older than that.

'That's cool. Bumping into my very own Mr Christmas on Boxing Day. That's neat.'

Everything seemed to be either *neat* or *cool* to Suzie. You could immediately tell she was different from girls around here. She seemed a bit more worldly-wise and grown up. Maybe it was because she was from London and a bit posh. Her dad was an airline pilot with British Airways. Her mum didn't work and so because he had some leave they had come up to see her grandad who lived alone in the cottage just across the way.

We walked up as far as Bluebell Wood and around the top of the third banks before Suzie said she really ought to be getting back. As we made our way, we swapped information on what we liked, favourite groups, telly shows and all sorts of important information. I told her I'd got Electric Warrior, but sensed that didn't particularly impress her. Suzie said her favourites were Cat Stevens and Barclay James Harvest. I'd heard of Cat Stevens but I had to admit I couldn't name a single record the other chap had made. I take it Barclay James Harvest was a man and not a group? Barclay Harvest? Yeah, perhaps James was just his middle name.

We still managed to chat for a good 10 minutes just down from the front gate of the cottage and I discovered that she was going back the following morning.

'That's a shame. I could have shown you some more stuff,' I said chivalrously.

'Well, I'm coming up in the summer for a few weeks I guess, so maybe then.'

'That'd be good,' I said, filling her in on exactly where I lived should she return.

'It should be a bit warmer anyway,' she said with a smile.

'Should be.'

'See you then,' she said, giving me a little wave and a huge grin.

'Hope things are okay with your dad when you get in!' And she was gone. She was really lovely. I might catch her in the summer but it was a bit of a long shot. What the hell? I decided to go back in and see if things had calmed down at all.

14

1972 - SHRINK-TO-FIT

'Now I've seen bloody everything . . .' Dad clearly couldn't hide his bewilderment at seeing me in the bath - in my new Levis.

'What in God's name do you think you're playing at now?'

'What do you mean?

I realised it was a rather futile question which had little, make that no, chance of pacifying him.

By my dad's reckoning the only things capable of making anyone sit in a bath full of water in his trousers was either mental illness or being absolutely pissed out of your brains. Given that I was 14, the latter wasn't an option, so I juggled with the prospect of slapping in an insanity plea.

'Go on. I'm all ears. What do you think you are playing at?'

'I'm just shrinking my jeans dad.'

'If they're too big, why don't you just take them back?

'They're not too big.'

'Go on . . . explain. I can't wait for this.'

'Because I want to make them fit perfectly and so you have to shrink them while you've got them on.'

'My giddy aunt.'

My giddy aunt was a regular daddism for his incredulity. I'd never met any of his aunts and certainly not any spinning around or collapsing in unconventional fashion.

'Is this a new phenomenon then?' he said stepping up his interrogation.

'No, everyone does it.'

'Well, I don't do it.' I resisted the temptation to say 'exactly.'

'Well, it's not the same thing really,' I countered.

'Well exactly what is it then? Do tell me.'

'They're Levis. They're made that way. You buy them to . . . well, fit . . . and then you shrink them to make them fit sort of perfect like.'

This wasn't the most appropriate moment to tell him I intended splashing bleach on them as well. He really would have gone absolutely off his tits if that minor piece of information had been lobbed in his direction. The very term Levis was lost on my old man. The only Strauss in his world was a musician not a maker of jeans. Chords, yes. Denims, no.

'Levis eh?'

'Yeah. Everyone's got them.'

'I haven't.'

'Well . . .'

'So you're going out in them like that are you?'

'Course not.'

'Well it wouldn't surprise me. In fact, to be perfectly honest, nothing you do these days really surprises me.' Now, that wasn't a surprise.

'Well I'll tell you what we'll do eh? You step out of there in your own good time and I'll get your mum to run the iron over them while you've got them on eh?'

He made his way out of the bathroom, mumbling to himself as he went. This was totally beyond him.

'Oh yeah, some girl called for you earlier on as well.'

'Girl?'

'Yeah, you know the things I'm talking about. She said she'd see you around.'

'Who was it?'

'Buggered if I know. I haven't seen her before. Long hair. Well spoken. Said she was up at her grandad's or something.'

'That'd be Suzie,' I said matter-of-factly.

'Is that Suzie Strauss - Levi's sister?' dad said with that taunting lilt in his voice.

'Well, whoever she was, she seemed quite normal which is a start. Girlfriend eh?'

'Course not - she's just a mate,' I said, which was slightly exaggerating things. I was dead chuffed she'd bothered to call though. I got myself out of my wet jeans and decided to just hang around by the cottage and see if she was about.

'That's made you move a bit sharpish hasn't it?' dad said with a grin.

'Never seen you move so fast.'

'Get lost . . .'

◇◇◇◇◇◇

I didn't have to look far. Suzie was helping an elderly man, I assumed he was her grandad, at the bottom of his orchard. She called out from behind the small redbrick wall the second she saw me.

'Santa . . . hiya!'

'Oh hi there. I heard you were back.'

'Yeah. Cool eh?'

'What ya doin?'

'I'm just helping grandpa plant a couple of these young apple trees. You around for a while?'

'Sure.'

'I won't be long,' she said, treading down some earth at the base of a young tree she'd planted right in the very far corner of the orchard.

'Here, have one of these,' she said tossing me a small apple from a battered basket down by her side.

'Ta.'

'Good catch.'

The grey-haired man told her to get on her way and we arranged to go for a walk and catch up on things. She looked

82

lovely. It was a baking hot afternoon, early in July. Suzie had a red tank-top vest on and a pair of faded, Falmers bell-bottom jeans. Her hair was a little shorter than I remembered. We made our way over the far side of the first banks and as we sat by the pool we watched the newts swimming around near the edge.

'Wow, I can't believe that. Aren't they great?'

'Don't you have newts in London?' I asked

'I don't know. Never really thought about it. I've never seen any anyway. They're cute.'

I told her about the Levis episode with dad.

'You're a nutter, Sant. You really are.'

'Oh, they just don't understand do they?'

'Nah, not to worry eh? I'm here now. I hope you're going to show me lots of stuff while I'm here. You've got three weeks of me.'

Three weeks. Fucking hell. I was looking forward to it, more than she probably knew. Mouse had got himself a job on a local farm that had taken him out of the equation quite a bit. He was earning a fortune - fifteen quid a week - and by the time he got home at night it was late and he was knackered most of the time. Mouse was working six days a week - Sunday was the only time I managed to catch up with him. Breadsall Farm was only a couple of miles away and he set off every morning at some unholy hour with his sandwiches under his arm in a Tupperware box. Foz and some of the other lads spent a lot of their days fishing, but it wasn't really my thing. I'd have plenty of time to spend with Suzie if that's what she wanted.

She agreed, Levis were great. Suzie said if you collected 10 of the orange or red tags off the back, they would send you another pair - completely free. I didn't know how she knew that but she was from London, so I took it as gospel. She was always saying people there had much more idea about clothes and stuff. But how long would it take to collect that many tags? And by the time you had, perhaps Levis would be out of fashion. It wasn't something to worry about for now. I'd got some fading with bleach to worry about - but not just yet. I'd wait a while until dad had come to terms with things.

Suzie had one drawback. She was in love with David Fucking Cassidy. The guy was everywhere right now. To a spotty 14-year-old with a feather cut, it seemed you couldn't turn a corner without seeing David or Donny smiling out from some magazine page. That wasn't to mention Michael Jackson, David Essex or even Gilbert O'Fucking Sullivan.

Suzie was David Cassidy mental. Not Donny - that would have been betraying the king of the Partridge Family. She had a David Cassidy patch sewn on her jeans. She told me she had 26 posters of him on her wall at home - the best was one of him in a patchwork shirt, sitting astride a Palomino.

'I kiss him every night and first thing every morning,' she said. Lucky bastard. The more I saw of Suzie the more I liked her. I couldn't imagine what it would be like kissing her. She was from London though and for that rather peculiar reason, I never envisaged she'd think about letting someone like me snog her. Anyway, it would have been betraying David no doubt.

Teenybop was well and truly here and though I'm sure she'd be quite impressed with a couple of the LPs I'd had for Christmas - Slade Alive and Alice Cooper's School's Out - I knew that her heart was elsewhere.

Is it just me, or is Slade Alive STILL one of the best live albums ever made? As for Alice, well I've only got to hear the single School's Out and I can see that distinctive desktop cover and recall my dad's take on it all.

I remember Pete Matthews not seeing Mr Hughes, the geography teacher, come in as he swung the window pole around like a microphone stand and blared out 'I wanna be erected. Ereeeeeected!!!!!'

'Do you really now Matthews?' said the master, barely able

to stop himself laughing.

'Aghhh . . . sorry . . .'

'You will be Matthews - or maybe you'd prefer me to call you Alice?'

We were gobsmacked. How the fucking hell did boring old Mr Hughes know Elected by Alice Cooper? How did he know anything about Alice Fucking Cooper? How did he know anything that was later than the Jurassic period? It was astonishing. He must have been in his thirties at least.

You see, my dad didn't know anything about such matters - unless he was just having me on.

'What's that racket?'

'Racket? Racket? That's brilliant dad. That's what that is.'

'I'll take your word for it. Who is it?'

'Alice Cooper,' I replied as dad craned his face closer to the TV in exaggerated fashion.

'You're not seriously going to tell me that's a woman?'

'Don't be stupid dad.'

'I'll give you stupid lad. What's she done to herself?'

'It's a bloke dad.'

'A bloke? A bloke? My giddy aunt - I've seen it all. A bloke called Alice.'

'Yeah. So?'

'So? A bloke called Alice with leather trousers that look like they've been clawed by a bloody tiger and . . . well . . . what does she, I mean he bloody well look like?'

'He's great, he is.'

'Great? I give up. I bloody well give up . . .'

Suzie was different. She wasn't like the girls around here. Maybe because I didn't see her much increased the appeal. I wasn't sure anymore. I wasn't sure of a lot of things these days. I'd even started to think Shirley Jones was attractive, though I hadn't told anyone. I doubt Suzie would be happy about that. Fancy wanting to shag David Cassidy's TV stepmum? She must be 35 if she was a day. She could even be 40. What was I thinking of? She just seemed really nice and for some reason known only to me, I found her increasingly attractive. It was quite worrying. What was wrong with me? Shirley Fucking Jones? For God's sake. I vowed not to tell anyone about that one. I'd started to have a different take on quite a few women on the estate as well. It was all becoming a bit unnerving. Susan Stranks off Magpie - there was another one. Not that she was on our estate. Just as well really, I'd have been sitting on the pavement at the end of her drive with my tongue hanging out. It would have been a bit of a giveaway. Having a crush on Susan Stranks wasn't quite so hard to fathom. I didn't have a problem with that one. One minute I'd be watching her helping with the feeding of the animals at the zoo or whatever, the next I'd got her decked out in stockings and suspenders, luring me into the long grass whispering 'seven for a secret never to be told.' Perhaps that liniment had somehow seeped into my system and contaminated me. I never used to get a hard-on watching Magpie. It was all getting very confusing.

One Saturday, Suzie had gone to see some relatives in Shrewsbury so wasn't going to be around for two or three days. We agreed to meet up when she returned.

By then I'd accumulated some cash from another of Mouse's get-rich-quick schemes. We'd made a fortune this summer after he cashed in on blackberry picking. He really was unbelievable that Mouse lad. My dad was convinced he'd end up a millionaire. He made a bit of money at school buying mint and toffee Yo-Yo biscuits when the school tuck shop had been closed and selling them to classmates for a penny over the odds. He was unbelievable. He was forever charging kids to fix their bikes or make a bike up for someone. A couple of his brothers had taught him how to do that. But his eye for an opening was becoming legendary and the blackberry scam was arguably his best yet.

We'd gone down to the fruit farm as pickers and had to blag the man in charge that we were 15 for a start off. Anyway, to cut a long story short, we spent hour upon hour picking blackberries into punnets - 24 to a tray on the promise of 10p a punnet. There was four of us - Mouse, me, Foz and Barry Bennett from across the road. But when we got to the selection station, the guy tried to get all funny with us and said they were no good to him because we'd picked too many that weren't ripe enough.

'That's rubbish,' Mouse said boldly.

'Take it from me son - I can't sell them. They're no use to me.'

'What do want us to do then?' a couple of us asked.

'You can have them. Take them with you, but they're no use to me.'

'What we going to do with 'em?' Mouse asked dejectedly.

'Same as you seem to expect me to do with 'em. I'm sorry but I just can't pay you for under ripe fruit.'

'That's a swizz,' Barry chipped in.

'Tell you what I'll do with you lads. I'll give you 50p each for the lot. I can't say fairer than that.'

Barry and me were looked at each other and were within a whisker of cutting our losses when Mouse spoke out.

'Get lost - you're trying to rip us off. We'll take them.'

'Take them then, but don't say you weren't warned. They're no use to anyone.'

'We'll see about that,' Mouse declared.

As the man moved out of earshot, the three of us looked at Mouse and wondered what the hell he was thinking of.

'What's going on?' Barry said.

'I'll give you 50p for the tray - deal?'

Barry looked at me and Foz looked at Barry. Mouse winked at me urging me to go along with it and he'd sort me out.

'Okay' I said. 'Deal.'

'Deal,' added Barry. 'I'm not carrying the fucking things all the way home.

'Nor me,' said Foz.

They accepted Mouse's offer to give them the 50p later on and apologetically rode off, leaving us with the four trays of blackberries.

'Fucking hell Mouse, have you gone off your head this time?'

'Nope. Trust me.'

'Again?'

'We'll need to leave the bikes here while we go over to those houses,' Mouse said.

'What you up to?'

'Well, there must be fifty houses over there in Station Road and I'll be blowed if we can't sell these.'

'What 96 fucking boxes?'

'Trust me.' It was a favourite expression of his. It was almost as if he liked testing just how far he could go.

'Stick the bikes under this hedge. Two trays each. Come on - let's go.'

'What you gonna do, stand on the street corner?'

'Don't be soft. Come on.'

We seemed to have walked ages when we got to a big imposing redbrick house and Mouse made his way up the drive.

'You're not going to just knock on the door are you?'

'Course.'

'Holy mackerel. You take the biscuit.'

'Watch.'

I stood halfway down the drive, half-listening to Mouse's sales pitch and watched on as an elderly woman pointed across the road to a small row of four bungalows. Whatever . . . no sale.

Mouse motioned me to follow him across the road

indicating that might be where our fortune lay.

I needed winning over and stayed a little way down the drive as Mouse got engaged in quite a long conversation with a grey-haired man of about 50. The man nodded. Mouse nodded. The man went around next door. Mouse waited and discreetly put a thumb up, urging me to come nearer.

The man returned with his neighbour and Mouse shouted me to bring my trays.

'Now lads, you're sure they're all above board. They've not been stolen now?'

'God's honest truth mister,' the two of us assured him.

'Well, like I said to your friend. I make wine. Jim here makes it too and he's sure that Fred next-door-but-one will have some. So how much?'

'What for? A box? A tray?' Mouse said in his normal business-like manner.

'We'll take the lot if the price is right.'

Holy shit, I thought.

'The lot . . . ermm, well . . .' Mouse said. 'What d'ya think?'

I could just sense the man was moving in for the kill. There was a bargain to be had here and you could sense he was well up for it.

'Fiver the lot - take it or leave it.'

Mouse stalled, just briefly, smiled at the man as if to say he admired what a hard bargain he'd driven and nodded.

'Okay. You won't be disappointed,' Mouse assured them cheekily, waiting as the two men sorted out the cash.

We walked down the drive, not too fast and not too slow and headed off back for the bikes.

Once out of earshot, Mouse turned and gave that massive cheeky grin of his.

'Not bad eh?'

Not bad? It bordered on brilliant. How had he turned the situation around like that? An hour ago the four of us were licking our wounds after being told we wouldn't be paid for hours of backbreaking work. Suddenly, life was sunny again and, make no mistake, it was all down to Mouse. Those who thought I was the bright one really should take a closer look sometimes. Now it was just a question of how we were going to carve up the proceeds.

'Am I brilliant? Or am I . . . brilliant?' Mouse said with a chuckle.

'You are!'

'Say it!'

'What?'

'Say 'Mouse you are brilliant - you are a genius."

'Mouse you are brilliant. You are an absolute genius.'

'That's better. So . . . 50p for Baz and Foz; a pound for you and three quid for me. That sounds about right doesn't it?'

'Great.'

'Don't be a numbskull. We were in this together. We go shares - two quid each.'

'Brilliant.'

The ride home seemed to take no time at all and we'd got the change to pay-up Barry and Foz after buying some sweets at the little shop just past the Malt Shovel.

'How's that Sant?'

'Mouse, you are a fucking genius.'

'I know kid. Hey, and who said money doesn't grow on trees? Well bushes anyway!'

I'd had a lot of lovely thoughts about Suzie - most of them now involved her in varying degrees of undress. Then . . . it happened.

It was just my luck that it was the night before she was due to go back. Her parents were driving up in the morning and her granddad had given her permission to go to the fair with a few of us. There was a gang going to meet up there - Mouse, Foz and a few others. We had a great night and Suzie had barely left my side. We went on the dodgems and been whirled around in the waltzers and the time flew so quickly, in the whirr of neon flashing lights and noise, that we suddenly realised we'd have to be making our way back. Suzie waved her candy floss in front of me and told me she ought to think about getting back. It was nine o'clock. It was going to take us 20 minutes to walk it, so I assumed she'd had instructions to be in by 9.30. Not so!!

She'd been told to be in by ten and explained that she didn't want to just rush indoors and say a hurried goodbye. Then, as we rested against the stile at the top of the lane, she nestled in towards me and kissed me full on the lips. God, this was fantastic. She tasted of candy floss and she seemed to know exactly what she was doing. I felt her tongue exploring my mouth and followed suit. God, this was fantastic. As I tried to put my hand on her breasts, she pulled away breathlessly and looked at her watch.

'I'll be in trouble, Sant! Better go, before you get carried away.'

'Ohh, okay,' I said the disappointment spilling out.

'Hey, there's always next time. I'll try and get up at Christmas if I can.'

I kissed her again and she slapped my hand playfully as she urged me to get down the alley as quickly as possible. It was almost five past ten and she'd be in bother if she didn't hurry.

I walked her to the gate, saw she got in and sighed. This was all just so very fucking well exciting. This was tangible excitement. I could bloody well feel it. Perhaps I'd shrunk my Levis just a bit too much.

15

1973 - PUPPYCOCK

David Cassidy is No 1 and droning on about how if only he could have a puppy he'd count himself so very lucky. Is he taking the piss or what? Virtually every girl in the western world wets her knickers at the very mention of his name already. He's worth an absolute fortune. Now he wants a puppy to start pissing all over the floor as well. Getting crushed at one of his concerts would seem to be the least of your problems - drowning was clearly the more immediate danger. Was David Cassidy really THAT good looking? If he was, how come he hadn't got his own cartoon series? The Osmonds had, so had the Jacksons. Even the fucking Harlem Globetrotters had their own cartoon series. I suppose he'd just point to The Partridge Family and say he didn't really need one and, grudgingly I guess, he probably had a point. Was there some plan for David Cassidy and Donny Osmond to rule the world? It was one of the conspiracy theories that deserved closer scrutiny. There were others, like was Bruce Lee dead and was the fella in Peters and Lee really blind?

Suzie would do virtually anything to prove her undying love for David. I was now the proud owner of a patchwork shirt just like his but Suzie had moved on to brown now because she'd read in Jackie magazine that it was his favourite colour. Fucking brown? What kind of a shite colour was that? Well, apparently it was and Jackie was to be trusted so now brown was the order of the day. It was her way of showing him her undying devotion. I felt like saying how was he ever going to know? Was she just wearing brown in case he happened to drop into Linshaw one day? It was fucking ridiculous. David Cassidy was ridiculous. Girls were bloody-well ridiculous. Jackie magazine was especially ridiculous for even mentioning it. Suzie admitted to me that she actually rehearsed just what she'd say to him if she ever met him. What was it with girls? Did I care what Rod Stewart's favourite colour was? Did I bollocks. Just what was the matter with them? I might be a way distant second to Cassidy on the looks and fashion front, but I did have a couple of massive advantages in that I was not only accessible, but also very much available. What chance had he ever got of snogging her? He lived thousands of miles away and didn't even know she existed. Life was so unfair sometimes.

Suzie had arrived just three days into the school summer holidays. I could remember that because it was just after the fight that had been the talking point of the entire area. If anyone wanted to know the day Melissa Ash and Mouse's relationship became cast in stone then it was that Wednesday afternoon when the little fella had come to her aid.

Melissa was stepping off the school bus from Wellington High School when Steve Hennessy, the unofficial toughest kid in the fourth year of Mouse's comprehensive, shoved her off the last step. She'd been carrying a wicker basket of scones made in her domestic science lessons. As she lurched forward the scones broke free from the plate and the crisp white tea towel covering them and spilled out onto the pavement. Melissa shrieked in anger and disbelief. Then, to compound matters, Hennessy aimed a size nine brogue at one and rugby-kicked it over the other side of the road.

'You idiot! You . . . you . . .' Melissa was beside herself but the tears got the better of her, when suddenly Mouse appeared and casually told Hennessy to pick them up.

'Fuck off you twat!'

'Pick them up.'

'Didn't you hear me? Fuck off. What's it to do with you anyway?'

'She's my friend, that's what it's got to do with me.'

'Well you pick them up then,' Hennessy sneered.

'I didn't knock them over.'

'What is it with you Ratcliffe? You gotta problem?'

'You're the problem.'

'Well, you gonna sort it then?'

Mouse flew at him, punching him to the side of the head before the two locked onto each other and ended up rolling around by the bus stop. Two adults broke them apart but the challenge was on. Mouse and Steve Hennessy were to meet at a more mutually convenient place and sort it out. The rec - the following day, 4.30. No one needed to put billboards up. Word spread like a bush fire. This was massive. Huge.

'Make sure you're there,' Hennessy taunted Mouse. 'And don't bring your fucking brothers with you either.'

'Won't need them. I'll be there.'

Some of the bystanders had helped pick up Melissa's scones but they had taken a bit of a bashing.

'You shouldn't have done that. But thank you,' she sighed. Melissa Ash couldn't quite believe that any boy would consider her worth fighting over. Truth be known, Melissa thought no boy had ever even given her a second glance. Now Mouse was going to go head-to-head with a foe already generally considered the favourite to emerge victorious. Steve Hennessy was a strong lad and you wouldn't even need the fingers of one hand to count those willing to stand up to him.

'They're only cakes . They're really not worth getting into any trouble over,' pleaded an anxious Melissa. She could feel her heart thumping with the anxiety and excitement of it all.

'Don't worry. He's had this coming for a long time. He's a loudmouth who needs shutting up.'

'What if he shuts you up?' I dared to suggest.

Mouse gave me that stare. 'He won't.'

94

The fight that was to see both of them suspended for the first two weeks of the following school year was a memorable affair. Hennessy had rushed straight at Mouse and looked to be getting the upper hand in the opening stages. Mouse was bleeding heavily from the nose after a right hook had caught him flush in the face. But just as the baying for more blood from Hennessy's jubilant pals reached fever pitch and Mouse looked to have little more to offer he connected with a ferocious uppercut and a sickening crack like an airgun shot, ripped through the air.

'Fucking hell d'ya hear that?' one of the onlookers groaned. Instinctively everyone knew something serious had happened. It wasn't in question. There was hardly a murmur.

Hennessy slumped over on himself, bent in the middle and winced audibly. You could almost feel the breath come out of him. Mouse seized on the opportunity and rained blows on him as he instinctively began to cover up. Even Hennessy's pals could sense their man was in huge trouble and started to close in, their concern for his safety now outweighing their dread of stopping the scrap prematurely. Mouse glanced at them and shook his head as if to indicate they'd better stop it and just as he pulled his right fist back to strike his foe full on the side of the head, Hennessy raised his hand indicating he wanted proceedings drawn to an abrupt halt. Mouse's satisfaction was branded on his face. It glowed from deep within.

Steve Hennessy slumped to the floor cupping his jaw. Eventually his friends marshalled him away. They weren't making quite so much noise now. A few hours later he was in hospital having his jaw wired. Mouse's thunderous uppercut had busted it in two places. The pair of them were hauled before the head and handed a fortnight's suspension. It was serious stuff, but Mouse Ratcliffe had just written himself into Linshaw folklore. The next day, Mouse was walking up Vinegar Hill when the sound of someone trying to start a car was interrupted by a call.

'Ian . . . Ian. Do you have a minute?' It was Peter Ash, Melissa's father, eager to thank Mouse and no doubt delighted he wasn't a teacher at such a rough school. Mr Ash was a maths teacher at Shrednall Comprehensive, a 20-minute drive away.

'Hello, Mr Ash,' Mouse said somewhat sheepishly.

'Ian. I'd just like to say a really big thank you for what you did for Melissa the other day.'

'Oh it was nothing,' Mouse said trying to keep his blackened left eye furthest away.

'No, it wasn't nothing. I would never condone violence but bullies should be stood up to. And by all accounts, you certainly did that. I do hope you are all right.'

'Yeah. Thanks, Mr Ash.'

'No, thank you,' he added, trying to get the engine to turn over again.

'Let's have a look,' said Mouse, twiddling under the bonnet.

'Now try it.'

Mr Ash turned the key and the engine fired first time. 'Crikey,' he said. 'What was it?'

'It looks like your suppression lead is loose. There's a casing on it, that you'll need to replace or the moisture'll get in and you'll never start it.'

'Thank you, Ian. Thank you, very much. You're certainly a handy fella to know!'

'Ah it's just something I picked up along the way. Bye.' Mouse continued his journey up the road.

And the summer that followed was hot in every sense of the word. Suzie had arrived just as the big scrap was still THE major talking point of the locality. Mouse continued with his farm job and Suzie and me explored almost every avenue of pleasure open to us. Days roaming around the fields by Bluebell Wood and spending hours in the long grass, led into evenings spent in the park or down in the street by Roly's Chippie just doing nothing much at all.

We went to see That'll Be The Day, which I thought, was just an absolutely cracking film even though it had David Essex as its star. Suzie explained that devotion to David Essex and David Cassidy WAS allowed because they weren't immediate rivals and, anyway, they were from different countries. It was impossible to love Donny and David Cassidy apparently. But you could love David and simply adore David Essex. I wasn't sure I totally understood, but that's how I remember the explanation.

It seemed like Suzie and me were now snogging to Olympic standard and she had eventually let me feel inside her top, but no more. By the time she had to go back we were both just turned 15 and getting more curious by the minute.

This Christmas I'd had mainly clothes. I wasn't particularly fashion mad or anything but I didn't want to stick out too much for all the wrong reasons. Some of the lads had Harrington jackets, crombies with studs in the pocket, Budgie jackets and the like, but my finances or desire didn't stretch to such extravagances. We were all off to the youth club disco New Year's Eve and I reckoned I'd be wearing my new Prince of Wales check bags, loafers and my green Brutus shirt with the button down collar. I didn't need telling that I wasn't No1 in the fashion stakes. To be fair, I didn't really need it ramming home that I wasn't No 1 in any stakes really. But, I hoped, I wasn't that bad. I was better looking than some of my mates surely. Yeah I was - there was no doubt about that. Was there? I suffered with the occasional spot but I wasn't a crater-face like some of them. Foz had a back like the surface of the fucking moon. I hadn't got any of that shit. He had to spend half an hour every night under a heat lamp to try and keep them under control. His back was a right mess. Mind you, he had got a right load of hairs on his dick, so maybe I'd got that to come. I'd only got about ten. When I say about ten I mean ten exactly. I was going to say, not that I'd counted them, but I just know you'd struggle to believe me. When it comes to such crucial matters there's no *'about'* about it really. It's like asking a top footballer how many FA Cup winners' medals he's won. He wouldn't say 'Oh *about* three - something like that.' It's one of those things you just happen to fucking well know. It's important until you get to the point where you've got so many it ceases to be an issue or you genuinely just don't know. That's what's most disturbing about nutcases like Harold Shipman or ruthless butchers like Amin, Pol Pot or Pinochet.

'So just exactly how many people have you been responsible for killing?'

'Oh, I think it must be about . . .'

And the chilling truth is they DON'T KNOW! That's when you know the guy really is a maniac. I couldn't wait for the time to come when I wouldn't fret if one pube fell out. Fantastic days. Bring them on! *Come on sprout you little bastards!*

Bring on the day. 'How many pubes you got?'

'How many? God, I don't know!'

It was 25p to get into the youth club disco being held at the Scout Hut this New Year's Eve. There was only pop and crisps on sale inside but Mouse, me and a few of the lads had clubbed together for three large bottles of Woodpecker which we had quickly seen off down by the seats just adjacent to the witches' hat on the rec play area. Some of the girls had gone on ahead but we decided to play it cool and arrive late. We weren't in any rush. The girls would be happy enough to go and have a dance - they always were. By and large, we viewed it as a pointless exercise until the last few records. Unless you were a really great dancer like Terry Cole, there wasn't much in it for us until the smoochy ones came on and even then most of us had to be virtually pushed into it.

I hadn't seen Suzie since the summer, her half-promise to return at Christmas hadn't materialised and I guess I was on the verge of going out with Teresa Harris who had made it quite clear that she wanted to go out with me. Tonight may well be the night, but I kidded around that I would be keeping my options open. What options? Who the fuck did I think I was? Current fashions and trends had only thrown me one sliver of good fortune - having a big nose and a bird's nest haircut was far from being uncool.

About six of us eventually made our way up to the Youth Club, heeding the warning that no one would be let in after nine. There were always rumours that lads from a rival area were coming to these functions and though that seemed to fill Mouse with relish and an unhealthy air of expectancy, it scared the shit out of me.

Mouse had tried, in vain, to persuade Melissa to come. He guessed her father wouldn't allow it. It might have been the case that she'd thought better than to ask him. Melissa's transformation from the scrawny girl with the eye-patch had been quite dramatic in the last 12 months. She had become very shapely and had a cute, pretty face. Mouse and her had become quite close in the summer on account of the fact that he'd got her a weekend job in the Breadsall Farm shop. Melissa worked behind the counter, and helped replenish the shelves when required. The owners had asked him if he knew anyone who was bright and honest who might like some work and the pair of them had been working together all through the summer. He got a bit agitated when we took the piss because he'd mentioned that the two of them quite often shared sandwiches in their lunch break. What Mrs Ash thought of darling Melissa tucking into one of Mouse's Spam and Branston sarnies, was a source of some amusement to us all. Mouse laughed but you could tell it rankled with him if one of us went on about it too much.

As we waited for Len, the youth club leader to rip out the raffle tickets, the sound of Leader of the Pack drifted through from the big room. Mouse, Foz, a few others and me made our way to the far corner where we basically hung around and picked faults with everybody else. I just didn't like dancing - full stop. There was a certain type of record you might consider having a dance to, but if I could get away with it, like most of the lads, I'd rather just give it a miss. Two or three of the lads would stick their thumbs in their pockets and do that suspect head banging dance if any Quo record came on. They were all the same so it didn't matter which one it was. Then you had songs like Saturday Night's Alright for Fightin', Jean Genie and Alright, Alright, Alright by Mungo Jerry which reluctant dancers like me could get away with and just make out that we were messing about.

Directly across the room from us was Teresa with a few of her mates and she was staring me full in the face and with a doleful look on her face was mouthing the words to the Limmie and the Family Cookin' song the DJ had just put on. I'm not particularly quick on the uptake, it must be said, but when a girl fixes you with a stare and starts mouthing 'You Can Do Magic,' even a clot like me figures he might have a chance. I quite liked Teresa. She was just on the acceptable side of chubby, with mousy hair bobbed into a neat pageboy cut. She was pleasant enough, but that was it really. *Quite liked?* Pleasant? *Acceptable side of chubby?* It was hardly Ryan O'Neill and Ali McGraw was it? Perhaps I expected too much. Terry Cole was catching everyone's eye with his artistic interpretations of Jean Genie and Roxy's Street Life. It had to

100

be said - he was a fucking show-off. Teresa came over to chat and finally persuaded me that anyone could dance to Rock On. There's one thing to be said for David Essex songs, all you have to do is kind of move your shoulders around just a little and you've cracked it. Fortunately, the DJ didn't appreciate what a coup he'd made getting me on the dance floor when he sticks Ballroom Blitz on and presents me with the perfect opportunity to get back into the corner and swig menacingly at my Coke. My heart just wasn't in it somehow when a tap on the shoulder made me turn around. It was Suzie looking absolutely stunning. My God, she was here. Suzie had made it. She kissed me on the cheek and smiled.

'Hiya!'

'Whoa . . . Great to see you. I didn't think you were coming.'

'I could see that,' Suzie said with a knowing grin, glancing to the girl with the page cut on the opposite side who was now giving me absolute daggers.

'Oh right.'

'Not cramping your style am I?'

'Course not. Come on, let's go and get a drink.'

Suzie held on to my arm and we weaved our way to the tiny 'bar' area where the Cokes were lined up.

'When did you get here?'

'Oh, it's a long story. We were coming at Christmas, then mum was bad, so we had to delay it by a few days, so we arrived this morning.'

'How did you know where to find me?'

'I called at your house and there was no one in but, just as I was waking away, there were a couple of girls on the corner who told me where I'd find you. So I nipped back home, made myself presentable and came up. If it's a problem, I can soon make myself scarce.'

'You're joking aren't you?'

'Well, not really. If looks could kill, I'd be . . .'

'Oh, take no notice. She's just a sort of mate. Nothing more.'

Suzie looked gorgeous. There was more than a passing resemblance to Carly Simon, which was certainly no bad thing. She had a pair of embroidered jeans on and a blue check cheesecloth shirt unbuttoned over a figure-hugging white vest. She was sensational.

Her breasts seemed bigger than when I'd last seen them just a few months ago. This had been a watershed summer in that respect. As we chatted over a coke, I suggested we should take a breather outside and she followed me to the bench over by the small bandstand in the park. As we sat down the recollections of the summer came springing back and I could almost smell Bluebell Wood and the long grass down the side of it.

We sat arm in arm by the bandstand and decided that although it was cold, we didn't want to go back in to the disco. We kissed and cuddled for a while and then realised it was time to be getting home anyway. She said she loved the smell of my Brut.

As we made our way back in the direction of the scout hut, the still air was broken by the sound of chattering

It was Teresa and a couple of her pals, clearly not entirely approving of my choice of chaperone.

'You can put your knickers back on now love. It's a bit cold to leave them off,' one piped up

'Night girls,' I said mockingly.

'G'night Sant. Sorry, didn't know you'd got company.'

'Charming,' Suzie whispered, clutching my arm tightly.

'Yeah lovely.'

'So, do you always have girls fighting over you then?'

'Oh yeah all the time. Haven't you noticed?'

'Well, yes I have actually. I've only been here five minutes and they're on my back.'

'I'm worth it,' I grinned.

'We'll have to see about that,' Suzie said teasingly.

As we passed the hut, it was just about wrapping up. You could hear Slade's new record 'Merry Christmas Everybody,' thumping out of the place. It was a strange sort of record for Slade to bring out, that one. Couldn't see that lasting.

16

1974 - CROCODILE SHOCK

The biggest selling group of 1974? The Wombles! Can things really get any worse? Boy, did they! Me and Suzie had so much fun - we kind of adopted Crocodile Rock as our summer anthem. Lord knows what anyone who saw us jigging along would have made of it. I certainly never knew me a better time and I guess I never will. We made hay in the most glorious summer for years. It was an absolute scorcher and things just seemed to get hotter and hotter in every sense of the word.

'Six weeks?' I said gleefully. The longest she'd ever been up for was two.

'Yep. Six whole weeks. I don't know what I'm going to find to do. I just like it up here. It's so different from home. Peaceful and . . . well different.'

'How come so long?'

'Well, mum and dad are going on a cruise and I had to make a decision. So here I am!'

'Didn't you want to go then?'

'Not for five-and-a-half weeks. It'd drive me mad. So it was a case of being shipped up here or go with them and I chose to be here. Do you think you can put up with me for that long?'

'I'll have a go.'

'Tell the truth, I was quite looking forward to seeing you as well. Hope you don't mind.'

'Nah, why should I?'

'Well, I'm sure you've got lots of other things you want to do this summer without having to entertain me.'

It was the start of one glorious summer. Me and Suzie had so much fun . . . holding hands and skimmin' stones led to all sorts of other new pleasures. Just a few days in and Suzie and me were inseparable, taking every available opportunity to snog our heads off in the long grass over the banks. She was really good at it too. I remember her gorgeous full lips and the faint fragrance of Charlie perfume like it was yesterday. Her beautiful firm breasts were quickly no longer out of bounds to me as we soaked up the heady summer sunshine, but all my best efforts to go any further met with firm resistance.

The fact that she always wore jeans seemed to deliberately hamper my manoeuvres. On the one occasion I'd got near the top of her long legs, she'd stopped me in mid-flight.

'Ah ah . . . stop Sant.'

'Oh go on, just . . .'

'Wrong place and certainly the wrong time . . .'

'Come on then let's go somewhere else,' I urged her.

'Sant! It's not a good time at all, believe me.'

Fucking hell, always some stumbling block. I glanced down at my watch. It was only twenty past three. What was she on about?

A few days later, Suzie's enthusiasm reached new heights and as we lay there over on a gentle slope at the back of the third banks, I made my breakthrough. She looked gorgeous and her denim skirt rode up over her thighs revealing the tops of tanned legs. This time she surrendered to my advances, allowing me to slip my fingers into her wetness with barely a murmur. Suzie smiled up at me, sensing my excitement. God, it was fantastic and I explored her warmth for what seemed like an age when she nibbled my ear tenderly.

'God I want you,' I gasped.

'I've told you to wait until I'm sixteen!' She pushed me away playfully and indicated perhaps we'd better get on our way. She was sixteen tomorrow - June the fourth. Happy fucking birthday!!

'We coming back here tomorrow?'

'Love to.'

'Okay.'

'Was that nice?'

'Oooh lovely Sant. You?'

'Fantastic . . . fantastic. You're lovely you are.'

'Oh you sweetie. Sant.'

'Yeah.'

'Why don't you bring something tomorrow?' she nuzzled her face into mine.

'I can do,' I said matter-of-factly.

'That'd be nice. I'll leave it with you.'

'Okay.'

God I was getting good at this. I was moving into expert territory - there was no other way to look at it.

I met her by the alley the next day and we walked hand in hand to a little spot just to the left of the flattened patch of grass where we had been.

'Happy birthday. I've bought you something,' I said with a smile.

'Oh . . . you shouldn't have.'

She unwrapped the small package and there was the broadest grin as she realised just what it was - a stainless steel zodiac ring like mine - but Gemini.

'You are sweet.'

'I know,' I said, rather pleased with myself. I've bought you something else as well.'

'Mmm can't wait,' she said temptingly.

Suzie was getting more adventurous by the minute and as I made my way towards the Holy Grail again, she gazed at me knowingly.

'Mmmm . . . so you have got something then.'

'Yep.'

'Oh good.'

'Where is it?'

'In my shirt pocket.'

She groaned as I felt her wetness and to my surprise, started to pull at my zip, easing it down and feeling my hardness.

'Fucking hell,' I sighed.

'That nice?'

'Yeah . . .'

'Come on then, get it out.'

'I thought you were going to do that,' I said triumphantly.

'Not that, you idiot. What you've brought. Get it out.'

'What now?'

'Yeah now for God's sake. Where is it?'

'In my shirt pocket.'

'Come on Sant, stop messing about.'

I was all of a fluster.

'Come on, I want it now Sant,' Suzie groaned.

'Okay, okay, okay,' I said sliding my fingers away to get to the left breast pocket of my cheesecloth shirt.

'Get it out Sant,' Suzie said urgently.

'All right,' I said somewhat flustered and moved it towards her.

'What the fuck?' she exclaimed.

'What?'

'You bloody idiot. Is that what you've brought?'

107

'I thought they were your favourites.'

'They are. A raspberry fucking ruffle! What you playing at?'

'Oh god, I'm with you.'

'Sant! You are a half-wit. What are you?'

'A half-wit,' I said sheepishly.

'Do I need to spell it out to you?'

'No. Sorry. I've got the wrong end of the stick.'

'Yeah, well that's all you'll be getting.'

◇◇◇◇◇◇

The raspberry ruffle incident merely served to make it crystal clear exactly what was on my shopping list. My God, I was going to do it!! I'd go to Gilbert's and nonchalantly ask for a pack of three after I'd had a haircut.

Gilbert kept asking me if he'd taken enough off and I swear if I'd delayed things any longer I'd have come out looking like Yul Fucking Brynner. In the end I came out with hair a bit shorter than I really wanted and a styptic pencil. I just clammed up when he asked if I wanted anything else. What if he told my dad? I was only 15 and he knew it. I'd go down the road to the chemists. If the woman with the curly hair and glasses who knew my mum wasn't serving I'd just buy some over the counter.

I sidled in to the chemists and casually glanced around before making my way to the contraceptives. The coast was clear. The woman my mum knew wasn't there. Now then . . . Nu Form, Fetherlite, Gossamer. The Gossamer ones were slightly dearer. I'd take those. Only the best. You shouldn't cut corners on such massive occasions. Lord, there were some black ones as well. Hey, perhaps they'd make your dick look bigger. Nah, they'd look silly. I held my nerve, got my money ready and moved towards the counter with my pack of three in my hand. I stood there. The woman was serving someone else, but she seemed very pleasant and unlikely to ask me any awkward questions. Suddenly she shouted towards the back counter.

'Teresa . . . customer sweetheart.'

No one told me that Teresa had a part-time job there. Oh my God, she was right there in front of me.

'Hi Sant, can I help you?' she said extending her hand. She smiled at my futile attempts to conceal them.

'Anything else?'

'Ermm, no I don't think so.'

'Would you like a bag?' she said with a sarcastic grin.

'Yeah, yeah, that'd be great.'

'Okay love, there you are and there's 50p change and your receipt.'

'Err thanks.'

Teresa pressed the bag into my hand and smiled softly.

'Have you got a job yet Sant?'

'Oh err, no . . . not yet.'

Fucking cow. She knew I had another year to go. Let me out of here.

'Oh well I'm sure something will come up shortly,' she said with a knowing wink.

'See ya then Sant. Have fun.'

Fucking hell. She hadn't said anything that would have alerted anyone else in the shop, but she knew I wasn't on a mercy mission for my dad. I made my way out of the shop and once I was up near the top of the alley I slipped them down the front of my pants just for extra safe keeping. Tomorrow couldn't come quickly enough.

Suzie looked fantastic. We met by the top field, as arranged, and made out way over to our usual spot. It was a Saturday and the need to be extra careful to avoid the attention of dog walkers and adults out for a stroll was all the more pressing. Knowing my luck I'd bump into Teresa and we'd end up discussing the varying merits of Gossamer over Nu Form or Fetherlite. Luckily there didn't seem to be too many people about. Not too many ventured as far as the third banks anyway. We were safe enough.

I'd love to say the whole wonderful experience went without a hitch but that would be stretching it. Suzie looked stunning in a black vest that just showed a hint of black bra strap. She had a tiny denim skirt on and flip-flops.

As our kissing became more intense, I could contain myself no longer and slipped my hand inside her vest top to manoeuvre my hand towards her bra clasp. After the hiccup of the day before this was no time for cock-ups, excuse the pun; I needed to be slick and resourceful this time around. I was round the back for an age when Suzie politely unclipped it at the front and allowed her gorgeous breasts to spring free.

'It's a front loader, you idiot,' she chastised me playfully.

'Sorry,' I said, eager to move on. How was I to know? Undo one? I didn't even know they fucking well existed.

Well, I got myself protected as it were, but only after one almighty game. Flipping heck! Is that a tricky procedure first time around or what? Johnnies weren't in the seedless grapes or plastic rubber class, that's for sure. Too much information. It proved to be an eye-opener, but I got there in the end. It was a bit of a nightmare, but you know, these things come with experience. It was like the end was split. Was that normal?

We'd become really, really close and as Suzie's return home drew closer, neither of us was looking forward to it one bit. Never mind having to go to sixth form college, what was I going to do when she'd gone? Suzie was lovely. She was just so different to the girls around here. Perhaps I could get a job and move down to London one day.

How it had turned into this nightmare I wasn't sure. Well, I should have had an idea, but this . . . I hardly dare think about it. There was little likelihood of me being afforded that luxury. From now on I would think of little else. What the future held for me, God only knew.

I was actually upstairs in my bedroom when the authoritative, rap on the door sent dad scurrying to open it. By the time I'd got to the curtains to take a peep, the sound of raised voices sent the alarm bells ringing. When I heard Suzie's dad introduce himself, I sensed this wasn't good news. When he said he wanted to kill me, that sort of confirmed things. I'd only met him in passing a couple of times and he'd certainly never been here. Why the hell would he come here? It wasn't to bring me a present that's for sure. This sounded serious.

'Where is he?'

'Who?'

'Your bloody son - that's who.'

'Whoa, hang on a minute here. What's going on?'

'I'm going to throttle him, that's what's going on.'

'Hang on a second mate. Less of that talk and before I even think about letting you in, you'd better tell me what the problem is.'

The man took one pace back, looked to the ground and took a deep breath before introducing himself.

'I'm Alan. Alan Day. I'm afraid I'm not here to wish you compliments of the season. I wish I was. . .' He tailed off as if he'd burst into tears or start head-butting the wall at any moment.

'Where does my John come into this? Well, if you're sure you've calmed down, you'd better come in.'

It was the last thing I heard properly before they made their way into their living room. It was quiet at first, then raised voices, then quiet again and as I sat deadly still on the end of the bed and tried to pick up snippets of the

111

conversation, a looming sense of anxiety made me realise I'd be summoned downstairs at some point fairly soon.

'Johhhhnnn. JOHN!!!' dad shouted from the bottom of the stairs.

'Get down here. Sharpish.'

Fucking hell. This was serious. I just knew it. I could feel my leg shaking. It's hard to explain, but from the moment that door knocked there was a distinct whiff of danger about this whole thing.

'This gentleman here has got something to say to you and I suggest you listen to him. VERY carefully.'

'Hello, Mr Day,' I acknowledged him sheepishly.

'I hope you realise you've just ruined my daughter's life.'

I just looked at him. A reply wasn't necessary. I waited for him to continue.

'Suzie is pregnant. What have you got to say about that?'

'Oh. I can't believe it.'

'Is that all you've got to say - *I can't believe it.*'

As it happens it was. I couldn't fucking well believe it. Was he expecting the Gettysburg Address or something? I couldn't think of a fucking single thing to say and a denial of any knowledge at this point seemed somewhat futile.

'Have you got *anything* to say for yourself?' he continued.

'Well, son?' dad tried to coax something out of me.

'I don't know what to say Mr Day. I really don't,' I said. I could feel my lip quivering with fear.

'Well that makes two of us. I'm absolutely beside myself. Say *something* for Christ's sake,' Mr Day begged me.

'I don't know . . . errr.'

'I take it you're not surprised that I'm here, rather than knocking on someone else's door then?'

'I'm not with you.'

'I wish you weren't with me. I wish I weren't within a 100 miles of this place, but I am. What I mean is, I take it you accept that you are responsible?'

'I guess I could be,' I said immediately sensing the slight inference looked set to trigger even more rage from my questioner.

'COULD be? Don't you believe what my daughter has said?'

'I didn't mean it like that. I mean, I don't know what I meant. I'm saying, if that's what Suzie says then . . .'

'Well, that's what she says. And she says it's you. It's your fault. This whole bloody mess is your fault.'

'Just hold on a minute,' dad stepped in. 'I'm not trying to dilute the seriousness of this in any way Alan, but just hold your horses a bit. If my John has done wrong then I'll do everything in my power to see that he does the right thing, but don't come in my house laying ALL of the blame at this door.'

'What do you mean?' Suzie's dad blazed.

'Well, if he's responsible, and I'm certainly not saying that he's not, he hasn't done it on his own, you know.'

'SHE wouldn't have got in this predicament without a lot of persuasion, let me tell you.'

'Let me tell you, Alan, if you're saying something has been done against her will, that's a different matter, but if you're not then just be careful what you're suggesting,' dad fired back.

'I'm not suggesting any such thing, but . . .' Mr Day rapped the table with the flat of his hand.

'Shouting and screaming isn't going to get this sorted,' dad insisted.

'I'll put the kettle on,' mum said, glaring at me as if I'd just trodden dog shit into the carpet, but worse.

'Shouting and screaming is the last thing I want to do, but I don't think you understand.'

'Listen, I'm trying. But this has rather been sprung on us,' dad said as calmly as could be expected.

'Sprung on YOU. Sprung on YOU. How do you think we feel? WE had such high hopes for her. We wanted her to go to university and everything and he's ruined it. He's ruined everything. I can't bear it. I just can't bear the thought of it.'

'Hold on. Hold on. Like I said, I give you my word that John and this family will not try to walk away from this delicate situation. I will personally see that and any provision we can make will be made.'

'I'm not here for your money. You can't buy me off.'

'I'm not trying to buy you off and I resent the suggestion, but will you just see sense for a minute. I know you're livid - and with every good reason - but all I can do is offer you any assistance that I can. There's not a lot more I can do. I'm as disappointed as you are, but what's done is done.'

'Believe you me; there's not a way in this world that you can be anywhere near as disappointed as me. You can't even BEGIN to understand how disappointed I am.'

'Okay, okay - stop right there. What I'm saying to you is this. You've every right to be mad - lord knows I'd be furious as well, but we've got to set that aside just for a minute.'

'Set it aside?' Mr Day said sharply.

'I was speaking figuratively. I mean, what can we do this minute to try and address this situation?'

'Castrate your son, might be a start, but it's a bit late for that.'

'Look, if that's the sort of stuff you're going to come out with then there's not much point continuing this conversation.'

'I'm sorry, but . . . what do you want me to say?'

'Well, it might be handy for a start off, like I said, if I knew where we might be coming from on this matter.'

'Well my daughter's bloody-well going to have a baby, that's where I'm coming from.'

'Yes, yes. But given that's the situation, doesn't it make sense for us to now try and do what's right for everyone concerned and try and come up with the best solution.'

'Don't you think it's a bit late for that,' Suzie's dad continued.

'Well, yes, but I mean there are a limited number of steps

to be taken here, so it's up to us to try and sort it out.'

'No, that's what I don't think you seem to understand. It's up to me - well, and the wife of course - to sort it out. Like everything in these cases, it's us that's left sorting out the bloody mess,' he went on.

'Well, yes . . .'

'And that's exactly what it is - a god-forsaken bloody mess. There's no other word for it. Well, there is, but I'd better not say it.'

'Right,' dad said curtly. 'This isn't getting us anywhere.'

'What did you expect? Just wave a magic wand and it would all go away?'

'No - and that's ridiculous of you to even suggest such a thing. But are we talking, forgive me for saying this, abortion here?'

'Abortion! Some chance of that. She's six months gone.'

'Oh right, I see. That's late.'

'Late? I'll say it's late, but we only had this confirmed yesterday. I've slept on it. Well tried to - I haven't slept all night - and came virtually straight here. There's no question of terminating anything.'

Dad looked at me, sitting there not daring to say a word, shook his head and gasped through pursed lips.

'Right then. Now look, when I say this it's certainly not a question of trying to buy you off, but all I can do is offer every little bit of help I can. All I can promise to do is help out financially in any way I can until he starts work and then, rest assured, I'll make absolutely certain that he's not allowed to forget his responsibilities.'

'And when exactly do you expect him to graduate as a brain surgeon?'

'Enough's enough Alan. I'm not having this,' dad sprang to my defence.

'The lad'll work soon enough and if it costs him then that's the way it is. Marriage isn't part of the equation, so I don't know what more I can do.'

'Marriage? Marriage. My daughter wouldn't marry him if he were the last person on this planet. Marriage? My God. It doesn't bear thinking about.'

'Who do you think you're talking to. You storm in here, ready to go pop, which I fully understand, and think you can just slag my lad off. I won't allow that. Whether you like it or not, these things take two you know. He's going to be made well aware of where he stands in this but, don't paint your daughter as some paragon of virtue who has had something terrible done to her.'

'Well, it seems that way.'

'Well how it seems and how it is are two different things and if you can't change your attitude then I suggest you go away and sleep on it again because I'm not having that at any price.'

'I'm going anyway. I can't stand any more of this. Marriage? Jesus Christ. That boy can't look after himself, let alone anyone else.'

'Enough, Alan, enough,' dad said pointing him towards the hall.

'Come back when you're more able to talk.'

'I'm not sure that day will ever come,' Mr Day sniffed, half way out of the front door.

'That's as maybe. But I'm willing to talk when you are,' dad assured him as he opened the door of his brown Ford Granada.

'I never want to see that lad again. Never. He'll never be anything. He's a waste of time,' Mr Day said defiantly, almost banging his head on the door-surround in his eagerness to get off.

'Never in a million bloody years. I don't ever want to see his face again.'

And with that he was gone, leaving my dad to give me one furious look.

'God you've been and gone and done it now, haven't you?'

The glass in the front door rattled as it slammed shut and dad pointed me to sit down without saying a word before making his way upstairs to the toilet.

Bruce Forsyth was hamming it up on telly. Bruce's antics and quick-witted repartee were normally compulsive viewing in our house, but while I waited for dad to reappear, I sensed anything to do with a generation game might be best avoided. Mum sat there ashen-faced, shaking her head as tears rolled down her face.

And there was Bruce, talking to a young woman of about 19, clearly in child and revealing that it was her second baby.

'I'll make a note of that,' says Bruce reaching for that card from his inside pocket.

'Sure thing . . .'

I couldn't help wishing Bruce would just fuck off.

Thankfully, dad switched it off.

'Well, well, well. Happy bloody Christmas!'

17

1975 - THE LETTER

Dear Sant,

Boy, oh boy, have we caused some shit!! If you think you have had a hard time, spare a thought for me. Dad has gone absolutely mental. He's still not come down off the ceiling about all this mess. I hear he gave you a hard time. I've had that for months now. Sorry, I didn't get chance to warn you he was coming, but by the time it all started happening, he was on his way. He just stormed down the drive, got in his car and the next thing we heard was him screeching away. I've honestly never seen him so mad. My mum isn't very happy, as you'd expect, but she seems to be getting a bit more used to it now. In fairness she's been really quite good because my dad has been like a demented madman about the place. There's just no talking to him - he just goes on about how I've ruined my life, my prospects, everything . . . he's raging. Guess I don't need to tell you that.

Anyway, the reason I'm writing is that we are moving shortly so even if you were thinking about getting in touch - don't. It seriously wouldn't be a good idea anyway. I'll try and let you know what happens as soon as I can. For now, if I was you, just keep out of the way. I've got to admit I'm a bit scared about all this Sant. What did I do to deserve this? I don't want to sound like I'm full of self-pity, but it all seems very unfair from where I'm sitting. I'm not asking for any help or anything like that. It's just that it seems like I'm on my own at times, no matter how understanding mum tries to be. There's just no talking to dad. He's on another planet somewhere. The thing was Sant, by the time I realised I was having a baby, there were hardly any options open to me.

Dad's gone absolutely bananas about it and I understand that, but honestly, I just didn't know. There was no bump or anything. I've read these stories about girls not knowing until the day they had it and never believed it. There was nothing - not a bump or anything. There is now. University is out of the equation for sure!! Anyway, just had to write to let you know I'm OK. I've left my address off on purpose so don't try and make contact for now. That might be one surprise too many for my old man.

I promise I'll be in touch as soon as I can and let you know the outcome. I'm due early March. Not long now. I'm hoping things will settle down in the not too distant future and things will be different for all of us. To hear dad talk you'd think I'd murdered someone. I think he might be ready to - YOU probably with me a close second!!!

I've told mum that if it's a boy I want to call it John - it's a nice name. I don't think I'll take your surname on though . . . just imagine John Christmas-Day!!!

I've had to take that ring off even though it is expandable!!! At least they won't have to cut it off!!

Anyway Sant, I'll be in touch as soon as I can

See you. Suzie X.

God I felt so helpless. It was only a few short months ago that all I would have had to think about was my O' levels. Now this. And I realised that even thinking that way was horribly selfish. Poor Suzie was in a right old fix and it was all my doing. My mind was all over the place.

Summer came and went with a whimper. I still hadn't heard anything. I hoped all was okay. I'm certainly not blaming Suzie's predicament for my relatively poor exam showing, but I'd expected to get more than five passes. Three 'C' grades and two 'Bs' were hardly likely to set the world alight - I'd expected to get maybe seven. My mind just wasn't on anything. How could anyone seriously expect it to be? I was feeling this a lot more than most people knew. Mouse knew and, strangely enough, Melissa Ash had been really lovely about it. I don't even know why I opened up to her. She was such a lovely girl - a listener.

Melissa had a good heart. You could tell she genuinely cared and I'd grown to see her for being the lovely person she was. I confess, when she was the scrawny little kid with the eye patch who never drank Coke and wasn't allowed to watch telly, she might as well have been off another planet, but now with the benefit of a little bit more maturity I was beginning to appreciate what a multi-faceted character she was. She could read music, played the guitar, cello and the piano, she embroidered and she could draw and paint. My God there wasn't much she couldn't do.

But March had come and gone and I heard nothing more. At least this Christmas had been less eventful than the last, but that didn't seem much consolation now. This time last year I'd been in really deep water, yet somehow the problem seemed to have just disappeared. That didn't stop me thinking about it. Just exactly what had happened? People probably thought it was okay by me, but it wasn't really. It's like it was hanging over me and yet there had been no proper conclusion.

I was a bit angry that I'd heard nothing more from Suzie. I realised this wasn't about me, but I couldn't help thinking it wouldn't have taken much to just let me know about the baby. No doubt her dad had something to do with it. I was a bit surprised she'd allowed herself to go along with it, but then again, it was her dad I suppose and it might just have been easier that way. I obviously had no say in it. Life goes on.

18

1976 - ANGELA RIPPON

I blame Angela Rippon. Newsreaders becoming a pain in the arse and performing in public started with her. Comic Relief and stuff has brought them all crawling out of the woodwork - you can't move for weathermen or newsreaders prancing around on stage pleading with you to donate your hard-earned cash. But time was -and it's an old-fashioned concept - when weathermen just read out forecasts and newsreaders just read out the news. It was all so simple back then. And it's Angela Rippon's fault that you know whether John Ketley can toss an omelette and Sian Lloyd gets her mush in every gossip column going and that's mainly because she was attached to a celebrity fucking MP. The only way an MP got to be a celebrity in 1976 was if Mike Yarwood included you in his act. This Christmas the only legs up for consumption by millions aren't attached to a turkey. No, the nation is going crazy over Angela appearing on the Morecambe and Wise Christmas Special and doing a dance routine. It's front page news.

Up to this point in time no-one had even thought about her pins. For as much as we knew and cared they could have wheeled her in every day half-an-hour before her stint and then pushed her back out when she'd finished. No one considered her legs. Tell the truth, everyone seemed genuinely surprised she had legs at all, let alone shapely ones. For years she'd sat at her BBC desk with no one really giving any thought to what might be hidden from view. She could have been the female equivalent of Douglas Bader and none of us would have been any the wiser.

Overnight, Angela had gone from reading the news to making it and the nation's grateful dads, including mine, expressed their approval.

'She's a very good dancer,' he observed, which was dad-talk for if he hadn't thought about giving her one before, he certainly had now.

She had quick-stepped her way onto his undisclosed Top 10 of fanciable birds which, I'm guessing, up to that point would have read something like this:

1 Nana Mouskouri
2 Shirley Bassey
3 Susan Hampshire
4 Cleo Laine
5 Judith Durham from The Seekers
6 Eartha Kitt
7 Sophia Loren
8 Mary Hopkin
9 Clodagh Rodgers
10 Any of the girls who appeared on Benny Hill

Mum knew what lay behind dad's complimentary take on Angela's foxy new image and said Vince Hill was the one who made her swoon. I could only imagine who might make up my mum's list, but it would have gone something like:

1 Vince Hill
2 Johnny Mathis
3 Jack Jones
4 Richard Chamberlain
5 Engelbert Humperdinck
6 Tom Jones
7 Gene Pitney

8 Burt Reynolds
9 Ryan O'Neill
10 Sacha Distel

So if you want to know why every year we get 'C' list celebrities offering to do all sorts of shit things to make money for Comic Fucking Relief then blame the Rippon girl. When some ageing bag off Eastenders or Emmerdale says she'll do a belly dance or something equally unfunny if people pledge enough money, you'll know the source.

Without wishing to sound an old twat, there were some genuine TV stars back then. They kind of knew their place. Now you get people like Jade Goody who have made millions basically because she's famous for being fat and stupid. How did that all come about? Well, once our Angela had come out from behind her desk and strutted her stuff it was open house. The very second she shuffled her papers, slapped them down on the desk and breezed onto the Morecambe and Wise show, that was it.

Now you get fuckwit male weather forecasters who just can't wait to dress up in stockings and suspenders with the failsafe that it's all for a good cause. It's very worrying and enough to signal an instant depression across the entire country for anyone with so much as an ounce of sense. Keith Chegwin is usually lying in wait somewhere as well. Screaming up and down someone's street like a demented five-year-old. If I saw him racing down my street, I'd have the bolts across the door in no time. No amount of coaxing would get me out. I'd vote for Britain being made a Chegwin-free zone, never mind my fucking street. If the man steps foot in your county, the police should make you aware of it. He could just be the most irritating twat in the world. I'm hard pressed to think of too many who'd beat him to that award.

But the big news in my life is that I now have a job. I hadn't managed to add an 'A' level to my acceptable five 'O's but I quickly learned that the art of deception is one to be encouraged when it comes to trying to land a job. I'd applied for a job on the editorial floor of the Linshaw Gazette, a small circulation weekly newspaper whose head offices were no more than a short bus ride from where I lived. The job specification for a messenger boy/would-be journalist was a minimum of five 'O' levels (including English, of course) and the rather sketchy proviso of 'we would like you to have two 'A' levels. What was that supposed to mean? I would like to have two 'A' levels as well, but it was not going to happen. So what does anyone apart from a total fuckwit say when they ask you at the interview if you are confident of getting two passes.

'Not a problem. English and General Studies. Yeah, can't see any nasty shocks there.'

'Good, good. It's just that we do ask for two 'A' level passes you see.'

Well, bully for you. But on account of the fact that this interview is taking place a good three months before the results drop through the door with a resounding bang, you're gonna just have to take my word for it. And by the time the results did come through I was already hard at work at the Gazette, hoping to chart a course through the ranks and end up getting a place as a trainee journalist.

It was a good nine months before Mrs McDougal, the woman responsible for training schedules, asked me what qualifications I ended up with. Oh fuck. So I just took the view that if failing my 'A's was going to cost me my job, I might as well lie. What a nonsense it is really. I just kind of wondered whether she, or anyone else, would ring my school or the national examination board and check these things out. They don't you know.

'Ah John, glad to have caught up with you. I need to get my training records up to date and I haven't got your 'A' level results.'

'Oh right . . . err. Two. I got them both but only 'C' grades

I'm afraid.'

I chucked the last bit in just for a real touch of authenticity. It was my kind of way of saying that things hadn't quite gone to plan.

'As long as they're passes - I only have to tick the boxes,' said Mrs McGregor.

'Nah, exactly.'

'Okey dokey. That's fine John. Thank you.'

'Thank you.'

Tick those fuckers then Mrs McGregor. I can only assume she never checked. If she did she kept quiet. But the added bonus to what I'd done was that once that tiny deception was on my records, it stayed there for all time. The folly is that I was never ever asked about my school examinations again for any job I ever went for, but if they had, then my two 'A' level passes would have been down there on record. It had been that easy. If I'd known I'd have given myself nine 'O' levels as well, just to really take the piss.

And so I started my chosen career on the princely sum of £22 a week which was a fortune to me after having had to rely on bits of part-time work and handouts from my dad for the two extra years at sixth form college.

Dad didn't talk about the matter much, but he admitted he'd been surprised I hadn't heard anything from Suzie. It was probably no bad thing, he argued. In his eyes the last thing a young man needed was having something like that hanging around his neck. Nonetheless, I still felt aggrieved that no-one felt I had a right to know.

It had been a source of considerable frustration to me that Mouse had been earning forty pounds and over for labouring on the farm, not counting the odds and sods he picked up for doing up or fixing motor bikes and scooters.

Mouse loved tatting with things. But he wasn't scared of hard work and he was as strong as an ox. Terry Law, who was a beast of a youth, had told me Mouse could match him, lifting anything he could on the farm, and more. He was astonished just how much strength the little fella had. He really shouldn't have been.

Mouse was a real jack-of-all-trades. He'd managed to secure three days a week work on the farm while doing odds and sods elsewhere and Melissa had been at the shop all summer to earn some money in preparation for going to university where she was hoping to read music.

Mouse picked her up in the battered yellow Mark Two Escort he'd somehow managed to get on the road. Mrs Ash was even rustling together a packed lunch for him after he'd let slip to Melissa that he couldn't always find anything suitable at home. Mr and Mrs Ash seemed to be very grateful for the way he took her under his wing.

She had blossomed over the past 18 months or so. She was no longer the ugly duckling with the lazy eye. She'd allowed her chestnut hair to grow long and she had shot up quite quickly and had become as tall as her two sisters.

Melissa announced that she was going to take a gap year before going on to university. The church had arranged for volunteers to go out to Africa to help with projects assisting poor people out there. She would be leaving in September.

Mouse was really quite concerned about it. She was going to Zandalaya wherever that was . . . there were probably cannibals and God knows what dangers there - and slimeball Guy Digby was in the party too.

19

1977 - GOD SAVE THE QUEEN

It could only happen in Britain. You honestly couldn't make it up. It's Her Majesty's Silver Jubilee and the Sex Pistols are No 1 with God Save the Queen. If it had been anywhere else, the government would have had the Pistols arrested, tried and fucking hung before one curled sandwich had been eaten at a street party.

You've got to remember these were times when the integrity of the Royals was only being questioned by Willie Hamilton and a few others. Charles was being primed to be King very shortly. Liz, God bless her, hadn't realised at this point just what a dimwit the guy was. He might have been talking to plants and if he hadn't shagged Camilla yet, he was about to, but we'd still got this notion that he'd been to university. Yeah, okay. He'd probably passed his Cycling Proficiency Test.

Anyway, the Royals were held in high esteem and, as I sit here on this Christmas morning, I'm even swigging my lukewarm cup of coffee from a Jubilee mug. I think its chances of ever appearing on Antiques Roadshow are next to nil. It's one of the millions of cheap souvenirs that have sent the country's tills rattling. We've all sung God Save the Queen and little did we realise back then, that but for her, the entire family would threaten to go into meltdown. It's hardly surprising really when you think about it. Take Charles . . . please, somebody!

The man who would be king. I think the last royal mug I

had was in 1969 when he was invested at Caernarfon and everyone seemed to be saying how handsome he was. Fuck me - are you lot all sure? He might well be the next face on millions of stamps but he's got jug-ears and a permanently dozy expression. But anyway, it seemed like Liz was waving her sword and suggesting one day soon she'd be putting her feet up. I'm still not sure she thinks he's ready, which considering he's knocking a hole in 60 and is her son after all, says about as much about him as you need to know.

What fucks me off more than anything about Charles is the way he rabbits on about rural life and how we should all fight to preserve it. I totally agree, but that doesn't mean I'm going to pay fourteen quid for a jar of his Duchy of Cornwall marmalade. Get real Charles.

And I'll tell you another thing he does which really pisses me off. He calls in at a country pub for a pre-arranged beer and then gives the Press an account of how horrified he is over the decline of the rural inn. Off he goes on about how the fabric of our very society is being undermined by the loss of such valuable institutions as the British pub. So he has half a beer and then fucks off without paying. If they all had customers like him, none of the poor bastards would survive. No one's got the bollocks to pull him up on it and if they did, he'd just shrug his shoulders and say 'I never carry money. Sorry!'

What a fucking excuse. And you just know that if he got his chequebook and settled the tab, the landlord wouldn't cash it because it's worth more just as a signature to put up on the wall and say he'd been in the fucking place. Tell you what Charles, Never Mind the Bollocks could well have been written for you.

The ironic thing about it all is that half the reason country pubs are on their arse is because people can't afford to risk drinking and driving. Our dimwit prince has got the luxury of a driver and still just pops in for half a bitter! He's got the perfect excuse to absolutely go on the lash but prefers to get home to talk to his geraniums. Wouldn't it be great if he popped in a pub and just said to the Press boys 'Right, take your pictures and get them sent off, then let's all get absolutely slaughtered?

The trouble with the Royals is they can't do 'normal' can they? It's not so much that they shouldn't - it's just how often do you see them trying to do something run-of-the-mill and end up making themselves look total twats?

A case in point - what was Charles doing as his mum and dad had their big day and the rest of Britain celebrated? Let me tell you - he was plastered all over the papers on a skateboard. What an absolute and complete tosser. God, they test your patience. Apart from Liz herself, there's not a day's work in the lot of them. I am a staunch supporter of the idea of the Royal Family - it's just the members that are the problem.

Phillip just can't keep his mouth shut. There's a certain comic element to him, mind you. You can just imagine Lizzie preparing for a State visit to China dreading exactly when he's going to put his foot in it. She just knows, like we all do, that the minute he's strayed off for a couple of minutes, he's going to make some reference to slitty eyes or eating dogs. It's brilliant. You just fucking KNOW he's going to do it.

Airmiles Andy just thinks he can shag and play golf every day and use our money to fly by helicopter to do it. Then gets the huff about why we seem to be so grudging? I've never forgiven Anne for being the BBC Sports Personality of the Year for 1973 and as for Edward, well, no more needs to be said. The only sporting thing he ever did was the Royal It's a Knockout fiasco. What a total twat he showed himself up to be. Like I said, they just can't do normal can they? And so Johnny Rotten and his mates were No 1, which, looking back was probably quite apt.

But as The Pistols crashed in, a couple of greats crashed out. It's Never Mind the Bollards for Marc Bolan - he was killed back in August when his Mini crashed into a tree. Quite what he was doing in a Mini still baffles me to this day. Elvis has fallen off the bog and into immortality at just 42.

John, a work colleague at The Gazette, has loaned me his copy of the Pistols album this Christmas and I've been trying to play it when mum and dad are out of earshot.

Mum almost fainted when she saw the cover. This was as far removed as 'For Someone Special' by Ken Dodd than you could ever imagine. If ever I looked in danger of walking out in the street with it, she'd give me that 'are you sure you don't want a bag' kind of mum look.

And though I was there when it all started, I essentially missed the whole punk thing. In the summer of '77 I was just short of my 19th birthday. I'd started work after five years at a grammar school and two years at sixth form college. I wasn't the ideal candidate for sticking a safety pin through my nose. I'd like to think I was also old enough to recognise most of it for the tuneless racket it was. Some of that lot survived, but only those with anything to say. Johnny Rotten came through it with flying colours and then he turned up in the jungle on I'm a Celebrity Get Me Out of Here with Ant and Fucking Dec and well . . . you just become more convinced that perhaps you were right after all.

Perhaps if I'd been an angry young man with no job prospects . . . no future, as Mr Rotten said, it might have been different. But it just wasn't the case and so any hidden frustration at not changing my name to Slasher Distel and gobbing over grannies has to remain hidden. I was kind of middle of the road at 19 and I'm kind of middle of the road now. It's not something you can help and I don't need assistance coping with it. I'm nearly 50 for God's sake. Show me a 50-year-old punk and I'll show you a twat . . . It really is as simple as that.

Rebellious? Putting Space Dust in a can of coke was about as shocking as I got. Then there were government calls to ban that. How did they ever get to know about it in the first place? I reckon an MP's kid must have snitched and spoiled it for everyone. So then their fathers go into the lobbies and try to drum up support for a ban on Space Dust before nipping into the loos and shooting a line of coke. That's democracy for you.

20

1978 - WITHERING HEIGHTS

I've always fancied shagging Kate Bush. It's just the waking up in the middle of the night with her prancing around on the landing in a white nightie that would spook me. I've always had a not-so-soft-spot for Kate but there's just that little something in the background that scares the shit out of me. Perhaps it's that weirdness that appeals to some deep hidden part of me. I can't explain it otherwise. Anyway, I've got her new LP - Lionheart - this Christmas and it's pretty good. There's Kate on the cover, dressed as a lion, looking every bit like she'd claw your fucking head off if you went anywhere near her. What is it with the girl? I mean, even if she doesn't knock your socks off, I think you'd be hard pushed not to describe her as attractive. Personally, I think she's gorgeous but, like I said, I think if you were ever lucky enough to sleep with her, I reckon you'd have to keep one eye open all night, just in case she suddenly went off on one. There is a little something of the night about the girl.

All that wailing and screeching 'It's meeeee Kathie . . . . .' sounds good in Wuthering Heights, but I'm pretty damned sure it'd put you on edge at half-past-four in the morning. Imagine peeping through the crack in the door and seeing her doing all that mystical dancing. Fuck me. The more I think about it, the more I wonder just what I'd say if she dragged me off to her mansion and begged me to stay the night.

'Look, okay Kate, not a problem - but I can't stay because I've got my cat to feed.'

Kate's got me thinking here. How many rich, beautiful women can you name who have that hint of darkness about them. There must be countless, but Whitney Houston, Diana Ross, Naomi Campbell and Britney Spears all spring to mind. Then there's Bjork, who's not so much beautiful but attractive in a child-like way. I mean the Icelandic minx has something but, again, she's made a career out of being fucking crackers. Same thing you see, imagine waking up in the night and she was missing from beside you. Peep around the door . . . there she is crouched on the landing going 'It's oh so quiet . . . shh . . . shh . . .' with her finger up against her pursed lips. How scary would that be? As for Whitney, Diana and Naomi? Well they are good looking birds but you just couldn't take them anywhere for fear of them kicking off.

One thing I'd say for Kate is, she's bright. I'm not sure you'd want Bjork or the others in your pub quiz team but Kate, now she'd have a chance. I reckon she'd be dead hot at that. Perhaps she could even help me do this Rubik's Cube that some sadistic bastard has thought might occupy me over the festive period. Actually, it isn't as difficult as it appears if you can just think laterally. I've worked out that if you carefully peel off the coloured stickers, it wouldn't take long to get all the colours on the right side. Knowing Rubik, which obviously I don't, there'd be one panel stuck on with special glue, so you'd be thwarted before you could get away with such a wicked deception. In my limited experience you tend to find nerds like that, think of fucking everything. And there was a kid on telly this morning, showing how he could do the cube in 10 seconds or something obscene. I swear to God I just felt like bellowing out 'YOU TW-AAAAAT!!!!' I should have done. It would have made me feel much better.

It's definitely been a year for infuriating games. You can't go in a pub these days without the sound of a Space Invaders machine in the background. I just can't get the hang of that either - there's a knack to it and it's not just a question of mental dexterity. There are certain key things to remember like getting the space ship with the 21st shot or whatever to get 300 extra points and all that bollocks. And now some fucking idiot is staging a World Championship and believes it should be classed as an Olympic event. Yeah, all right mate. Dream on.

Things like that just want me to make me tear my hair out. I wonder what Dr David Banner would make of it? He'd chuck the machine a few hundred yards if it came all that nonsense with him. The Incredible Hulk is big news right now and one of the best things on telly. But tell me, please, just where did he get that dusty wig from? It's not one of Elton's old ones is it? Has he been Hoovering or something? I've never seen so much dust. Mind you, you wouldn't want to be the one to point it out would you?

'Hey Banner. Where did you get that dusty fucking wig from?'

'Don't make me angry. You wouldn't like me angry,' he says. What a fucking understatement! Suddenly off pop his shirt buttons and he's ready to go absolutely nuts.

Maybe that bird off Dukes of Hazzard could have a good go. Daisy Duke . . . now she made Saturday tea times a much more pleasurable experience. What a pair of pins she had on her. I'd read somewhere she'd insured them for 20 million dollars. Wow. I bet it was easier to get insurance for those than ever trying to get one for the General Lee the way those two half-wits drove the fucking thing around. Imagine pulling up outside the insurance brokers in that garish orange thing and saying you'd like a fully comprehensive policy. It'd be worth it just to see their faces. They weren't the brightest pair Luke and Bo were they? Mind you Daisy wasn't exactly university material either come to think of it. I don't think she was in it for her intellectual capabilities. It always made me laugh when they referred to her as being 'full of spunk.'   It's an Americanism that just doesn't cross over. Mind you . . .

See, there are a few Americanisms that still don't quite sit comfortably over here. It's like their attitude to therapy. They just see it as the fashionable thing to do - just go see a shrink or admit yourself to a clinic. It doesn't work that way here. We still think it means you're at least half way to going nuts - and quite often we've got it right.

How many movie stars book themselves into rehab for a few weeks and we are kind of indoctrinated to think it's perfectly fine. Look at Britney. What a doll. All that school uniform stuff, suggestive lollipops and 'Oops I did it again.' What's she done again? Broken her lolly? Scuffed her knee? Accidentally knocked her glass of pop over? Nah, she's just cut all her hair off and thrown a bit of a wobbler, that's all. People were saying that husband of hers wasn't the brightest, but I struggle to see that. Our Kev gets to screw the arse off Britney, the world's sexiest pop star at the time, gives her two kids and then gets a massive pay-off! What kind of a job is that? I didn't see that one advertised. I bet the cosmetics firm, which paid her an absolute fortune to launch an expensive new fragrance, were really happy. Great result eh? I bet some executive can't believe his luck that he thought he'd got the No1 role model only to find her stock is about to absolutely plummet. Can you imagine his fucking boss?

'So, how's the new range going?'

'What the Britney one? It started off really hot, but it has slowed down a touch, if I'm perfectly honest.'

'Slowed down a touch! Do you think the bald look has helped us? I mean it would be interesting to know exactly when some of our potential customers thought that perhaps Britney looking like Kojak wasn't someone they wanted to be identified with. Slowed down! May I make a suggestion?'

'Certainly boss.'

'Why don't we rebrand it and call it Coot eh? In the meantime, get the fuck out of my office!'

21

1979 - FOOTPRINTS

"One night a man had a dream. He dreamed he was walking along the beach with the Lord. Across the sky flashed scenes from his life.

For each scene he noticed two sets of footprints in the sand. One belonged to him and one to the Lord.

When the last scene of his life flashed before him, he looked back at the footprints in the sand. He noticed that many times along the path of his life there was only one set of footprints. He also noticed that it always happened at the saddest and very lowest points of his life.

This really bothered him and he questioned the Lord about it. 'Lord, you said that once I decided to follow you, you'd walk with me all the way. But I have noticed that during the most troublesome times in my life - and times of great upheaval - there is only one set of footprints.

'I just don't understand that at the times when I most needed you, you weren't there.'

'My precious child' the Lord replied, I love you and would never leave you. During your times of trial and suffering when you needed me most, there IS only one set of footprints there but don't you understand why?'

'No Lord, please explain.'

'That my child was when I was carrying you.'

'It's lovely Mouse, really lovely.'

'Isn't it just one of the nicest messages you've ever read?'

136

'Yeah mate. Very thoughtful.' Cards were cards to me, but Melissa's card had clearly been a source of great comfort to Mouse. At just 55, Geordie Ratcliffe had gulped one lungful too many of that deadly black coalface air and had died three days ago. Mouse was devastated, not least because he'd been the one who'd taken him the cup of tea in the morning and found him there. A choking blanket of disbelief and sadness had smothered the entire family. Mouse was beside himself. He seemed to have taken it worse than anyone. It had hit him really hard. Finding his dad there like that had clearly traumatised him.

'He just looked so peaceful. Like he was no longer struggling,' Mouse repeated himself.

'I know, it's hard to explain, but he looked almost like a child. Kind of at peace. It was strange seeing him like that. I always remember my old man being such a strong sod. He was such a powerful bloke . . . but he just looked kind of vulnerable, I guess.'

Mouse's mum took Melissa's card from him and placed it back carefully on the brown veined tiled mantelpiece.

'Thoughtful girl,' she said nodding. 'Shame she can't get to the funeral, but it was very thoughtful of her that.'

Melissa Ash was breaking up her university studies to go back to Africa again and had been to see Mouse personally to express her sympathy. He was really disappointed that she was going back to Africa even if it was only for three months this time. What with her studying at Winchester, it seemed like she was now of another place. She didn't get home that much these days as it was. Only something of this magnitude could have put that to the back of his mind. Even then it was never far from his thoughts. She'd kept in touch periodically from college and promised to drop him a line when she got out there. But if the last time was anything to go by, by the time it arrived through the letterbox, she'd be back.

Mouse shuffled through the kitchen and out towards the

scullery, motioning me to follow him.

'Just need a breath of fresh air,' he said as he stood out by the small patch of lawn and leaned against the washing post.

'Remember when dad made that trolley?' he said pointing in the direction of the shed.

'Yeah. Great that was wasn't it?'

'Fantastic. Don't know if I've ever had anything as good as that.'

'That was the big thing about your dad though.'

'What's that?' Mouse asked, merely seeking confirmation of what he knew I was going to say.

'Well. He was just so fucking good with his hands and his . . . imagination. He always seemed to come up with some really cool things, didn't he?'

'He certainly did . . .' Mouse smiled, taking comfort from the observation.

'We might not have had a lot of money in this house, but mum and dad always managed to come up with something special for each of us.'

'True enough mate.'

'Tis true enough. He'd always battled against the odds my old man. He'd struggled with his chest for absolutely ages. I can't remember a time when he didn't have a real cough to be honest.'

'Yeah . . .' I nodded.

'But you know what, he was a wise chap. 'Ian,' he'd say to me. 'Remember one thing it's not the dog in the fight - it's the fight in the dog.' He used to say that to me . . . and it's true you know. He fought his corner and never gave a toss.'

I'd never heard Mouse say that before. It was an unbelievably profound statement and explained an awful lot about the inner steel of the Ratcliffe family. I had never come across anyone with the spirit and resolve of Mouse. He could be an awkward cuss at times, but when the chips were down, boy, I'd back him against almost anyone. I could honestly say

138

that I'd never seen him deliberately go out looking for trouble but if it came his way, he was, to use his dad's analogy, an absolute terrier. And not just in a physical way. He was a far deeper thinker than people gave him credit for. He was always stashing away little titbits of information and storing them away for future use. Mouse was my mate and maybe I was biased, but he was quite a remarkable thinker at times and certainly no one's fool

But this had floored the family. Geordie's baccy tin and lighter were still on the Formica coffee table as if he'd just popped out for 10 minutes. He was all around the place from the floor to the nicotine-stained ceiling, but Geordie wouldn't be coming back.

Melissa said a prayer for Mouse and the family and then made her way to the village centre where she had agreed to help out at the ramshackle building that doubled up as a school.

Chabra was the main town in the Cheeka Province that sat just 100 miles west of Lake Zanda. Melissa fell in love with the place almost straight away. She knew people back home struggled to believe her when she told them just how beautiful it was. Just because it was one of the poorest countries in the entire world, she knew everyone imagined it to be some kind of dust-blown hellhole, but nothing could have been further from the truth. But Zandalaya did have some really serious problems and, for that reason, was a place where many missionaries and relief workers made their way.

Melissa smiled, recalling how Mouse had teased her about being careful not to find herself in a big cooking pot. He was funny. She could almost hear him.

'Hey, Melissa. There's this cannibal and his mate eating their tea and the one says 'I'm not sure I like your wife.' And so the other one says 'Just eat the chips then!'

That was typical Mouse. Melissa hoped he was all right but for now she'd got enough on her plate trying to help the local people who had been brought to their knees by drought again.

Zandalaya was no different to so many other regions in many parts of Southern Africa. It wasn't so much a lack of rain or intense heat - it was too much or too little of each at the crucial harvest times.

It was inevitably one thing or the other. The maize crop was the most important single harvest to the rural poor in Zandalaya. Too much rain and the maize rots; yet too little at the critical flowering stage and the crop is wiped out.

Zandalaya was actually a water-rich country with the magnificent Lake Zanda spanning almost a third of its total mass. Measuring over 300 miles long and 45 miles across, the stunning fresh water lake was one of the biggest in the whole of Africa and so big it had mile upon mile of sandy beaches.

But for all that, one of the key problem areas was irrigation. That would be a solution for so many of the curses which befell this lovely land, yet with only one per cent of arable land enjoying any form of irrigation, it wasn't difficult to pinpoint why food supplies often dried up completely.

There were other problems ripping away at the very infrastructure of this fragile land. Thousands of refugees from the war in Mozambique had settled in the south and never returned. Aids was taking a terrible toll too, leaving many farmers too sick to work often leaving others with less time to work the land because of the need to look after sick relatives. River blindness was another thing threatening to rip the heart out of the community. The irony of that awful disease was that it only struck in the really fertile areas of land close to fast-flowing rivers. They were the breeding grounds for the black fly, which infected so many people and subjected them to a lingering condition, which meant their eyesight disappearing over a 10-15year period. It was a destroyer of families and communities, which often had to flee prime land to get away from the deadly invaders. There was always a problem of some sort it seemed.

But Melissa loved being around the place and among the people. Her alabaster pale complexion and her soft dark hair fascinated them. And they marvelled at her coming so far to try and help them. They were truly grateful and their gratitude made her realise more than ever than there was more to life than muddling around Linshaw. Melissa was in no doubt that God had called her there and could already see a time when she might not return home.

22

1980 - REVOLVER

John Lennon is dead. Unbelievable. Some Billy No Mates loser has gate-crashed The Beatles story and taken the life of one of popular music's true greats. I have a problem with that. What right has Mark Fucking Chapman to be part of the story? None - absolutely fucking none. It's plain wicked. It's a nonsense. I just hope he doesn't get to keep that autograph Lennon signed for him. Seriously - where the fuck did that end up? Did Chapman hide it away and plans to sell it as his retirement nest egg when he eventually comes out of jail? Is it in the New York Police Department files somewhere? It has to be one of the most valuable pieces of Black Museum memorabilia around. What price that signature? To think that Lennon signed it outside the Dakota building for the man who was to kill him just minutes later. It's astonishing. I wonder if he signed it 'Best Wishes.' It's surreal. As Lennon himself would say . . . imagine . . .

'Hi John.'

'Hi man.'

'Could you sign this for me please?'

'Sure man.'

'Thanks.'

'Anything on it?'

'*Best wishes* would be good.'

'Okay.'

'Would you mind dating it - oh yeah, and the time would be handy.'

'You what?'

BANG.

And with one senseless, cruel click of a trigger, Mark Chapman's name will go down in history. It's obscene and not because I think Lennon was the saviour of the world or anything so extreme. I don't think everything he did was brilliant. But he certainly earned his place in history unlike the toerag who cut his life short. I'm just embarrassed for the whole of mankind that I even know Mark Chapman's name or what he looks like because he's nothing but an inconsequential wanker.

Lennon wrote some great stuff but he did come out with some shite as well. All that bed and hair nonsense. But he was his own man and he was undoubtedly one of the all-time greats. Chapman has no right to be in that story. There's something distinctly uncomfortable about the whole process.

There are countless examples where people just going about their own unspectacular lives get caught up in a bigger story through no fault of their own. And their name or the name of the place where they live is forever stained. How many poor sods called Ian Huntley or Harold Shipman have been going about their ordinary lives troubling no one and suddenly find their name has become so problematical that they feel the need to dash off and change it? It must be an absolute nightmare being asked your name for the most innocuous of reasons and then waiting for the surprised look to come. Waiting for the quick double take as you say, 'That's right. Sutcliffe . . . Peter Sutcliffe' and then watching them run for cover.

There must be dozens of clean-living Peter Sutcliffes who flatly refuse to pay by cheque in B&Q if they go in to buy a hammer or a set of screwdrivers.

It's the same with places. Time was not that long ago when you could say you came from Hungerford, Soham or Lockerbie and no one would bat an eyelid. Now everyone's heard of them - and for all the wrong reasons.

And so, thanks to Mark Chapman, the main image this Christmas is of the ex-Beatle playing that white piano with his pig-ugly missus floating around the place.

It's been a funny old year for shootings. Up to this unthinkable turn of events the whole of the supposedly civilised world had been wrapped up in trying to guess who shot JR. Yeah Larry Hagman as JR Ewing had become the most famous shooting victim in Dallas since John F Kennedy. There's been a right old frenzy about it and the bookies took millions on the outcome. Can you believe it? Fuck me, if the guy who wrote it didn't lump stacks on, he wants shooting.

The big drawback is that now every politician both sides of the Atlantic is banging on about what they intend doing about gun crime. Psychologists are crawling out of the woodwork to tell us that it's because boys are programmed from an early age to believe that playing with guns is okay. I just don't get it. I played with guns and I've never had the slightest urge to shoot anyone. Guy Digby had the biggest, meanest gun around all those years ago and he hasn't gone around killing people. It's ridiculous.

It's a pretty bleak Christmas all round, what with one thing and another. I've had a major bollocking from work - and I mean major. Everyone in the office is talking about it and I'm the unfortunate one who missed the mistake so I'm left carrying the can. It was an unforgivable error really and even though I suspect deliberate sabotage by someone at the paper, it's still no excuse.

The whole sorry episode had actually kicked off the Friday before when the first article appeared in the Gazette. It had escaped my notice - which was the whole point really - but not for long. Hearing the editor groan 'God's fucking teeth,' seconds after clearly grovelling to someone on the phone, was a sure indication someone was for the high jump. How could I have known it was to be me?

We had carried a full-page feature on Colonel Hugo Beaufort-Smythe, the High Sheriff of Shropshire and revered war hero, who was turning on the Christmas lights in town this year.

The feature spread to a full page with a couple of pictures taken of him at his country spread. There was one picture of him standing in front of shelves full of books in what appeared to be his very own private library or study, medals adorning his chest and another of his standing at the entrance to a massive grand room with three huge chandeliers as the central feature.

'Fuck, fuck, fuck, fuck, fuck!' The tirade was all the more shocking because Peter McGregor was not renowned for swearing at all. Clearly something was very, very wrong. We all looked at each other like rivals in a game of Russian roulette wondering where the gun barrel would stop clicking. Bang!

'Who proof-read page 11 with the feature on Colonel Beaufort-Smythe?'

Oh, fuck, that was me.

'Errm, me Peter.'

'Fucking hell Sant. We've made the most enormous cock-up. He's raging and with good reason. Fortunately I think I've managed to convince him that they were genuine mistakes and we'll carry a proper apology next week.'

'Mistakes? Plural. What's the problem.'

'Well, in fairness to the old duffer, he quite saw the funny side of the picture caption. He had quite a laugh about that. But considering he's fought in virtually every fucking battle this country has had this century, it's the mistake in the copy which has got steam coming out his ears.'

The dozen or so editorial staff who were in rustled their way to page 11 to see the offending article. Very quickly it became apparent, just what the problem was. Under the picture with the chandeliers, the caption read:

THE GLENAVON ROOM - where Colonel Beaufort-Smythe holds his balls and dances.

'Oh no,' was the collective gasp.

'Hey, listen, that's not the fucking problem believe me. He had the good grace to laugh that one off; it's THIS . . . he's doing his nut about. Peter folded the paper inside out and pointed to the start of the paragraph quite high up the article which started:

'But there's more than enough daily duties around Ragford Hall to ensure this battle-scared veteran keeps busy.'

'Battle SCARED! Battle fucking scared? Jesus Christ, this guy has got more medals than Lord Mountbatten and we've described him as battle fucking SCARED!'

'I'm so sorry,' was all I could think to say.

'Well it's done now and there's nothing we can do about it this week. Next week's edition yeah? I've agreed to give the Colonel a front-page apology.'

'Christ, front page? Don't you think that's emphasising that it was our mistake a bit?'

'It was our fucking mistake and I've got the most-decorated man in the county not so much wanting to dance with my balls, but to fucking well cut them off. Get it sorted.'

'Okay boss,' I said eager to appear suitably remorseful. Ah well, at least the old twat had settled for an apology rather than issuing a writ for libel. That was to come just over a week later.

'No, no, no, no, no fucking NO!' Peter McGregor came storming out of his office with a face like a smacked arse.

'If one of you fucking lot is trying to put me out of a job, you might just have fucking well done it this time. Who did the front page last night?'

'Right, I want whoever saw that page off and whoever

wrote the fucking apology for Beaufort-Smythe to get their arses into my office - NOW!'

Oh Jesus, what in heaven's name could he be complaining about now? That's the trouble with the landed gentry, you give them an inch and they want to take a yard. He's got himself a front page apology - something that would not have been afforded the common man. It's obviously not prominent enough for him or perhaps he wanted it with a gold border around it. Fiona Nesbitt got up and made her way towards Peter's office, closely followed by Joey Johnson the poor cub reporter who had landed the job of penning a suitable apology to appease the Colonel.

'And if you say to me it's just one fucking letter that's gone astray, I won't be responsible for what I might do!' Peter yelled as he followed young Joey in.

I picked up the paper found the apology to the Colonel and started to read.

'Oh fuck,' said one.

'Oh no . . .' said another.

'Ugh!' said another.

I don't want to sound terrible but I was just glad this one wasn't my mistake. I'd had enough of a bad time about last week's error. At least this one had nowt to do with me. Under a small non-descript COLONEL FEATURE heading you find on apologies, you would have sworn it had been done deliberately. It was bad. It was very fucking bad.

'In last week's Gazette we inadvertently referred to the honourable Colonel Hugo Beaufort-Smythe as battle-scared when as we are sure all our readers would have realised this should have read bottle-scarred. We apologise for any confusion that may have arisen.'

Confusion. There was no shortage of that when the aggrieved old duffer stormed into front reception demanding to see the editor. If it hadn't been for the fact that he's 84, I swear to God he would have punched his lights out. Peter tried vainly to convince him it was a genuine error and that he would afford him the rarely offered gesture of another front page apology. The Colonel was having none of it.

An out of court settlement of ten thousand pounds, an apology and the editor's dismissal was the eventual outcome.

And because I'd been in some way responsible, this particular Christmas had a strange muted feel about it.

It shouldn't have done - Mouse and Melissa had surprised everyone by announcing their engagement. Everyone knew they were seeing each other whenever they could these days, but her trips to Africa combined with studies meant they had often been forced to conduct their relationship at a distance.

Clearly things had accelerated far faster than anyone could have possibly assumed. They were absolutely wrapped up in each other and their happiness was etched on their faces. They were to marry next year. Lord knows what Mr and Mrs Ash thought about it all. They'd always been really fond of Mouse, there was no getting away from that, but as a son-in-law? Who knew? There were no indications of any discontent to be fair and the scheduled date of July 29 had to be switched to a week later because of a certain Royal Wedding taking place that day.

23

1981 - CREASE IS THE WORD

I wonder if Charles and Di had cheese and pineapples and Black Forest gateau at their reception? I don't think so somehow. But I'll tell you what, for all their vast resources of money and staff, they couldn't have had as lovely a time as we had at Mouse and Melissa's big bash. It was fantastic - right from the word go. And not a crumpled dress to be seen anywhere. Just exactly what was that creased, slept-in fucking nightmare? Not Princess Margaret - Di's dress. Imagine being told you had been given the honour of making one of THE dresses of all time and coming up with that monstrosity. People were too scared to say anything for fear of being out of touch but it looked like she'd rolled around in it the night before.

Mouse and Melissa on the other hand were seamless. Two people destined to be together forever. It was as stunningly simple as that.

Mouse and a few of us met up at The Farmers for a quick drink before the ceremony as arranged.

As best man, I ordered the first round and enquired as to whether he fancied something a little stronger just to settle his nerves.

'Brandy?'

'Nah, I'll have a coke.'

'Coke!'

'Yeah. That's all - just a small glass.'

'Fucking hell son, you're getting wed in a couple of hours

149

-aren't you nervous?' Foz said.

'Nope.'

'Not even a little bit.'

'Nope - can't wait.'

'Thought you'd be all over the place,' said Marty.

'Why would I?' Mouse said, a hint of irritation peeping through.

'Well, you know, getting married and all that. It's not something to be taken lightly. Most blokes are nervous wrecks.'

Mouse looked ready to give one of his famed Mouse glances, but seemed to think better of it. He smiled broadly and pointed gently at Marty.

'Listen. I ain't most blokes. I'm going to that church absolutely in no doubt about what I'm doing. The only thing I'm nervous about is that she'll have second thoughts about marrying a little twonk like me and call it all off.'

'Hey, good on yer mate,' said Foz.

'So why would I be nervous? I can't believe she's marrying me. I'm in a daze and have been from the minute she said yes. You know something? I can't even believe I ever had the guts to ask her.'

'Three cheers for the Mouseman!' Marty bellowed.

'There's only one thing I wish I could change about this whole day. And that's dad. I wish he could be here. When he saw that girl of mine coming down the aisle, his heart would have been as a big as a bucket. I'd change that, all right. But he'll be there with me - I know that.'

Foz raised his glass aloft. 'To Geordie.'

'To Geordie,' the shout went up.

I patted Mouse on the shoulder, impressed but not in the least bit surprised by his impromptu speech.

'Hey, and thanks for being best man Sant, just in case I forget to thank you later.'

'Thanks? You don't have to thank me, mate. It's an honour.

Thank you.'

It was a strange one really. I kind of felt I was losing a bit of Mouse but in a nice way. I knew how deeply he felt about Melissa and that he was going to be very happy but we'd been together a long time. It was a new era for everyone. Shortly nothing would be the same. Perhaps that's the way it is meant to be.

Melissa looked radiant. How good was this girl? She'd made all the dresses, hers in shimmering white and the four bridesmaids' -in lavender - with just a little help from her sisters. The Emmanuels should have taken note.

Mrs Ash, friends and relatives had slaved away for ages completing all the catering and somehow managed to get it to the community centre via a fleet of cars and several repeat journeys.

The spread was superb and Mr Ash, who was by now really letting down his hair, had made a truly wonderful speech.

Everyone wondered what he was going to say when he started going on about 'There is one thing I just cannot forgive Ian for . . .'

It was strange hearing Mouse referred to us as Ian throughout the ceremony, but calling him Mouse would have been just a teeny bit inappropriate.

Mr Ash was unequivocal in his praise for Mouse and said he was honestly the proudest and most pleased man in the world because he knew in his heart that his daughter had truly found her soul mate.

'There is one thing however, that I cannot find it in my heart to forgive Ian for . . . introducing my lovely daughter to Spam sandwiches. Spam with cheese, Spam with Branston, you name it. But that apart, I can't think of anyone who I would rather see my youngest daughter choose to spend her life with. He truly is a quite remarkable young man.'

I swear to God Mouse was close to tears. I know I was. Mr

Ash had got it spot on. These two were absolutely made for each other. They just were. What more needs to be said?

My attachment to Christine was more delicately balanced. We'd been seeing each other for 12 months on and off after I met her at work. It wasn't so much that she was my soul mate as she had huge tits.

Christine worked in the advertising department after moving to the area from Kent. I'd first been attracted to her by the size of her breasts. Call me shallow, but they were magnificent by anyone's standards. She was quite diminutive in stature and slim, but she had a habit of wearing skin-tight tops that fully showed off her two biggest assets. It wasn't until years later that I'd come to realise they were two of only a handful of good points. The decision to move in together had come about almost as a convenience thing and, looking back, was destined never to last.

With that decision having been made, we'd seen a neat semi-detached house we both liked just a mile outside Linshaw in a tiny cluster of houses known as The Meadows. Now that we were within weeks of completing the purchase, telling mum that I was planning to live in sin was something I could put off no longer. I just knew she wouldn't be happy. Crikey getting a girl pregnant had just about topped it but mentioning that I planned to live in sin would be another searing disappointment to her.

Mum just couldn't get her head around the idea at all. She just couldn't come to terms with the notion that her beloved son would even contemplate *'living in sin.'* It might have been 1981, but enlightened times these were not. Plenty of people were doing it, but that didn't mean it would meet with any sort of approval from the likes of my mum.

It just wasn't part of her life-plan. In mum's great scheme

152

of things there was a big hat, a lovely reception following a pretty church wedding and dad in his cuff links - the whole shooting match. To just move in with someone - and have sex with them - just wasn't something she ever quite accepted.

I'd always known it wouldn't be easy to broach the subject, so I ended up just kind of blurting it out one day at a completely unplanned mid-point between the Sunday tea-time salmon sandwiches and the tinned fruit cocktail. I mean, what was I thinking of? And on the Sabbath too. Not that my mum was vaguely religious, I hasten to add. Had she known it was coming, we'd have been lucky to be offered a slice of frozen Arctic Roll. This was serious stuff and not something to be trifled with. The fact my normally meek-and-mild mum would even consider offering a contrary opinion about any such private arrangement, underlined just how dimly she viewed it.

It wasn't that she disliked Christine even if she did feel she showed off far too much cleavage, and a little too often for her liking. I blame mum for my fascination with that - it's that rabbit jelly mould thing as a kid. It must be the wobble factor.

So, mum placed the trifle dishes down on the table, deliberately trying to be seen to not bang them down and remain calm about the situation.

'I just didn't think you were the type to do that - that's all.'

'Do what exactly?'

'Well, live in sin,' she said firmly, astonished that I couldn't see exactly where she was coming from on the subject.

'And anyway, what do you mean *'type?'*'

'That type.'

'I don't get you. I just don't get what that's supposed to mean. But get it off your chest because I'd rather you say what you really mean,' I said nobly.

Actually, I really didn't want to hear what she had to say on the matter, but it was the best I could come up with.

'Oh, call me old-fashioned but it's not what I expected from you at all. You hardly know each other really.'

153

I got the distinct impression that I could have told her I'd been arrested for flashing and she'd have been a lot more understanding. This wasn't going down well at all.

'Listen mum, I know this isn't going to get your approval but it makes a lot of sense and, anyway, that living in sin stuff, really is a bit outdated.'

'It never happened in my day, if that's what you mean. Mind you, teenage girls getting pregnant wasn't commonplace either.'

Gulp! 'Times have changed.'

'And not for the better. No one bothers anymore. Everything is too much trouble.'

'No one bothers about two people living together mum. You're right - no one bothers about that.'

'I bother' mum said indignantly.

'Well, yes you do, but no one else does.'

'Well, do what you want, you usually do. It just won't get my blessing. Sometimes you disappoint me John. I don't ask much, but I feel like you don't take the family's feelings into consideration. Times might have changed but you needn't expect me to be happy about this and that's all I'm saying on the subject.'

Not getting mum's blessing was like having the Pope wag a stern finger at you. I wouldn't have minded but she only went to Church for christenings, weddings and funerals. The only time she'd been independently to that, to my knowledge, was back in 1969 when Songs of Praise came to Linshaw. St Mary's was packed to the rafters that day. But that apart and the fact that she always put a few coins in the Christian Aid and Oxfam envelopes which came through the door, she hadn't been ordained to do blessings. What bothered her more than anything was what Mary at No 26, or Isabelle at No 54 thought about it.

It was almost as if we couldn't afford to get married, so we'd gone for the cheap option. It was all that nonsense rolled into one - and more. Mum wasn't happy - end of story. Then she played her trump card.

'Well Ian and Melissa did it the right way.'

'They're different.'

'How are they different? You were inseparable you two. What's so different about him? Don't get me wrong, but he hasn't had quite as nice an upbringing as you. And he didn't go to the grammar school either.'

Fucking hell. Mouse's sanctification was all the more incredible taking those facts into consideration. How had he managed it?

This didn't rest comfortably with her. I wondered what Suzie would have made of it. I'd stopped giving it too much thought now. I felt strangely out of all that. That didn't lessen the fact that I still felt a deep resentment at not even being told the outcome. Our child would be six now. It just wasn't right.

24

1982 - SOCKET TO ME

There's one thing you can bank on - the minute you start setting up home, your Christmas presents get as boring as hell. They seem to take on a completely new life of their own.

Hence, I am now the proud owner of a drill, a Black and Decker Workmate and a socket set. If you're not handy these are the kind of things from hell that people buy for you, with the best of intentions, in the hope that you will suddenly become useful. It doesn't work. Show me a lad who takes to a hacksaw straight away and I'll show you a man who will be interested in DIY for life. To my mind, if you don't get it straight away, you've had it. I just glaze over now. I can honestly say that whenever I've had call to use a hacksaw the blade has been broken well within two minutes. It's something you can either do or you can't. If someone starts spouting about a rawl plug with a butterfly back to grip the wall, I'm away. I just float into another land, while my companions compare notes on different grades of sandpaper.

Tools and stuff are a bit like shoes you have bought for you as a kid. They get them a bit bigger so you can grow into them and by the time you have they've fallen apart. Go in my shed and you'll find more hacksaws without blades, hammers without handles and screwdrivers covered in paint, because they've been used as stirrers. It's unbelievable. And handy people just don't get it do they? If they are good enough to come around to do a job for you they usually punctuate every other sentence with a 'Have you got a?'

156

I feel like saying 'Of course I fucking well haven't. Why would I ask you around to come and help me out with this that or the other if I'd got the tools to do it myself?' Useful people are a pain in the arse until you need them.

The thing with tools - proper tools - is how often would a dimwit like me need to use it, if I could do the job in the first place? One? Try never. So what is the point in me buying, say for example, a torque wrench, when I haven't got the faintest idea what to do with it? I might as well buy myself eyeliner. Hands up, I've got a sneaky regard for people who are handy, but I think you either take to that sort of stuff or not.

The nearest I got to being handy was when I subscribed to a weekly magazine series called The Knack which showed you some really crap things to do. Things like how to remove a chimney breast, dealing with damaged gullies, building brickwork arches and the like. Great things but when I had to ask someone how to get the darned magazines in the special binder, I knew it was time to call it a day.

And half the time I not only don't have what they are asking for, but I don't even know what the thing looks like anyway. It's nonsense. So, anyway, onto my presents. First, a socket set. What the fuck are they for? Seriously. You might as well have given me a Scandinavian phrase book for the amount of use I'm going to get out of that. Tools and accessories really disarm me. There are certain things that I just can't use. It's like drill bits. They're a source of constant bewilderment to me. I will quite happily try to drill a hole in a wall with a woodwork bit if necessary. And I'll look bemused when it snaps off and nearly takes me eye out. I will use the hammer attachment to put a hole in a piece of chipboard and go bananas at the resultant devastation. And, just for good measure, I won't know where the chuck key is for the darned thing because I'm not handy enough to know that you should keep it in a handy place. I hate drills. I hate them in the hands of dentists and I hate them in the hands of dickheads like me.

And so, that leaves the Black and Decker Workmate, which I must admit I've found quite handy for standing on. That's when I've managed to get it on its feet. I've had more blood blisters and trapped fingers trying to get the fucker open, than anything. Many a time I could have tossed it across the lawn had it not been attached to my shirt or trouser leg. The little plastic grippers for holding wood have long since been lost.

It's like those metal-framed gun things you are supposed to load up with a tube of bathroom sealant. How exactly do they work then? What about mitre boxes? Wow. I almost had a nervous breakdown trying to cut some coving with one of those bastards. And never trust a man who even owns a pair of mole grips. You have to have a certain kind of mind to master the art of using those. To me anything named after a stupid blind animal which spends its time living underground eating worms and fucking up golf courses, has to be suspect.

This Christmas is going to be a mixed one for all the families with relatives in the armed forces. The Falklands War has been the one big talking point all year and, needless to say, while most of our lads and lasses will be coming home - if not for Christmas, then soon - some won't be coming back. It's all so bizarre. It wasn't that long ago that hardly anyone knew where The Falklands were. I honestly believe if you'd taken a straw poll in the streets, for every 100 asked, maybe a couple could have told you.

It was all so surreal from the very first minute and I don't think it was until HMS Sheffield was hit that everyone woke up with a jolt and thought 'Fuck me, this is a proper scrap.' Up to that point, we'd all assumed it would sort of go away and then, suddenly, it kicked off and everyone began to learn new places and terms like San Carlos, Goose Green and Exocet.

Until then, most of us assumed The Falklands were perhaps near The Orkneys or The Isle of Wight. When I first heard the Argentinians had invaded them I thought I'd heard it wrong. Argentinians? British islands? Were they on holiday and just didn't want to go back? Penguins? Was there a zoo there or something? Why are we thinking about sending battleships to get rid of them? Couldn't we just send Keith Chegwin? He'd have them fleeing in no time. But it all turns out to be Maggie Thatcher's finest hour as we send a taskforce thousands and thousands of miles to give the Argies a bloody nose. This was colonial Britain at its very best.

There was a big fuss about a headline in The Sun that screamed 'GOTCHA!' above the story of how we had managed to sink The Belgrano. It must have been about that time then that the PC loonies started to take over. I don't get it. You are at war with a country and you sink one of their vessels, why not put GOTCHA up as the fucking headline? All the prissy do-gooders point out that 1200 servicemen lost their lives and it's not appropriate. What is appropriate? You tell me. For once, we didn't go out looking for a scrap. The Argies started it and we finished it. It was our way of getting one in before Diego Maradona stuck his fucking nose in and floored us with the Hand of God? He cheated us out of the World Cup and we just sit back and say that's kind of okay. But the headlines back in Buenos Aires was all about how God had come to their aid and given us marauding Brits a right kick in the bollocks. How irreverent a term is that? But he seemed to get away with it for some strange reason.

We do ourselves down sometimes. The fucking Germans want to change the EU constitution from one vote per country to a system reflecting the population of any given nation. Big surprise there. With 82 million people that would mean them effectively ruling Europe just like they tried to when Hitler was around. Cheeky bastards. It's like the Polish minister said, their population would have been millions more than it was now if it hadn't been for the war.

25

1983 - TOMATO RELISH

It's getting worse - I'm now the reluctant owner of a greenhouse heater. You just never think these things will happen to you. In the spring I took charge of a greenhouse and it's been mainly downhill from there. Here's a piece of advice - if you really want to feel the full economic and culinary benefits of one of the darned things then move next door to someone who has one. Make sure you compliment them on the wonderful appearance of the courgettes or tomatoes and you will be quids in. People with greenhouses give you stuff. It's just one of those things you get to know. It's a double-edged thing, because it makes them appear, and feel, generous, plus it's a fantastically subtle way of showing off. If you own the fucking thing, it ends up costing you a fortune and at the end of the day, how many tomatoes can two people eat? You have to buy growbags, plus special food for the fussy sods. Then you have to protect them from too much direct sunlight and frost and all kinds of bollocks. You can get little collars to put on them too stop some grub climbing the stalk and getting his fangs into them. Then all the fruits of your labour tend to come at the same time, so you end up letting it rot or giving it away. The real people who benefit from the darned things are neighbours and friends. They end up getting half a dozen tomatoes and a lettuce for bugger all and you end up paying a fortune for the things. It's a ridiculously strange phenomenon you only tune into once you have joined the greenhouse set. And once you have, the days of going to Tescos and just

160

buying a handful have gone. Now you deal in units of three dozen minimum. You want a lettuce? Here, have ten before they go off. People start to avoid you for fear of having to take yet more tomatoes off your hands.

It's barely exaggerating the point to suggest greenhouse keepers assume the mantle of deranged drug pushers.

'Here try some of these,' you say.

Once that house of glass is up, you're knackered. Before long, you'll be trying your hand at growing marrows, courgettes, cucumbers, the fucking lot. Next step - pricking out seedlings. Suddenly you'll be making a point of listening to weather forecasts in case there's a frost on its way. And so now, I've been given a paraffin heater to make sure my little babies stay warm. I have become a lost cause. I've already invested in some bubble wrap, I keep old newspapers and the benefits of a cardboard box can't be over-emphasised. You end up buying books and all manner of strange bits of equipment. And then you discover, horror of horrors that your cucumbers are bitter because there's been an outbreak of same-sex propagation going on that no one warned you about. Bitter? I'm furious. Fucking hell, I've got homosexual cucumbers and no one told me! If anyone had told me a couple of years ago that I'd be even contemplating the merits of analysing male and female flower heads and carefully transferring pollen with a camel hair brush I'd have had them certified. Now, it's me one step away from the men in white coats. I swear I'll be dragged off to some institution screaming: 'You've got it all wrong - it's the gay cucumbers wot did it!'

A dark world beckons - men in grubby caps, putting you right on the legions of mysterious insects that can ruin your summer. They are all around you; they're even in the soil, the bastards. There's no escape. If you successfully traverse that minefield, the next step is Chutney World. You'll have that much stuff that the only way to deal with it is to make chutney. Jar upon jar of tomato chutney or piccalilli. I've never had the desire to eat tomato chutney before, so why should I start now? Marrows? Who do you know who eats marrows? I'm going to eat my marrow because it has cost me thirteen fucking quid - that's who. You'll be in the pub and someone will slip you a recipe on a crinkled piece of brown paper. You are officially a member of that secret society of greenhouse owners. Let's cut to the chase here. I had possibly 30 tomatoes this year and they have probably weighed in at three quid a fucking tomato.

Once you've got to the stage of nigh on being a vegetable, you're sucked into the bedding plant syndrome. You'll have hanging baskets and liners galore any day now. And just wait until you start writing out your own labels to stick in the several thousand bedding plants you're now responsible for. Discovering whether you need potting compost No 3 or No 5 and how much grit to put in gradually starts to be an obsession. You become suicidal.

There's an easy solution. Don't get a fucking greenhouse. It really is that simple - trust me. I guarantee, if you have a neighbour or a bloke in the pub with a greenhouse, you can get yourself sorted. Just drop your Little Gem into the conversation and you'll be inundated with produce in no time.

Just say 'There's nothing quite like the taste of tomatoes fresh from the greenhouse,' and they're smitten. They will adopt you.

If you have any allotments near you, stroll past on a Sunday morning and compliment the guy in the cap on his broccoli and you'll get some. Ask what potatoes he thinks are best for the type of soil and he won't be able to resist giving you some.

As for plants, well, it's a remarkable concept, but you just go to a garden centre and buy a whole tray of the fucking things for a couple of quid. Even better, they'll make hanging baskets for you and give you a bracket if you're lucky.

Be warned - if you can't wait for the day when you get into

a greenhouse, as sure as night follows day, you'll never be out of it before long.

Glass houses and stones are never far away from each other when you work for a newspaper and though the most recent spate of errors weren't anywhere near as dramatic as the sorry episode with the Colonel, the Gazette's location in Duke Street had lent itself to a rather clever play on words.

More than a reasonable amount of mistakes were getting through. Sid Thompson, the editor appointed to replace Peter, the man slain in his duel with the Colonel, called a meeting on the editorial floor and addressed his troops.

'Listen in please,' he said, shirt sleeves rolled up and an edgy, exasperated tone to his voice.

'I'll keep this brief. But as I'm sure some of you are aware, the twats on the Star have apparently had a big sign made up which points this way and says 'The Hazards of Duke Street.'

He continued: 'Very funny, but sadly there's a ring of truth about it that should concern us. There are a lot of errors creeping through which border on criminal. I trust no-one is deliberately turning a blind eye to these literals, but believe me, if they are, then pack it in because it's ceasing to be funny. I know some might seem amusing, but they are making us a fucking laughing stock.'

Sid didn't need to repeat some of the most infamous cock-ups that had somehow managed to creep into the Gazette in all their glory.

We'd carried a front-page piece on a pilot who had escaped certain death by *ejaculating* from his stricken jet.

Then a few weeks ago we'd had an absolute nightmare when an advertising feature was married up on the light tables with just a couple of single columns of editorial. That one was a really unfortunate series of events, but the bottom line is that someone should have spotted it. What happened was, in time-honoured fashion, the editor is given a dummy copy of the coming week's paper with pages and columns crossed out because they are to be filled with adverts. Things change, to everyone's annoyance, but on this particular occasion page 46 had seven of its nine columns marked to be left blank for an advertising feature, leaving two awkward thin columns to be filled by editorial. Sid decided with few options left open to him, that he'd fill the end two columns with obituaries.

Little did he know that the blank space was to be filled with a gardening feature and so right next to the obituaries with small single column pictures of some of the deceased was a 72pt headline which screamed 'NOW IS THE TIME TO GET DUG IN.' Furious relatives jammed the phone lines demanding a more sensitive send-off.

So clearly Sid had got a bee in his bonnet about something that had slipped through this week, and yet again, the selfish side of you kicks in and you just pray it's not something that can be traced back to you. Newspapers can be a little self-preservation society when it suits.

Sid continued: 'Like I said, I know these things can be seen as amusing and really good topics for a laugh down the pub, but it's leaving us open to all sorts of stick and it's not going unnoticed by the proprietor.'

Most of us nodded our support as he broke off briefly, before hitting us with the latest bombshell.

'Anyway, I won't be pointing this particular gaff out to him and I just hope no one else does or my head could be on the chopping block,' Sid said tossing a copy of the paper down with a big black ring marked around the offending article. It was a record review on our rather crappy showbiz type page. I had to muffle any desire to laugh.

Someone had clearly enjoyed the album, but how could you fail to from a group called Kid Creole and the Cococunts!

26

1984 - BIG BOTHER

It's 1984 and George Orwell was warning us about the perils of Big Brother. Bear in mind this was long before Jade Goody and Co burst onto the scene. It's Big Brother this or Big Brother that, thanks to George. Everyone in the country is fed up to the back teeth of Big Brother references. Did George Orwell really know what he was subjecting us to when he came up with 1984 as a title for his book? For the whole 12 months it's been like every story on the telly or in the papers has had something to do with Big Fucking Brother. It was going to take something colossal to divert Big Brother's watchful eyes . . . then BANG!!

It's New Year's Eve, 1984, and I've really, really enjoyed this Christmas despite Bob Geldof's best efforts to totally fucking ruin it. Every time you turn the telly on there's been footage of pot-bellied kids wailing with hunger and, call me selfish, it does your head in after a while.

Christine, me, Mouse and Melissa are in the Peking Dragon in Shrewsbury and there's not one of us who could force down a single prawn cracker. We've eaten for Britain and I didn't want reminding that millions of people in the Third World are starving to death. There are people out there who would kill for a prawn cracker - which really is the ultimate statement on how serious things are. I can't imagine anybody getting worked up about them. What are they exactly? No one has ever explained them to me. I'm not sure anyone knows. Has a prawn ever been anywhere near the fucking things?

Well, I digress, but right now, my hidden guilt determined that I didn't want Geldof or Bono walking in the restaurant asking me if I'd enjoyed my meal. I was certainly relieved they were playing that ridiculous Chinese music in the background and not 'Drive' by The Cars. I didn't want to put my head in the sand on this, but after a festive season in which I seemed to have attempted to smash the world gorging record, I'd prefer not to have starving kids rammed down my throat.

There was no escaping it. I'd say one thing for Geldof he was fucking persistent. I'd struggled with the last few bits of my mum's delicious Christmas pudding. Every time I saw a shiny, little black currant, I kept seeing flies. The Peking Dragon was packed. There must have been well over 150 people in the place and at every table there seemed to have been mountains of food. I thought we'd got away from the African crisis until Melissa mentioned it.

'Mmm . . . that was lovely, but I don't half feel guilty,' she said.

'Ah, you shouldn't,' I insisted trying to pacify her.

'I don't see how you can't. I've just eaten enough for six people and there are people out there who haven't got a bean.'

'Don't you mean bean sprout?'

'Santa! Come on. I don't want to spoil things, but it doesn't do any harm to realise just how lucky we are at times, don't you think?'

'Yeah, course. But there's only so much you can do, you know.'

'Well, I haven't done anything. Not yet, anyway, but I'm going to,' Melissa continued.

'Well, like what?'

'Oh I don't know. But there's millions of people starving to death out there - you can't keep sitting back hoping it will go away.'

I tried to brighten things up. 'I'm not surprised if they've only got these things to bloody well eat with,' I said, holding a chopstick aloft. I never said the F-word in Melissa's company. She wouldn't have said anything, but I just knew she didn't approve of it and I thought too much of her to cause offence.

'Santa! Honestly.'

'Well, I'll happily give the Chinese credit where it's due, but eating implements are not their strong point. Walls? Bloody brilliant. But eating utensils, I just don't know where they went wrong.'

Melissa giggled, though I knew she found some of my views irritating at times.

I had a point. I dare say the Orientals would argue chopsticks had been around for centuries before the knife and fork came in, but that didn't mean you had to fly in the face of progress. For a nation whose staple diet was rice, chopsticks made absolutely no sense at all. I mean to say, the penny farthing was around long before the motorcar, but I sure as hell knew how I'd like to make a journey of any distance. It was about time they admitted they'd been bettered and gave chopsticks the chop.

'Santa . . . that's a bit of a sweeping generalisation don't you think?'

'Well, not really. Scooping up rice with these things - it's virtually impossible. And another thing, what about these?' I leaned over to get one of their spoons.

'These aren't much better are they? How are you supposed to get these in your mouth? They've got sides like the Great Wall.'

Christine slapped my arm playfully and told me to behave. I just couldn't get these pictures out of my mind of them riding battered old bikes in their millions and pulling each other around in rickshaws (and eating rats) and everyone was telling me they were going to be the next super power. I couldn't honestly see it myself. If they wanted to take over the world the easiest way for them to do it would be to poison the takeaways. We'd be on the back foot before we even knew something sinister was going on.

'It's only because you can't use chopsticks,' Melissa said.

'I admit it. I can't. I find them extremely difficult to use. If I had to eat a meal with chopsticks it would last me a week. The only way I can ever get any food into my mouth with a chopstick is if I stab it.'

'That's because you're a pleb,' Christine interjected.

'I know. But it's just that some foods are ridiculous. I get sick and fed up of the French and the Italians ripping the arse out of British food and treating us like we are culinary idiots when you look at some of their stuff and it's just . . . well, it's just . . . daft.'

'Like what?'

'Well spaghetti for a start off.'

'Ooh, I love pasta,' Melissa cooed.

'Well, so do I. But considering the Italians have a worldwide reputation for being stylish, I struggle with that. I mean you just can't eat the stuff without looking like a three-year-old.'

'You are a silly so-and-so,' said Melissa

'It's true. You whip an Italian's Gucci jacket off and I can guarantee you, he's got Bolognese sauce all over his shirt.'

'Go on then, what about the French?'

'Snails - I rest my case. Oh, and horses while we're at it. And they go on about us. It's bonkers. Germans? Well they eat all sorts of garbage - spicy sausage that resembles your grandad's dick and has been hanging up for years. And they dare criticise our grub. I can't believe it.'

'Sant, if you had your way, the world would live on fish and chips and steak and kidney pie.'

'No, that's not the case, but I'm just sticking up for us because it's like everyone wants to give us a bashing.'

It must have been the wok I'd had for Christmas - the latest in a seemingly never-ending line of those presents you use once and then sling in the back of a cupboard, never to be seen again.

It wasn't even in a box. Christine had wrapped it up for me and gave me that kind of look as if to enquire as if I'd got any idea what it was. How stupid did she think I was? I half expected Rolf to come out from behind the rubber plant and say 'Can you tell what it is yet?'

Barmy. I swear to God I was the only sane person on the planet sometimes.

We paid the bill and the waiter gave each of us a fortune cookie and waited for our eyes to light up. Do I really need to say anymore?

27

1985 - FOOD FOR THOUGHT

Christine has bought me a diver's watch . . . a really handy gift for someone who gets the bends in a paddling pool. It just underlines how little she knows about me really and, anyway, there's not a Christmas present you could have which wouldn't seem rather futile and pointless in the great scheme of things. Bob Geldof has seriously jolted the world - and full credit to him for that. I grew up as a kid to take the piss out of starving kids. It's true. We've all heard the jokes. It was just a question of changing the name of the fucking country as far as I was concerned.

'Now for today's football scores - England 8, Biafra didn't', simply became England 8, Ethiopia didn't and suchlike. I'm ashamed now, but that's the way it was. I grew up in an environment where you just assumed the people of whatever country it was, were too stupid to do anything about the problem themselves. I honestly think no one should ever under-estimate what Geldof did. He totally embarrassed millions of us, told us we were pig ignorant and selfish and then got us to say thank you for doing it. Top man.

I know he didn't do it on his own and the world should thank Midge Ure and the rest who toiled away to get Live Aid on, but he was definitely responsible for giving the world a good shake. And right there was Freddie Mercury - come the moment, come the man. That show took some stealing, but he managed it. How good was he? There he stood in his glory, silhouetted against that Wembley sky. Who would have thought that some of the pot-bellied kids on that video footage would outlive him? It's bizarre, but his memory lives on, if only for that. And there were so many high spots and on one day in history, it was like the world united and became a better place. And giving to charity wasn't somehow wet or for other people. Everyone was doing it. Kids gave up their pocket money and no one thought they were pansies. Men with tattoos and a bull terrier, dug deep and women with tattoos and bull terriers dug deeper still. It was marvellous.

Like I said, there's nothing this Christmas could throw up that would be even halfway worthwhile. Christine had bought me a book by some American guy - one of these how-to-get-rich things. It's called 'I Made a Zillion Dollars In Just One Year' or something similar and, you know what, I doubt I'll ever pick it up. I've got an aversion to books like that and, I think, with good reason.

First, why would anyone who had found the magic formula for making squillions of pounds want to share it with the rest of the world? And if you had genuinely made such vast amounts of money why would you want to take up hundreds of hours toiling away at a book for? It's a barmy notion. It's like those twats who write books about how to write a best-selling novel. They can't have written a bestseller or they wouldn't be trying to make a few quid writing a book telling you how to do it. It's crackers and I refuse to be taken in by it. If they knew the magical formula why would they want to hand it over? It really doesn't make any sense.

Anyway, I know it's going to sound terribly ungrateful and all that but back to my all-action scuba diving, orienteering-type timepiece. I had to make out how chuffed I was when, really, I can't stand the fucking things. For one, I think they look ridiculous. They're so big. You can have forearms like Popeye and it still looks like someone has strapped an alarm clock to your wrist.

To be honest, and I realise it is a sweeping generalisation, but I'm always a bit suspicious of guys who have those big watches. It's like private number plates - you know, that kind of need to make a public declaration of just what type of person you are. I just don't go for watches that can still tell the time at a thousand feet. Believe me, I've drowned long before that point. I don't want a heart monitor, pulse-rate checker, compass or anything that tells me what altitude I'm at. Give me one that can tell you the TV listings and I might go for it. I'm no couch potato but I'm just wary of some of these outdoor pursuit types. Two minutes in their company and I just feel like telling them to 'fuck-off.' They're like missionaries for exercise and can't resist the temptation to convert you. You always get some twat who wants you to give him a fiver because he's going to do the London Marathon. Fair enough, I give in. Then, next degree up, is the person who wants to do six peaks in six days or whatever it is. Worse still, the absolute nutcase who wants to run a marathon, followed by a fifty mile swim, followed by a hundred mile bike ride and then walk up Ben Nevis in a pair of flip-flops. Yeah, okay, fuck off.

They just get on your tits and yet because it's a supposedly healthy pursuit, you're made to feel guilty for knocking it. I hate the lot of them . . . people who drive around in open-top vintage sports cars with silly Biggles caps on and insist on telling you it's the only way to drive. No it fucking well isn't. I once had the misfortune of bumping into a group of about eight classic sports car enthusiasts as I was having a quiet pint in a pub. And they started on me. They put their Biggles helmets on the bar and verbally accosted me for even daring to suggest that it wasn't for me.

'Now I know you're joking,' says MG bore.

'I'm not joking as it happens,' I reply indignantly.

'What? You'd rather drive a Ford Mondeo than my 1938 Piscutati six-cylinder?'

'Well, eleven months of the year, yeah.'

'You're winding me up.'

'Listen, which bit don't you get? The only thing that needs winding up around here is that pile of junk. I'll take your car for about one month a year - when it's sunny - the rest of the time forget it.'

'Oh there's nothing like a bracing drive around country lanes in January.'

'Yes there is. Driving around country lanes in January with the heater on, the radio on, the roof on and with some assurance that the damned thing isn't going to break down.'

They just looked at me like I was mentally deranged. Like, I just didn't get it. And you know what? They were right. I don't fucking well get it. Not one bit. On a lovely sunny day - fantastic. The rest of the time - stick it.

It's like potholers. What kind of a crackpot pursuit is potholing? Don't get me wrong, I can be impressed by a nice cave and a few stalactites but just don't ask me to squeeze through a six inch gap to get there. I like my caves with an ice cream and a tour guide, otherwise forget it. The trouble is these types are a liability yet don't realise it. If ever I got into parliament, I'd just scrap the mountain rescue service altogether. So what if people get stuck up a blizzard-hit mountain in mid-winter and can't get down? Leave them there. Any idiot, who wants to climb a peak armed with a flare and a piece of Kendal Mint Cake, shouldn't expect to be rescued. Climb it if you want, just don't expect me to come and rescue you. I'll be on the sofa with a mug of warm tea and the central heating on full blast. Would I feel guilty or partly responsible? In a word - no.

There's no end to them. There are people who get publicity for trying to cross the Channel in a bathtub. Either do it or drown, that's my take on it. If you want to do it, do it. Just don't expect to be picked up in choppy waters when the fucking thing has tipped up that's all.

Anyway, so now I'm walking around wearing a diver's watch and you know what? It can tell me the time in

Venezuela. Mmmm . . . that could be really handy one day.

Mouse seems suitably unimpressed, but he's been in a distant state of mind for some time really. And so, as we're having our customary drink in the Farmers on Christmas lunchtime, he comes out with it.

'There's got to be more to it than this.'

'Than what?' I asked.

'All this bollocks. Just going from one day to the next, working your arse off and never really getting anywhere kind of much.'

'What's got into you?' I said, concerned by Mouse's rather gloomy air.

'Ah it just makes me wonder, that's all.'

'What?'

'It just seems like we we're leading pointless lives in a way aren't we?'

'Well, speak for yourself Mouse.'

'Na, you know what I mean. There's got to be more to it than this . . .'

'It's that fucker Geldof who has got to you isn't it?' I said somewhat uncharitably. Mouse smiled.

'Well, not just that, but don't you think he's got a point?'

'Well of course he has, but then again he sang about not liking Mondays and I find them okay for the most part. Come on!'

28

1986 - GRIPES OF WRATH

'You Can Make Wine in 21 Days!' It wasn't the exclamation mark that made me wonder whether the author was a guy from Nazareth. I turn inside to find he's actually some saddo from Stoke-on-Trent and the impact dwindled just a touch. The very least I would expect is for the author to come from Chardonnay or Rioja. Are they places? Why can't the Spanish pronounce 'J'? That's always pissed me off ever since we had to change the name of Jif to Cif. Were they bothered that the switch made it sound like some horrid sexually transmitted disease in English? Were they bollocks. It's just another example of having to bow down to other people. Anyway, I digress. Those are the sort of sad remarks you would expect from an amateur winemaker and my only defence is that I dabbled in such a dubious pastime for only a shamefully short amount of time.

Christine has decided it would be a great idea if we, or more to the point I, got kitted out to produce our own Chateau Corblimey. I should have known when I saw an absolute stack of various sized boxes under the Christmas tree, that things couldn't possibly be as exciting as they first appeared. I'm now kind of duty-bound to start experimenting in one of the Devil's pastimes and pretty soon I will be looking at nettles, raisins, parsnips, cowslips, elderberries and dandelions in a completely different light. I was always told that if you picked a dandelion that you wet the bed - not that you made a fucking lethal drink out of it and then pissed the bed. It was my own fault. I happened to express a passing interest in the economics of home winemaking and ended up with enough equipment to sink the QE2.

It's a hobby that can just take over your life. There I was trundling over fields, returning hours later with so many elderberries I was struggling to lift the darned things. It's at moments like that you get to realise why Mouse and me found such an easy outlet for the blackberries we'd picked all those years ago.

The thing was, that when I got home, I hadn't any scales to weigh them. I toyed with the idea of getting on the bathroom scales weighing myself and then weighing myself carrying two buckets, but it just seemed so inexact.

Then I had a brainwave. I emptied a bag of sugar into a saucepan and carefully poured the berries into the bag. With each one coming in at more or less two pounds, I'd soon have the job done. Stupid? Yeah, I know it appears that way with hindsight, but it made sense at the time. Hey, cut the tittering. I'm 28, I went to grammar school, so I'm not thick you know. Okay, it was a thick idea, but the principle seemed okay at the time. Why can't people just leave idiots alone? I'd got to the point of wondering whether I could patent the idea before Mouse interrupted and started going on about a pound of feathers and a pound of metal. That was when he wasn't pissing himself laughing. And my multi-function watch was no use at all.

Anyway, there was no way back. The point of no return had long since been passed. I had too much stuff and equally as much enthusiasm to bin the fucking lot right now. This was the world of settled people. People who'd rather spend the evening painstakingly sterilising bottles than popping out for a pint. This was the world of cosy domestic bliss, where you sat out on the patio and sampled the delights of last year's vintage dandelion. This was respectable - poisoning your friends with a particularly venomous Parsnip and Beetroot was considered quite acceptable.

'You Can Make Wine in 21 Days!' The title had drawn me in. In just three weeks, we'd be drinking the fruits of my labour and I couldn't wait. In no time, friends would be calling in on the off chance that I would offer them the best my cellar had to offer. And all for two bob a bottle. It was an opportunity not to be missed.

I'd got demi-johns, sterilising solution, fermentation buckets, a bottlebrush, filters, a hydrometer, funnels, labels with pretty countryside scenes and a corking tool. I was ready to go.

God it fucking gets to you! I was rushing to the floor of the airing cupboard every time I came in to see if there was the slightest sign of life. I lived in fear of the dreaded vinegar fly.

Experts informed me that the longer you kept your wine, the better it got. Bollocks to that. If I could have just given guests a long straw and a demi-john that would have been fine by me.

My enthusiasm for the pastime died more quickly than my appalling Ribena-coloured concoctions. It's such an arse-achingly lot of bother to get bottle-upon-bottle of cheap booze when you can just nip down the supermarket and get a belter for three quid.

I ended up selling all my equipment in the local newspaper as a job lot. And so the excursion into cheap wine making had probably ended up costing me fifteen quid a bottle or something equally ridiculous. I wouldn't mind if I was keen on wine, but I still don't really know the first thing about it.

I guess it's just something you have to go through. I comforted myself that most people had gone through that stage at some time in their lives. I remember even my old man making bins full of Tom Caxton beer and triumphantly announcing that his wonderful brew came in at around four pence a pint. Then he threw up everywhere one night and mum went mad so that was the beginning of the end of that.

When he spilt some on the coffee table and it took the varnish off, it signalled the rapid decline of his days as a master brewer.

I've started doing things my dad did all those years ago that I thought were a total waste of fucking time. And you know what? I was right. In some cases you should be able to put a young head on old shoulders.

I remember my dad absolutely crippling himself on a blazing hot summer's day digging out a hole for a garden pond. Jesus . . . he had blisters the size of paint lids.

'What the hell you doing dad?'

'Digging out a shape for our new pond.'

'What we want one of them for?'

'Because they're nice. They're restful.'

'Don't look very restful to me' said the awkward and naive 16-year-old me.

'No pain, no gain. These things don't just come overnight you know. I know you think things just appear . . .'

Oh, oh, time to go before I get the *'a little help wouldn't go amiss'* bollocks.

'And, I'll tell you something else smart arse . . .'

I know dad, believe me I know. A little help wouldn't go amiss. Needless to say I fucked off sharpish before dad had hauled himself up from the hole to even try for a bit of hired help. Vamoosh . . . I was out of there. Dad could barely walk for a week. He couldn't do anything as strenuous as open a coffee jar. Did I learn? What do you think?

I've got a pond liner just waiting for a hole. I'll make little ledges for the marginals, make sure I've got loads of oxygenators and most probably go and splash out on a pump.

Boy, I'll have forked out a fortune before I've even got to the fish. I'll probably get a garden pond fish book telling me of the best ways to stock it and who knows? I might even get a plastic heron to ward off unwelcome visitors. What did you say? Exactly. What the fuck happened to me?

29

1987 - UPWARDLY MOBILE

The office mobile phone went off and every single person in the bar at The Farmer's Arms looked around as if some strange alien being had walked through the door.

'Sorry, sorry . . .' I said holding my hands up apologetically and making my way towards the door.

'Yuppie!' yelled Frankie, who was playing darts at the far end. I smiled.

'You can tell who's making all the money,' Stan hissed sarcastically. It was Christmas Eve lunchtime and reluctantly I was still taking phone calls. Did it ever stop? The brick-sized Motorola phone was a cause of constant amusement wherever I went these days. But, unfortunately I was on call and that's why I had the one which was a kind of 'pool' phone for our section at work. They were quite handy though and they had me wondering if they were to be the next big thing.

'Don't you find those things a bit of a nuisance?' Mouse asked.

'Well, there's two ways of looking at it. Yeah, they go off when you could perhaps do without it, but they keep you ahead of the game as well.'

'They ought to for the price. What d'ya say that thing cost?'

'Just over two grand, I think.'

'Fuck me. Your office must have more money than sense.'

'Depends which way you look at it.'

'Two grand - that's the way I look at it. Stick 10p in a pay phone and be done with it.'

'That's okay if you want to sit by a pay phone all day.'

'Well you've got your home phone.'

'Yeah, but I'm not there,' I pointed out.

'Yeah, but Christine is and she could give them the number of this place and it would save all that nonsense.'

'Nonsense?' I replied indignantly.

'Well, I know what you're saying but, unless everyone has got one, there's not much point really.'

'Well, everyone will have them one day I would imagine.'

'I'm sure you're right,' said Mouse

'You'd better believe it, mate.'

'What? Two grand? I can't see too many people lugging one of those things around in their arse pocket.'

'They'll get smaller.'

'Yeah but . . .'

'And, they'll come down in price.'

'You could well be right?'

'I know so - it has to happen.'

'Oh, it's perfectly possible.'

'No doubt about it,' I said firmly.

'They'd need to get a hell of a lot cheaper though. A hell of a lot . . .'

'They will. The time will come when everybody will have one of these things,' I said, holding the brick with the bayonet-type aerial aloft.

'And they'll be the size of a credit card. You wait and see. They are the future. If anybody wanted to make a ton of money that's the business to be in.'

'Why don't you do it then?' Mouse said

'Someone will come along and make fortunes no doubt.'

'Well, why don't you beat them to it?' Mouse asked.

'Cos' I don't really know anything about mobile phones for a start off.'

'Well, what do you need to know? You'd only be selling them, not making the darned things. Might be worth a shot."

'I think they'll be massive in the not-too-distant future. You think about it.' I raised my finger as if about to deliver my most telling point.

'Right. When we were kids, who had a phone in their house? Hardly anyone.'

'True enough,' Mouse agreed.

'Okay, so a few houses start having them in - hey, and they weren't cheap back then either.'

'Yeah.'

'Well, okay it's taken a few years, but now everyone has the phone in. It's progress. If you'd have said to someone twenty years ago that virtually every house in Britain would have a phone in, they'd have thought you were crackers.'

'You're right,' Mouse was forced to agree.

'And that's the way it is. And now they have all those people buying all those phones and spending hours on the phone chalking up call charges, talking total bloody nonsense for the most part,' I continued.

'Mmmm.'

'So if you think that they are not going to take off, think again. There's absolutely no way, if you think about it, that they can't take off. A bookie would say it was a racing certainty.'

'Mmm, interesting,' Mouse agreed.

'It's natural progression. Forget phones. Take TVs. Take anything you want. You name it - stereos, radios. You just look . . .' I was getting excited.

'I get the principle. But they are beyond the pocket of the man in the street.'

'Right,' I said indignantly. 'How much do you think a TV cost when they first came out? A bloody fortune, yeah? And what's more they were the size of a double-decker bus.'

'Yeah, true.'

'Radios. Stereos. The ordinary man couldn't afford them at first and they were fucking massive. Not now. They're so common place you don't even think about them.'

'Good point.'

'Remember when we were kids and Guy Digby had the first colour telly for miles around.'

'God, yeah.'

'Same thing. Colour TV - big deal. Now, if you haven't got a colour TV you're living in the dark ages. I'm telling you, phones are the big deal of the future - and it won't be long either.'

'How come you're not into them then?' A telling question, if ever I heard one.

'Tell the truth, I would, it's just time. I'm so busy, I haven't the time or I might.'

'You have to make time. Give your job up and have a go at it.'

'I'm not that adventurous Mouse.'

'Well, don't live to regret it, that's all I'll say.'

'It's just the expense of the bloody things. But once they've come down in size and they're cheaper, then I think everyone will be having them,' I said.

'And it'll be too late then,' Mouse said instinctively.

'It's the early bird that catches the worm. I know it's an old saying, but business is full of people who sat back and waited for someone else to give it a go.'

Mouse had this habit of making you feel almost boring. It was fine for him, he'd always flown by the seat of his pants. He bought this and sold that and had now ended up with quite a big shop selling second-hand stuff called Second Chance.

'I never saw myself as a phone entrepreneur,' I smiled.

'I'll bet a lot of rich men never imagined having so much money they didn't know what to do with it. But some just had the guts to follow their instincts,' he said.

'You make it sound so easy.'

'It's not supposed to be easy. If it was easy, everyone would be doing it. It's like when people hear the phone go off

182

and immediately say 'Yuppie.' Fair enough. But think about it. Why do yuppies have them? Because they are making money - that's why. One call at the right time, and you're talking big money. So a couple of grand for a phone is peanuts to those guys. Like you said, once they get cheaper, everyone will have them.'

'I don't see how they can't take off to be honest."

'They'll be fucking giving them away, trust me,' Mouse grinned.

'Well, I know what you mean.'

'In the future, you'll get a mobile free with a packet of cornflakes.'

'Yeah!'

'You wait and see. Your old Aunt Mabel will have one. Nearly everyone in the country will have one. It's hard to believe, I know, but . . . you just wait.'

'Well, that's over 50 million people Mouse.'

'I know! There's a lot of money to be made out there.'

'And you want to give them away!'

'Hey, Sant, time'll come when you won't be able to give them away. Believe me.'

And I did believe him. There would be those who were to question my judgement. It would be no use me telling them about Mouse's impressive track record - making money from selling the Yo-Yo biscuits when the school tuck shop had to shut down for a month, the blackberries and the Christmas logs. I had every faith in his ability to recognise an opportunity. He did it all the time, but this was the first instance where I'd seriously thought of perhaps putting my bollocks on the line

'Why don't you do it then?' he said. 'You should go for it.'

'Yeah but I've got a job and everything. I wouldn't have the time,' I said typically unadventurously.

'Well, you'll have to give it up. I can help with some of the financial backing to get you started if you want - provided

183

there's a good interest fee of course! You'll need to be out there on the road, at the sharp end. I'm too busy to help out with that.'

At the sharp end - I liked the sound of that. It sounded dangerous. If I'd known just how sharp it might get, I would have resisted the suggestion.

'I'll think about that you know.'

'You should. All you need is some get up and go and you're halfway home. I think you'd be on a winner. Get yourself a decent name - a really good one that gives the impression you are bigger than you really are. Off you go.'

'Phones Unlimited?' I said.

'Na, you need something more memorable than that.'

'Like what?' I said a shade indignantly. I was the newspaper man after all.

What about Fonez, with an 'F' and 'Z' - something like that. The Fonez Factory! How about that?'

I liked it, I had to admit. The Fonez Factory. Yeah, it sounded good.

'It's got a nice ring to it,' I chuckled.

'Exactly. The Fonez Factory?'

'I'll give it some thought,' I said.

'Hey, and if you want to use the shop as a business address to make it seem more official, feel free.'

'Thanks Mouse,' I said. He'd changed his shop address to International House, to give it an authoritative feel.

'Take a tip from me Sant. Either do it or don't do it. He who hesitates . . .'

'I can't just do it like that though. I need to think about it.'

'There's nothing wrong with thinking it through. But it's the first rule of business, to be in there first. You wait about until everyone realises it's a cert and you'll be dead in the water. It's all about being first.'

'I'll see if I can put some cash aside and start up in a few months.'

'It'll give me time to put my notice in and stuff,' I said.

'Exactly.' Mouse said raising his glass.

'A toast - to the Fonez Factory.'

I raised my glass along with my hopes and contemplated the adventure I hoped would launch me on the way to my fortune.

Christine was suitably underwhelmed. In fact, she was fucking furious.

'You've what!'

'It's a great idea. I'm gonna call it the Fonez Factory. This could be our big break.'

'Our big break? Ours! Are you off your head? Do you seriously think people are going to suddenly be walking around, with a large brick attached to the side of their heads and pay a couple of grand for the privilege? You are stark raving bonkers. You want your head examining.'

'Think about it carefully.'

'Oh I have. You want to remortgage the house in the name of some hair-brained bloody idea. And where exactly will this factory be?'

'Well, for a start off, Mouse has agreed to let me use his business address.'

'Business? It's a bloody bombsite! It's a junk shop for God's sake.'

'It's just a business address until things take off.'

'You are unbelievable. I've heard of some stupid ideas, but this takes the biscuit.'

'This could be the making of us Chris. Trust me.'

'Don't talk about us in this. I don't want anything to do with it.'

'Oh come on. Where's your sense of adventure.'

'It's got lost somewhere in that scrap yard your mate wants

to pass off as a business. That should really impress business people when they come to see your international headquarters.'

'It'll only be for a while.'

'Why don't you call it the FONZ Factory and be done with it.'

'Heeeey. Cool,' I said holding my arms out, thumbs raised Henry Winkler-style, in a bid to lighten the proceedings.

'No it's not cool. It's very uncool actually,' she raged.

'Fonz was the coolest man on the planet.'

'No he wasn't actually. He was a 30-year-old wanker in a leather bomber jacket. He was a twat. More to the point, he was a twat who never grew up. I think it would be very appropriate.'

I clearly wasn't going to win her over on this one.

30

1988 - CUT OFF

My decision to go into business was the final straw. In phone terms I'd been cut off. I wasn't even engaged. Nor was I likely to be now. It was just too much for Christine and on July 4 she finally decided to walk out on me. It's not that I'm big on dates normally, but on the day you were handed back your independence, it seemed wholly appropriate. Everything had got to her, she said. Not least my efforts to sell the 12 mobile phones I had bought. Mouse had helped with some of the cash and I'd given up my steady job at the newspaper. It was all too big a strain on Christine, who ventured to suggest that maybe I had lost my marbles after all. The early indications are that she was right. I was struggling to sell the darned things and right now, Christmas was looking bleak.

Had it not been for Mouse's bit of help - and his insistence I was on to a sure-fire winner - I'd have been tempted to jack it all in. He remained positive that if I could get in at ground level and get a foothold in a burgeoning market, I'd be quids in. Right now it was more a case of quids out. I was working night and day to try and get rid of the darned things. Eight months I'd been at it and I had managed to shift four. Mouse drove me on even when I could see very little light. The bank was getting impatient.

Banks really can be your worst fucking nightmare and they were threatening to pull the plug just when I needed them behind me most. They steadfastly refused to extend my overdraft limit and were bouncing the odd cheque here and there as if to fire me a warning shot. The minute they pulled out of a single mortgage payment that would be me finished. I was facing up to the fact that I was within days of going to the wall.

'Stay positive,' Mouse said with a grin. 'No pain, no gain.'

It would have been easy to give in and if I'm honest, but for his relentless optimism, I probably would have thrown my hand in. This Christmas might well rank as one of my worst. But for Mouse, propping me up with a small 'wage' to help me out, the wheels would have come off. Suddenly, steady employment in the newspaper office, seemed 24-carat luxury. All this flying by the seat of your pants, was okay for people who didn't mind messing their pants occasionally. Otherwise, it certainly wasn't for the faint-hearted. Mouse exuded that gritty, over-the-trenches kind of mentality, which you just had to admire. That is, unless, it was one of his plans that was putting you on the breadline.

'Stick with it. Trust me.'

I did trust Mouse - it was just my bank manager who didn't. I'd been loaned the thick end of 15 fucking grand largely using the arguments that Mouse had put forward in The Farmers last Christmas lunchtime. That could prove to be the most life-changing couple of pints I'd ever had, one way or another. Mouse had put in some more. The only way I could get discount on the phone units from Motorola was to buy in quantity. I'd taken a dozen with the promise of more. They wanted us to take 50, I agreed to take 25 top whack, but in stages. Each phone was £1,300 with a sell-on value of almost double. We'd recouped in the region of £10,000 and things weren't looking great when I took a call that helped turn things around a bit. It was Boxing Day and the caller was almost apologetic. He needn't have been. James was a guy I'd spoken to in London in the summer. He was a well-to-do stockbroker and was interested in making an order.

'Twenty? Absolutely not a problem,' I assured him

resisting the temptation to head butt the lampshade.

'Cash deal? Absolutely. If you're talking cash, I'll knock them out for you at a special price. Call them two grand apiece. I can't say fairer than that.'

The deal was agreed. Forty thousand cash. I was up and running. From this moment on, it would be up, up and away. Fonz Factory indeed. I wondered if the day would come when Christine might regret kissing me and the Fonez Factory goodbye.

At last I had something to tell Mouse, never mind the bank manager who had become increasingly frustrated at his fruitless attempts to get hold of me. He argued that if I was in the mobile phones business, it shouldn't be difficult to get hold of me, but I didn't want to hear what he'd got to say. He never had anything positive for me these days. Just warning after warning and increasingly stressful conversations about the spiralling rate of bank charges. It was a nightmare. At least this order would keep my head above water until well into the New Year. It would have been a good time to cut and run. I could get out now and clear everything off. I'd get a job easily enough, but Mouse insisted I stay strong.

'Keep your nerve when everyone around you is losing theirs,' he said with a bar room philosophy that I found easier to go along with in principle than in practice.

'See this cash as the way to get fresh stock,' he said.

'It's all right for you. I'm less than skint right now,' I said.

'You have to make sacrifices. No one said it would be easy. Every rich man has had to go to the wire.'

'This next year is the crucial one,' he assured me. 'If you can ride it out, get more stock and get a couple of lucky breaks you'll be up and running. The rest will be lagging behind.'

The only break the bank manager had been contemplating thus far was a clean one - somewhere between the base of my skull and my shoulders. I'm not sure if he'd have the resolve to run with this adventure too much longer.

'Ah fuck him,' Mouse said dismissively. 'That's why he's the manager of a poxy little district bank. Tell him to have faith.'

I ended up getting the stock regardless. I whooped jubilantly when the call came with more orders. A company associated with James' firm wanted fifty. Fifty fucking phones! It was a hundred grand's worth of business and with each passing day it became clear that I might now be getting into something bigger than I had ever imagined.

Mouse and me went down The Farmers for our pre-Christmas lunch couple of pints with a sense of jubilation. I hadn't made much profit yet, but the signs were good. I'd paid him back his investment with interest and repaid the few hundred he'd stuck my way just to keep the wolves form the door. Even the bank manager was keeping off my case for now.

'I'll tell you something Sant. Just stick with this now and I think you might be surprised.'

'I know where you are coming from but . . .'

'There's no buts about it Sant. You waited an age for that first call from James. Now that's bought in another couple of bits of business. Now you just wait and see.'

'Yeah, but you can only wait so long Mouse. I'm just about breaking even and then any money I get is ploughed back into the next lot of stock.'

'That's business,' Mouse assured me.

'Yeah, but isn't the idea to make money?'

'You're making money. You just can't see it yet. You've got capital now. Anyone who wants to move into this business, won't have the cash unless they are really big players.'

'Oh Christ don't say that.' The last thing I wanted to hear was about *big players* coming in.

'You are building a name for yourself. At the same time you are acquiring contacts and learning the trade. Also, you are getting a foothold in the market. With a little bit of a tail wind behind you, I reckon you'll be well in profit this time next year.'

'Next year! I fucking hope so, Mouse. I really do hope so.'

'Hold your nerve now. Keep the faith - you'll be okay.'

Mouse raised his glass and tipped it against mine.

'The Fonez Factory.'

I remembered what Christine had said about Henry Winkler. Perhaps I was just a sad dreamer minus the leather bomber jacket. But something about this did still feel quite cool - NOW. I'd do as Mouse said, hold my nerve and give it 12 more months.

I need this to work for more than just me. I needed it to be a success if only to stick two fingers up at the schoolmasters who thought I'd never do anything much. I needed it to work so that one day maybe I could say to Suzie's dad that I did have it in me to make something of my life. And now I needed it in me to show Christine she should have had more faith.

Fonz Factory indeed. . .

31

1989 - LOAD OF BANKERS

You know something? You owe a bank two hundred quid and they have no hesitation letting you know it's *your* problem. Why not try owing them two hundred thousand - suddenly it becomes *their* problem.

They only like to back winners - and only when they are winning. In the meantime, it's like observing an institutionalised Robin Hood, robbing the poor and handing it out to the rich. The reason for venting my spleen? Well, it's a Christmas gift I have just received.

I've had a Christmas card and a beautiful leather-bound diary - from my bank manager! Can you fucking well believe it? He should have just signed it 'Turncoat Twat' and I would have known what he meant - there wouldn't have been any need for the bank's logo.

This has been one hell of a year for Fonez Factory and me and everything is moving so fast it's unbelievable. With every passing day, my view on the financial institutions gets dimmer and dimmer until a black hole appears in front of my eyes. What an absolute bunch of tosspots.

My bank manger is now falling over himself to lend me lots of money. And the reason for his generosity? Because I'm showing all the signs of having pots and pots of it myself. I've just opened my fourth shop, which is way ahead of schedule, but mobile phones are suddenly booming. They are getting smaller and smaller as my bank account gets bigger and bigger. Signals are getting better by the day and all the signals are that they are starting to get very popular.

I remember Mouse saying that one day everyone would have one and while that outcome is some way distant, you can see this business is heading that way. They started being the sole preserve of so-called yuppies, but they've smashed down the boundaries far beyond such an elite market now. Who knows, time may come when every four or five-year-old will have one? Don't laugh, it could happen. Then I'll start doing them in Barbie designs with attractive girlie pink luminous cases and maybe camouflage ones or something similar for the boys.

It's all going absolutely crazy and I'm almost having to curb just how fast I build for fear of it all crashing around my ears. I've got staff in the shops, and sales reps doing great business around the country, and early in the New Year I'm going to have an advertising campaign in some of the national papers. I wonder what my former colleagues on The Gazette will make of that?

I haven't any real trappings of minor success yet because I haven't had the time. I'm still driving around in a Ford Sierra with 86,000 miles on the clock. That kind of stuff isn't a priority right now. I've got a real affection for this car. It has stuck by me through times when the last thing I needed was for it to break down on me. I couldn't afford to have it repaired and drove it on pretty threadbare tyres for months. It's ironic really because the bank manager is almost insisting that I buy a brand new one and offset it against my tax for the year. Now money is coming in, people who should know are almost demanding I get a brand new motor. I will do, but it pisses me off a bit. Getting rid of this 1.6L Sierra will be like losing a close mate. I'd slept in it a few nights not so long ago when I couldn't afford to stop over anywhere. Motorway service stations are just great to have a shave and freshen up in before going on to your destination. More often than not, I'd park her well away from the offices where I was calling for fear of anyone seeing just what I was driving around in. I feel almost guilty about that, but image matters in this type of business. I didn't need any external messages that perhaps I wasn't doing so well. If my little cracker had said 'fuck you, I'm breaking down,' I could hardly have blamed her. It was never anything personal, sweetheart!

Anyway, the upshot is that my bank manager wants a word with me to my convenience rather than a 'get your arse up here' and he'll make sure it's to his convenience. I eventually find time for him - I like that.

'I know you are a very busy man, but have you looked at your accounts recently?'

'Well not that closely, no.'

'Don't you think it would be a good idea?'

'Isn't that what people like you are supposed to do for me?'

'Well, I'm not your accountant John.'

'It just feels like it sometimes!'

'We don't want to go over old ground on that one do we?'

Actually, I felt like telling him, I might do. If I could have been arsed I'd like to shift all my money out and put it in another bank. But they're all as bad as each other. Anyway . .

'You really need to start utilising it better to be honest. You've got a lot of cash, just sitting there and if the business is expanding as rapidly as it appears to be then I'd be happy to set up an appointment with our business expert who I'm sure could point you in the right direction.'

'You gonna charge me?'

'No, no, it's a free service for selected customers.'

'Oh good.'

'Next Tuesday, any good? Ten in the morning?'

'Who will I be seeing?'

'It'll probably be Wayne. He's very good indeed. He's got a degree in Business Studies.'

'Has he ever run a business?'

'Well err . . .'

'Well err . . . no, I take it?'

'He's been at college studying. That's why we employ him.'

'Apologies, I was only kidding. I'll have a word with him. Tuesday you say?'

'Yeah, ten?'

'Done. See you then.'

I reckon if I told them what type of biscuits I liked with my coffee, they'd be there when I turned up. I wasn't like that. I wasn't a vindictive person in that sense. I liked to have a bit of fun with them now. Now I can afford to.

Melissa smiled. She'd seen it coming. They'd only been out here a couple of days and yet she had seen the strain of day-to-day life in England drain out of her husband. She'd never doubted he'd feel perfectly relaxed here and was pleased he now fully appreciated where she was coming from when she'd tried to explain things about the struggle of the Zandalaya people. He'd promised to do everything he could, but a lot of the things that needed doing wouldn't come cheap. The biggest thing wasn't just buying materials, but getting them out to the village because of its remoteness. A proper school would be great but there were a few more things that were far more important. Fresh, running water was the main priority. Mouse told her he was convinced it couldn't be that difficult to get a borehole down to it, if they could just get the equipment there. That might be the stumbling block. Lake Zanda was fresh water for a start. There must be a way of harnessing the torrents that fell on the region in the wet season between December and March. More pertinently, that water must be sitting there underground somewhere and if they could just get a diesel pump borehole down to it, it could transform the village.

Right now, the womenfolk and young girls had to walk a round trip of around five or six miles to get jugs of water from an outlet to the north of the village. Mouse was certain it wouldn't be insurmountable to do something that would transform their lives so dramatically. The school could come later. He was going to see the current building in the morning.

'Is that it?' Mouse said, a horrified expression sweeping his face.

Some of the village children were sitting on the dusty floor under a thatch canopy supported by poles. This was Chabra Village School. Nothing other than slate-type boards and bulky primitive chalk. No desks, no seats, no proper teachers. All the children looked happy and their broad smiles just made Mouse laugh. It was infectious.

'It's not ideal,' Sancha, the village guide, agreed.

'Hardly,' said Mouse.

'One of the main problems is during the rainy season. The very minute it starts, school has to be abandoned because it all leaks through the roof.'

'But doesn't it rain like every day for three months?'

'Something like that - like I said it's not ideal,' Sancha continued.

God there was so much to be done here without even scratching the surface. From what Mouse could see, water was the main problem. So much of it and yet not enough at the crucial time it was really needed. The village just couldn't cope with another failed maize harvest.

'Water, water, everywhere and not a drop to drink,' he mumbled to himself. From what he could see the problems were massive - but they weren't insurmountable. These people needed help and he'd do everything he could.

Mouse hadn't enough time this visit to get too much

196

sorted, but he spoke to Eddie who seemed to be the main spokesman for everyone and promised to try and arrange for some things to be done. It would take money. More money than he had, that was for sure. It would take hard work as well, but he wasn't afraid of that and once he'd got the men of the village organised, he was sure labour wouldn't be a problem.

Mouse couldn't help but admire the resolve of the people in often life-or-death situations. Their small, mud-brick houses were always presentable and they tended their fields with meticulous care, hardly daring to think that their crops could be wiped out.

Some sort of irrigation system was what was really needed. The village also needed some way of holding on to water when it fell. This wasn't a place that didn't see rain for years - quite the opposite. He couldn't get over how green the place was. Zandalaya really was quite breathtaking and he could fully understand why Melissa had been so taken by it.

He promised her he would come back. It was like something was calling him there to help. It was like all those little things his dad had shown him when he was a kid, were coming to some proper use. The village people already seemed to think he was some sort of miracle worker. What would they be like when he came back with things like screws and nails and something resembling proper tools?

32

1990 - OF MOUSE AND MEN

'I wanted you to be the first to know Sant. I've found God,' said Mouse rather matter-of-factly.

'I'm surprised you can find anything in this tip,' I said, surveying the dump that also went under the name of Second Chance. There were sofas, filing cabinets, chairs and tables of all sorts and sizes and he even had a small single-decker bus outside. The headquarters of Fonez Factory had sometime since moved to an impressive building a couple of miles down the road.

Mouse had quite a thriving business going. I wasn't quite sure how he made it all pay, but he did. He always seemed to have cash available for his next venture, but there was a different air about him now.

'I don't think you heard what I said did you?' Mouse pressed the matter.

'Yeah, you've found . . .'

'I've found God, Sant. This is something I've been holding back for a short while now. Just while I made sure I suppose. But I just felt it was only right that you were the first to know.'

'Oh right, that's good of you. You've err . . . what?' I said, suddenly realising the magnitude of it all.

'I've pledged myself to Jesus. It's something that's been ongoing for some time now Sant. I just wanted to make sure that I was absolutely definite about what I was doing.'

'In terms of what?' I asked.

'Well, in terms of my life, my future, the business,

everything really.'

'And?'

'Well, I'm not going to rush into anything, but I can certainly see the business becoming a bit of a stumbling block before too long.'

'In what way?'

'Well, just a hindrance to me and the way I think I'm going to be leading my life. In that way.'

'I'm not with you exactly?'

'S'no big problem Sant. I can just see me winding down on the business side of things and, well not retiring exactly, but putting my time to better use.'

'You're only a bit over 30 Mouse.'

'I know. I can just see a time - pretty shortly too - where I will want to bail out, so it was only right you knew first.'

'But you are making decent money.'

'I guess that's the whole point really. I'd just rather make better use of my time - oh, and the money of course.'

'Meaning?'

'I want to move aside.'

'What are you planning to do then? No one retires for 50 years. It's the other way around Mouse. You work for 50 - then call it a day!'

'Look, if I could get by without the money, I would. But I just need to put enough aside to know that I'll have some to keep Melissa and me fed and watered for a while and I'll take it from there.'

'But none of this would have been possible without you. It seems such a waste, Mouse.'

'Quite the opposite. What I'm doing is a waste. It all seems so pointless. There's an awful lot of things I want to do.'

'Like what?'

'Well, like helping people who have nothing. Stuff like that. I feel like I've been searching for something for a long time now. And I've found it. It's like I need to put my life -

myself - to good use. There just has to be something more worthwhile and I want to explore those sort of things.'

'What - out there you mean?' I said

'Yeah. There's a big world out there Sant. There are a million and one jobs to do and I'm here tatting about with second hand sofas. Making ten quid here, twenty quid there, driving a grotty old van around - always searching for the big deal . . .'

'And . . .'

'Well I think I've found it. I can't explain it. Being there among the people, I just felt like, well a sense of purpose. You know like dad made stuff for me as a kid?'

'Yeah.'

'Well kind of like that. I might not have much money, but I could really make a difference to those people. And they really appreciate it, not like some of the scumbags and chancers around here.

'Thanks!'

'Nah, you know what I mean. It was like the folks out there in Africa really appreciated some of the things I did. And it was nothing really. It was like . . . like I'd been taken there for a reason. It's hard to explain. It was like things suddenly fell into place. I was thousands of miles from home yet, it had called me there. There seemed to be a reason to it. Some sense . . . do you get that?'

'Ermm, well. You're my mate. I'll respect anything you decide to do. But don't rush into anything. That's all I'd say.'

'I appreciate that,' Mouse rested his hand on my shoulder.

I knew Mouse well enough to know he'd have thought it all out for himself. Despite the shock of it all, in a way, I wasn't surprised. He had always been as deep as a pitshaft. I knew him better than anyone bar Melissa and I immediately sensed there would be no turning back. I didn't want him to do it, but that was just being selfish. He was answering a calling that would take him away, but I was powerless to stop him.

'If you've made your mind up then you should go for it. You are too much of a mate for me to stand in your way. That doesn't mean I want you to go pal.'

'Look Sant, I'm not going anywhere this very minute. I've got the shop to get rid off. Wind down the stock and all that sort of stuff.'

Mouse really did mean this. He was talking like he'd be off sooner rather than later. I was losing more than just my best mate and the man who'd been my business mentor. My pal was bailing out. He was off thousands of miles to a place I knew nothing about. I presumed we'd see each other again once he'd gone but who knew?'

'Soft sod,' Mouse said with a smile.

'Well.'

'You'll come out and see us won't you? You'd love it out there.'

'What if you get eaten by a lion? Or one of the locals for that matter?'

Mouse chuckled. 'You've got more chance of getting eaten by one of the locals around here these days.'

'Fair point. Just one thing Sant - promise me.'

'What?'

'You stick with this business of yours now because I can see you making a ton of money very, very soon. Don't sell up to the first smart alec who comes along because they will get all the rewards. Then maybe you can give me a loan! You've sacrificed a lot to get this far.'

'Well. Like what?'

'Well your job . . . Christine . . . you've earned your crack at this. Stick it out. I feel part-way responsible.'

'You are part-way fucking responsible. Yeah, now you're fucking off? Is it something I said? Should I change this deodorant? You would tell me wouldn't you!'

'I'm telling you, you've done the hard work and you're in at the ground level. I'll do you a deal . . .'

'What's that?'

'Right, this is it. Promise me one day, when these phones are bloody everywhere, that you and me will talk. I'll be there in some bloody mud hut and you'll be here in your mansion and we'll talk on Fonez Factory handsets and it'll sound like you're next door. How's that?'

'Deal,' I agreed. I was upset. I don't mind admitting it. I was really fucking upset. I was pleased for him. I was worried at the same time. And I was full of questions on just whether this would all work out. Mouse had always been around. Call me selfish, but things just wouldn't be the same without him here.

'Just one thing Mouse, that's all.'

'What's that?'

'I'd like to help you get started up out there and stuff.'

'Like what?'

'I'd like to give you a helping hand. It's the least I can do. If it hadn't been for you, I wouldn't be in this position now. Things are going really well.'

'You don't have to do that you silly sod.'

'I know. It's because I don't have to that I want to do it. I really respect what you and Melissa are doing. I'm gonna help you build that bloody school, if it's the last thing I do.'

33

1991 - FFATAL ATTRACTION

Just watching the voluptuous blonde directly opposite dribbling oysters down her chin was virtually giving me a hard on. I chivalrously handed her my napkin.

'Oooh thanks,' she giggled, just happy to have halted the trail sufficiently quickly to prevent any chance of it snaking down into her cleavage.

'Don't mention it. They can be tricky. Nice, but tricky,' I said trying to ease her concern.

'Mmmm I love them. Just such messy little so-and-sos if you're not careful.'

Several thoughts whirred through my head - none of them even remotely appropriate. I resisted any attempt to be suggestive and settled for the more subtle approach.

'Have you tried them with horseradish and Tabasco?'

'Never. Are they nice?'

'Gorgeous. Absolutely fantastic,' I assured her, motioning her to take another.

'Do you think I should?' she said with a smile.

'Oh absolutely. By the way, pleased to meet you. My name's John.'

'Ffion,' she nodded back. 'Pleased to meet you too.'

'Ffion? How lovely,' I replied, actually thinking it was just about one of the most snobbish, stupid bloody idiotic names you could ever burden a child with. Why two ffucking ff's?

'Thanks, it's Welsh.'

I decided to drop it and get back to the oysters. Ffion was,

I was guessing, in her early 20s, tall and leggy with immaculate teeth. She had a cute, girly bob cut and noticeable long crimson nails. She didn't appear to wear much make-up at all, the little she had on having been meticulously applied.

'So, what do I do?' she said, jiggling the oyster on the small plate in front of her, awaiting advice.

'Here,' I said taking it from her. 'Do you want the horseradish and Tabasco?'

'Ooh yes please. That sounds rather good.'

'Okey dokey. A little bit of that. Followed by . . . a tiny drop of that. There you go.'

I handed Ffion the oyster, carefully eased clear of the shell and now sitting with a small nest of freshly made horseradish and a couple of drops of Tabasco.

'Oh don't watch me,' she shrieked. 'I'll probably make a right mess.'

'You'll be fine,' I assured her.

Ffion carefully scooped the shell towards her pursed lips and gulped it back in one, blinking her eyes as the sharp tang of the horseradish and sauce hit the back of her throat. She quickly wiped the creases of her mouth to remove any excess and raised a clenched fist in the air triumphantly.

'Good?' I enquired.

'Mmm. Very good,' she nodded.

'They ought to be,' I said.

'I know. They are so expensive. It's ridiculous really,' she agreed.

I wasn't paying. Ffion was one of a group of sixteen at the table in Makai's - arguably the finest seafood restaurant in London. Most of them I assumed were staff at Clintonville's - a communications company I did major business with. Keeping me happy was probably worth around £2m a year to them, so I didn't baulk at the odd complimentary round of golf and hospitality or some fine shellfish and champagne.

Oysters are funny things. Show me a girl who steadfastly

refuses to take a white, salty, oyster down her throat in one swift movement and the chances of her giving you a blow job are seriously slim. It's not just that aphrodisiac thing at all. Eating oysters is virtually a sexual act in itself. Any woman gulping oysters like there's no tomorrow might as well have a t-shirt on saying 'I give great head.'

Champagne is a similar thing. It's not the actual alcohol content that's the decider, though obviously that helps. It's the whole fucking façade with champagne. Personally I can take or leave the stuff but you get in the company of guys buying champagne and you might just as well watch rutting stags clashing antlers.

There's the whole premise that you can afford it for starters. How big is the bottle? How big are my fucking antlers? Then you have the opening and pouring ritual. It's sex in a glass if you think about it. The whole role-play with the stuff is just so pretentious. If you don't like it you are either considered a pleb or a cheapskate who can't afford such an indulgence. As it happens I can, but give me a glass of Chardonnay and I'm sorted. Did I really say that? I did, yeah. Chardonnay eh? In this particular analogy that's the equivalent of long johns, I guess. Ah well.

Where were we? Champagne. Right. Yeah, with bubbly it's the whole shooting match. How expensive is it? What year is it? How big is the bottle? Then what do you do? Give it a bit of a shake and then carefully ease the cork out of the end and all scream in delight as white stuff spurts out and ends up all over the place. Liquid sex.

And, big surprise, Ffion loved champagne too. She was a charming dinner companion, who I discovered was the beautician for the MD's wife who had just come along for the ride, figuratively speaking.

'Oh, I've got a diploma in it,' she said defensively when I enquired just what background she had in doing women's nails.

'I'm sure,' I said eager not to cause offence.

'I've got quite a few certificates for all that kind of stuff, you know . . . nails, lips, make-up, hands. The lot really.'

'That's marvellous,' I said hurriedly.

'You probably think it's really stupid,' Ffion continued.

'Not at all. I have my nails done all the time,' I said with a grin.

'Male manicures are very popular now.'

'Really?'

'Mmm really.'

'I must have them done sometime,' I joked.

'Hey you should. You can tell a lot about a man from his nails you know,' she said motioning for me to stretch my hand across the table.

'Yep. Not too bad. Clean. Not bitten. Good half moons. Pretty good all round. Seven out of ten'

That was me. Clean and unspectacular. I'd always been clean and unspectacular, right from the days when I smelled of Super Matey and Vosene. I'd settle for that. You definitely wouldn't want to be a callous-ridden, warty, nail-chewed one-out-of-ten. A wart might dictate a big fat zero, in fairness. Neither would I particularly want to be a Liberace perfect 10 either. That wasn't becoming of a man, white-collar job or not. Seven. That was fine.

Ffion showed me the watch her brother had bought her for Christmas and I established that there was no boyfriend on the scene. Perhaps she'd like to meet up for lunch one of the days next week?

'You would? Oh great. I'll give you a call - I'm just going to be tied up for a few days.'

'Business or pleasure?'

'Bit of both I guess. I'm buying a house and I've fixed up to see a few. I've had to hold fire a bit because of the Christmas holidays, so that's held me up a bit.'

I helped Ffion out of the crisp December air and into a

waiting cab.

'I'll give you a call then.'

'That'd be great. Look forward to it.'

So would I. She was extremely fit. She was young, vibrant and, I would imagine a touch on the expensive side. Oysters, champagne, the works. What the hell, I could afford it. Live your life John. Have some fun. You can't take it with you.

The genuine buzz of excitement at the thought of taking Ffion out made me realise I'd been developing the business at the expense of everything else. I wasn't lonely. If I was, I didn't like the sound of such a term. But there was no escaping the fact that since splitting up with Christine, I'd just thrown myself into work and associated things even more. It's like I didn't have any time for spur-of-the-moment nights out anymore. And anyway, the bulk of your true mates were happily married or with partners and not always around. Mouse had found God. Why did he always take the easy route! No, I definitely wasn't lonely in the strictest sense of the word, I told myself. How can you be lonely when you are absolutely fucking loaded anyway? I chose to dismiss that one for now. I hate playing the depressed millionaire bit because it just wasn't like that. But the effort and time put into the business in the last couple of years had seriously curtailed my social life. Taking the gorgeous Ffion out just had to be done. She was not only stunning; she was waiting for a call. Wow!

As I slipped back into the restaurant to join the remainder of the party, there was no way I could have known just how expensive that call would eventually work out to be.

34

1992 - TAKING THE PISS

SHOP ASSISTANT: Can I help you?

VIVIAN: I was in here yesterday. You wouldn't wait on me.

SHOP ASSISTANT: Oh?

VIVIAN: You people work on commission, right?

SHOP ASSISTANT: Yeah.

VIVIAN: Big mistake. Big. Huge. I have to go shopping now.

◇◇◇◇◇◇

Isn't Pretty Woman just one of the best films ever? It's Christmas 1990, and it's No 1 at the box office. It's not hard to work out why. And you don't have to be loaded to appreciate the above passage, so wonderfully acted out by Julia Roberts as she goes back into the Beverly Hills designer store that had judged her wholly unsuitable just 24 hours earlier.

We'd all love to have those moments, but invariably just don't get the chance. While I have no immediate desire to dispense with the services of my bank, the fact that they are now sucking up to me in such dramatic fashion, does give you a certain feeling of power. The I-told-you-so card doesn't have to be played. Boy, do they know I told them so. It's lovely when some things don't even need saying. My bank manager has been calling me for ages and I just haven't had time to see him. But I've not answered his calls for a while, just to let him know it wasn't personal when he was chasing me for the opposite reasons. He's worried, it seems, because I now have too much money floating about in my personal account and feels I'd be better off taking some more detailed advice.

Ask a man if he's a millionaire and he says he's not sure and it can mean only one of two things. He's either a bullshitter-extraordinaire or he is. I guessed I might be. Don't you just love that phrase? It occurred to me a few months ago that things were heading that way, but the Fonez Factory has just been so flat-out with work that I have hardly had a minute. How fucking grand is that? You know your problems must be diminishing when the main one you have is to take stock of your situation to see if you've crashed through the million pound barrier. I had in terms of business - by miles. But turning over, say £8m, doesn't mean that leaves a cool seven figures shoved away in your personal account. I had already decided I needed to re-evaluate everything but one thing was for sure - The Fonez Factory was a money making machine. I now had over a thousand staff over 120 shops and an ever-expanding retail and distribution outfit. By April next year it was estimated turnover would have shot past the £10m mark. Ten million? Fucking hell. How could I have foreseen that when I was struggling to sell one of the damned things? I could hardly believe it myself.

Estate agents . . . don't they just take the piss? They are all basically wannabe solicitors. Gerald, as he's asked me to call him is showing me around a house that's on the market for the thick end of half a million quid and he's just pointed out the outside tap which he thinks I'm going to get excited about. You can get an outside tap fitted for probably thirty quid and he's pointing out as if to say 'this house really does have everything!' And, in fairness, it does. Mill House sits in 25 acres of Shropshire countryside, has six bedrooms and is absolutely magnificent. It even has a swimming pool and that's something I'm finding attractive for some strange reason. I never had myself down as a show-off, but I must be. I certainly wouldn't be forking out a small fortune for something I would rarely, if ever use. Funny things, swimming pools. They're a bit like faggots really. I like the thought of them, but they just don't bear up to close scrutiny.

Faggots are one of my all time favourite dishes but I swear to God if I ever saw exactly what went in them, I'd never go within a million miles of one of the fucking things again. And that's my take on pools. Puzzled? Well don't be. There's a definite connection between faggots and swimming pools. My wealth has accumulated at a far more rapid rate than my desire to do 30 lengths every morning. Jesus, I like the occasional dip, but it's not my favourite pastime. I enjoy it to a point, but don't ever toss me overboard even a hundred yards from the shore and lay bets I'd get back. So why would I want a pool? God knows really. It's just something you do when money ceases to become any real object. You soon realise that it's more of a cosmetic acquisition than one you will use every day.

It's like I said, if you knew what went into most pools, you'd be fucking horrified. You wouldn't even put your foot in one, let alone expose every orifice of your body to the frightening ingredients of the average holiday swimming pool.

Just imagine right, that you were sitting on your sun lounger and some lunatic stood on the end of the diving board and proceeded to piss in the pool from a great height. No one would even contemplate going near the thing let alone swim in it. Right, let's push this particular example to the enth degree. So, a guy gets on the diving board and announces that he's going to have a piss in it. He quickly follows this up with an address to a horrified audience that he's got some additional stuff that he's going to tip in just for good measure.

'So ladies and gentlemen, I beg your attention. Here I have a bucketful of used plasters; some ear wax, 20 verucas, fifteen bucketfuls of suntan lotion, two buckets of snot, some athlete's foot cream complete with a dash of athlete's foot, some pile ointment, saliva, just a shake of debris from people's bottoms, a bucketful of pubic hair and throw in some dirt from between your toenails. 'Thank you for your undivided attention ladies and gentlemen, I now declare the pool open.'

Funny? I think not really. That's what goes into your average hotel swimming pool and just for good measure the deadly brew is allowed to ferment at a nice baking hot temperature of 70-plus degrees just to give the bacteria every chance to thrive. It's a fucking horror story and if you've ever wondered why the woman in the next room has got a dicky tummy, ear infection or a mystery rash. Look further than the paella. I won't go in a swimming pool that's been frequented by anything other than friends and family - and that still doesn't deem it ten out of ten on the hygiene list. It's a personal thing. It's a bit like egg sandwiches or vomit - you never find your own quite so offensive.

Don't get me wrong - egg sarnies take some beating. I'd sell my soul for an egg and cress sarnie when the mood takes me, but if someone else ever opened up his or her sandwiches on a hot coach, I'd quite happily chuck. It's like being sick on a bus. When I did it as a kid, I always thought everyone else was making a bit of a fuss about it. What the fuck is wrong with these people? It's all very personal. Your own never smells so bad. Even skunks think their kids smell like Chanel No 5 you know.

So even if your hotel is five star, don't be blinded to the fact that you don't have to have sharks circling around for swimming to be a total liability.

I swear I was tainted as a kid. When I was about seven or eight it seemed like every other news bulletin featured some fat girl covered in lard attempting to swim the Channel. And the poor, bloated child would get stung half-to-death by jellyfish and all because her dad was there in front of her in a rowing boat bellowing encouragement through a loudhailer. Fuck me, they would just ring Childline now, but that wasn't around in the late-60s. It was a time when a whole host of inconsequential and extremely disturbed fathers thought the way for their fat child to get on in life was to swim the English Channel. What ever happened to those poor cows? Are they all in institutions now? God knows, but it affected me at an early age and I've never quite got my head around it.

It was right up there with Opportunity Knocks, Take Your Pick and Terry Scott dressed up as a child singing My Brother. This was early reality TV and fat girl swimmers covered in lard and jellyfish stings were all part of it. Great eh?

35

1993 - TOP GEAR

If I needed a reminder of just how far I'd come then this Christmas present was surely it. Ffion has handed me the keys to a brand new car and it's parked outside on the driveway. She must be thinking along similar lines too - it's not often you can treat your hubby to a gift that costs the thick end of a hundred grand. Especially when the last kind of gainful employment you had was part-time in a beauty salon and that was over four years ago.

For me the gleaming silver beast was like coming full circle but in a most glorious and unbelievable way. I can still remember the thrill of getting that Corgi James Bond DB5 all those years ago and being mesmerised by it. I loved everything about it - the machine guns which poked out of the front, the tyre shredders, the bullet proof shield which popped up to cover the back window and the revolving number plates. But the one thing every boy of a certain age recalls was that fucking ejector seat. How cool an accessory was that? Wow, just imagine pressing that button and seeing someone you'd suddenly taken a dislike to, flying out of the roof and onto the hard shoulder of the M6. That little blue man in the passenger seat had done more air miles than Alan Whicker by the time I'd finished with him. That James Bond car really does just have to be one of the greatest boys' toys of all time. Thirty years on and I've got the real thing. It can't get much better than that, surely?

I'd never been able to do any of that sort of stuff with my

child. Lord, I didn't even know whether Suzie had a boy or a girl. I'm a bit upset about that right now because this year he or she would have celebrated their 18th birthday. I wondered if they ever gave me a second thought. You would have thought so. I certainly hoped so, but I was just powerless to do anything about it. I was angry with Suzie because once she'd had the baby all contact was broken off. She could have just let me know - that's all. I don't think it would have been too much to ask.

Thirty years on and I was about to sit in my very own Aston Martin. Metallic silver. Connolly leather in oxblood and parchment. Burr walnut panels. That fuck-off elegant radiator opening. This beauty was 0-60 in 5.7 secs and had a top speed of 157 mph. The Aston Martin DB7 Vantage was arguably the most beautiful car in the world. Can a car be beautiful? Yeah, I'm not a guy who drools over machines, but this was astonishingly beautiful. That's why when the idea had been put forward, I chose the Aston above everything else. Keep your Ferraris, Lamborghini's and Porsches. My car of choice was the brand new Aston - £84,950 worth of gleaming testosterone. I liked the look of it and I liked the sound of it. The cost didn't matter, which is just as well.

I got in it, smelt the leather and reached for the top of the gearstick. I pressed the badge but no, the passenger seat didn't shoot out of the roof. Perhaps someone needed to be in it. Perhaps I was just seven again. This car was gorgeous. I just had to take it for a spin. I turned the key and grinned broadly as I heard the unmistakable growl of the engine with the crunch of the gravel acting as backdrop.

'My name's Bond - James Bond,' I chuckled as I made my way out of the front gates. I'd head for the dual carriageway, just a couple of miles down the road and see if I could let it rip.

As I pulled up at the first set of lights a youth pulled alongside me in a bright yellow Fiesta and I tried not to glance sideways for fear of appearing to show-off. It's difficult with one of these beauties. How can you not show off when you're sitting in a brand spanking new Aston?

As the lights changed, the youth screamed away and then slowed a little as he got held back at the next set of lights. I could see he was trying to say something to me, so I wound down the window.

'Should have got one of these - could have saved yourself a few quid,' he cackled, adjusting his cap.

'Yeah, about eighty-five grand!' I said with a snigger and mouthed him to fuck off.

Ffion's main present was something I'd rather have nothing to do with - apart from pay for it that is. She wants to have a nose job and just wouldn't be deterred so, for what it's worth, I've gone along with it. She says she's always been so self-conscious about a teeny-weeny bump on it that is so teeny-weeny I've never been able to see what the hell she is talking about. Anyway, having got her way, she's going to book herself in as soon as she can in the New Year. And, she's decided, she might just have a little bit taken off the end, seeing as she's in there. I didn't think it would be a good idea to ask if they do two-for-one deals, and just gave my reluctant backing to her plan. What is it with women and plastic surgery? What is it with cosmetic procedures in the first place? I only have to look at Michael Jackson and it sets me worrying. Presumably he has access to the world's finest, money-no-object plastic surgeons. Yet what a mess he looks. Fuck me; if that's what the best people can do, what happens if you fall into the hands of a rogue operator?

Presumably that horrid Bride of Wildenstein woman has been paying top dollar to end up looking like a lion that's been hit by a safari truck. Apparently, Jocelyn Wildenstein, embarked on a phenomenal string of cosmetic operations because she wanted to look cat-like. The story goes her husband had been screwing someone else and she thought the only way to ensure he didn't stray was to take on feline characteristics. Someone really should have told her you don't spell cheater like that. What cosmetic surgeon would want either of those two advertising their work? Who in their right mind is going to own up to doing that? It's always been a rule of thumb to me - judge something from the best and take it from there.

It's like with Aston Martins - and I'm not being a snob here. But if you want to judge exactly where a town stands in the national pecking order - go and have a mooch about and see the car showrooms it boasts. You show me a town with a Bentley, Porsche or Aston showrooms and you don't need to be Einstein to know there's wealth around. That's not sticking up for the darned place. It could be full of rich people who are absolute twats, but the indicator is there. You won't find nice car showrooms in a shit area - it just doesn't happen. It's like buskers. Nice towns like Chester and Cambridge invariably have great buskers - jazz saxophonists, talented jugglers and the like. Go to a dump and you'll just get some wanker with a dog and a crumpled hat in front of him. And to me that's like plastic surgeons. Try and see the jobs done by the best and use that as the starting point. If Jacko can't get it done better than that, what chance is there for the rest of us? His face is falling off by the looks of it, so count me out. How bad does it have to get? And yet now it seems, the world's women are queuing up to go under the knife. It just doesn't make any sense to me.

It's like Botox - fucking hell. They have Botox parties now. Whatever happened to Tupperware? Yeah, parties where loads of 'girls' get together for a night out and get the woman from No 56 to inject their foreheads with one of the most lethal toxins known to man. How fucking crazy is that? All over the country, women are taking on this astonishing glazed appearance because one of the totally unqualified neighbours has given them a shot of poison and charged them for the privilege. You honestly couldn't make it up. Thousands of women now have startled expressions - and all with the help of some idiot woman from up the road who is only staging parties to try and claw back the money she lost in some pyramid buying scam she was idiotic enough to fall for. She does it in the evenings because in the daytime she's busy working down on the checkout at Spar.

Suddenly, the woman from No 56 is an expert at administering the venom from a cobra's arse, or wherever it comes from, into her friends. They're chasing a dream and it's quite frankly a nightmare. Everyone tells me how great Joan Collins looks and she's 70-odd. And hey, yes she does look great and credit to her, but I bet she always goes missionary in bed. And whatsmore, I'll tell you why - because for all her money there isn't a surgeon alive who can perform a successful arse lift. They might be able to raise cheeks and eyebrows, chins and all manner of things. But you dare ask Joan which way her arse points and it's more likely to be Australia than Alaska and that's for sure.

I'll guarantee Joan doesn't go doggy for fear of presenting you with something that resembles a bloodhound. There's scores of them. Tina Turner is another. You can just imagine some young stud being summoned into her boudoir and thinking he's just taking a trip to heaven.

Off comes the wig to be carefully placed on the bedside table along with the nails, the fake eyelashes and god knows what else. Get on the table son, there's more of her on there.

There's nothing wrong with shagging a celebrity for either the sheer kudos or to make some cash, but it's a rocky old road. The ideal scenario if you want to make some cash is to really screw a member of the Royal Family - Paul Burrell has done okay out of it. Poor Di. What a hapless little cretin. Rock? He was a fucking shoe cleaner, that's what he was.

Don't you just want to puke when he minces around the place trying to convince everyone how close he was to her? Rock? Is that some sort of royal code word for skivvy? He's not a rock - he's a glorified waiter. Sorry, he's an ex-waiter, who now thinks he's a celebrity. And he portrays himself as some sort of moral guardian to Di's secrets. Now he's waltzing around the world with a diamond earring claiming he didn't nick all that stuff from the Royal Family. The conniving little arsehole makes me sick. And he goes in the jungle on that reality show and I swear to God all those bugs had to go home with no meal stars for their mates back in Bugland because they just couldn't stand the thought of a single second with Burrell.

36

1994 - PRIVATE PLATES

Ffion was adamant she wanted to buy me a private number plate. When she could see how against the idea I was, she accused me of being miserable. I just don't fucking like them - full stop. What is it about a private number plate that can send a seemingly sane, intelligent man, completely ga-ga? I really honestly don't know what it is with the darned things. It's that sort of 'I'd just like you to know that I'm kind of doing well' type of thing or, only marginally less scarily, a certain comic statement which invariably doesn't quite come off. I just don't quite get them and so while I would never question anyone's right to have one, they're not for me.

I think they're pretentious, right. I firmly believe so-called important people who have them, possibly aren't as important as they think, and for those who have them because they're just unbelievably rich, you don't need one pal! If you've got a brand new Roller and a fuck-off big yacht, believe you me, having JON 1 or whatever on your car won't matter a jot to me. I'll kind of take it as read that you might just be worth a few quid.

But if you're famous, why the fuck do you need one? And if you do have one, then don't ever let me hear you complain that people bother you all the time. It's like having POP 1 on your car and then making a song and dance about it when every time you get out of the fucking thing there are dozens of people peering at you.

But I still maintain if you feel the compulsion to have a

private plate, you're not *that* famous. Let me ask you something, right. Do you think Osama Bin Laden drives around in those caves with OBL 1 on his motor? Does he bollocks. But I'll bet you one thing, if he drove down Oxford Circus in that, he'd bring the crowds to a standstill even if they couldn't see through the black, bulletproof glass. Now *that's* famous.

When people know who you are before you've even got out of the fucking thing. Did Hitler have AH 1 on his Volkswagen? That's the whole point. He didn't need anything on his car to say 'Hey, I'm the leader of the Nazi party.' There are just some things people know. So, in brief, if you're that famous you don't need one and if you're not then stop pretending and just fucking well grow up.

I've never actually asked but I would be pretty confident in saying that the very reason really famous people avoid private number plates is the threat of kidnap or something equally horrible. I'm sure Paul McCartney doesn't have FAB 1 on his car not just to stop being pestered but so that some twat who might want to kidnap his kids or whatever isn't given an immediate pointer as to who is in the car. Anyway, Lady Penelope not Lady Mucca had bagged that one already. She would be better off with LEG 1 - that would be a bit of a giveaway.

Just imagine having a really desirable plate, being held up by armed gunmen and then having to be asked who you are! How embarrassing a kidnap attempt would that be? Just having to ring someone up to tell the robbers that your kids really are worth holding to ransom. That's the road you are straying down once you go down the private plates route. Be warned.

Then there are the so-called funny number plates. You know the 'I'm a wacky twat' type of plate. There are a limited few which just about scrape under the acceptable barrier, but it's a low bar believe me. You see Jimmy Tarbuck has got the plate COM IC, which despite Bernard Manning's assumption that he should be done under the Trades Descriptions Act, I think kind of passes the acceptable criteria. Paul Daniels reportedly has the plate MAGIC and if I was being charitable I'd say that comes under the same banner as Tarby's. But on account of the fact that I can't stand the repugnant little midget, I'll speculate that the plate TWAT 1 had already been claimed.

You just have to be really careful with so-called comic statements. One man's meat is another's poison. It's like the guy in the office who wears a Minnie Mouse tie or has got Pluto on his socks. He might as well have a sandwich board on saying, 'do you think I'm funny?' But equally, he shouldn't be surprised when he gets pelted with rotten fruit to yells of 'No you fucking well aren't.'

Why not have a hat with a fan on in the warm weather? Now that's humorous. It's like people with senseless pursuits like bog snorkelling. Doesn't that sound fun? Well actually, no it doesn't. You'll always get some idiot who not only wants to crawl face down in a rancid, cold, shitty ditch, but can't wait to tell you all about it.

'Honestly, you should have been there . . .'

'Listen pal, no I shouldn't have been there. You know what I was doing on Saturday afternoon when you were scratching the skin off your knees and elbows and swallowing forms of crustaceans which haven't been seen for years?'

'Well, no... .'

'Right, well I went down my local, had a few beers, came in and lay on the settee in my nice warm house and watched the football results coming in. And you know what? The bog snorkelling championships from wherever weren't even mentioned once. Now *that's* what I did.'

Anyway, I digress, back to private plates. And so under that little mob you have an even more worrying couple of brackets. You've got the person who isn't that famous or that rich, but is doing okay and just thinks you might like to know. Just in case, you get to actually speak and find out that he's the district manager for a firm that sells baked beans, he wants to let you know that he's getting there. Enter PXG 746 man. I only use the X because some fucker with a plate like PJG or PSG or P fucking BG will try to sue me for thinking they are social misfits. So PXG 746 man, what's it like to be only the 746th most important person with the initials PXG in Britain? And if PXG 1 became available, do you think you'd be able to afford it? Exactly. No more questions Your Honour!

There are no hard and fast rules here, it's a personal thing. I'm not saying I'm right, it's just the way I feel about it. One guy even offered me the theory that the only people who had a problem with private plates were those who couldn't afford one. I rest my case . . .

And the strange thing, which says more about the whole system than anything ever could, is that all the plates that might give you a snigger aren't issued because the powers-that-be won't allow it. It's a bit like Groucho Marx saying something like he'd never want to be in a club that would consider him as a member.

Some might think Mouse and his work out in Africa were at the bottom of all this, but it wasn't the case. The business was going just fantastically and the money was pouring in and yet the opportunity to squander it on insignificant crap, seemed to grow by the day.

And you know what? Having money and managing money while handling relationships is the hardest thing to juggle of all. Friends and acquaintances see you differently and gradually all the borders become blurred. I struggled with all this at times. Ffion would have quite happily sanctioned me buying some pathetic private number plate for, say twenty grand, yet we would have had an argument if I'd told her what I'd just done. That was the moment it all dawned on me that this relationship had hit the buffers. What had I even been thinking of in the first place? Married or not I, perhaps wrongly, considered that sending the cheque off wasn't really anything to do with her. Mouse was going to have that school and community hall for people who would really appreciate it. I would make sure of that. Seventy thousand quid was nothing. It wasn't the price of a decent number plate. So P155 OFF.

37

1995 - CHICKEN SUPREME

Now here's a thing. So, there's me fed up with being stressed out selling mobile phones and making enough money to wipe out an African country's national debt and there's this poor guy who hasn't a penny piece giving me a gift which can only be described as priceless.

Eddie hasn't got much to speak of. He struggles to make ends meet and often has to go hungry for the sake of his family. Yet he's just invited me into his home and served up his chicken - yes, the only fucking chicken he owns. I could have cried. It made any thoughts of private number plates and expensive cars a total nonsense.

I couldn't wait to see Mouse and Melissa and the lifestyle they'd thrown themselves into. A lot had happened to all of us in the five years since we had last seen each other. We had kept in touch and they were aware that the Fonez Factory had gone ballistic in terms of expansion. This was more than just a social trip for me.

I'd taken a scheduled flight into Johannesburg and was spending a couple of nights there to tie up one or two things for The Christmas Foundation that would be headed up by Mouse and Melissa. The work they had been doing in Zandalaya was quite incredible but they badly needed financial help and this latest cheque should see them right for many years to come. Two hundred thousand pounds - it was the least I could do to help my mates and the fantastic, worthwhile projects they wanted to pursue. It wasn't a case of showing off. No one back home knew about it and I knew the cash would be gratefully received. The Foundation had already helped them start to plan important things like an irrigation system, fresh water and a temporary school. The next step was to provide a grain barn so they could cope with any harvest failure and water tanks and then build a proper school for the village children. They needed some sort of medical facilities too and hopefully, once the Foundation was properly structured, they should be able to oversee countless worthwhile projects.

Mouse had offered to come and pick me up but I declined. It would have been a long journey for him and anyway, the thought of a bone-jarring 10-hour drive over rough tracks and barely definable roads filled me with dread. Melissa had laughed when I told them I planned to charter a small private jet to bring me in. She assured me the whole village would be out in force to see such a spectacle. It was quite a big deal apparently.

She wasn't joking. As we made our approach, the pilot informed me that the village nestled just over a small hill he was pointing to. I hadn't been able to get my head around how green the place was and the sight of all sorts of gazelles, zebra and giraffes along the way had been something to behold. I didn't regret taking the plane in at all. As the Piper made its approach to a small dusty field that offered a suitable place to land, whole families seemed to be watching, eagerly awaiting our arrival.

Mouse raced over and hugged me. I don't know what they had been feeding him on but he'd put on quite a bit of weight since I'd last seen him. The food couldn't be too bad! We hugged and then Melissa came over and the three of us embraced.

Then hordes of smiling people - women, children, men - were waving at me, offering their hands and one large smiley woman put a garland around my neck.

'You're quite popular around these parts,' Melissa smiled.

'You are this mysterious figure who helped them get things they could only have dreamed of. These people would walk a hundred miles to see you - I'm not joking,' she said.

'Wow. I feel like I'm the King of Zandalaya,' I joked.

'Hey, in their eyes, you might just as well be,' Mouse said.

I was a bit overwhelmed by it all. One man insisted on taking my case and another offered me a piece of fruit.

'You couldn't persuade Ffion to come out here then?' Melissa said with a grin.

'Nah, there were just too many things she needed to sort out at that end, so it just wasn't possible,' I fibbed. The fact was that Ffion was rather dismissive of the whole idea of helping people out here. She had more important things, like her nails and hair, to tend to.

'It's just not my thing,' she'd said and she was right. I couldn't think of anything that was less Ffion than having to make do with things in rather primitive surroundings. I wasn't sure how much it would be my thing to be honest, but I was quite looking forward to it in a bizarre kind of way. It was just fantastic to see Mouse and Melissa again and it would be good being able to see and appreciate first hand, exactly what it was they were hoping to do.

I arranged with the pilot to pick me up in two weeks time to get me back to the airport for my return flight. It was kind of great having nothing to worry about for a couple of weeks and I was looking forward to the experience.

'God, I'm starving,' I said to Melissa. 'What's on the menu?'

'You!' she laughed.

'Hey don't joke . . .'

'Who said I was joking?'

'Starving? You don't know the meaning of the word,' Mouse corrected me.

'You don't look to have done too bad on it mate,' I replied slapping his belly.

'Ah, I'm contented see.'

'Yeah, I can see that. You must be really contented.'

'Anyway, how come you didn't come in on your own private jet, Mr Big Time?' Mouse said sarcastically.

'My regular pilot's on holiday,' I quipped.

'Hey, I just want to say words can't tell you how grateful we are for everything you've done. This village has fresh running water, the lot now, and it's largely down to you Sant.'

'Hey, slow down. You're the ones who are doing everything. I just supply a bit of money, that's all.'

'A lot of money,' Mouse chipped in.

'Well, thanks to you and the advice you gave me, I've been fortunate enough to accumulate quite a lot of money. It's not a gift - it's yours by right.'

'I almost took you under!' Mouse exclaimed.

'True. There is that. But it all worked out in the end.'

'So what's for tea?'

Melissa informed me that a guy called Edward had insisted on preparing a meal for all of us at his house, up near the top edge of the village.

'No cannibal jokes,' she warned me.

'Would I?'

'Yes, you would actually. Edward's really looking forward to doing this. It's a big thing for him. It's not every day he gets the chance to cater for the King of Zandalaya. I think he's quite nervous.'

He shouldn't have been. The meal was magnificent - a type of chicken stew cooked in a black cauldron-type of pot and served with a kind of cornbread, which was sweet and very filling. I thanked him very much and he explained the various roles he carried out in the village. It seemed like he did a bit of everything and he was lavish in his affection for my two pals. I'd only been in the place a few hours and you couldn't fail to see the love everyone felt for these two. Children, who were smiling already, lit up, as they passed. It was wonderful to just experience it. The kids had nothing - just about the clothes they stood up in, yet every single one had a massive smile on their face. It was such a contrast to the moody, threatening, types who you were often forced to pass back home.

We spent a pleasant couple of hours at Edward's before making our way back to Mouse's house where I was staying.

'That was really, really good,' I said.

'Yeah, it's quite a spread he put on for you there. I wouldn't want you to think it's like that every day here.'

'Come on, you've been giving me a sob story and you're all shovelling it away like pigs,' I laughed.

'You know something?' said Mouse.

'What?'

'You are really honoured. That chicken we've just eaten.'

'Yeah. Oh please don't tell me it was his pet or something!'

'No, stop it! But next best thing. Edward only has one chicken. That's how big a compliment that is.'

'You're kidding me!'

'No.'

My God. How kind was that? The guy has one chicken and next to no money and he treats us to it. I couldn't think of anyone back home apart from my mum who would have done that.

'They'd all do it here.'

'You're joking.'

'I'm not. They really are the most fabulous people.'

The money supplied for the borehole project had

transformed life beyond recognition for the village people. At last they had fresh running water from the large hand pumps that the South African contractors had put in. It had cost more than it should because of the logistics of getting a drilling team out there, but that was of no consequence. The contractors had taken the piss when it came to the price but they knew I had limited options about getting a team out there to get the work done properly. In the end, you just pay it and get the job done.

You just take running water for granted. I had three downstairs toilets back home. How could you even begin to explain that to these people? They already looked upon me as some kind of royalty. Why would I do this for them? They couldn't understand it. I wanted to. I wanted to do it for them. And for me. And for Mouse and Melissa. I felt good about it and perhaps it eased some of the guilt I'd started to feel about being rich beyond most people's comprehension. I admit there was a selfish aspect to it. It made me feel bloody good and somehow worthwhile.

Mouse explained that prior to the boreholes being drilled, women of the village would be forced to leave their children and walk six miles daily carrying a five-gallon jerry on their heads to get water. They would return to feed their kids, knowing they had the same journey to make the next day . . . and the next . . . and the next.

It wasn't that surprising that they thought I came from another planet . . .

38

1996 - GOTCHA

It had been a far from amicable split. We both knew it was all spiralling out of control long before I had a fit of uncontrollable anger and murdered the darned pet she had given me just a few days earlier.

Guilty as charged, I took a hammer to the unsuspecting thing and bludgeoned it to death. It offered little resistance other than a pathetic grunt as I rained down blows on it.

'Take that, you bastard.'

'And that.' Thump.

'And that.' Thwack.

'And never darken my door again!' I yelled, hurling what was left of my recently acquired companion down the garden. The little fucker had only done a big shit, not seconds after complaining it was hungry. It was more than I could bear. But when it woke me up in the night to let me know exactly what it had done, well, that was it.

'I just can't believe you've done that,' wailed Ffion.

'Fucking stupid bastard thing,' I countered.

'That's as maybe, but it didn't deserve that. I hope you feel better now.'

'I do actually. Much, better. Much, much, better to be completely honest,' I replied with a manic grin.

'You're pathetic.'

'That's as maybe,' I said, wondering if this was how serial killers got started.

'It's not as if it could bite you back or anything like that,'

Ffion declared with a glare..

'It'd have been biting a hammer if it had.'

'Pathetic. I've never seen anything like it.'

'Good.'

'Why didn't you just give it to one of the kids down the road or something? You didn't have to do that to it.'

'Because giving it to one of the kids wouldn't have given me the satisfaction I have just had from pummelling that little fucker to death. Good riddance!'

I'd checked how hungry it was; I'd fed it and I'd even cleaned up after it once. I hadn't had time to play a game with it before it was no more. My Tamagotchi was dead - flying back through cyberspace to meet its maker.

Right, hear this:

Tamagotchis hatch from tiny eggs after travelling millions of miles through cyberspace to learn what life is like on earth. NO THEY DON'T

Tamagotchis will always return to their own planet. NO THEY DON'T.

Tamagotchis will quickly grow into lovely virtual pets with proper care and feeding and will display a wide variety of personality traits. NO THEY DON'T.

That's what the box said and that might be what Ffion cares to believe, but let's get it straight, they are nothing more than an irritating nuisance designed to get on any sane person's tits in little or no time at all. Why the fuck Ffion thought one would ever amuse me was scary. They were pure torture from a nation who knew a thing or two about that.

What sort of fuckwits paid good money to own one of the darned things? I'd read stories in the papers about how counselling services had been set up in some parts of the world to help people who had lost their Tamagotchi prematurely. Mine had passed into another world prematurely and I felt wonderful. No counselling for me, though Ffion seemed to think otherwise.

It was the beginning of the end - the £800 Petaskis bag actually proved to be the final straw. She had seen the look of incredulity on my face as I slaughtered the Tamagotchi and clearly could see the inner rage seeping through to the surface as I expressed disbelief at the price of the small bag draped across her forearm.

'Eight hundred quid!'

'So.'

'So . . . they must see idiots like you coming that's all I've got to say about it.'

Rage would be the wrong word, just anger that people could take liberties like that and make you feel wonderful for having let them do it. It was beyond me. I never drew the line on her having anything she wanted but eight hundred notes for a fucking handbag, well . . .

'You can't take it with you, you know?' she said a shade too dismissively for my liking.

'What the bag?'

'No, your precious money,' Ffion hissed, the clear implication being that I was prone to more than the occasional bout of stinginess.

'Take it with me? I wouldn't have any to take anywhere if you had your way.'

'You'd have me shopping at the Oxfam shop if you thought you could get away with it.'

'Ffion. Stop talking bollocks and grow up. Just because some of your dippy mates think nothing of paying the thick end of a thousand quid for a bag, doesn't mean that I have to go along with it. Their husbands must have more money than sense.'

'Well they haven't got anywhere near as much money as you.'

'I'm not fucking-well surprised.'

'They aren't in the same league as you, yet they don't seem to mind.'

'Well, perhaps they were given it, but I earned mine and I just can't see the sense in it - that's all.'

'I'll take it back in the morning.'

'Forget it. Don't give me that *I'll take it back* nonsense. I wouldn't dream of it, but just engage your brain next time before you splash out that kind of money.'

'I can't believe you said that?'

'I'll say it again if you like.'

'It's a Petaskis. That's what *they* cost.'

'Is that an anagram of piss-take?'

'Oh very clever.'

Then, she made the classic error of dropping herself in it, thinking she was putting forward a classic defence.

'It was the only one that went perfectly with the shoes I . . .'

'Oh, the £600 Jimmy Shoes bargain you just happened to stumble across the other day eh?'

'Choos. Jimmy Choos. I know you'd be happy for me to go around in a pair of flip flops.'

'That's just not true and I resent the implication.'

'What implication?'

'That I'm mean or something.'

'I never said that.'

'The inference was there.'

'That's your mind that is.'

'Well, anyway. Would it be ridiculous of me to ask if you don't think fourteen hundred pounds is a little over the top for a pair of shoes and a bag which will probably be used half a dozen times and then get relegated to the bottom of the wardrobe?'

Ffion did a bemused/hurt look better than most. She did perplexed to Olympic standard. She seized on a chance remark I'd made about Mouse being able to provide fresh water for an entire village for roughly the same amount.

'Oh well, that's sorted then - I'll have a borehole next

Christmas. That should be fun. I don't say to you when you are eating steak, that you could feed 50 kids for the price of that, do I?'

'Fair point, but hardly the same argument really,' I said, refusing to be sidetracked on this particular issue.

'So what is the argument exactly?' she goaded me.

'I'm sick and fed up of you living the Hollywood fucking lifestyle and just spending ridiculous amounts of money on . . . well crap most of it.'

'Really?'

'Yes, really. The thing that fucking annoys me isn't the spending of it so much but the way you make me sound mean for ever having the audacity to question it. I provide the cash around here and, despite what you may think; I don't want you to shop at Matalan. But there is a limit.'

'Sounds like I've reached it.'

'Just *think* sometimes. That's all I ask. There's kids out there who . . .'

'Oh, just fuck off Sant. I feel like I married Bono or Sting or something. I buy a dress and I'm in the shop working out how many malaria tablets, I could buy for that amount. You get on my tits.'

Bono? Sting? God she knew how to hurt. If she meant my money had given me a more acute sense of social conscience then she was right. To my mind it was a case of have a nice handbag, have a really nice handbag - but just don't come back and tell me it's cost a thousand pounds because I just don't get it.

Ffion stormed off in tears . . . again. I really couldn't stand much more of this. I needed to see someone . . . and I knew just the man.

Wayne Richardson was a renowned divorce solicitor I bumped into occasionally at the golf club. He's always joked that if I needed his services, I knew where he was. It had been a laugh at the time. An immaculate man in his early 40s with a mop of chemically enhanced jet black hair, Wayne was known as the man who would leave no stone unturned in his effort to clinch the best deal for his clients. We agreed to meet in the bar one quiet Tuesday afternoon when there was hardly anyone around.

'I thought I'd told you, even you can't afford my advice,' Wayne laughed and ordered two pints of lager shandy. I'd sorted him out with a decent deal on some phones for his firm, so although we weren't close pals by any stretch of the imagination, we were friendly enough to be able to talk on the understanding that it went no further.

'Listen, Wayne, nothing's on the horizon right now, but I can just see it all going tits up to be honest. If it does, it does and there's nothing I can do about it, but obviously I was wondering what it might cost.'

'Well with no kids and her having played little or no part in the business, you won't be looking at anywhere near a 50-50 split if that's what you're worried about.'

Actually, it fucking well wasn't! Fifty- fifty! Hang on a minute. Just attach me to a drip and siphon off four pints of blood while you're at it. Fifty-fifty? It hadn't even entered my head. I think Wayne had got the message.

'In relative terms with no little ones involved, you would get off reasonably lightly I would have thought.'

'Reasonably lightly . . . like?'

'Hard to say really, but I'm guessing she would argue that she needs to be kept at least some way to the standard she's become accustomed to and if she's not worked for a while then . . .'

'How much Wayne? And before you say, do I need to go back to the bar first?'

Wayne nodded and continued to scribble on a spare beer mat. I returned, placed the drinks down and waited for his verdict.

'Well,' he said, pulling one of those faces you see a mechanic pull when he's just about to drop a bombshell.

'Well?' I urged him to hit me with it.

'Well, she's a young woman with her life ahead of her so . . . you really need to be looking at a clean-break arrangement. A one-off payment and that's it. I'd be surprised if you got it down to much less than . . . put it this way, if I were acting on your behalf and was offered a straight cut, no strings arrangement . . . then . . . err, I'd be happy at anything in the low seven figures.'

'Seven figures! And you're on my side! For fuck's sake, what's going on?'

'That's the way it is. From what you've told me about your assets and projected income, that'd be an absolute snip. I'd honestly urge you to take that if it was offered. If you get away with two and a half million, you've had an absolute result. Times have changed.'

They certainly had. Ffion's only job in the last seven years was going out spending my cash. It's not as if she did anything else. And now because she's got used to having a cleaner, a gardener and an extravagant lifestyle, I'm supposed to provide that for life. What an absolute load of bollocks. She would be looking to walk away with several million if I was *lucky*!!

'And the worse case scenario?' I dared to ask him.

'I don't think any divorce judge in a case like that, with no kids involved, would think of straying over the twenty million mark.'

Twenty!!! My God.

'Are you serious?'

'Serious business, divorce. Listen, you've got huge assets. She's got to have a roof over her head. Then she needs some kind of income to sustain her to a reasonable standard. Work it out yourself. A few million could be on the low side.'

A roof over her head? He made it sound like a mud hut out in Africa. A million pounds would sort out Mouse and Melissa's African village for ever. What that sort of money could buy, was anyone's guess. But it could certainly save thousands of lives, prevent countless more from going blind and make sure they had schooling and clean, fresh running water on tap. It was scandalous. Money was scandalous. Obscene. It really was starting to get to me. And the more I protested about such injustices, the more I stood accused of having a mean streak. I'd give Ffion *fifty* fucking million if she promised to donate the lot to charity. But she wouldn't. She'd carry on breezing around the place in a soft top sports car with a swanky plate and spending thousands of pounds a month on clothes and having her hair done. I found it hard to stomach

There had to be other ways but the Tamagotchi solution, appealing as it was right now, wasn't one of them.

39

1997 - CHEAP SHOT

It might have seemed like a cheap shot, no pun intended, but it was actually only a joke. I didn't realise some nutcase would actually go and do it. I'd just made a passing remark that if I had my way most of these design gurus like Gianni Versace would be lined up and shot. Fucking hell . . .

You can't even crack a joke these days, but it was enough to send Ffion off on one. Was I happy now? No. Far from it actually. Give me a break. I was just making a point that I thought most of these tossers who are acclaimed as chic designers or artists were actually more Emperor's New Clothes than stunning new clothes. It's a sweeping generalisation, granted, but I reserve the right to say 'Hey that's shit' and not be looked down upon as some pleb unworthy of an opinion. How often had I seen those models tottering down the catwalk in stuff that was, quite frankly, ridiculous? Yet because some top name was attached to it, the photographers and critics were there in droves convinced they were at the cutting edge. It just strikes me that if someone spouts enough bullshit, then they can not only convince half the world it's great but they can convince countless other half-wits to pay fortunes for it. Delia Smith mentions a particular type of omelette pan that has had sales in trickles for years and suddenly they can't knock them out quickly enough. I'd seen if first hand with phones, so I shouldn't really knock the theory, but it just grates at times.

Look at art. I can admire a sensational piece of painting,

drawing or sculpture with the best of them. But if it looks like a chimpanzee has done it then count me out. It's like Tracey Enim's unmade bed. I heard art critics with supposedly far more intelligence and perception than me extolling the virtues of that. And if you think it's shite, then you stand there like some brain-dead eight-year-old daring to say that the king is in the altogether. Unmade bed? It's a pile of fucking junk. Just like that assortment of bricks was a pile of junk. It's the expression of someone with little to say and I'm not having it.

And so, while I certainly didn't have any desire to see Gianni Versace mown down on his front step, it doesn't mean I was happy that my missus would pay extortionate amounts of money just to have a dress with his label in it.

'It's just that, well, it's like these designers seem to think they put their name to it and can charge you ten times as much for half as much material. It's a nonsense.'

'I don't think a thousand is over the top for a Versace. Look at Liz Hurley . . .'

'Yeah.'

'Well, that dress - the one with the safety pins - that was one of his.'

'So! Liz Hurley is a movie star for starters and the ironic thing about it is that she was probably paid to wear it, or at worst, given the fucking thing.'

'Don't be ridiculous. Who'd give her an exclusive Versace dress for God's sake?'

'Well try Mr Versace himself for a start off. Everyone goes on about the dress she wore on the red carpet and bingo!'

'Do you think so?'

'Open your eyes Ffion. They give stuff like that away or lend it out . . . whatever.'

'Well how can they make that pay?'

'Because then gullible people go and pay over-inflated prices for the darned things.'

'Oh right. That's unbelievable isn't it? I wish he'd give me some stuff.'

'So do I.'

Ffion's penchant for throwing cash around - my cash - was taking on alarming proportions. She did always look lovely mind, but it came at a frightening price. Sometimes it was a cost I just couldn't quite get my head around. And doubtless, I wasn't always being told the whole truth. I'd lost count of how many bargains she'd picked up. There was always fifty per cent off this or twenty per cent off that. I didn't always actually realise just how much we were saving until Ffion pointed it out. This particular bargain was a cocktail dress she had bought for a New Years Eve party. Sure, it looked great, but the price of it was just astro-fucking-nomical.

'Is money all you think of?' she asked.

'Well, no actually. But someone has to.'

'Every girl has a little black dress. If you have nothing else, you have to have a little black dress.'

'Nothing else!! You must have ten little black dresses to my knowledge.'

'Yeah, but not like this one.'

'Really.'

Ffion seemed to think I would be quite happy for her to shop at British Home Stores and that just wasn't the case. I didn't doubt for one moment that the likes of Gucci, Versace and their like were in a different league, but the price of some of the things was just ridiculous in any language.

You get designer everything now. Designer cooks, designer decorators, designer vets, designer gardeners, even designer nannies. Andy Warhol was right. Every which way you turn there's a 'guru' of some description. Someone you've never seen of before suddenly pops up and the TV presenter describes him or her as a lifestyle guru or a behavioural guru. What the fuck are terms like that supposed to mean?

It's like Versace. I knew of him. It would have been hard not to really. His name had really come to the fore last year when Liz Hurley wore *that* dress- the black number with the staples down the side - for the premiere of Four Weddings and a Funeral. And then he really went high profile earlier this year when he was killed.

All the tops stars were at the funeral. That must have been great for business. Lady Diana was there sitting next to Elton John. Who would have thought the next funeral they'd be at was hers?

Diana died back on August 31 and the nation was still in mourning. Fucking hell, it was still hard to believe really. That story would run and run even though you'd have thought every angle had virtually been done to death.

I couldn't help wondering just how the top brass at Mercedes first got to hear about what had happened in the early hours of the morning in Paris. Can you just imagine the conversation? Top Mercedes executive rings the boss. It's not only Sunday morning, but it's seven o'clock Sunday morning? We'll call them Tom and Jerry just for convenience (the Jerry is not a German thing, ok?). The phone rings.

'Ughh, hello.'

'Tom? Hey, sorry to bother you. It's Jerry in New York here.'

'Jerry! What the fuck time is it?'

'Seven a.m. UK time, I guess. I've waited hours before calling you.'

'This had better be good Jerry.'

'I can't promise that. You seen the news?'

'Seen the news. I haven't even seen the stairs yet. What the hell is going on?'

'Prepare yourself. I'm telling you there's going to be one of our cars on the front page of every newspaper in the land.'

'Hasn't anyone told you there's no such thing as bad publicity Jerry.'

'I wouldn't bank on that Tom.'

'Holy shit!!!!'

'You've got the TV on I take it?'

'Fuck me sideways.'

'I told you.'

'Bollocks, bollocks and thrice bollocks. It's one of the safest cars in the fucking world.'

'Listen. I know that and you know that. But the whole darned world might need some convincing.'

'How unlucky is that? Lady Di - the most famous woman in the world - gets killed and it's in one of our fucking cars!'

'There's a lot of conspiracy theories doing the rounds already.'

'What, that it was BMW or Audi or something?'

'No, there's all sorts of nonsense being bandied about. French driver, Egyptian boyfriend and a German car. Can't think why the English think something might have gone on.'

'To be honest right now, I just can't think of anyone you'd least like to have killed in one of your cars. If Mother Teresa was in there as well, I just don't want to know.'

And the strange thing was that less than a week later, with the wreckage still being cleared, Mother Teresa pops her sandals. Unbelievable.

And so England's beautiful rose is cut down in her prime and ends up getting outlived by Mother Teresa!

Can you just imagine walking into a bookies and asking for a bet like that.

'Can I help you sir?'

'Yeah, I'm looking for a bet and I wonder what odds you will give me on Lady Diana being outlived by Mother Teresa please.'

'I'll check. Gaffer says he'll lay you a million-to-one.'

'Fair enough. I was wondering if I could do a single, a couple of doubles and a three-way accumulator.'

'Who on sir?'

'I'd like Lady Di to be outlived by Mother Teresa, Pope John Paul . . . oh, and yeah, throw in the Queen Mum as well.'

'Gaffer says you must be out of your mind. Ten-million-to-one. Tell you what - name your own odds.'

The argument about the dress was the final straw. Ffion had decided life had become far too stressful for someone of her delicate disposition.

'You are going off golfing with your silly mates for two weeks and I don't go on about that do I?'

'The entire fortnight only comes to the cost of a fucking handbag. Don't bring my golf into it.'

'Oh I wouldn't dream of it. I've had enough. When you come back I'll be gone. Out of your hair. Out of here. Is that what you want? Don't even answer that. I'm leaving.'

'Okay.'

'Okay? Is that all you can say, bloody well okay?'

It was as it happened, but I thought better than to stress the point. Jetting off to Portugal couldn't come quickly enough. In the unlikely event of Ffion having thrown herself off this particular gravy train by the time I got back, then that would be just one almighty relief. This relationship had run its course.

'So, I've got two weeks to get out then. Is that it?'

'Look, I didn't put a time limit on it - you said that. Take as long as it takes.'

'Kiss my arse,' she roared. 'I hope you'll be very happy rattling around your big house on your own. Mind you, you can play with your Scalextric if you get lonely!'

It was unworthy of a reply. I headed towards the front door and out to the pub.

'I'll be gone by the time you get back,' she bellowed down

the drive, though I didn't imagine she meant by the time I'd got back from the pub. The next morning couldn't come soon enough.

I pledged that I wouldn't allow the distractions of the last few days and the possible cost of a divorce to distract me from my break with the lads. I could play golf badly enough without any help. What was a couple of million after all? I'd probably get back and the house would be burned down. No, in fairness, she wouldn't do that. We'd agreed she'd pop her keys through the door when she was finished. Just the keys not a paraffin-doused rag. Everything would be fine. I was sure of it.

My perilous domestic state at least made for good banter with the lads. It seemed like no time at all that we were heading home from Faro airport. The fantastic Vilamoura golf complex, which had been home for a brilliant couple of weeks, would soon be a distant memory. It wouldn't have surprised me if Ffion had still been there. It struck me that her taste for the high life might prove reason enough to try and rescue a relationship that was as clearly as hopelessly off course as so many of my golf shots. As I pulled onto the drive, the immediate signs were that there was no one home . . .

There was certainly no car on the front to suggest anyone was around. Things appeared just fine on the surface. It was just as I'd hoped really. I hadn't got her down as the spiteful sort. Actually, that's not strictly true. I had feared she was capable of something sinister, but was prepared to give her the benefit of doubt. She was a woman for God's sake. As I opened the door, I spotted a small white envelope, rather oddly shaped, which I found to contain Ffion's keys. But I couldn't help noticing a strange, somewhat musty smell about the place. There was only the faintest aroma in the hallway. Perhaps I'd left some fruit in a bowl somewhere and it had gone off. I was always doing something like that and in fairness to Ffion, I doubted she'd have given it a second thought. If she had, why bother? I'm not sure I would have in her circumstances.

I opened the living room door and was left dumbstruck by what was before me. What was only recently a newly laid £69.99 per square yard beige Axminster carpet was now a sea of green vegetation. The fucking bitch. She had sprinkled the entire living room floor with mustard and cress seeds and, I presumed, given it a light watering before allowing nature to do the rest. Hell hath nothing . . . Hoover? A hover might be a lot less bovver.

40

1998 - SCALPED

Mum thought that having turned 40 a few months ago, it might be amusing to buy me a Remington hair trimmer for Christmas. You know the thing - a tool to quickly rid you of any unwanted nasal hair or anything that might have sprouted on your ears. Funny eh? How fucking useful are they? You know you are on a slippery slope when someone buys you a 'joke' present and it turns out to be one of the best things you ever stumbled across. It really is a fantastic tool and I honestly don't know how I've lived without one over the past few years. Mums really do know best don't they?

I still feel Ffion has scalped me even though my solicitor argues I've had the result of the year by accepting a one-off clean-break arrangement of £3.5m. Three-and-a-half million quid I've had to fork out to Ffion and it fucking hurts. Not the amount but the principle and the fact that she can look me in the eye and say that she's been exceptionally easy on me. Scalped?

What is it with some men and their hair? I'm receding a bit and there's a pink patch creeping through at the back, but overall, I genuinely don't have a problem with it. I don't want it to all fall out and I don't particularly want to wake up and find it's silver, but I'll take what comes.   I won't be having grafts and I certainly won't be exploring having a weave, hairpiece or anything even more dramatic. I'm not that vain and, more to the point, I couldn't be arsed with all the fuss.

Elton John is a total enigma to me. How can you work out

a bloke who is more than happy publicly declaring he's gay but has a real problem acknowledging he's bald? It's bizarre. I like Elton. He seems to have been around almost as long as Rolf Harris and he's an engaging sort of bloke. But it's a bit dodgy knowing what's off-limits with him. Seems to me you could ask him about what it's like to fall in love with a bloke and he'd give it you blow-by-blow, so to speak, but point to the dead fox on his head and he'd give you that 'Bald? Me? How very dare you?' sort of look. It's odd. Sorry to just hit you with that, but let me explain . . .

I'd popped in for a haircut just a few days before Christmas, as you do. Don't you just fucking hate it when the person who has just cut your hair decides it's a good idea to hold up a mirror and let you see what the back is like? Aghhh! There's a solar panel showing through. I don't go to the barber's and pay good money to be upset. I don't actually expect them to tell me I look like Brad Pitt, but lay off the 'I presume you are aware of this' bit. I don't see that area unless some twat points it out to me. I walk around quite happily, not even giving it a second thought. Actually I'm not too bad about it in the great scheme of things. I've always said from early adulthood that there would never be any way I'd go down the Just For Men route or consider wearing a toupee. What's the point? It just strikes me the whole procedure is too much time and trouble. Too much fuss. And I'm not being horrible but if Elton can afford the best hair treatment programmes money can buy and ends up with that fucking thing, what hope is there for anyone else?

I like Elton - always have. I'd be about twelve, I guess, when some of the bigger lads at school could be seen clutching copies of Tumbleweed Connection. That was the first I'd heard of him, but boy, he was setting out on a long and eventful career. He's a talented bloke. He seems to have a really great sense of humour. Why the fuck doesn't he just ditch the wig/weave/weasel/whatever, shave off what tufts remain and breeze onto Parkinson or whatever and say 'Guess what? I'm bald!' We've fucking known that for years you stupid arse. Why has it taken you this long to come out?

And that's why Elton's stance on the whole subject renders me speechless. For God's sake Elt, just live with it man. The little fella's been around for most of my life and I take comfort in that. You've got your rock stars who have just always been there and the likes of Sting, Paul McCartney and Rod Stewart kind of stick around like old mates.

I love Sting's music right from The Police to Fields of Gold and all that stuff - I just wouldn't want to get cornered by him at a party that's all. Just imagine it - you want to talk about Don't Stand so Close Me and all he'd want to go on about is some ancient tribe in the Brazilian rainforests. It would just spoil it for me if I was in his company and I was secretly wishing he'd just fuck off and bother someone else.

Rod's the same. Some a bit younger than me might find it hard to believe but there was a good few years when thinking Rod Stewart was fucking great was nothing to be embarrassed about. Rod was one of the lads - a beer-swilling, serial shagger who swanned off all around the world having an absolute blast. Time was when his whole life seemed like one non-stop party and yet he retained the magical quality of appealing to both women and blokes. You just knew he'd shag your bird if he got half the chance, but us lads forgave him that. Us 14-year-olds were there swinging around the window pole in class and trying to croak Stay With Me back in the early 70s. A lot of us had feather cuts knowing it's the nearest we'd get to being in The Faces. We'd sing with a hairbrush or swing a broom handle around and sing Maggie May or Cindy Incidentally and Rod got extremely rich in the process.

When someone bangs on about Oasis or Robbie Williams, it's well worth remembering that Rod didn't just crack America, he fucking well shattered it. Atlantic Crossing? I'd say. There was a time when there wasn't a blonde in California who didn't start tearing her clothes off just at the very mention of his name.

Sure, we lost him for a while when he dressed up in those ridiculous leopard-skin pants, but he's kind of back a bit now, covering all those classics and singing songs much more befitting his age.

And Macca's the same really. You can't help but have a soft spot for him. I can't be doing with those Lennonists who want to always put Paul down. He was every bit as good as Lennon but he's done some shit as well. It's inevitable . . . you can't have a career that spans 40 years and not come out with some crap. He's just suffered a bit because of marrying the one-legged bird. She did the impossible and became more hated than his first wife. The nation only warmed to Linda when she was dead. Up to that point we'd all secretly resented her for being in Wings. There she was, banging that tambourine and then giving us ridiculous veggie sausages. It was all too much for us. Macca was ours - no one would have been good enough for him.

And so when Linda died we all kind of got to love her, just for being Macca's true love. Along comes fucking Heather and suddenly Linda is sanctified. Have you tasted one of her meals? Exactly. And then she goes and dies so young it was just about the worst PR the veggie movement could ever have had. Don't marry our heroes. We don't like it. Oh, and while you're at it, if you do, don't try and serve us the food you're giving them. We certainly don't like that.

It seems to me that once you reach 40 you became more and more conscious of your mortality. You realise that even if you are going to be lucky enough to make it to 70, you are well over half way there. You don't need hairs sprouting from your ears and nose to make you feel any worse.

I switched the ignition off, clasped my hands to the sides of my face and contemplated the enormity of it all. Just 40 and I'd been struck down by a stroke. How could God fucking well do this to me?

My right leg was twitching frantically and went into a weird kind of spasm if I even attempted to move it. I was having a stroke - there was no other explanation. Christ - and in Milton Keynes of all places. I didn't know anyone here. This would be a horrible place to die. It seemed a horrid enough place to live. But to die there. Alone. On a supermarket car park. It didn't bear thinking about. I tried to compose my thoughts. I was sweating profusely as I reached for my mobile and instinctively rang 999.

'Hello, emergency services . . .'

'Ambulance. Quickly please. I think I've had a stroke.'

'Okay sir, can you give us a location.'

'Yeah. Right leg.'

'No sir, where are you?'

Jesus, where was I? 'I'm on a car park. Sainsbury's. There's a cinema opposite. Milton Keynes. Help me please . . .'

'Can I take your registration number please?'

I gave her the car number and tried my best to relax and take in her next question.

'Yeah, it's silver. A silver Mercedes.'

'Okay, sir the ambulance is on it's way. Now, help me to help you. What exactly has happened sir?'

'I've been to see someone. Work. Oh that doesn't matter. I got in the car and tried to pull off and my leg err . . . my right leg is just twitching all over the place. Every time I try to move it, it jerks all over the place.'

'Okay, sir. Try and stay calm. At least your speech seems okay, so that's a good sign. Loosen up your shirt for me and just try to relax as much as possible.'

Relax? Fucking hell. Right now, the only plus is that my speech is okay. I might be confined to a wheelchair for the rest of my life, but at least I'll be able to talk to people. I'll have had a result if I'm not reduced to dribbling my dinner down my face. Stay calm!

'Okay sir, I'm sure everything is going to be fine. The ambulance is entering the car park so could you please try and tell me whereabouts they can find you.'

'I'm by a kind of skip thing. Yeah, a bottle bank maybe.' God, I was going to die by a bottle bank in Milton Keynes. The indignity of it all. Being stretchered out across a supermarket car park with hundreds of people watching me, my tongue lolling around uncontrollably as I took my last breath. I couldn't stand the thought of it. I could hear the ambulance nearby. I prayed they'd switch the siren off. I didn't want everyone alerting. In seconds they were alongside me.

There was a tap on the passenger side door and I pressed the button to disengage the locks.

'Hello sir. Are you okay?'

Course I wasn't fucking okay. I was having a stroke, twathead. A small crowd gathered on the premise that they wanted to help, but I knew they were just being nosey. Word was going around that someone was having a stroke and in these parts that definitely qualified as a spectator sport. The door opened.

'Okay sir, stay calm. I'm not going to move you just for now. Right, tell me exactly what happened, while I take your blood pressure.'

It's my right leg. It just started twitching violently. I went to put my foot on the accelerator and it just wouldn't go down and then . . . and then . . . it just started shaking. It was horrible.'

'Okay, sir. Okay. Can you move this way slightly for me? Your blood pressure seems okay. A little high, but that's to be expected.'

The ambulance man carefully took my tie off and unbuttoned my shirt completely, nodding his head towards his colleague who was at the driver's side window.

'Now what we're going to do is this. I'm going to try and lever my arm underneath your bottom and Bill there will try and ease you out of the door. Don't try to move, we do this every day.'

Not to me you don't. Oh please don't drop me. I spluttered 'ok' and as the man I now knew to be Bill, gently opened my door, I felt a sudden sense of relief as my movement returned to my stricken leg.

'My God.'

'What is it?'

'I can feel it again. It's a miracle. I can feel my leg. It's moving - but not of its own accord.'

Bill started laughing, which I couldn't help thinking was a touch inappropriate, but what the hell.

'I think I know what's happened here sir.' Bill spluttered. I might have got my movement back by some strange divine intervention but the hilarity was starting to grate.

'What is it?'

'Can you look down sir?'

Was this some kind of test, the outcome of which was only of significance to them? I looked down towards the bottom of my leg. Oh bollocks. No!

'Easily done sir' observed Bill.

'Surely not. Suddenly a stroke - albeit a mild one - seemed a welcome proposition.

'I haven't?'

'I think so, sir.'

'Oh fuck. I . . .'

'It's okay. Easily done.'

My shoelace was undone and was now flapping around defiantly having been freed from the door the very second Bill yanked it open.

'I think you've just trapped your lace in the door sir.'

'God, I'm really sorry.'

252

'Hey that's what we're here for. Glad to be of assistance. Anyway that's one to tell the lads when we get back.'

'I am so, so, sorry.'

'Think nothing of it sir. Take five minutes and just relax for a while and then start again eh?'

'Thanks.'

Bill and the man whose name I never got to know got back in the ambulance while the crowd still seemed somewhat bemused and, perhaps, just a little disappointed

I declined an explanation, buttoned my shirt back up, thanked my two rescuers and decided to make my way sooner rather than later.

Embarrassment subsided to relief. I had not had a stroke or anything resembling one. I was not going to die or even be partially paralysed. I was not going to spend my dying moments alone in Milton Keynes watched by an appreciative audience. The day was getting better by the minute.

41

1999 - MILLENNIUM

Robbie Williams had the right idea - bring out a song called Millennium two years in advance. Brilliant. Britain has gone Millennium mad and everyone sees the chance to make a fast buck. Some saw it quicker than others. But a lot of them have caught a fucking cold.

And while interest in The Millennium might have waned, the fever to cash in on it only started to waver when people realised we weren't mugs. And so all the clever bastards who booked function rooms 10 years in advance and then tried to flog them at extortionate prices, had their fingers burned. I think it was that as much as anything that signalled such a massive turn in the way I thought about things. Greedy bastards charging five quid for a lukewarm hot dog in Trafalgar Square; clubs and pubs trying to charge ridiculous amounts for entry to the biggest night of the century.

And it was triumph for common sense when the majority of people seemed to say 'stuff your events' and organised things amongst themselves.

And maybe it was the letter from Mouse that rammed it all home to me. The people around him in Malawi had no real concept of time, dates etc. They just relied on the seasons and whether they could provide enough food for their families. And so, Mouse was saying that whatever I might be doing on Millennium night to enjoy myself and think of him, doing absolutely nothing.

And I thought about the whole concept of not even

knowing it was 11.59 on January 31, 1999 and considered what a luxury that must be. Not having to give up chocolate biscuits because there aren't any and not making a New Year's Resolution to lose weight so you can get into a Size 12 dress because it just doesn't matter out there. It's not important. And as I got to think about it, I saw all this nonsense for what it was - just not important. Fucking hell, Mouse, what were you doing to me? It would have been nice to be out there with him and Melissa. I couldn't help wondering what they were doing right now . . .

'Zandalaya . . . a craw fish pie and a file gumbo.' Melissa twisted the words and strummed her slightly battered acoustic guitar. The embers of the campfire illuminated her tanned face. Mouse swayed gently, cross-legged and sang along to Melissa's modified version of The Carpenters hit from his position directly opposite. Singing by the glow of the campfire had become a regular pastime. The group sat in a circle, gnawing away at pieces of cornbread and the fish platter that Edward had both caught and prepared. Eddie, as he liked to be known, was sitting immediately to Melissa's left. He could quite easily have doubled up as the lead singer of The Stylistics. He had an Afro which would have done itself proud in the Jackson Five and begged only one question - when had he last had it cut? Eddie had a smile like a freshly sliced watermelon and one of the cheeriest dispositions you were ever likely to come across. He seemed to have untold roles within the community ranging from parish priest to councillor, local mayor and town crier. Eddie was just a plain and simple top guy. His wife Kasarla sat to his left, smiling and swaying to the beat of the guitar. Next were three of the volunteers who had been seconded to the village a couple of weeks ago as part of their college syllabus. There was Meg, a slightly plumpish

girl of around 20 with dark hair and rosy-cheeks that looked like she had just been well-scrubbed. Next were Ricky and then Jack, two Aussie Christian Aid volunteers in their mid-20s who had come to help out with the final stages of construction at the school. Then Mouse was to be found half-way around the circle. Next was Syreeta, a local woman who doubled up as a medical advisor cum spokesman for the witch doctor, a revered man who lived just outside the village. Next were four more volunteers - Sally, a slim, fair-haired lass of around 21 from Sheffield; Martha, a harsh featured girl from Austria; Louise, a smiley-faced student from Loughborough and Gerald, a serious-looking scholarly-type with a rather unkempt beard from Manchester, who was about 40. He was in charge of the group and was gently shaking a tambourine, seemingly confident that the rest of the group would flag long before he would.

It had been a lovely night and most people seemed in agreement about one thing - singing Jambalaya against the backdrop of a cool African night made it sound far better than they could ever remember it from the Carpenters days. Most of them were feeling quite tipsy by now - courtesy of the locally distilled Muala, a spirit derived from an apple, which could be found all around the province. A kind of halfway house between an apple as we would know it and a crab apple, it wasn't great to eat. But when it had been given the villagers' local treatment and allowed to ferment with locally produced brown sugar, the resultant liquor was something to be respected.

Melissa was urged to do one last number before most agreed it was time to turn in after yet another long, hard day. She started strumming the intro to 'Leaving on a Jet Plane,' and everyone in the group joined in. Eddie and Kasarla gently hummed and tried to smile their way through it in the absence of any word sheets and within 20 minutes of the song being finished there were only three or four people left.

◇◇◇◇◇◇

The next night after an evening meal comprising mainly of spiced sausage called Boerewors, vegetables and rice, the bulk of the party decided to have an early night. Mouse and Melissa were just about to toss some water over the flickering ashes when the two Aussie boys came over, sat themselves down and offered to make some coffee.

'That'd be good,' said Mouse motioning for them to pull in closer.

'You having a good time you guys?' Mouse asked.

'Marvellous. It's a cooler place than we ever imagined to be honest,' said Ricky.

'Yeah, we're having a ball,' added Jack.

'Well you both seem to have settled in just fine. Sometimes it takes some getting used to,' said Melissa.

'Anyway, if you'll excuse me, I really could do with getting my head down.' Melissa kissed Mouse on the cheek and bid the other two farewell as she headed for the house.

'How long did it take you two to adjust then?' Jack asked.

'Mmmm . . . good question. Not long really. It's just different you know? Things you take for granted at home, you just don't get here. But, hey, it's still one of the most wonderful places on earth to me, anyway.'

'Yeah . . . it's spectacular for sure,' Ricky added.

'Mouse?'

'Yeah.'

'The School . . .'

'Yeah?'

'Have you ever met the guy who's funded it all. John Christmas. Have you ever met him?'

'Yeah, you could say that,' Mouse smiled. 'He's my best friend. What's more, the best friend any man could ever have.'

'Really?' Jack said with an appreciative smile.

'Yeah, really.'

'Go on . . .' Ricky urged his friend.

'Well, it's just that. I think . . .'

Mouse interrupted. 'I think I know what's coming.'

'Know what?'

'Oh err. . I know what you're going to say.'

'I'm not sure about that,' Jack said somewhat taken aback.

'Well, I'm pretty sure.'

'I think he's my father.'

◇◇◇◇◇◇

'I'm sure of it,' Mouse grinned. 'When you laugh son, you couldn't be anything but.'

'You know him really well then?'

'Oh yeah. He's going to be astonished at all this, I can tell you.'

'I don't want him to know. Well, not yet, anyway. I'm not sure how he'd take it.'

'He'd be a relieved man, Jack. He'd love it believe me. He's thought about you a lot over the years. He just didn't have a clue where you were. He doesn't even know he has a son.'

'Promise you won't say anything, Mouse, please. Not yet, I beg you.'

'Okay, okay.'

'It's just that he's obviously a wealthy man and I just can't help wondering if he'd think I'm trying to track him down because of that.'

'I'm sure he wouldn't.'

'Please don't say anything …'

'I promise. But, you could do a lot worse than make contact because this has burned away at him for a long time.'

'I had no idea.'

'Well I know he had a letter from your mum Suzie just before you were born, but that was it. He heard nothing more.

It hurt him badly. He's had to live with not knowing.'

Jack continued: 'The thing is, you see, mum died giving birth to me so I never knew her. I didn't even realise until I was about 14 that my parents were actually my grandparents. They brought me up.'

'Died? Suzie? Oh my good Lord. That explains so much,' said Mouse. 'I can't believe it. How terrible. Your father knows nothing about that - I can tell you that for certain.'

'I've only actually known for seven years or so about my mum and that was only because I needed my birth certificate for something. Then that's how it all came out.'

'Right. How sad. Poor Suzie.'

'I don't think they were planning to keep it a secret forever, but I think their hand was forced a little.'

'And so they told you?'

'Well, yeah. John Christmas is the name on the certificate, although I was brought up as Jack Day. I guess it was just their way of dealing with it. Apparently mum insisted that John's name be put on the certificate. But she never came round after having me and so it all remained a bit of a secret for all those years.'

'Yeah, well, they were no more than kids - the pair of them. We only met your mum a few times.'

'You met her? Oh, what was she like?'

'She was lovely. Really pretty, with a smile which lit the whole place up. Like I said I didn't know her that well. But I can remember her coming up to Linshaw as a teenager and meeting up with Sant.'

'Sant?'

'Yeah, sorry. Sant - it's short for Santa. Everyone knows John as Sant.'

'This all seems so weird.'

'Tell me about it!'

'So, how much did you know about . . .'

'Well, not much really. This story all gets confused about

the time of Christmas, it would be Christmas, let me see . . .
1974 I guess. Yeah, 1974. Your father, well Suzie's dad,
actually, came around to Sant's and went bonkers . . .'

'So that would be John's parents' house then?'

'Oh yeah. He was only a kid. Barely 16. That was virtually
the last he heard of it, I think. Yeah it was. Your family moved
away and all contact was lost . . . though, like I said, I know
he had a letter.'

'Oh right.'

'That was it - nothing more. But from what you've said, it's
not surprising. Poor Suzie. I had no idea. Well, how could I?'

'Course not,' Jack said somewhat quietly.

'What's he like then?'

'He's a great guy - a really great guy. He'd love to see you
- I'm absolutely sure of that.'

'I need to think about that.'

'Look, I promise. I think he has a right to know, but I also
respect your right to deal with it however you see fit.'

'Thanks.'

'Don't worry about the money issue. He's not like that.'

'Yeah, but I take it he's pretty seriously loaded.'

'Yeah - seriously.'

'I'd rather he wasn't rich to be honest. I know how it would
look after all these years suddenly contacting someone and
mysteriously discovering that they have money. It'd be better
if he didn't. I've read that he's in the multi-millionaire bracket?'

'Oh yeah.'

'Yeah, you could say that.'

'I read an article about him and The Christmas Foundation.
I got it off the Web.'

'Well you don't get that off your dad, that's for sure.'

'What?'

'Sant's a great guy, but for a man who made his fortune
through cutting edge phones, he's not exactly a wizard on the
world wide web.'

42

2000 - THE BANK BOUNCES

The deal is done . . . I've just taken the phone call which has transformed me from a jet-setting tycoon to Britain's richest unemployed citizen. Unemployed? I'm virtually unemployable. Just 13 years since starting the Fonez Factory, I've sold it - for £898m. Yeah, that's right - EIGHT HUNDRED AND NINETY EIGHT MILLION quid. It's official. If I were to write a cheque right now, the fucking bank would bounce. I'm 42 years old and my financial team inform me I'm officially so rich, it would be nigh-on impossible to get rid of my money. Apparently, there's virtually no pastime around which could absorb that kind of cash. The only way I could get rid of it would be to develop a chronic gambling addiction but, as they inform me, there aren't that that many people around who could actually afford to bet with me. Drugs, alcohol or fine living would kill me long before they could damage my bank balance. It's as scary as it is comforting really. It's taken almost 18 months to get everything sorted out. From that first chance conversation with Mouse in the Farmers Arms all those years ago, Fonez Factory became the biggest independent retailer and distributor in the business. My biggest competitor wants my entire chain of 350 shops, the distribution centre - the lot. His company has put together the package of a lifetime to make me walk into the sunset. And for over £800 million, I'm happily making plans to go. At the press of one decisive button, the money has cleared and my arch-rival has completed the buy-out. He openly declared in the Sunday Times the other week that he was delighted to be seeing the back of me. For £898m I'll happily show him my arse. It's incredible to think that the company now has a turnover of well in excess of a billion pounds. At the point of handing over the reins Fonez Factory employed just over 8,000 staff. There's a tinge of sadness in one way. It's a bit like handing your baby over. I'd nurtured this thing right from its infancy. I'd bought into the idea when Fonez Factory didn't have a single phone, let alone a factory. It didn't even have a name. Now with a network of retail outlets the length and breadth of the United Kingdom the baby had grown into something of a monster. There was a tinge of sadness in the parting of the ways, but enormous relief to be getting out. There really wasn't much I couldn't do now. I'd always said that at some point I wanted the free time and cash to be able to go to all the major sporting events of my choice - the US Masters, an Ashes series, a football World Cup. Now I was free to realise such dreams. I'm 42 and wealthy beyond my dreams.

All this had come about from buying just a handful of 'brick' phones and taking a gamble. What about all those people who sniggered and told me they wouldn't take off? I'll leave them to live with that. They could have been right. The whole thing nearly took me down. There was a time when I couldn't flog one of the darned things. Yet within a couple of years I'd sold a million quid's worth and I was on my way.

Now I'm within touching distance of being a billionaire - a hundred and twelve million quid short to be exact - but who's counting?

And you know the key to it all? Not me. It's the people I've employed every step of the way. Boy are some of those loyal staff going to be happy tonight when I give them their envelopes.

We are having the party of all parties tonight and some of my loyal and hard-working senior managers will get cheques which will make them millionaires overnight. They don't even know that yet. When I carved up the sale of the business, I oversaw a plan to make sure every single member of staff was rewarded. Every person who works for the company - right down to the toilet cleaner - will receive a cheque for at least £1,000 and rising dependent on years of service and position.

My 350 store managers are in for a huge surprise tonight. It will be worth the money just to see their faces. I know they haven't got a clue because the only other person who knows is Jackie, one of my very closest staff and she's like Fort Knox. They will all be getting cheques rising up to £25,000 dependant on service.

Then come my thirty senior managers who will become millionaires, just as I promised them they would when I took them on. They'll get the last shares issue that means that while they don't get it instantly, they are set up for life - eventually. I prefer it that way. A man can go off the rails if he's given it all at once. All except me of course.

I've always been straight with people I've been looking to take on and some of them looked at me as if to question MY integrity. But I knew deep within that if they trusted me and showed me I could trust them, they would be rewarded massively. There's a strange thing about the way people run business in this country and I'd like to think I bucked the trend. First off, when you start with nothing like me, then don't surround yourself with anybody who would be surplus to requirements. People ask me how I know my business so intimately, even though it's so big. It's because I'm hands-on and it's because there isn't a job I can't do. When you've travelled the country in a clapped out car, cleaned the toilets, tidied the desks and done the books along with other mundane duties, then you get to know your business inside out.

But secondly, and most importantly, bring in good people. Honest people, who will work with you and for you. And reward them. Why is it in this country that companies seem to get a good guy in a good position and then allow him to be taken away by a rival firm prepared to pay him more? What kind of lunacy is that?

From the minute Fonez Factory started to take off, I oversaw every single recruitment for at least three years and then made sure anyone I elevated to a senior position, knew exactly what my take on it was.

I've paid superb money to my staff from day one, but I've staggered it. I work on the theory that a really bright, good operator is only going to work for the same things as all of us. He or she has aspirations for a nice house, to start a family and to try and ensure they have financial security in their future years sorted out as quickly as is decently possible.

I pay good people well and have never baulked at that. I pay him or her handsomely because I know that if I do that then their wives or husbands are happy and that gives me a contented workforce. And I made sure that the financial incentives for them are staggered over a period of years so they had no desire to leave me. Poor operators? Chancers? Cheats? Just fuck them off. It's as simple as that. Bad guy in the office with a bad attitude? Fire him. Simple. I have no loyalty or sense of duty to people like that. Come with me and share some of the wealth generated, but take the piss or get a bit smart with me and you're out. Poor or mediocre people drag a company down like poor or mediocre people drag a party down. Poor or mediocre people will drag a town down, a football team down. It's what they do. Avoid them at all costs.

If you get good people in and they are of value to you, then value them. It's not rocket science is it? Why the hell do I want a smart operator of mine to be lured away? I've often joked with my competitors that they couldn't afford to take my staff and when they first tried, they realised I wasn't kidding. So if one of their employees catches my eye, I simply go out and get him. They just don't get it do they?

What a party this was going to be tonight. I wasn't usually into champagne and caviar and all that shite but tonight was different. This was the night I could see the looks on my staff's faces as I kept my side of the bargain.

I've taken over the Rio Grande Hotel for the night. But I've done the lot, paid for staff, rooms, bars everything. It's all on me and for once I don't care.

Wow! I thought of all the people who said I'd never make anything of myself. There was more than the odd teacher - Suzie's dad, the bank manager. As Julia Roberts said - big mistake. Huge. I'm officially the richest unemployed person in Great Britain. The one thing about acquiring massive wealth is that it does increase your capacity and resolve to be able to tell people to 'fuck off.'

Just being in the Sunday Times Rich List is sort of cool. If you needed a measure of just how far you've come, it's a good gauge when they round your estimated wealth off to the nearest five million. There's loaded and seriously loaded. It's true that money doesn't buy you happiness but I've been with it and without it, and I sure as hell know which one I prefer.

But I am grateful that it really isn't my God. My English teacher all those years ago used to quote Chaucer by saying that love of money was the root of all evil. And he could have a point.

Having tons of it can play games with your mind, if you are a reasonably intelligent person. It's an obscene amount to get your head around and my contributions to the Christmas Foundation have helped me come to terms with that. There's a lot more I want to do as well. I'll never be without again, that's one thing I do know. But I reckon the accumulation of vast wealth can steer you in one of two directions. I don't believe there's any middle ground - you either become mean beyond belief or you get generous. Those traits are in your character regardless of how much money you may have. I've seen poor people whose generosity has astounded me. Chances are I'll see a lot more - and I intend to reward them for it. My principles remain the same, regardless of where I am.

I've seen people with money coming out of their ears who wouldn't buy a down-and-out a cup of fucking tea and I've seen people with virtually nothing who'd share their last piece of bread. It teaches you stuff.

You'd be an idiot not to learn from the people I've come across in my business life - especially those who know the price of everything and the value of nothing.

43

2001 - HARRY POTTY

I find a book is always a welcome Christmas present - they can be so personal. And so I rip the paper off to discover I'm the latest potential recruit to the Harry Potter Fan Club. I am now the owner of Harry Potter and the Philosopher's Stone and as I mulled over the whole Potter phenomenon, my mind couldn't help wandering. . .

Picture the scene. It's the mid-90s in Edinburgh and a humble workman, who for the sake of this particular adventure, we'll call Bill, is ready to take a well-earned lunch break.

Bill: 'I'm off for an hour if that's okay. I'm desperate for a quick bite to eat.'

Boss: 'Alright mate. Where you going?'

Bill: 'Dunno, might just nip up to the caff.'

Boss: 'Oh yeah. And I wonder what the attraction up there is then?'

Bill: 'Give over.'

Boss: 'You're trying to pull that bird you've seen up there aren't you?'

Bill: 'Which bird?'

Boss: 'That blonde bit of stuff who's always in there. Nicholson's isn't it? The café up by the North Bridge?'

Bill: 'I don't know what you're on about. Silly old sod.'

Boss: 'Hey you can't kid me. I've seen ya . . . that blonde piece who's always in there scribbling away.'

Bill: 'Give me a break.'

Boss: 'I'll give you a break. You can have it now, but don't give me all that old bollocks. Get off with ya.'

Bill makes his way to the café in Nicholson Street and makes his way upstairs. The room is empty but for a waitress and the attractive woman, who looks to be in her mid-30s sitting at a corner table awash with papers.

'Cup of tea please and err . . . and I'll take a piece of your fruit cake please.'

'That'll be one pound eighty please. Sit down and I'll bring it.'

'Thanks. Anywhere?'

'Yeah sit anywhere my love.'

Bill surveys the room and decides to sit at the table just across from the scribbler who he's nodded to numerous times previously.

'Hi. Am I okay sitting here?'

'Sure.'

'Didn't want to disturb you. You always look so busy.'

'No, you're fine there. I was going to take ten minutes anyway.'

'Oh please, no, don't let me disturb you.'

'No you're fine. Please,' she insists, smiling warmly.

'I've never seen you stop before.'

'Well, so much to do, so little time. You know how it is.'

'Yeah. So what is it exactly you do here all the time?'

'Oh God, how long have you got? Well, without boring you to death, I'm writing a book.'

'Really. Now THAT is interesting.'

'Well . . . I'd like to think so, but it's just a question of trying to get someone else to think that. That's the tricky part.'

'No publisher then?'

'No. Not yet. Keep trying . . . don't be put off . . . and all that other stuff they keep telling you.'

'Must cost you a fortune in coffee,' says Bill.

'Yeah. Still, it's cheaper than trying to heat that flat of

mine. At least it's warm here.'

'Right. So, I'm a bit ignorant of these things . . . how do you get paid?'

'I don't! Twelve publishers have turned me down.'

'Twelve? Ouch!'

'Exactly. I get benefits and I've got a grant that helps, but, I'm not exactly in Danielle Steele territory if that's what you mean.'

'Well, you never know. Come on then, fill me in, what's it called?'

'Well this one is going to be called Harry Potter and the Philosopher's Stone. It's one of seven that I've got in my mind, but err . . .'

'Well, the title's . . . different.'

'Different? Yeah, you could say that.'

'What's it about then?' asks Bill undeterred.

'Well, I won't bore you with all the details but it's about a boy wizard who goes to this school called Hogwarts.'

'Okay.'

'Well, he has special powers. I get him to catch a train at Platform Nine-and-Three-Quarters so he can catch the Hogwarts Express and then he goes off on all these adventures and stuff. I suppose you could say, it's a bit specialised.'

'Well, fair play for persevering with it. Must be quite hard to get it all down. And what are all the drawings then?'

'Oh that's my rough sketch sort of thing and the rules of a game he plays at Hogwarts.'

'Game?'

'Yeah, it's called Quidditch. It's like an airborne ball game, played on broomsticks and there's like a World Cup sort of thing.'

'Oh right. Right, so this squidditch, it's like football or something I guess?'

'Quidditch,' she corrects him politely. 'No it's more sort of, well, they play it on a long oval field with three goal hoops at each end and basically they play it with three balls at a time. They fly while they do it.'

'Wow. Sounds tricky,' Bill says with an assuring smile.

'Yeah. They have a quaffle that is like a bright red ball with a sticking charm placed on it. There's a golden snitch too . . .'

'Ohh right.'

'Bit hard to explain really. The golden snitch has got wings on it and it darts around at high speed. It's kind of complicated - there's two heavy iron balls which are called 'bludgers' and there's like 700 ways to commit a Quidditch foul, so it's not easy to master.'

'Yeah, I can imagine,' says Bill, devouring the last piece of his fruit cake.

'Oh well, that's enough of all that. I expect you find it terribly boring. I'm sorry to have even tried to explain it.'

'No it's fascinating. Really fascinating.'

'People probably think I'm mad, but I like it and I happen to think other people will.'

'Yeah, well that's all that matters. You keep at it. More power to your elbow.'

'Thanks. It's meant for kids, but I think adults could maybe get into it too.'

'You'll have to try it out on some. You got any kids?' Bill says, trying not to be too obvious.

'Just the one. She's a bit young to appreciate it.'

'Maybe your husband can give you his opinion. We're all kids at heart us blokes, you know.'

'Might be a bit tricky . . . I'm not with him anymore.'

'God, I'm sorry.'

'Oh, don't be. I'm not!'

'Well maybe we could go for a drink one of the nights?'

'That would be nice.'

'Can I have your number?'

'I'm not on the phone - too expensive. But you know where to find me!'

'Yeah. Okay, I'll maybe sort something and see you soon eh?'

'That'd be nice.'

Bill makes his excuses and goes back to work, promising to catch up with her in the next few days. His boss is lying in wait.

'All right lover boy. How did it go?'

'What?'

'Don't give me what? Was she there then?'

'Oh, give over.'

'Did you get talking to her then?'

'Yeah.' Bill said indignantly.

'Is it on then?'

'If I want to yeah.'

'What do you mean *if I want to*?'

'She's up for it.'

'You got her number?'

'She's not on the phone.'

'Dahhh.'

'She's not on the phone, honest. She's a single mum.'

'She's blown you out.'

'No honest. No, I reckon I could be in there . . . but.'

'But what?'

'She sounds a bit odd - mad as a March hare, I wouldn't wonder.'

'Odd?'

'Yeah, she's writing some book about a boy wizard or summat. Couldn't quite work out what she was on about. Coming out with some right old stuff.'

'Eh you never know, she might be the next big thing. You never know mate.'

'Yeah okay, take the piss. Knowing my luck I'll make a date with her and she'll turn up on a bloody broomstick.'

'No pleasing you is there? A bird with her own transport? Don't knock it.'

'Get lost. It's not that. But I mean . . . she's got a kid, her flat's so cold, she spends half the day in that caff. It's not exactly promising is it?'

'She might keep you one day.'

'Yeah, well I doubt that very much. She sounds a bit of a crackpot to me. Harry Potter? Slightly potty more like.'

FOOTNOTE: The blonde with the cold flat did manage to get the book published. At the last count she had sold approaching 500 million books and was listed by Forbes as being the only US dollar billionaire to amass her fortune from just writing books. She is now ranked even higher than The Queen on the British rich list and could, if she wanted, buy the whole of Edinburgh. She brings in a bit of extra revenue from films of the books; books about the films about the books and films about the making of the films about the books. Bill still earns four hundred quid a week doing labouring work and was last seen looking up at Edinburgh's North Bridge with a rope in his hands.

44

2002 - HEIR MAIL

I sat on the sofa sobbing uncontrollably. My God, how had everything all turned out this way? I should be the happiest man on Earth - instead emotions that had been hidden deep within me were threatening to turn me inside out through shock.

What was even stranger was that I had no control over the bizarre set of circumstances. I sat there dumbstruck. The two letters might have been written by two different people and been sent almost thirty years apart and yet they were inextricably linked. I'd been to the small leather box where I'd kept Suzie's letter and retrieved it. It had a stranger ring than ever now. Now I had read this one:

> 117 Southview Blvd,
> Wallagong,
> Melbourne.

"Dear John,
Well, where do I even begin to write a letter like this? Tell the truth, this must be nearly my 100th attempt and somehow every single one has ended up in the wastebasket.
It's a hard enough task in the first place without the added complication of not knowing whether you know of my existence or not. I guess I might as well just steam right in (in true Aussie fashion!) and get this off my chest. I was going to say I think I'm your son, to try and broach the subject tactfully,

but nothing seems to sound right. The fact is, I am your son. Well, there it is, that's got that little matter into the open. I'll give you time to pick yourself up off the floor and apologise for my clumsiness. Truth is, how do you come out with something like this?

Anyway, if it's any consolation, it's not any easier from this end. You must forgive me, but I have only a rough idea where the trail of this story might have gone cold for you.

Believe me it's taken an age for me to pluck up the guts to write this letter. Despite having so long to think it all through, it never seemed to get any easier.

Let me make a start. My name is John Day, though I was brought up to answer to Jack, which has kind of stuck with me all this time. I was born to Suzanne Day, formerly of Esher, Surrey, who I know to have been a close friend of yours in the mid-1970s. I was born in Australia in 1977 after the family emigrated there. I was brought up in Melbourne, which is not only my home, but a great place too! Anyway, I've been intrigued to know more about you for as long as I can remember, which is not quite as long as you might imagine.

The whole business started to become an issue with me from about the age of 14 when the 'parents' who had brought me up sat me down and told me a story that they felt I should know. It turned out that while they were my mum and dad, they weren't if that makes sense. The pictures I'd seen around our home that I'd always been led to believe were my sister were actually of my blood mother Suzanne. It turned out they were actually my grandparents. The thing is - and again please forgive me, if you don't know - my mother died in childbirth and so parts of the story only began to emerge later. Then when I eventually tracked down who you were I discovered to my horror (if you know what I mean) that you were a very successful and wealthy man. That didn't help at all because then I thought you might question my motives for wanting to get in touch. Honestly, I have no intention of making anything

274

difficult for you and the money is the last thing on my mind.

I have been told you are a good man. I met your friend Mouse Ratcliffe out in Zandalaya a few years ago and have kept in touch periodically. As we are both Christians, he pledged to adhere to my wishes and not let you know I had been out there. I trust that is the case. By the way, great work and assistance you have done out there. Well done.

Please don't think badly of him or me. It wasn't some plot to keep it from you, just a question of timing. Well, here it is, the letter I hope you receive with some happiness just to know that I'm doing okay. My wife's name is Rachel. Things are good for us and we want for nothing. As I said, please do not misinterpret my reasons for getting in touch. I realise this must have all come as a big shock, but I do hope you can appreciate this has not been easy for me.

I am well aware that this series of events happened many years ago and when you were a very young man. I quite appreciate it, if this is now a part of your life that you have confined to the past and no longer want to re-visit. You have my word that if you indicate that is the case, you will not hear from me again. A lot of water has passed under the bridge, as they say, since then. All these years later, it's almost like we are both innocent victims of a unique set of circumstances. I haven't bothered sending e-mail addresses or phone numbers. That would have been too presumptuous. I can be contacted at the above address and look forward to hearing from you, if you so wish.

Yours Jack.

I found myself reading the two letters alternately for what seemed like hours. I was in an absolute daze. It was like someone had punched me. I felt physically sick. Suzie dead? And all this time I hadn't known. Was I responsible? I felt like I was. A son? Wow, this had all happened so fast. Well, not so much fast, but in one short, sharp jab, which had knocked me sideways. I felt winded. Angry. Jubilant. Sad. Joyous. Tell the truth, I didn't know what I felt. This was the oddest experience I had ever been through. I picked up Suzie's letter and read it again. She'd never got back to me and I'd eventually held that against her. Now I knew why. I'm sorry Suzie for ever being angry with you . . . truly sorry. Forgive me. I couldn't believe that lovely girl I'd spent so many happy hours with was no longer with us. She had died just a few months after I'd last seen her. That wonderful summer of 1974 had been her last.

Dear Sant,

Boy, oh boy, have we caused some shit!! If you think you have had a hard time, spare a thought for me. Dad has gone absolutely mental. He's still not come down off the ceiling about all this mess. I hear he gave you a hard time. I've had that for months now. Sorry, I didn't get chance to warn you he was coming, but by the time it all started happening, he was on his way. He just stormed down the drive, got in his car and the next thing we heard was him screeching away. I've honestly never seen him so mad. My mum isn't very happy, as you'd expect, but she seems to be getting a bit more used to it now. In fairness she's been really quite good because my dad has been like a demented madman about the place. There's just no talking to him - he just goes on about how I've ruined my life, my prospects, everything . . . he's raging. Guess I don't need to tell you that.

Anyway, the reason I'm writing is that we are moving shortly so even if you were thinking about getting in touch - don't. It seriously wouldn't be a good idea anyway. I'll try and let you know what happens as soon as I can. For now, if I was you, just keep out of the way. I've got to admit I'm a bit scared about all this Sant. What did I do to deserve this? I don't want to sound like I'm full of self-pity, but it all seems very unfair from where I'm sitting. I'm not asking for any help or anything like that. It's just that it seems like I'm on my own at times, no matter how understanding mum tries to be. There's just no talking to dad. He's on another planet somewhere. The thing was Sant, by the time I realised I was having a baby, there were hardly any options open to me.

Dad's gone absolutely bananas about it and I understand that, but honestly, I just didn't know. There was no bump or anything. I've read these stories about girls not knowing until the day they had it and never believed it. There was nothing - not a bump or anything. There is now. University is out of the equation for sure!! Anyway, just had to write to let you know I'm OK. I've left my address off on purpose so don't try and make contact for now. That might be one surprise too many for my old man.

I promise I'll be in touch as soon as I can and let you know the outcome. I'm due early March. Not long now. I'm hoping things will settle down in the not too distant future and things will be different for all of us. To hear dad talk you'd think I'd murdered someone. I think he might be ready to - YOU probably with me a close second!!!

I've told mum that if it's a boy I want to call it John - it's a nice name. I don't think I'll take your surname on though . . . just imagine John Christmas-Day!!!

I've had to take that ring off even though it is expandable!!! At least they won't have to cut it off !!

Anyway Sant, I'll be in touch as soon as I can
See you. Suzie X.

45

2003 - JONNY BE GOOD

Every dad treasures the day he first takes his son to a match, I just had to wait nearly 30 years to do it. But what a match to start-off the whole experience.

The small but stocky blond figure pulled his right foot back and what happened next has only one natural speed - slow motion. In real time it seems to take an age, but it's still far too fast. Moments like these deserve to be embalmed in a state of slow motion for ever. In the same way that some black and white films would never look quite the same in colour, Jonny Wilkinson's kick should be in freeze-frame for eternity.

'He hasn't?'

'He fucking well has! Has he? Yeeeees! It's over.'

'Strewth. I can't fucking well believe it,'

'Come on my son!! Jonny Wilkinson walks on water.'

'My God.'

'He won't help you now son. We've done it. England have fucking well done it. Unbelievable.'

The bulk of the 80-odd thousand crowd have been stunned into silence. The sea of green and gold has instantly been calmed as the scale of what has just taken place sinks in.

My son is shaking his head in disbelief while I'm unashamedly punching the air with delight. Well, he's an Aussie for God's sake and Jonny - OUR Jonny - has just sent a drop goal sailing over the posts with 26 seconds to go to win the Rugby World Cup for England. Here, right in front of our eyes in the magnificent Telstra Stadium in Sydney. It really doesn't get much better than this. It's a fantastic time to be a Pom. I told Jack he shouldn't have ditched his heritage quite so quickly. King Jonny has done it. Swing Low Sweet Fucking Chariot. When I pledged to myself that I'd go and watch some of the great sporting events in the world, I didn't think it would take in sticking one up the Aussies right in their own backyard. And with a goal coming from the very last kick of extra-time - it's the stuff of fairytales. November 22, 2003 and Christmas has come early for Brits everywhere. All around me hardened beer-swilling rugby-mad Aussies are struggling to hold back the tears. Aussies don't cry. But fuck me; they're close to it. The Poms have put them to the sword and on their own patch just for good measure.

It's all material for good-natured piss-taking just as you'd expect. They don't like it up 'em, the Aussies. We don't get to celebrate too often but when it comes HERE and in THIS fashion; it'd be rude not to gloat. Take that you baaaastards!

But that's the good thing about rugby crowds - you can have the craic without someone wanting to punch your head in. It's a civilised game rugby - played by solicitors and accountants who never question a referee's decision. Real respect. They'll bite your ear off, try to snap your neck with a high tackle or rake studs all over you as you lie on the ground, but they're proper gentlemen. It's thuggery with standards. Most of them double.

It's a defining moment in my relationship with my son. I guess all dads dream of taking their lad to a match. I'm guessing I was about eight when my father used to take me to watch a side, then known as Wellington Town. Okay, so I waited until my lad was 29, but I would like to plead extenuating circumstances. How bizarre was all this? It felt good though. Just being able to spoil him with the promise that not only was I coming over, but that I'd managed to get a couple of tickets for the Rugby World Cup final, gave me unimaginable pleasure. How could I have even dreamed it would be The Poms versus the Aussies, full on for glory? I've never found getting tickets for major events a problem - but then again, you tend not to when you're loaded. It's obscene really, but I'm not complaining. And the strange thing is, it's nothing to do with being able to outbid anyone to land them - people give them me. When you've got clout like the Fonez Factory, people chuck stuff at you. It's like 'Would you care to be our guest at the Monaco Grand Prix?' or 'We'd love to fly you out to the US Masters in Augusta as our guest!' Fucking hell - it's a no-brainer. It's that Julia Roberts 'now really spoil me' bit. It's like my big grievance with banks - when you don't need charity, you get it. They still send me loan offers through the post. I've got over eight hundred million quid, what the fuck would I want a loan for? People would fall over themselves to get me to go to The Open golf and lay on all the hospitality. They'd even actually be excited if I accepted their invitation to be flown to the venue and gorge myself on fine food and wines at their expense. If I said I was struggling to get up there because of pressure on time, they'd just lay on a helicopter. It's grossly unfair really, but hey, I'm not complaining. My business was important to them. Time was when no-one gave a shit. When I could have used those sort of events for some serious networking, no one ever invited me. Bollocks who cares? I'm here now and that's all that matters.

It's been really great meeting up with Jack and Rachel - a pretty olive-skinned girl who he's known from his high school days. She says she can't get over the similarity between us but, like most blokes, I can't really see it. He's better looking for a start and a lot thicker set than me. I don't know if it's all those rough Aussie sports he was brought up on, but he's got the look of a guy who would take some knocking over. Jack's around 6ft 3in - an inch taller than me and, I would guess weighs in at around 16st. I don't know what that is in kilos. We only went metric 32 years ago, for Christ's sake. He's got dark hair like his mother, cropped to within an inch of its life.

There's a look of Suzie about him when he laughs. He's got forearms like Popeye, due to spending a couple of years working in a sawmill as he made his way through university. All in all, as I catch glances of him, he's a fine figure of a man. I take little credit for that, sadly. He appears to have grown up to be a pretty regular fellow and I'm grateful, but in no way responsible, for that. In fairness, from what I've seen over the past couple of weeks, there can't be many better places in the world to be brought up than Melbourne.

I confess to knowing little, make that nothing, about the place, until this dramatic family soap opera started to unravel. Jack and Rachel live in a modest but nice chalet-type home in Roscommon, a suburb of the country's buzzing second city. Melbourne sits comfortably around the shores of Port Phillip Bay with the rather unusual Yarra River coursing its way right through its heart. When Jack and Rachel said they would take me down to see the 'upside down' river, I really couldn't imagine what they were talking about. But the Yarra is a distinctive strange brown colour giving the appearance that it's somehow been turned over and its bed is on the top.

From the little I'd seen, it was easy to see the appeal of such a beautifully designed, cosmopolitan place. The leafy bayside community certainly seemed to be a template for mixing modern and more traditional architecture. Within it was an impressive array of restaurants and bars and the few locals I spoke to at any length made it quite clear they proudly believed theirs was one of the most civilised cities on the planet.

To be honest, I'd always viewed Australia with some suspicion and that's nothing to do with Rolf Harris or Dame Edna. It has animals you find nowhere else in the world - and most of them are fucking deadly. Forget that image of cuddly

Koalas, Bondi Beach and endless barbecues, up until very recently it had been my idea of hell. The only good thing I could think to say about it was that it was 24 hours away on a plane. The snakes that aren't poisonous just fucking strangle you to death. I don't like sly animals like that. I don't need to be told a lion is dangerous because I can work it out for myself. You don't have to tell me to keep out of the way of elephants because they are very heavy and have big tusks. I can see that. Australian animals are a bit sneaky. Even the kangaroos are likely to box you around the ears at the first available opportunity. How can you ever be totally comfortable in a place where there are spiders which crawl into the nearest available orifice and inject you with a venom capable of pole-axing the world's strongest man in about six seconds? It's not just on the land either - ask Steve Irwin. I mean to say, he spent his entire life with the darned things and still ended up copping it. Imagine that - a stingray that shoots a deadly barbed spear into your heart. Britain just doesn't have natural phenomena like that. The Severn Bore is about as dramatic as it gets and I don't mind admitting I take great comfort from that. Active volcanoes, hurricanes, deadly animals . . . well, you can fucking well keep them.

That's why I've always been suspicious of people in Britain who keep strange pets. Never trust a man who keeps an iguana. You don't have to take my word for it, but as a rough rule of thumb, you won't go far wrong. Show me someone who bonds with a tarantula, scorpion or a corn snake and I'm suspicious.

The really strange thing is that my dad was often telling me how he and mum so nearly emigrated Down Under in the mid-60s. There was some scheme to recruit people there and you could go for just ten quid. Apparently the Australian government were virtually handing out passports to anyone with a trade and were more than happy to subsidise the travel to get people over there. Bit ironic really, considering how we sent them boatloads free of charge in the days when Britain really did deport people fucking properly.

You see, even Australian history is suspect. I mean what the hell was all that about? Creepy crawlies apart, what made any right-minded magistrate or politician think that the way to really punish someone was to send them on a boat trip to a land of golden beaches and sunshine? Just imagine some sheep rustler from Yorkshire being put on a boat and eventually emerging on a sun-kissed beach on the other side of the world. What kind of punishment was that?

And dad said to me on a number of occasions that if they hadn't eventually decided to back out, he and mum would have gone out there and started a family.

And so I ended up beating them to it. How weird did that family stuff still sound? Rachel, who has Aboriginal ancestry, has just told me she's four months pregnant. My god, I had spawned a new mongrel breed. Hey, that's quite chic these days. Time was when I was a lad that if next door's Labrador got your pedigree poodle pregnant, you would reach for the shotgun. Now, they call them Labradoodles and want to charge you an absolute fortune for a pup. They're more expensive than the pedigrees. I'm in fashion for the first time in my life?

It really is odd how perceptions change. How could I have known all those years ago when I was watching Love Thy Neighbour and Till Death Us Do Part that one day I'd have part-Aborigine in my family? I hope the kid doesn't inherit my sense of direction. It could go on walkabout and never return. All the messages are different these days. Mind you, when I was a teenager the geography master was forever telling us that the world was heading for a new ice age and that one day we'd all freeze to death or get mown down by a glacier. Thirty years on and everyone's saying global warming is going to fry us. Is it any wonder we are all left feeling so fucking confused?

◇◇◇◇◇◇

From my brief stay, I could imagine Melbourne being a far more exciting place to grow up than any small town back in England. Yet Jack made me promise to show him some of the places where I grew up, when he could arrange to get over. I could understand that. And I guessed it would be as poignant as it would interesting for him, because he had absolutely no knowledge of the place.

'I've just got to come over one day. And real soon,' Jack said excitedly.

'No problem. Both of you come. It would be my pleasure.'

'It's a place I just have to see. I don't know if you can fully get your head around that, but that's how it feels to me.'

'I can understand that,' I assured him.

'You know it's like . . . well, exactly that. It's like I'm looking at my past as a jigsaw and there have just been whole areas of it missing. And now I'm fitting pieces in and, for the most part, the picture I'm putting together is something I like. It's not something to run away from. I feel like there was this thing to be hidden away and it's just not like that to me. Seeing you and the things you can tell me, it's all really helped me piece things together.'

I nodded and chewed my bottom lip. What could I say? It struck me this was as happy an ending as was possible under the circumstances. Suzie and me were so carefree roaming around the fields by Bluebell Wood, how could anyone have predicted it would all turn out like this? A bizarre set of circumstances had conspired together to take the story this far. And there was no doubt plenty more mileage in it yet. This story could run and run and long after I was dead and gone, and hopefully future family members would marvel at how wonderfully romantic it was, though it still doesn't seem quite like that to me.

My stay was drawing to a close. It had been fun and had flown by. I understood totally the circumstances why it had taken Jack so long to get in touch. I was quite touched that my financial situation had been a problem to him. I gave him a bollocking for it, but I suppose I wouldn't have wanted him to think any other way really. I didn't want to try and buy my way into his life and, likewise, he was at pains to point out that he was well on the way to trying to find me when he realised I'd amassed considerable wealth. It was no longer a problem. He'd be coming over as soon as possible and I'd fill in some more of the pieces for him. To say it had been fantastic to see him would be an understatement. A deep ache inside which had been there for years, had been soothed. It had been great to see my boy. I still couldn't help thinking of Suzie . . . that first meeting, newts, the youth club disco and her smiling at the entrance of Bluebell Wood.

46

2004 - LONELY THIS CHRISTMAS

Christmas in hospital. It's been another eventful year. I became a grandad in April. Rachel and Jack have christened him John. I'm delighted. They don't even know I'm in hospital because I was rushed in two nights ago. Apparently I've been very lucky. The surgeon told me that had my appendix burst; it could quite easily have killed me. How lucky is that? He explained that I really was quite fortunate because if they rupture, the toxins held there can burst into your bloodstream and completely poison your system. And what exactly does your appendix do? Fuck all, actually, from what I'm able to determine. It's some superfluous oddity that's likely to catch grape pips and whatever and hold onto them until they have gone really rancid and poisonous enough to terminate your life. To say I'm not happy with my appendix might be something of an understatement. As far as I'm concerned the appendix, wisdom teeth and fucking grape pips for that matter are going into my personal Room 101.

Actually I was an unashamed disciple of seedless grapes regardless and now I realise that, I'm even more inclined to give the guy who developed them a knighthood.

Aren't seedless grapes just one of the best innovations of all time? I'd love to meet the person who came up with that idea and give them a massive pat on the back. Not in that forceful *'you're choking - have you swallowed a pip?* sort of way. No, I'd just love to congratulate them on such a fucking superb transformation of a fruit that up to that point had well and truly got on my nerves

If only they could adapt the same principle to produce boneless fish - now that would be something. Okay, so they'd wobble around in the water a bit, but that's their problem, not mine. No matter how big a fan you are of fish or grapes with seeds in, it just strikes me that for the most part they are a fucking waste of time. Call me picky, but once I've found a bone in some fish I'm all over the place. I just can't settle. Images of the Queen Mother come flashing before my eyes and in my mind's eye there's a bone the size of a jouster's lance lurking there waiting to spear me.

Maybe the real reason I'm so taken with seedless fucking grapes is that grudging acceptance that my teeth are no longer in the Bluebird toffee league. I'm knocking a hole in 50 and so maybe I'm unconsciously weaning myself onto any sort of foodstuffs that don't look capable of putting up a fight. The days when strawberry and lemon bon bons or gobstoppers as big as your fist didn't fill you with dread have long since passed. Perhaps it's not that you grow out of some of those sweets but that your body, more to the point your teeth, starts to reject them. The days when peanut brittle didn't cost you a fortune at the dentists are a distant memory.

Do your taste buds just disappear? Do I now have a different set from when I was ten? Surely not. I swear to God I could still demolish an Aztec Bar or an Icebreaker. What was that other one called? Yeah, Swisskit, that's right. They used to advertise that all the time. 'I'll risk it for a Swisskit!' Blimey, what happened to them? They must have disappeared about the same time as Country Style - another favourite of mine, which vanished off the face of the earth. Was I really the only person eating them? They certainly can't have been as popular as I thought. And where did Bar Six go? The good old Bar Six had been confined to the chocolate knackers yard along with the likes of Old Jamaica and Mint Cracknel. Mint Cracknel - now there was a classic. Did the health and safety brigade get their fucking hands on those? I loved them - shards of bright green glass that could slice your gums open before the wrapper was fully off. They were superb.

Why weren't we consulted? Kids seem to be asked their opinion on everything these days, yet it's like someone stripped our heritage away without even thinking us worthy of asking. Who actually decided that Marathons should be called Snickers? When did it become silly or downright unhealthy to ask for a bag of rainbow kali which you could drop in your pop until until it fizzed all over the brim? It's lost in time but I can't help thinking we should have been asked prior to any change.

And now I tend to sidestep chocolate things and plump for fruit. It's better for you. You buy into the healthier lifestyle thing. You end up walking around city centres clutching bottles of mineral water. You start thinking about doing the London Marathon. Oh fuck, it's that Jimmy Savile thing again

I know he's raised stacks for charity but he just gets up my nose. You can't see clips of a charity run without that white-haired tosser suddenly appearing in front of the camera. I swear to God if he ran past me, I'd trip the bastard over. It's bad enough getting passed by someone who must be at least 86, but to see him waving a big fat cigar as he did it would just about do my head in. Why isn't he clutching a bunch of seedless fucking grapes?

Seedless grapes just weren't around when I was a kid. Fruit was awkward. Banana sandwiches were about as exotic as it got for us. Even they went mushy and brown if you didn't eat them pretty quickly.

So, I'm not sure exactly when I'm going to be out but I'm just grateful to be alive. That's my Christmas present for 2004 - being alive. Well, Barry White would swap with me that's for sure.

The Walrus of Love is dead. Yeah, the fat sweaty sod who topped the charts that Christmas back in 1974 when I was having my biggest nightmare, has popped his clogs. Forgive me for holding a grudge but I don't suppose he gave me a single thought when he was warbling away and having the time of his life. If it hadn't been for that association, I guess he could have been a bit of a hero of mine. Let's face it, anyone who perspires so profusely, has a figure the size of a block of flats and can still be considered a love god, has to be admired. The Walrus of Love indeed. Yeah, Barry Fucking White, 25 stone if he's a day, has gone to that big disco in the sky. Those wings should go perfectly with his suit if it's any consolation.

It has to be one of life's greatest absurdities how he could ever be considered a sex symbol. Come on folks, great voice - granted. Great songs - granted. But a man to make women swoon? It's a puzzle to me. Jesus, this guy can't even sit on the toilet properly. And there he was, sweating away, and just to really take the piss, he was going to the audience and dangling his perspiration-soaked hankies to his adoring public. And they were fighting over them! These women were virtually clawing each other's eyes out to get one of Barry's sweaty snotrags. Explain please . . .

If I hadn't seen it with my own eyes I would have sworn it was a total piss-take. Jealous? Me? You fucking bet I am. If I was ever vain enough or ambitious enough to toss a sweaty hankie into a crowd of women, I guarantee you one of them would come over and slap me. So if that's fair, then I'm a Dutchman. Superstars get away with fucking murder, I'm telling you. It's like they operate under a completely different set of rules. Which is annoying enough when you are not even taking into consideration the fact that they are seriously loaded.

I never fully realised just how attractive I could be until I had cash. It's like how many haggard old millionaires or pig-ugly footballers do you see with really top looking birds? Fucking loads of them. I wonder why that is then? Perhaps I'm just bitter thinking back to the days when I had nowt. Perhaps

I'm just getting a bit morose because The Walrus of Love has chosen to add his name to an ever-increasing list of pop stars from my era that are now no longer with us. I didn't need the stroke scare in Milton Keynes or a grumbling fucking appendix to ram home just what a fragile line we walk. Death seemed to be everywhere I looked just lately. Les Gray passed on a few months back.

It'll be lonely this Christmas . . . well, it will in his household. Les, the happy-go-lucky lead singer with Mud, has died and it's things like that which start to make you more aware of your mortality. Christopher Reeve has gone a few months ago as well.

Marc Bolan's long gone, Freddie Mercury, Elvis, and Brian Connolly from Sweet. Time was when I was a teenager I'd have swapped my life with any one of them.

I guess that's what it is when someone like Big Barry snuffs it, the frailty of it all is brought home to you. We're all getting older and we don't need things like this happening to ram it home to us. Swap? What with me? No fucking deal now mate.

It's like with Superman. That horse managed to do what 50 mega-tonnes of Kryptonite couldn't manage. When poor Christopher came a cropper that was it for me. I'd watched in awe as he flew over tower blocks; whizzed around the planet and rescued Lois Lane from certain death at Niagara Falls and then suddenly he falls off a fucking horse and he's eating his dinner through his arm.

And so when proud mums stick their kids on top of these beasts, I think they're seriously misguided. I mean would you put your six-year-old daughter on top of a car and push it down the road? Course you fucking well wouldn't. Have you ever seen a horse with 'L' plates on? Exactly.

You know more teenage girls are paralysed through falls from horses than car crashes. Yet little Lucinda gets a hand up onto one of these beasts and thinks a protective helmet will do the trick. If it were a working class pursuit, they'd have outlawed it years ago.

I can't remember exactly when Les and his Mud mates crept onto the scene, but now he's crept out and it's sad really.

It wasn't cool to like Mud when I was a teenager. I'm not sure if it was ever cool to like them. But they did give you the impression that they were just taking the piss and having a good time and so deserve respect for that alone. Hey, and he did sound quite a bit like Elvis.

John Denver's another one we've lost. What a cruel way for him to die. The man who wrote Leaving on a Jet Plane, killed in an air crash. Someone really is taking the piss. Almost Heaven . . . it was when he lost control in that light aircraft. The Blue Ridge Mountains must have been on him in no time.

Maurice Gibb has gone too. He's up there with kid brother Andy giving it loads in their white suits. Stayin' Alive . . . well, not quite boys, but we know what you mean.

And just for good measure, Sacha Fucking Distel has left us too. I struggle to forgive him - he was one of those compulsory shit acts the BBC inflicted on us on Top of the Pops. My mum thought he was great, which was a good enough reason to hate him when I was 13.

And anyway, anyone who shagged Brigitte Bardot before she had a face like an old saddlebag and stunk of rescued animals deserves everything he gets. Au revoir . . .

Sacha can go in a special section along with Benny Hill and Lena Zavaroni. I don't know what you'd call it. How about the people-who-fucked-up-Top-of-the-Pops section?

The disturbing thing about it all was that I remember when I was a teenager thinking how odd it was that a lot of the stars mum and dad liked were dead. What was that about? Bill Haley? Dead. Gene Vincent? Dead. James Dean? Dead. Buddy Holly? You guessed it. Dead. I used to taunt my dad asking him if there was anyone alive he liked. And he said one day, I'd know how that felt and I probably just laughed. And yet now just off the top of my bloody head, I could think of loads. It's quite disturbing. I can't count the number of times I'd wished Little Jimmy Osmond had choked on his own vomit, but all these years later I suddenly wished him a long and happy life. Partly through pure selfishness and because I'd seen him on telly recently and as much as my mind told me to still hate him, he seemed a decent enough chap. Yeah, if ever I'm lucky enough to see the headline 'Little Jimmy Dies at 94.' At least I'll know I'm in telegram from the king territory.

47

2005 - MISSING PIECES

'It's just like I have this need to fill in some of the pieces. They've been missing for so long . . .' Jack said with a rueful smile.

'Hey, let's make this really great,' I urged him as we made our way out from in front of mum and dad's old house and came to the mouth of Orchard Grove. My parents were still in good health but as my business took off I helped them buy a lovely bungalow set back in its own grounds on the outskirts of the village. Things had changed around here for sure, but there were still plenty of things I reckoned I could show him. It was kind of strange really, but I could thoroughly understand his eagerness to get a taste of his past through seeing some of the places where Suzie had been. It was a beautiful, bright June morning and we'd agreed a rough plan whereby we'd finish up at The Farmers for a pint or two and I would try and fill him in on everything I could recall.

'Let's just go right here, only a little way,' I said as I went down to the dead end where Maggie's shop and the chippy used to be. I knew they had both long since gone, but it seemed as good a starting point as any. Any references I made to his mum were always as 'Suzie' because he'd grown up well into his teens calling Mrs Day mum and the term didn't quite come naturally to him.

'Okay,' I said putting my tour guide hat on. 'Well, down here . . . that house there used to be a shop called Maggie's where we'd go and get sweets and stuff and that big space there, well, that was where our chippy was. Mouse and me spent some time there in our time. Two bags of chips and some batter bits. You can tell how long ago it was, ring-pulls weren't even around, so if you had enough money for a can of pop they used to have to open it for you in the shop with a sharp pointed can opener.'

'Really,' Jack said with an incredulous smile.

'Yeah, really. Ancient eh? They'd put two holes in the top on opposite sides. They were the days when the cans were so strong you could drop the darned things on the pavement and they wouldn't split. God, do I sound like an old fart?'

'Yeah, but it's great,' Jack assured me.

'God I can almost smell the place.'

Jack grinned and tapped me on the arm as if to assure me it was exactly the kind of stuff he wanted to hear.

'That building there was a pub. The Green Man. Been closed a few years now. Can't remember exactly when that place shut down.'

We did a u-turn and made our way back up Vinegar Hill towards the Farmers and we turned left at the top and round the side of it to where we could see the cottage that had belonged to his great grandad. He'd died some years ago and the place had been completely renovated. Half of the small field now housed a couple of detached homes but to the back of the old place was the large garden where I'd first seen Suzie.

'It was here, Jack, that I first bumped into Suzie. I'll always remember it. Mouse wasn't around much in those summers because he was always working every hour God sent at a farm a few miles from here. I was just sort of wandering around when I saw this very pretty girl helping out in the orchard.'

'Where? Just here?'

'Right there,' I said pointing. She was helping to dig a hole to plant an apple tree right there in that corner. In fact, I'll bet that must be the very tree she planted look. It's a lot bigger now obviously.'

Fucking hell, I could feel a Bobby Goldsboro moment coming on. See the tree how big it's grown and all that.

'D'ya think this is it then?' Jack said pointing to a tree which must have been easily twenty feet high.'

'Yeah, I do. Weird eh?'

'I think it's really lovely.'

We stayed a while until Jack indicated it was time to move on. He looked a bit choked. We made our way out towards the first ponds, the banks and on to Bluebell Wood.

Just to the far side of the second banks the wood was a carpet of blue with a fragrance that took me right back to those summers all those years ago. I could almost see Suzie standing there laughing, urging me to come in further.

'We spent a lot of time over here. Suzie loved these flowers. Such good times. Really, really lovely times. We'd spend whole days here, just messing about and having fun. It was really great,' I assured him. I didn't need to seek his approval, but I suppose I was. And Jack was receptive to all the things I had to tell him.

'This is like pieces of a jigsaw being carefully put into place for me. It's really cool too, nothing like I imagined really. I don't know what I'd expected.'

Neither did I. It had been years since I'd been here. Suzie and Mouse were around every corner. There had been changes, but not that much. We came out of the wood and turned back on ourselves to follow the railway line up towards the stone bridge that would take us to the old rec.

Half of it had gone, but you could still pick out places where we had idled away long summer days, playing football and eating Tip Tops. The old swimming baths and paddling pool had been filled in and there was no sign of the little shop down at the bottom.

'Suzie and me would spend hours over here. Just mucking about and doing . . .well, nothing much really. They were good times you know. She used to love it here. We did have some laughs.'

Jack didn't say a lot. He seemed to be letting it all wash over him, feeling her presence and trying to picture her as a young girl at these very spots.

'It's lovely, but strange. Quite odd. So different from where I was brought up. I just regret never knowing her. Never being able to ask her about this stuff.'

Two hours passed quickly and we agreed to make our way across the old stile and stop off in the Farmers on the way back.

The pub had changed quite a bit, but not so much that I wouldn't have recognised it if I'd been blindfolded and plonked in the place. We made our way to the bar.

'You know it was here that the whole idea of the business came up. It was Mouse's idea to be honest. He was always a shrewd little sod you know.'

'Ah he's a great guy,' Jack agreed.

'Yeah, if it hadn't been for Mouse the whole Fonez Factory thing would have been a non-starter. He persuaded me to go along with it and the rest, as they say, is history.

'Just shows you doesn't it?'

'Not half. It didn't take off overnight. At one point, I don't mind admitting, it was touch and go. It was mainly Mouse's assurances that the business could boom, that I stuck with it.'

'Is that why you are so close?' Jack asked.

'No, not really. We've been mates from day one, but he always had this kind of, well I guess you'd call it street intelligence, which always got him through. He'd turn his hand to anything and somehow it always seemed to come off. The business thing? Well, that was just following a hunch really. It was no more than that. A bit of bravado and a huge slice of luck and I was in at the start of it all. I'd like to say there was some big master plan but it was never really like that if I'm honest.'

'Life-changing moments eh?' Jack said with a broad smile.

'Tell me about it. Tiny acorns, mighty oaks and all that stuff.'

'Or apple trees,' Jack quipped.

'Yeah . . . or apples. I wish Suzie could have seen that tree. It's so odd seeing that again.'

'I feel more at ease now,' Jack said. 'I feel like . . . well, it's a kind of spiritual thing, but I just feel she'd be pleased I came here.'

'I'm sure she would. I'm sure of that.'

'Listen, there's something I've held on to for a long time, but I'd like you to have it.'

I raised my eyebrows and grinned at him, not knowing what to expect.

'It's just a little something, but I'd like you to have it,' Jack said reaching into his left hand pocket. He unravelled a frayed piece of tissue and told me to close my eyes and hold my hand out.

'What is it?' I laughed.

'It's just something that I kind of feel belongs here now. It's not mine. It belongs with you,' he said placing the object in the flat of my hand.

'You can open now,' he urged me.

'Oh my God. Good lord.' I could feel the tears welling up in my eyes as I looked at it. I looked at him and made my way towards the door. Jack followed.

We hugged outside as I made my way to the small bench across the road and sat myself down.

'God, I bought her that from a little market stall in Linshaw,' I sighed looking at the stainless steel Gemini ring I'd given Suzie all that time ago. I was completely overwhelmed and looked skywards sighing heavily.

'Wow. I'd forgotten all about that.'

'It was passed on to me. I was told that it was something you'd given her and so it's been kept safe all this time.'

I was lost for words. Jack could see I was choked and

allowed me my silence as he clutched my hand.

'I'll treasure that.'

'I know. I have.'

'Unbelievable.'

'It's like another piece falling into place,' he said.

'You can say that again. Come on . . .'

It was time to maybe get back now. That had knocked the stuffing out of me. Suzie's ring. Well, I never . . . She'd mentioned it in the letter, but I'd imagined it had long since been lost. I hadn't given it another thought.

48

2006 - THE BEAUTIFUL GAME

I can't recall seeing the beautiful game ever played quite so beautifully. Two-dozen-or-so barefooted lads ranging from maybe eight to 15, darting around the dusty clearing that doubled up as a football pitch. Only the occasional straying goat having to be coaxed back by one of the players, or one of the old men in battered straw hats, signalled a break in play. Mouse had told them I had coached a lot of the very best footballers in England, which if he hadn't been a Christian, I would have pulled him up on.

So I stood in the centre circle acting as referee with a special mandate to kick the makeshift ball, if it came in my direction. None of them knew I had a surprise for them later - some brand new footballs. Not that having to play with a ball made from plastic bags bound tight with string and tape seemed to hamper their enjoyment. Mouse had asked if I'd bring some. I'd popped over to his house a little earlier but he wasn't in, so they would just have to wait a while. I could barely wait to see their faces when I showed them a proper heavy-duty plastic ball. They would never have seen anything like it. What a far cry from so many of the spoiled brats back home in England. There were no eight-year-olds with David Beckham haircuts here, no fancy-dan top-of-the-range Adidas boots, no replica team shirts with sponsors' names on and no interfering parents moaning because their little Wayne or Jason hadn't been picked in his preferred role as sweeper. There was so much unnecessary pressure on our kids today -

and most of it came from their own parents. How times had changed - and not for the better, it seemed to me. I don't know what it was with kids these days, but somehow- and somewhere - Britain's children seemed to have lost the knack of being happy. As I revelled in the broad smiling faces and the chattering of unadulterated enjoyment, I couldn't help wondering if we couldn't learn more from these kids than we could ever teach them.

I could wince just thinking about the sorry state we've got into. The adults and coaches have taken over at home because it's not safe for kids to be left to play outside without supervision. And now youngsters aren't given time to fall in love with the game because they are shepherded into organised games at organised clubs run by overly ambitious and very organised coaches. And the parents turn up in droves and talk soccer-speak about how eventually they think their little diamond will favour playing in the hole just behind one of the strikers. And it's all bollocks and makes me realise that days playing war, cowboys and Indians and racing on Mouse's trolley were infinitely more special than I could ever have appreciated at the time. Whatever happened to just going out to play or making your own way to and from school? Did the dark men who might snatch your kids really end up winning? I suspect they did.

My dad never put me under any pressure to do anything other than my best. He played football with me but wouldn't have dreamt of interfering. As I watched the village kids chuckling and giggling as they played, I reflected that perhaps the Hungarian soccer legend Ferenc Puskas had got it about right when he said: "I am always eternally grateful to my father for all the football coaching he never gave me!' Spot on.

It seemed like we had lost our way in our pursuit of excellence and that for all the latest equipment and fancy gadgets, we'd lost the very soul which had once made us the best in the world at so many things, not just football.

Suddenly I spotted Mouse, pacing methodically around the pitch and making notes. I called to him but he seemed quite involved with what he was doing so I left him to it. Eventually he came over.

'What ya doin' Mouse?'

'Oh, I'm just pacing out some measurements in the village for a kind of map I'm making for some of the locals.'

'What do the locals want a map for?' I asked.

'It's just for some of those who are older or have difficulty seeing properly. I'm marking different routes out in paces so they will know exactly how far certain specific points are.'

'You are a good egg aren't you?'

'I try. Anyway, what was it you wanted?'

'Just wondered if I could come and get one of those balls.'

'Sure.'

Just watching the village lads was tiring me out, so I made my excuse to leave for a few minutes on the promise that I'd be back. Two of the boys - Singer and Sonny - insisted on coming with me as we made our way across the road to Mouse's chalet. Sonny was one of Eddie's sons and he'd adopted Singer when he was orphaned. The little boy was found wandering around one day a couple of miles outside the village. He was all alone and no one managed to establish whether his parents had died or whether he had merely been abandoned. But he was a happy soul most of the time and Eddie had given him the name Singer because he was always humming little tunes to himself. Singer and Sonny were both about seven and had become inseparable. That meant they were both with me, tugging at my shirt tails as we got to the house. The balls had come flat for ease of transport. I'd brought ten because I knew that, hard wearing as they might be, they were going to get some frightful hammer.

'They're in the back here somewhere,' Mouse said pointing in the direction of a long room on the far side, that   he

301

obviously used to store all manner of things.

' Now where did I put those balls?'

'They're there,' I said pointing to a small table just in front of him.

Sonny and Singer were waiting at the doorway and followed me back across the road, begging me to tell them what I had got.

'Right, I'll show you,' I assured them sitting myself down on the ground under the huge mango tree just down from where the football boys were playing.

'What is it?' Singer said with a smile.

'It's a new football.'

Singer and Sonny sniggered, so I showed them the adaptor, placed it into the valve and attached the pump.

'Blow it up,' I urged, Sonny, motioning to him to work the pump in and out.

'Go on then Singer, your turn,' I said as Sonny looked at me as if I was trying to trick him. Singer couldn't quite get to grips with it either.

'Here you are - give it here.' I began pumping the orange ball full of air. The boys' faces lit-up as they watched the ball inflate and they squealed with delight as it began to take on its proper shape. Once I'd got it to its right size, I bounced it off the hard ground, straight towards them.

'Go on, run on,' I said, seeing they could hardly wait to get back to their friends and show them what they had. As I made my way slowly towards the opening that led back to the footie pitch, my progress was interrupted by deliberately exaggerated squeals.

'It is isn't it? It is. Don't tell me . . .'

As I turned around to catch sight of who the noise was coming from, a pretty woman in khaki Bermuda shorts, a green Army-surplus type cotton shirt and blond hair scrunched up under an orange baseball cap was smiling up at me.

'It's Sting isn't it?' she said bursting into laughter. Whoever the mystery woman was, one thing was clear - she'd been talking to Mouse. I'd merely joked to him that the more I thought about the immorality of rich people having swimming pools they never used while water here was such a priceless commodity, made me sound more and more like Sting every day. I was even wandering around in sandals all the time now and Edward had given me a tiny bracelet of beads, which I wore on my right wrist. Fuck me, I would become vegetarian and start ranting on about rainforests next. I was halfway to becoming a lost cause.

'That's me,' I said with a smile and extended my outstretched hand towards her.

'Sting. International rock star and all round good egg. That's me.'

'Thought so,' the woman replied scrunching her nose up sweetly.

'I'm Sant. Pleased to meet you. I'm err . . .'

'The King of Zandalaya!' she chipped in again.

'That's only in my spare time.'

'Boy, you must be so busy. How do you even find time to make records and go on tour and all that stuff?'

I shrugged, and nodded in her direction, inviting an introduction. Mouse had said something about volunteer teachers being here, but I hadn't bargained for one of them bearing more than a fleeting resemblance to a younger Goldie Hawn.

'Hi, I'm Eva. I am really pleased to meet you. I'm working down at the school. You know . . . the one you built.'

'I know it!'

'Hey, I'll stop taking the micky. You're a top guy. What a great thing to do - and provide me with a job into the bargain. We all owe you!'

'You teach there?'

'Yeah.'

'Everything all right? Facilities wise and stuff?'

'Well . . .' she said, shaking her head in a deeply concerned fashion.

'We could use some soft toilet paper, but apart from that . . .'

'I'll see what I can do.'

'Well if you could fix that, that would be fantastic.'

'I'll do my best. Everything else ok?'

'Fine. Brilliant. It's great. I teach at the coolest school in the world you know. And now the great man himself is here. All my Christmases have come together . . .'

'Funnneeee . . .'

'Sorry, I bet you get that all the time.'

'Well, not for a while actually, but then not too many people here know what Christmas is I guess, so it's no big deal.'

'I can feel a song coming on,' Eva said, promptly starting to hum the Band Aid song as she asked me if I would mind her joining me down with the football lads.

'Course. Be my guest.'

'Guest of the king - can't be bad,' she chuckled, tugged down the peak of her cap and started to walk alongside me.

The minute the kids realised who was with me, the game stopped as they ran to greet Eva and show her their new football.

'Wow, isn't that great?' she said struggling to cope with the amount of children trying to hug her.

'I'm the Queen of Zandalaya' she said with a chuckle.

'I can see that. You've just brought that game to a halt.'

'Yeah, it's what's known as queen stopped play. It happens a lot out here.'

Eva kneeled down and embraced Sonny and Singer and their pals. It was one of the loveliest things I'd ever seen. So that's why they called it the beautiful game.

I promised to pop in to the school in the next couple of days, though I already suspected I would go tomorrow and made my way across the road to see Mouse and Melissa.

'I just err . . .'

'Met Eva?' Mouse said with a smile glancing across towards Melissa.

'Oh, we only bumped into each other, did you see us?'

'See you? We heard it. Listen, you don't need an Eva alarm around here. The kids let you know. They're like geese. That girl can't go anywhere without all of us knowing exactly where she is,' Melissa said.

'She is - she's like a magnet,' Mouse agreed. 'We're so lucky to have her. She's only been here a few months and already I wonder what we'd do without her.'

'Why is she going?'

'No, not to my knowledge. But I mean, it would be unreasonable and unrealistic to think she'd stay here for too long.'

'Suppose so.'

'You're okay Sant. She's definitely not going for the next couple of weeks,' Melissa said, giving me an approving wink.

49

2007 - GLOBAL WARNING

Water, water, everywhere and not a drop to drink. Desperate people stranded and having to be airlifted from their homes, aid workers paddling through the neck-high water to look for anyone trapped and the threat of disease everywhere. Rescue services are tossing bottles of water to grateful people queuing in the streets. Freak floods are wreaking havoc and it seems like no one wants to know. It's a good enough reason to fuck off back to Africa and leave England's atrocious summer behind. What was going on? And to make matters worse, it's given the global warming bores plenty to go on about. Do I really give a fuck?

This was to be the Christmas to top the lot. I was going to see my grandson for the first time. He was three now and I couldn't wait to catch up with him. I'd brought one or two silly gifts along for everyone, so I was feeling like Santa in every sense of the word. There were some unconventional pressies which had been received with great enthusiasm none the less - some jars of Colman's English mustard; HP brown sauce; a dozen tins of Spam for Melissa and Mouse; curry powder and loads of packets of jelly sweets along with some soft toilet rolls - luxury. I'd bought along loads of daft things like crossword books and also Sudoku, which I knew Mouse and Melissa wouldn't have heard of, but would have great fun with. Melissa and Eva were also very taken with the bottles of nail varnish I'd brought along. All the ingredients had been put in place for truly memorable festive celebrations. We had arrived at the lodge on Kaya Zala only last night and its beauty was beyond anything Mouse and Melissa had been able to convey. Kaya Zala was a small island sitting just 100 yards into Lake Zanda but separate from the mainland by a stretch of water rumoured to be at least a thousand feet deep. For this trip I'd chartered a jet to Johannesburg, then had a large container transferred to another private jet and flown in to the town. We had gone ahead of it and it was being brought on by truck sometime in the next couple of days. It was three days before Christmas and in the middle of the warm and wet season. How long the truck would take to get to us would depend on the roads. In this part of the world, too often the roads became rivers and the rivers became roads. The access to this part of Lake Zanda was quite good generally, largely on account of the fact that the lodge and surrounding areas was a playground of the country's ruling elite. Mouse had been told he could stay here any time he wanted in thanks for the work he'd done out there. He'd never taken them up on it before, but this was to be special. He and Melissa were going to take a week's break, I'd arranged for Jack and Rachel to fly in with John junior and Eddie his wife and their boys along with Eva. Everything was in place. Jack, Rachel and John Junior had arrived in the village three or four days ago, just after I'd flown in. There had been an air of excitement about the trip even since the idea had first been put forward way back in March.

Kaya Zala was simply stunning - unchanged since the days when Livingston explored these parts. The lodge, which consisted of seven round cottages joined together by either corridors or paths, had been entirely built by hand. The teak-framed buildings were set, on different levels, into a granite headland. All the cottages had private terraces with direct access to the crystal clear azure water. On the east side of the complex was a bar terrace with an infinity ledge looking over the lake.

Ancient trees surrounded the island and narrow, stepped

walkways led down to a boulder beach where there was a small hut housing half a dozen kayaks.

I sat on the infinity ledge and watched spell bound as fish eagles skimmed the top of the water before hurtling away with another meal. This was truly paradise. Little wonder that Zandalaya and neighbouring Malawi had been dubbed The Warm Heart of Africa. It was impossible not to be captivated.

John Junior sat on my lap and made me promise to take him in a kayak, while Jack and Rachel helped themselves to a drink from the supply I had brought along.

Some of the things in the container were to stay boxed up until Christmas but the supply of drink and mixers along with a lot of tinned food was being put onto the tabletop in the kitchen area.

I couldn't help wondering what Suzie would have thought about all this. What a strange remote place for a family reunion.

Melissa came out on to the terrace while Mouse and me made our way down to the water's edge. She mouthed at him to be careful. Always worrying was Melissa.

'Isn't it just unbelievable?' Mouse said.

'Phenomenal. Absolutely breathtaking,' I agreed.

'Yeah and no doubt there's all those people back home thinking I've gone off my rocker living out here.'

'True enough,' I said with a smile.

'Hey Sant, I know I've thanked you, but listen, a few days in paradise can't repay you for what you've done for this place.'

'Mouse, let me tell you something - and I mean this. This place has given me more than I've ever given it. And listen, if it hadn't been your say-so, I'm not sure I wouldn't have still been working at the Gazette or something similar. Helping out here has been an absolute pleasure.'

'You're a diamond Sant.'

'You too Mouse, but let's get back up there before we both

start going all slushy on each other eh?'

Mouse patted me on the back and for the briefest moment, we looked at each other as if to acknowledge just how far we had all come from those days back in Linshaw.

'It's almost like something called us here. Here, of all places,' I said.

'God called me here - and you indirectly,' Mouse replied.

I liked the sound of that. I might not have been a God-fearing man but it was certainly nice to have a back-up. Perhaps I wouldn't be spit-roasted in quite such an agonising fashion if Mouse and Melissa could put a word in for me.

In the two days before Christmas we all spent some time kayaking in the crystal blue waters and walking the long strips of beach that were just back across the jetty.

On Christmas Eve night, I took the opportunity to ask Eva if she'd like to go for a walk down to a cove we had all been to yesterday. It would take a good couple of hours there and back and we'd return in time for some food, drinks and a music night that had been arranged. Eddie was in his element having been given the task of catching some fish for the barbecue and Eva and Melissa were planning to play the guitar later. With Jack, Rachel and John Junior crashed out on the bed after all the activity; Eva seemed pleased to go for a walk down the coast.

We'd gone a fair way, talking about nothing much at all, when Eva turned out to face the vast expanse of water and suddenly declared wistfully: 'You've got a good heart, John Christmas.'

'Thanks. What brought that on?'

'Sometimes people just need telling. You laugh and joke around and make out you never take anything too seriously, but you've made a real difference here. You didn't have to do it. The people here love you for what you've done.'

'They worship you,' I said deflecting the praise.

'I only teach them. There would be nothing here without

Mouse, Melissa and you. The fresh water, the farming methods, the school - it's all down to you lot.'

'It was nothing. Really nothing.'

'I think it was everything. I wouldn't even have been here but for the school. It was the school that brought me here and changed my life.'

'Well, it was worth it if only for that.'

Eva smiled and scrunched her nose up as she did when she didn't quite know what to say. I grabbed her hand and ran towards the cove, gently pulling her with me.

When we eventually stopped I asked Eva if there was something on her mind. This was the first time she'd seemed her usual self virtually since we had been at the lodge. She had appeared a little distant on occasions, but nothing I could put my finger on.

'Oh God I haven't been miserable have I?'

'I didn't say you'd been miserable did I? I said you hadn't been quite your normal self that's all.'

'Oh I wasn't aware of that. Sorry . . . maybe it's because . . .'

'What, come on spit it out.'

Eva pretended to spit and gave me a warm hug. 'It's probably just that, well, I'm a bit of a spare part really. There's Mouse and Melissa and you've got your family with you, so I'm just on the periphery of things a bit I suppose. Nothing much really.'

'Listen, don't ever feel like that. It's not like I've got a big family thing going on. I'm just getting to know them really. It's pretty bizarre when you think about it. But don't let me ever hear you say that.'

'It was no big thing. Sorry.'

'You have my personal permission to thump me if you ever feel in the slightest bit on the fringe of things okay?'

Eva thumped me on the top of my arm and challenged me to a race back to the jetty. My days of racing were long since past me, but I tried anyway and just about managed to keep up with her.

We were breathless as we flopped down on the balcony seats and helped ourselves to a couple of beers.

'What you two been up to?' Jack said. 'Or shouldn't I ask. Listen to the pair of you.'

Eva smiled and called down to Eddie on the boulders beneath us.

'Dya wanna beer, Ed?'

Ed nodded and she tossed it carefully over the edge for him to catch.

'What songs you going to do for us tonight then?' Jack asked.

'Oh all sorts I dare say. Melissa and me do have a soft spot for The Carpenters though, so there'll be plenty of those no doubt.'

Eva looked at me for my approval and I nodded. I couldn't think of anything more fitting than the sound of Carpenters songs with the lake splashing gently against the shore. Time was I wasn't such a fan. They always seemed such an odd pair, Karen and Richard Carpenter. Talented for sure, but there was just something slightly strange about them. Karen would have been an ideal barbecue guest, though - pitch perfect and she wouldn't wolf all the grub.

The girls were chatting so Jack, Mouse and me went down to the boulders to see how Eddie's fish was progressing.

'Ask him if he's got any batter bits Sant.'

'Barrabiss?' Eddie said clearly puzzled.

'Batter bits - nothing quite like them. I can smell them now Mouse.'

'And me.'

And so we reminisced about the days back in the village in those lovely days when we just *thought* we knew everything. And as we recalled hot summer days back then, we were forced to admit they weren't quite as glamorous as this one had turned out.

With our thoughts stuck on Tip Tops, Jublees, Sky Rockets and Funny Face ice creams, how could we ever have known then that one day such an unlikely twist would pitch us all together here?

As we ate, the subject of favourite movies came up after we'd all broken off for a couple of minutes to watch a small shoal of colourful orange fishes which I said reminded me of Finding Nemo.

'Great film,' declared Mouse.

'Right then, everyone. Favourite movies. You've got one choice and one choice only. Sorry Eddie, you'll have to sit this one out!' Mouse chortled.

Eddie laughed out loud. He'd never seen a movie. Predictably, he didn't seem too perturbed about missing out on that particular pleasure.

'You start Sant.'

'For me, it would have to be The Sting. It's a close call between that and The Shawshank Redemption, but if I've only got one I'll go for The Sting.'

'I don't think I've seen that,' Jack said.

'Surely you must have!' I exclaimed. 'There's something missing in your education if you haven't seen The
Sting.'

'Well my dad wasn't around for quite a while,' Jack said bursting into laughter.

'Cheeky sod. Well - it's Robert Redford and Paul Newman who are conmen and it's just got the best ending of any film you'll ever see. It's brilliant. I'll get it for you.'

'Next!' Mouse barked.

'Mary Poppins,' Melissa cooed. 'My all-time favourite . . . you next Jack.'

Jack stroked his chin as he quickly tried to mull over his options. It wasn't easy, just on the spur of the moment like this.

'I know . . . I know . . . The Green Mile - that's mine.'

'Yeah! Good one!' Mouse agreed.

'Oh, that's such a sad one,' I said.

'Brilliant though, you next Eva.'

'I loved Splash! That's just my all time favourite along with Sleepless in Seattle. But I've only got one, yeah? Splash - definitely.'

'Yeah that was a good one,' I agreed. 'When Tom Hanks jumped into the sea at the end. Superb.'

'Did you know?' Eva continued, 'that in the one scene where the mermaid eats that lobster whole in the restaurant, they actually had to make one out of tofu because Daryl Hannah is a strict vegan.'

'Really?' Melissa said.

'Yep, top bit of trivia that,' Eva said proudly.

After we'd eaten, Melissa got the guitar out and started to play.

'Let's think. Well here's one I know you all know . . . *'Zandalaya crawfish pie, file gumbo.'*

We were all tapping away and Mouse forgave me for shouting him down when he had tried to come out with some kind of sermon about the funny thing was that Jesus was a carpenter.

'Oh shut up Mouse,' I hollered and my little preacher pal just held his hands up apologetically.

Melissa laughed and went straight into Cat Stevens' Moon Shadow before finishing her stint with You've Got a Friend. She handed it to Eva who rocked her shoulders to and fro and started to sing in the most melodic voice I had ever heard. She was remarkable and Melissa looked at me as if to say 'How about that then?' I was mesmerised.

'Told you she was good didn't I?' Melissa mouthed to me, but I was gone. She finished Only Yesterday and went straight into Please Mr Postman before giving a haunting version of Janis Ian's At Seventeen. Isn't that just one of the best songs

ever? I applauded warmly. Then as she started Yesterday Once
More you couldn't help noticing there was a twist of sadness
coming from her very soul. She'd told me on the beach that she
had almost been married quite a few years ago and that it
hadn't worked out, but didn't want to expand on it, so I left it
well alone. Eva signalled she was about to hand over and so
decided to finish with a haunting version of Judy Tzuke's Stay
With Me Till Dawn.

And as the rest of the party made their excuses and left,
some rather unsteadily, Eva and I sat hand in hand on the
balcony overlooking the water until the sun did come up. This
place seemed timeless but the natural things which people
with no comprehension of watches relied on, never let you
down.

Like a huge orange penny gently lifting itself from the
lake, the sun came up over Kaya Zala island and prompted me
to think I had never been so at ease with myself. No alarm
clocks, no mobile phone ringing and Eva - a truly enchanting
woman. I couldn't recall ever feeling quite like this.

As the sun came up we kissed on the infinity ledge and I
told her it was without doubt the most stunning Christmas I
had ever known. No snow, no robins, no tinsel or notes up the
chimney. But I felt destiny had brought me into her arms. She
cried when I joked that if I had my way she would come back
with me.

'You are my mermaid,' I said.

'You don't look anything like Tom Hanks,' she giggled,
cupping my face in her hands.

'I'd like that Sant. But I belong here. I could never come
back with you and live a life of luxury. Soft toilet paper, hot
showers and bubbly baths filled up to the brim. What appeal
does that have for a girl? How could I leave all these people
behind?'

As the sun rose higher like a huge smouldering balloon, I
realised my fate was being taken out of my hands. I was no

longer in control and I felt vulnerable. Eva was the woman I was meant to be with and yet she was of some other world. No money or power would change that. For all my wealth and possessions, suddenly I had never felt weaker.

We walked down to the water's edge hand in hand and Eva smiled at me as we sat ourselves on a huge rock, jutting out over the water.

'Shall I just flip in and swim off,' she smiled.

'I'm not a great swimmer, so don't bank on me following you,'

'Hey, it's like in the film. You'd be safe in here with me.'

We kissed and looked deep into each other's eyes.

'Mouse said this could be over a thousand feet deep you know.'

'You won't come to any harm with me,' she laughed.

Maybe that was what was worrying me. I'd found paradise and in a few days, I'd be leaving it. So much of all this didn't make any sense any more.

This felt deep. Very deep. Easily a thousand feet.

Next morning, Melissa caught me unawares as she sauntered on to the infinity ledge with a glass of orange juice. I'd had barely a couple of hours sleep. I had things on my mind.

'Oh hiya,' I said, looking at my watch. It was 6.30am.

'We don't do time here. Sunset, sunrise and all that sort of stuff. Apart from that, time doesn't matter quite so much.'

Melissa looked around to check no-one was near and suggested we take a walk down to the water's edge near the rocks.

'I need to have a word with you Sant before you get into this whole thing too deep. There's no easy way to broach this Sant. I wasn't going to say anything, but . . . well, there's

315

something you should know.'

'My God, what is it?'

Melissa dropped the bombshell of all time and then swore me to secrecy.

'But . . .'

'No buts about it Sant. Not a word.'

'Yeah, but . . .'

'Listen Sant. I love you with all my heart. There's nothing I'd like more than for you to come back here. Soon - and more often. You are just too important to both of us - well all of us here - to keep you in the dark on anything. I just wanted you to know and I didn't want you put in a compromising position where you came back as some sense of duty.'

'I wouldn't do that.'

'You could feel some sort of obligation. That's the last thing anyone would want.'

Melissa hugged me and made her way back up the steps to the chalet. I held my head in my hands and wept. I'd be back. I'd known before this conversation that I would. Now I was absolutely positive.

50

2008 - NOTHING RHYMES

The world has been turned upside down - the best golfer in the universe is black and the best rapper is a white guy. And my world has gone arse about face with it. I have a son and grandson I didn't know I had; I'm loaded and in love with a woman whose idea of luxury is soft toilet paper and a bag of wine gums while my best mate is going blind. Fucking hell. Explain all that to me.

It was only when Mouse knew I was definitely going back to Zandalaya that he managed to spit out his devastating news. Maybe the fact that we were talking on the telephone somehow made it easier for him. He didn't know I knew. He'd contracted river blindness and was losing his sight. Though it was a gradual thing, he could be totally blind in the next few years. I told him he should maybe consider coming home, but he was having none of it. It made me question God to be honest. How could that happen to someone who had done so much to help others? It didn't make sense and it certainly wasn't fair. I promised to sit down and have a word with him the minute I got there. He seemed more concerned that I met up with Eva who, I was quite pleased to hear, had been counting the hours till I got back. Typical Mouse.

This is my 'Splash.' I've fallen head over heels in love with a woman who is not of my world. Eva is a woman you can 'spoil' with a £6.99 bottle of nail varnish. So how the fuck am I supposed to work that one out? I've a bank balance that stretches to EIGHT figures now and want for nothing . . . or so

I thought. And the one woman in the universe I'm mad about finds none of that stuff in the least bit attractive. She likes me for what I am. The fact that I'm a billionaire is totally irrelevant. How mind-blowing is that? She's not even lured by some of the smaller luxuries I could provide, like the occasional hot bath or a microwave. Yesterday I even bought The Carpenters' Greatest Hits. That could just confirm that the world - or mine, at least - has gone stark raving bonkers.

Mouse was bleating on about only going back if I really wanted to. He kept insisting how much they all owed me and that I didn't have any obligation.

'I know that Mouse, now shut the fuck up,' was the only reply I could really think of. It seemed hardly appropriate given the circumstances and that he's a devout Christian, but he got the message.

No-one has been able to tell me what to do for a long, long time. This is a decision entirely of my own making. The boarding gate at Heathrow airport is my harbour. This is my Splash. I'm going back to Zandalaya for God knows how long. Everything I have back home counts for nothing if I'm not with Eva. Every possession can't be enjoyed properly without her. My money won't be wasted - there are more than enough fantastic projects to get involved in. I couldn't just leave it to waste away having worked so hard to get it. But I'll make sure it still goes to good use. I've seen first hand the kind of difference it can make.

I'm going to get Mouse to Johannesburg as well and see if there's anything that can be done for him. I've bought Eva a present I just know she's going to love. Two hundred quid it cost me! She'll think that's extravagant beyond measure, but what the hell. I just know how much she will love this guitar. I should have known there's no such thing as a no-strings relationship. I bought one for Melissa too - just couldn't bear the thought of them fighting.

Taking my seat on the plane, I reflect on the events of the last few days. The phone call to Jack and his delight as I told him of my plan. I unzip my travel case and take out the picture that arrived just the other day. There's Jack and me with Rachel and John Junior along with Mouse, Melissa, Eddie and Eva. It's almost like my life story captured in one definitive snap - a perfect Christmas in a faraway place. I can almost hear Rod belting out 'Every picture tells a story don't it?' in that gravelly voice of his. And what a story this one was. It had more twists and turns than I dared think about. Mouse and Me? We were just two raggy-arsed kids from a normal little village who had gone on to do some quite incredible things. He was for the high jump when I got my hands on him. Trying to keep something as serious as that away from me.

'So that's why you were pacing out the village that day?' I asked.

'No, no honestly. That was something I'd been planning for a long time.'

'Well look. I'm going to make some enquiries and get you off to Jo'burg mate. There must be someone who can do something about this. Money's not an issue, so let's try everything we can eh?'

'I would just feel a bit guilty that's all?'

'Guilty? Why?'

'Well, there's a load of the villagers who've got it as well. It's like I'd be getting preferential treatment.'

'Well, if we can sort you, we'll get them all sorted as well. Does that make you feel better?'

'Yeah!'

'You can be the village guinea pig. If there's any guinea-pigging to be done, you're the man!'

'I'm the man! I can't thank you enough Sant.'

'Listen, don't fucking start all that nonsense again. There's absolute pots of money sitting there waiting to be put to good use. Consider it done.'

'I sometimes wonder what we could ever have achieved out here without you mate.'

'Look, I know you'd do the same for me. It's not even an issue. We've been mates far too long for all that. That trolley your dad made for you, cowboys and Indians, war over the banks, blow football It's a long time you know.'

'It sure is. I loved that blow football.'

'I know you did. I've got a confession to make.'

'What's that?'

'I couldn't stand it!'

'You're kidding me.'

'Nope. Honest.'

'I can't believe that you've said that.'

'I had to get it off my chest. It's something I've kept hidden for years'

'Oh well, it's best to know these things.'

'But we've always covered for each other pal.'

'True enough.'

'It's like you used to say - 'be my eyes.' Well I will.'

'Fucking hell Sant,' Mouse sobbed, tears streaming down his face.

'What?' I asked, shocked that Mouse had used such a strong word.

'Just promise me one thing,' he said wheezing with laughter in his unmistakeable Mutley style.

'What!'

'Just promise me you won't start singing Two Little Boys,' Mouse spluttered. We both cracked up and had tears streaming down our face as Eva and Melissa bounded over, hugged the pair of us, and begged to be let in on the joke . . .

PRAISE FOR: BORN TO BE MILD